# Footsteps *in the* Sea

ALSO BY ANN NEVE

*Ride upon the Storm*

*Song of the Skald*

# Ann Neve

# Footsteps in the Sea

Matador
5 Weir Road
Kibworth Beauchamp
Leicester LE8 0LQ, UK
Tel: (+44) 116 279 2299
Fax: (+44) 116 279 2277
Email: books@troubador.co.uk
Web: www.troubador.co.uk/matador

ISBN 978 1848761 612

British Library Cataloguing in Publication Data.
A catalogue record for this book is available from the British Library.

Cover image of Happisburgh (Haisbro) Lighthouse courtesy of Happisburgh Lighthouse Trust

Typeset in 11pt Bembo by Troubador Publishing Ltd, Leicester, UK
Printed and bound in Great Britain by TJ International Ltd, Padstow, Cornwall

**Matador** is an imprint of Troubador Publishing Ltd

*For my late brother-in-law, James O'Keefe, and all the others who risked their lives on the Arctic Convoys*

*'God moves in a mysterious way*
*His wonders to perform;*
*He plants his footsteps in the sea*
*And rides upon the storm'*

William Cowper 1731–1800

*The poet is thought to have written his famous hymn after watching a storm gather over the sea at Happisburgh, (Haisbro), Norfolk*

# ACKNOWLEDGEMENTS

I read a great many books and articles whilst researching the background for this novel; in particular, I am grateful for and acknowledge the work of the following:

Georges Blond, Richard Brown, Adrian Hoare, Derek E. Johnson, Frank Meeres, Helen D. Millgate, Tony Overill, Leonard C. Reynolds, Colin Tooke, Richard Woodman and, of course, the Great Yarmouth Mercury and the Time and Tide Museum, Great Yarmouth.

# 1939

# I

Alec Tovell strode purposefully out of Stalham Station but came to a sudden halt when he found himself surrounded by a group of pretty young girls. He did not object to the enforced delay and chatted happily to his captors for several minutes. Then he chanced to glance across the street and see an old man leaving the *Kings Head* public house. When this gentleman caught sight of the young people he stood still, grinned and shook his head.

'Must go now, girls. I can see my lift over there.' With a wave of his hand, Alec dashed across the road. As he approached, he called out, 'Morning, Uncle Ted. Are you tut-tutting at me?'

'Just like your father! He could attract young women like moths to the flame. You're the spitting image of him, Alec. And you tower over me just like he do. How many hearts have you broken since you were last here, you young devil?'

'Are we going to stand around all day discussing my supposed love life, or are you going to give me a lift home?'

'Course I'm going to give ye a lift home, bor. Chuck your stuff in the back. Thought you might be too high and mighty these days to want a lift in a hoss and cart.' As he spoke, Ted Carter hauled himself onto the vehicle and untied the reins.

'If I ever get high and mighty, Uncle Ted, you can throw me in the duck pond like you used to do when I got out of hand as a littl'un.'

'Oh, you were a rascal, alright,' agreed the old man. 'Always into mischief ….'

'Move over then. I'm driving,' said Alec, climbing effortlessly onto the seat of the wagon and taking the reins. Once they had left the town behind and were on the country lane that would take them through Lessingham towards the coast, Alec glanced affectionately at the wiry old man and asked, 'When are you going to retire, Uncle Ted?'

'Retire? When I drop down dead!' his companion replied tartly. 'Cor, blast, bor, can you imagine me sitting around the house all day with nothing to do? That would drive me mad, that that would. And then there's the young master to consider. He'd have a hard job managing without an experienced man like me.'

'The young master - he must be fifty if he's a day,' scoffed Alec.

'Don't you be cheeky now,' Ted retorted. 'To me he'll always be the young master 'cos I worked for his father and for his father afore him. They'll have to drag me off that land feet first if I get my way. That is, unless I go in the pub. I've spent most of my leisure hours in that there place. Yep, going in the *Admiral Lord Nelson* would be all right too.'

'If I'd known the mention of retirement would make you morbid, I wouldn't have asked,' said Alec, laughing. 'Here, take the reins a minute while I get out of my jacket. This August sun is a real scorcher.'

'Been a long hot summer so far,' Ted commented. 'That's been great for getting the harvest in but that probably means we're in for a long hard winter. Anyhow, what do you think of Navy life?'

'I'm getting used to it,' Alec replied. 'Don't forget I was in the first intake after they passed the Military Training Act last May. Once my six months are up I'll be back in civilian life – unless, of course, we're at war by then.'

'Mr Churchill's been warning them for years. I don't pay no regard to that "peace for our time" squit that Mr Chamberlain sets such store by. You can't trust that Hitler. They gave him the Sudetenland, dint they, to keep him quiet? He said he'd be satisfied with that but then what did the bugger go and do? He sent his bloomin' army to invade Prague. You can't believe a word he say. I reckon the government knows that really. Why else have they been encouraging men to become Air Raid Wardens? Last week someone said in the pub that a Gas Van was going round the schools to test that the littl'uns' gas masks were working alright. He also said Norfolk's been declared a safe area for evacuees to come to – except for Norwich and Yarmouth, of course. And a lot of local men are joining the Auxiliary Coastguard or the Auxiliary Fire Service. Yep, it's a rum old do to be sure. Haven't decided yet what I shall join.'

Alec glanced across at his companion and saw that he was deadly serious. 'You can't be spared from the Life-saving Brigade, Uncle Ted.'

'Well, that's true of course. If war's declared this will be an even more dangerous coastline than it is now. As if the sea and those bloomin' Haisbro

Sands are not enough to contend with, we'd have convoys going past here with U-boats after 'em. And it's the perfect spot for an invasion. Everyone thought the Hun would land on Haisbro Beach last time. Reckon you're right, young Alec. An experienced man like me is needed with the Brigade – especially since the RNLI gave our lifeboat away to Sea Palling.'

'That still rankles, does it, Uncle Ted?' Then, seeing another vehicle approaching, Alec added, 'We'd better find a passing place and pull over.'

'Leave it to Bessie,' said Ted. 'She don't like motor cars – that she don't. She'll soon find a spot to pull over.' The car slowed down as it drew near and the driver waved cheerily to the occupants of the cart. 'That's young Doctor Lambert. We dint have a local doctor for several months 'til his mother persuaded him to come down here and take over his father's practice.'

'And how old is young Doctor Lambert?' asked Alec with a grin.

'Oh he can't be more than forty-five,' answered Ted calmly, not noticing the emphasis Alec had put on the word young. 'He's a nice enough fella but he don't drink, y'see. His father never missed a night at the *Admiral Lord Nelson* – not unless he was out on an emergency that is. Yes, I miss having a yarn with Doctor Lambert.'

'Father said the same thing. He wrote to me last year to say that the doctor had died. I have fond memories of him too. He could always make me laugh when I was a little boy – no matter how sick I was feeling.'

The pair was silent for a while, each man lost in his own thoughts, but as they neared Whimpwell Green and the family smallholding, Alec asked, 'Are you coming in for something to eat, Uncle Ted?'

'No, better not,' Ted replied. 'Thanks all the same but your mother fed me yesterday and I don't want to overstay my welcome. Anyhow, they haven't seen you since Easter and they'll want you to themselves.' Taking the reins, Ted brought the cart to a halt and watched whilst Alec climbed down, collected his kitbag, waved and called out his thanks. 'Perhaps I'll see you and your father in the pub later,' Ted shouted as he urged the mare on her way.

'I've only got a forty-eight hour pass,' Alec explained to his parents as they sat round the living room table, 'but it was better than nothing. I'm half way through my training so the next time I come home it should be for longer.'

'It's wonderful to see you; I don't care for how long,' said his mother.

'And you look fit and well. Navy life must suit you,' added his father.

'I don't mind it but I've no wish to make the Navy my career as you did the Army, Father.'

'You won't need to. With a first from Cambridge, plenty of doors will be open to you. Have you decided what you want to do yet?'

'Yes. That's my main reason for coming home even though it's only for a few hours: to tell you the good news. You know that when I graduated, Mr Collins arranged for me to have teaching experience at the school where he'd retired as headmaster. It seems I performed so well that Mr Collins has been able to secure me a trainee post as a junior master at a public school in North Norfolk. The vacancy will arise next January when the present post-holder takes up a position elsewhere. The headmaster didn't even want to interview me. He was Mr Collins's deputy for several years and apparently trusts his judgment implicitly.'

'That's wonderful news, Alec,' said his father. 'But I'm not surprised Mr Collins has such influence. Who could ignore the recommendation of a war hero and a scarred VC holder?'

'He's never cashed in on that,' replied Alec quietly. 'He doesn't even like being addressed as Colonel Collins.' Then turning to his mother, Alec asked in a lighter tone of voice, 'You won't mind if I go to see my godmother and tell her the news, will you? I promise I won't stay long.'

'Of course I won't mind. She's been quite lonely since Mr Brewster died and she'll be as pleased as we are at the news. You owe her a lot, Alec: all those hours she spent giving you extra lessons when you were young. And if she hadn't told Mr Collins how clever you were you would never have gone to stay with him and Mrs Collins.'

'I know, Mother. And if Mr Collins hadn't coached me I would never have got into Cambridge. I've been very lucky. And let's not forget Father's influence. He's the real academic in this family. If he hadn't spent hours with me, and Bobby and Lizzie, drumming our lessons into us when all we wanted to do was play, where would we be?'

'You would have been alright but not as happy as you are today,' said his mother affectionately.

'I'll go next door this evening and see Lizzie.'

'No need: she and the baby will be here when you get back,'

explained Ginny. 'Your sister always eats her meals with us when Peter's at sea. No point in her cooking just for one.'

'Why don't you take Rajah Two,' suggested Tovell. 'He could do with the exercise. I don't seem to get the time to ride him as I should. Must be boring for him just trotting around his paddock.'

'Thanks, Father. I will. I'll give him a quick canter along the beach after I've seen Aunt Lydia. He loves splashing around in the sea. He's still a youngster at heart – like me!'

Lydia Brewster walked down the garden path with Alec to where he had tethered the horse just inside the front gate. 'Thank you for sparing the time to come and tell me your wonderful news, Alec. Let's hope you will be able to take up the position.' She gestured towards Haisbro Lighthouse, standing a few hundred yards from her garden. 'Before I close my curtains at night, I look up at that beacon and pray that it's a beacon of hope. From what we read in the newspapers, it's seems that war is almost inevitable, but if it comes so many lights will be snuffed out. I've watched you grow up, Alec, and my grandchildren and all the young people who live around here. You have the right to a life.'

'We'll have a life. Don't you worry,' replied Alec warmly as he stooped and kissed his godmother's cheek. 'You're as handsome and elegant as ever, Aunt Lydia, but I think you're getting shorter – or perhaps I'm still getting taller.'

Lydia laughed. 'You're a giant it's true, but I'm afraid I am shrinking. Ladies of my advanced years usually shrink, you know.' She gave Alec an affectionate hug and then, changing the subject, she asked, 'Are you going back along the cliff top?' When he nodded, she added, 'I still walk along the cliff path most days as far as Cart Gap. I like to stand and look across to where we used to live when Mr Brewster was Station Officer at the Coastguard Station. You shouldn't dwell on the past, I know, but what else is there when you get to my age? So many years spent there; so many memories. But enough of that! You take great care, Alec, and come and see me again when you're next home.' She held the gate open for him as he mounted and urged the horse out onto the road which led to the cliff top. They waved to one another until the hedges obscured them from each other's view.

Once on Haisbro Cliffs Alec dismounted and walked to the cliff edge.

He looked down and saw children happily playing on the beach and paddling in the sea, their laughter wafting up to him on the breeze. The day was perfect: cloudless blue sky and sparkling sea. Suddenly, the strangest feeling came over him: that he must commit this scene to memory for it would be a long time before he saw its like again – if ever. Abruptly, he turned around, his back to the water and found that he was facing the lighthouse. At once he remembered how his father had told him, when he was a little boy, that the memory of his mother standing in front of Haisbro Lighthouse had cheered and sustained him through the long years of the last war. Alec looked up and recalled what his father had described: the lighthouse painted in bands of red and white, towering over his diminutive mother like some giant guardsman. The lighthouse had worked its magic for his father and he had come home at last; if there was a war, he prayed it would work the same magic for him.

A nudge in the back from Rajah Two brought Alec back to the present. 'Sorry, boy! I promised you a run, didn't I?' Climbing easily back into the saddle, Alec let the horse canter at first but as the cliffs sloped down towards Cart Gap, he allowed him to break into a gallop. By the time they reached the gap in the marrams and trotted down onto the beach, Alec felt better. The exhilarating ride, the wind in his face, had blown away his sense of foreboding. Once in the breakers, his spirits lifted even higher when he caught sight of another rider letting her mount enjoy splashing around in the shallows. 'Hey, Podge!' he called out. The girl looked round, waved and immediately brought her horse alongside his.

'Hello, Sailor! Didn't think I was going to see you this summer. Where have you been?'

'This is the first time I've been home since Easter. I got called up – just the six months training thing. I'm half way through it.'

'Which service did you join?'

'The Navy.'

'What, not the Army? Was that to spite your father?'

'Of course not. I would never do anything to spite him. I joined the Navy because I've always liked messing about on boats. I've told you, both my uncles are fishermen and would let me go to sea with them when I was a boy. And both my brother and my brother-in-law joined the Royal Navy as soon as they were old enough – never done anything else. I've been brought up on tales of their adventures on the High Seas. The Navy was a natural choice.'

'That's funny, isn't it? "Sailor" has always been my nickname for you. I must have had a crystal ball when I named you that.'

'You've always said it was because of the hideous sailor suit I was wearing when we first met.'

'It was! You looked ridiculous kneeling in the sand trying to build a castle when your outfit was too small and too tight for you. It looked like your pants would burst open at any moment.'

'That suit had been my brother's. We couldn't afford to waste anything, my mother was always saying.'

'Well, if I get called up I shan't join the Army and that will be to spite the family – Grandfather especially!'

Alec laughed. 'Still the rebel, eh? Haven't you rebelled enough? Turning your back on a suitable match; insisting on going to university then making matters worse by studying not the arts, but the sciences! And of all subjects – engineering! How unladylike! You're a disgrace to the good family name!'

'Oh! Stop teasing me! Things are unpleasant enough at home. That's why I've been here all the vacation – not just a few weeks - staying with Nanny Barker.'

'Sorry, Podge. You know I don't mean it. I admire you for what you're doing. It was hard enough for me to overcome the barriers but it must be a great deal harder for you. Don't let's fall out. And what's all this about you being called up? I didn't know they were thinking of calling up women.'

'They're not – yet! But we were in Great Yarmouth this morning; you know how much Nanny Barker loves that place. We always go on day trips there when I'm staying with her. We caught the early train as usual but as soon as we got off at the station we realized something was wrong. There were people everywhere with their luggage waiting to catch trains home – in the middle of the week. We walked through to the seafront but we didn't get far. There were barriers up and policemen all over the place. Nanny got quite worried so I asked one of the officers what had happened. He said they were stopping people from going any further because they were about to blow a hole in the Britannia Pier – to stop the enemy from landing vehicles on it – and that all visitors must go home.

He said every place of entertainment had been closed by order of the government; so the summer season was over even though it was only August. I thought war must have been declared whilst we were on the journey but he said, "No, these are just precautions." We went back to Beach Station and got on the first train we could. Nanny Barker's neighbours have been making dug-outs in their gardens for weeks. Maybe they were right. I thought I'd bring Bella down to the water's edge just in case it's our last chance before the authorities close this beach too. She loves playing in the sea – just as much as Rajah Two.'

Alec said nothing for a few moments, remembering the sense of premonition he had experienced earlier on the cliff top. 'If it comes it'll be our war, Podge,' he said quietly. All thoughts of teasing this plump tomboy of a girl he had shared many an escapade with during their growing-up years, had vanished from his mind.

She immediately adopted his serious tone and replied, 'You'll be in the thick of it straightaway, Sailor. You say you've already done a lot of your training. Hope you won't regret choosing the Navy. You could be at sea very soon.' She leant forward and patted Alec's horse, avoiding looking directly at her friend as she added flippantly, 'This animal with the daftest name ever will miss you. C'mon, Rajah Two! Bella will race you to the Town Gap and back!'

# II

Ginny heard the truck pull into the yard. Immediately she rushed out of the back door and called to Tovell and Ted Carter as they climbed down from the vehicle. 'Where have you been? You've missed the broadcast.'

'Don't you fret, gal! We're here now. Couldn't leave half a tankard of beer undrunk, could I now?' said Ted, unperturbed, as he sidestepped Ginny, hurried through the scullery into the living room and settled himself in an armchair beside the cooking range.

Tovell smiled apologetically at his wife. 'You know what he's like when you're trying to get him out of the pub. They had the wireless on in the public bar ready for the Prime Minister's broadcast but I knew you'd want us to hear it together. I'm sorry we weren't in time. We're at war, aren't we?'

Ginny nodded. 'Lizzie was with me. She was upset, of course. She's upstairs in her old room now feeding the baby. She'll be down in a minute. She didn't want to hear the news on her own.'

'What about Rachel? Is she here?'

'No. She decided she'd better go to her mother's – to Mary's. Don't forget Rachel's brothers are in the Services too.'

Tovell put a comforting arm around his wife's shoulder as they walked together into the living room. They sat down on opposite sides of the table; Ginny leaned forward and nervously smoothed out the creases in the chenille cloth, avoiding Tovell's gaze. He could see that she had been crying. He looked across at the old man, busily filling his pipe. 'We missed the broadcast, Ted, but war has been declared.'

'Knew it would be. Only way to stop that devil Hitler!' replied Ted enthusiastically.

At that moment, Lizzie came down the staircase in the corner of the room, placing her feet carefully on the narrow treads, her baby clasped firmly against her shoulder. Tovell got up at once and went over to her and ushered her towards the other armchair, opposite to where Ted was sitting.

'You and little Molly sit here,' he said kindly. Once she was seated, he stooped and kissed the baby gently on top of her head, noticing as he did so that Lizzie's eyes too were swollen and red-rimmed.

'We'd better tell you what Mr Chamberlain said,' announced Ginny, straightening her back and striving to keep her voice even. 'He said that this morning our ambassador in Berlin had handed the German Government a final warning that unless we heard from them by 11.00 am that they were prepared to withdraw their troops from Poland, we would be at war. We didn't hear from them so that's it.'

'He did explain that we'd done all we could to establish peace,' added Lizzie, making an effort to join in the conversation, 'but now we and France must honour our obligations to Poland and go to her aid. '

Seeing that Lizzie looked on the verge of crying again, Tovell intervened. 'The speech he made to the House of Commons two days ago – the newspapers reported it yesterday – made that clear. He made the point then that we had no quarrel with the German people - other than that they allowed a Nazi Government to rule them. And that, I suppose, is down to the fools who made the peace treaty after the last war so humiliating for the Germans that it was easy for someone like Hitler to gain power. But as Chamberlain said, we're much better prepared than last time. He mobilized all the armed forces and the Civil Defence organizations on Friday too, and like I told you all, he must have ordered children to be evacuated from the cities then as well. When I delivered our produce yesterday, there were children everywhere in North Walsham Market Place. They were ushering them into the church and giving the poor little kiddies bags of food to eat. It was the same in Great Yarmouth. Paddle steamers were bringing them from London. I saw a lot of young mothers too carrying babies and toddlers. The billeting officers in Yarmouth certainly had their work cut out yesterday, finding overnight accommodation for them all before transporting them inland. And I had a heck of a job getting into the Market Place to deliver to the stalls. They were digging up Church Plain to make way for public air raid shelters. That really brought it home to me.'

'That should never have got to this. He should have been stopped afore this,' said Ted vehemently. 'The third of September 1939 – there's another date for the history books. But we'll have him now. That shouldn't last long. I reckon it'll all be over afore Christmas.'

'Ted, listen to yourself! That's what you said last time,' Tovell pointed out, laughing.

'I said it too,' Ginny admitted. 'Everyone said it – except you, Tovell.'

'Well, there's nothing wrong with being optimistic but we ought to consider that it might not be over quickly. I suppose I ought to rejoin the Army.'

'No!' shrieked Ginny. 'Haven't you been in enough wars? You've done your bit. And anyway, you're far too old. You're sixty, Tovell, or have you forgotten? It's not your war.'

'It's everyone's war and we've all got to help. I know I'm old but I could still train the recruits – the conscripts.'

'Both my sons and my son-in-law will be in the thick of this war plus nephews and the sons of many of my friends. That's contribution enough – and enough to worry about. I spent every day of the last war dreading what might happen to you. It's not fair to expect me to suffer like that again, especially not with Bobby and Alec and Peter ...' Ginny covered her eyes with her hands and could say no more.

Tovell leaned across the table and placed a hand on her shoulder. 'I'm sorry. I didn't mean to upset you. But try to understand that I feel I must play a useful part.'

'You can, Father,' said Lizzie. 'Mr Chamberlain emphasized that it's vital that people in factories and those supplying the necessities of life should continue in their jobs. What could be more necessary than producing food? If the war goes on we'll be short of food just like last time. Peter and I have a lot of land at the back of our house just going to waste. You could make a break in the hedge between our two properties and use that land for crops.'

'Thanks, Lizzie. That's a good idea. Ted will give me a hand, won't you, Ted?'

'Course I will. Glad to, bor. But if I know you, that int going to satisfy you for long; you'll soon have some other scheme up your sleeve.' When Tovell pulled a face at him, the old man changed the subject. 'You did invite me to Sunday dinner, dint you, gal? Is that beef I can smell roasting in the oven?'

The regulars at the *Admiral Lord Nelson* mulled over the events in Poland.

To a man, they felt for the Poles trying to defend themselves against tanks and aircraft and wondered when the help that the British and French Governments had promised was going to materialize. By the eighteenth of September, they learned that the previous day Russia had taken decisive action – but not to help the beleaguered country. She had invaded Poland herself, from the east, saying she needed to protect her White Russian nationals by taking back the Poland she used to have before the Great War. Under attack from both sides, Poland could not hold out and by the twenty-seventh of September, Warsaw had surrendered – half of it in ruins. There was much speculation in the public bar that night that the fall of Poland meant Hitler could turn all his attention to the Western Front. But with the War Budget having been released by the British Government that same day, conversation tended to concentrate on more immediate and more personal concerns. Ted Carter expressed the feelings of all his drinking companions when he exclaimed, 'Cor, blast, bor! A penny rise on beer and baccy up a penny ha'penny! What I wouldn't like to do to that Hitler!'

'While you're sorting out Hitler, don't forget that Friday is National Registration Day,' said Tovell, laughing. 'If you fail to fill in the return you won't get your identity card and you won't be registered for food rationing.'

'Now that's a real worry!' Ted agreed. 'Not the identity card bit – at my age I'm not bothered if some botty little official shoots me as a spy – but not to be able to claim my rightful share of the grub …'


Ginny was relieved when a long-awaited letter came from Alec. He described how his training was coming to a hasty conclusion and his hope that he would be assigned to a large warship which would see immediate action. He had a message too for his father to pass on to Ted Carter. *'Tell Uncle Ted that on the day after war was declared, we were told that his hero, Winston Churchill, had been re-appointed as First Lord of the Admiralty. Ted would have liked the way it was announced: the signal, which was to all the Fleet, merely said, "Winston is back". As soon as it was broadcast across the base, a great cheer went up.'*

Ginny was so pleased to receive the letter that she left the house and went to look for her husband, knowing that he was working on the overgrown area of land which Lizzie had suggested he make use of to grow even more food as his contribution to the war effort. She had not even reached the boundary between her land and her daughter's when she saw Tovell hurrying towards her with an animal wrapped in his jacket.

'I found this poor thing chained to a tree on the other side of Lizzie's hedge. It was lucky I heard it whimpering: it hadn't the strength left to make much of a noise. From the state of it, it must have been there for days.'

'Oh! How can people do such a thing,' Ginny exclaimed as she hurried along the path ahead of Tovell and opened the back door. He placed the bundle on the draining board whilst Ginny hastily filled a shallow bowl with water. She held it so that the dog could drink whilst Tovell supported the animal's head. 'What can I give it to eat? It must be starving. There's a little of last night's stew in the larder. Would that be alright do you think?'

'Yes,' replied Tovell, taking the bowl from Ginny and allowing the dog, still cocooned in his jacket, to lie back again on the draining board. 'But I should chop the meat up fine and mix it well with the gravy. If he hasn't been fed for ages he may have trouble eating. He wanted the water but hadn't the strength to lap it properly. I'll try him again with that whilst you're preparing his meal.' When Ginny emerged from the pantry, Tovell added, 'I bet whoever owned this poor thing couldn't or wouldn't afford a vet's bill or the cost of a bullet, to put him down. If I get my hands on him I'll chain him to a tree and leave him there so he can find out for himself what a slow agonizing death is like.'

The dog showed some interest when Ginny began to dice the meat and lifted its head slightly and looked at her as she worked on the other side of the large stone sink. Tovell took the opportunity to give the animal some more water and when the food was ready, the dog managed to gulp it down. 'Better leave it at that for the moment in case we make him sick,' Ginny concluded. 'He's very wet and cold – not surprising considering the rain we've had the last couple of days. Carry him into the living room, Tovell, and lay him in front of the cooking range. I'll find some old towels to wipe him with and a blanket for him to lie on, so you can have your jacket back.'

'Does he remind you of anyone?' asked Tovell as he placed the dog gently on the rug in front of the hearth.

'Of course he does,' replied Ginny with a smile. 'He's a black Labrador like Blackie. You want to keep him, don't you?'

Tovell nodded. 'If he survives after what he's suffered, he deserves to live.'

'But the authorities would never let you keep him. Think how many pets have been destroyed so far, to save food. Our cats have escaped the cull only because they find their own food – or so we've claimed – and do a necessary job in keeping vermin down on the smallholding.'

'The authorities have been too hasty. I dread to think how many children have cried themselves to sleep these last few weeks because their beloved pet has been put down. Anyway, I'll say he's a working dog – a guard dog.'

'You'll have a hard job convincing anyone of that!' said Ginny, laughing. 'Look at his poor sweet face. You couldn't have a gentler animal.'

'Oh, I'll think of something; don't you worry,' Tovell asserted.

Ginny knelt on the floor and began to un-wrap the jacket from around the dog. As she did so, the animal moaned. 'Look at these weals. He's been beaten. There's dried blood on his coat. I'll have to bathe those wounds.'

'The bastard who dumped him must have used the leash on him first,' said Tovell. 'It was one of those leads which are mainly a metal chain. I left it attached to the tree and just undid his collar. Remind me to go back for it in case some children find it.'

'And another thing,' Ginny added, looking up at Tovell. 'He isn't a "he" – he's a "she". So what are you going to call your new girlfriend?'

'That's easy! What else? Blackie Two, of course,' replied her husband, leaning forward and kissing the tip of her nose.

'I should have guessed! First we have Rajah Two and now we have Blackie Two. You won't make a habit of bringing home waifs and strays, will you?'

So the first few weeks of the war passed and Tovell, always an avid reader of newspapers, followed its progress intently. The British Expeditionary Force had been dispatched to Northern France just as hastily as it had in 1914. 'I hope we're not making the same mistakes as we did last time – wrong assumptions,' he said to Ginny. 'The papers must have been told not to report where our troops are deployed but I bet it's on the Franco-Belgium border. They'll be assuming the Maginot Line is all the defence France needs from Germany. I hope they're right. Anyway, we need to defend Belgium. Hitler's told them and Holland that he'll, "respect their neutrality". If his past record's anything to go by, that means he's poised to invade them.'

'They're certainly expecting an invasion here,' commented Ginny. 'I went to see Mrs Brewster this afternoon and there was a lot of activity in Beach Road. They were constructing a gun emplacement, so she'd been told. Our lovely cliff top is a right mess: barbed wire all along the edge and more pill-boxes being built. She said the beach has already been mined.'

Tovell nodded. 'I got stopped by the Army on my way back from delivering in Stalham. The coast is out of bounds; you have to prove you have a right to be there. You could see by the barriers they had piled up on the side of the road that the intention is to set up road blocks instantly if necessary. Stalham and North Walsham seem to have completed their public shelters and First Aid posts. They've put up new signs on a white background – because of the blackout, I suppose – and there are white arrows painted on the pavement to direct people. I expect it's the same in all the towns by now. Did Lizzie collect little Molly's respirator today?'

'Yes. Poor little baby, she didn't think much to being pushed into it. She made sure everyone heard her protests. Let's hope she never needs to be put into it for real. At least everyone, from the very young to the very old, has a gas mask now.'

'I passed Ted on the way home. He says he's found out from some blokes in the pub what those wooden huts they're building near White's Farm are going to be: it's some kind of hush-hush place for the RAF. The last war was supposed to be the one to end all wars. Nothing much has changed in twenty one years, has it?'

'Nothing except the boys have grown up and are in the thick of it,' said Ginny ruefully.

'Come here, you,' said Tovell, taking her arm and leading her towards his large armchair beside the cooking range. Blackie Two followed and stretched out on the hearth rug with a contented sigh. 'Come and sit on my lap.' When she made a half-hearted protest, Tovell continued, 'You're still my little darling, aren't you? The years can't change that. A cuddle is still a comfort, isn't it?'

17

'Of course it is, you old silly. I know it's pointless to worry about them and I realize that they are probably relishing seeing action, but I dread the thought of those telegrams arriving again ...'

A few days later, the first of the dreaded telegrams arrived. Ginny was not the recipient. The first the Tovells knew of it was when their daughter-in-law, Rachel, came running down the path to where they were working on their land.

'Whatever is the matter?' cried Ginny, seeing the tears streaming down the girl's face.

'My brother, George ... My sister-in-law's just had a telegram ... "Lost at sea – presumed dead".'

Ginny threw down her hoe and rushed to embrace her daughter-in-law. 'I'm so sorry, Rachel. And your poor mother ... Tovell, I must go to Mary. I'll come home with you now, Rachel.'

'Was your brother on the *Royal Oak*?' asked Tovell. The girl nodded, too distraught to say any more. 'I heard on the news this morning that she was sunk by a U-boat. I had a nasty feeling your mother had said that George was on the *Royal Oak*. History's repeating itself already and the wars only been going six weeks. Damn those U-boats.'

When Ginny returned from comforting Mary, her friend and former neighbour from the days when she had lived at the Coastguard Station, Tovell told her that the report of the sinking of the battleship, *Royal Oak*, had stated that a daring German commander had sneaked into Scapa Flow, discharged his torpedoes and escaped out into the open sea again. 'Now you understand why I said history was repeating itself. Those devastating attacks last time, at the start of the war, which killed so many coastguards in the reserve ships, were also down to a daring German commander who achieved what was thought impossible. The Hun certainly breeds 'em! Hope we catch them up more quickly this time.'

The war conducted verbally around the public bar of the *Admiral Lord Nelson* was as heated as ever: people moaned about the confusion caused by the removal of road signs; about the upset, and the injuries, which occurred as a result of the blackout; about the restrictions imposed upon their movements by the Army. Off-duty Air Raid Precaution wardens complained that people were becoming too complacent and many were not carrying their gas masks with them as they should. The air raids had not materialized in the numbers or the force which had been expected so many of the evacuees, who had been bundled out of the cities for "safer"' areas which had not always been ready to receive them before war was declared, began to drift back home.

'Why hant he invaded?' was the general cry. 'Thought this was supposed to be a lightning war – like the invasion of Poland. Reckon that'll all be over by Christmas.'

Whenever Tovell happened to be present at these deliberations, he was quick to point out how unwise it was to make such an assumption. 'I've heard that said twice before: at the start of the Boer War and the last war – wrong both times. They mean business. Look how they're attacking our shipping. They know we don't produce enough food to feed ourselves; that we depend on imports. They intend this war to go on long enough to starve us into submission.' He was also concerned at the way Ginny was worrying constantly about her eldest child, Bobby, searching newspaper reports and listening to wireless announcements about attacks by U-boats.

And so the drinking companions discussed the latest maritime news: the U-boat successes and our own victories in hunting this submarine menace attacking our convoys and laying mines in our estuaries. Then, at the end of November came news of invasion; but it was an invasion of Finland, not Britain, and the invaders were Russian, not German. There was much sympathy for the brave Finns and speculation as to what Russia was up to, given her recent attack on Poland. There was rejoicing too, in mid-December, at the news that our Fleet in the South Atlantic had trapped the *Graf Spee* in Montevideo Harbour. But, as ever, the talk soon reverted to more personal issues such as whether to keep pigs in case bacon became rationed and where cyclists could acquire batteries since shops had run out of them following the realization that a torch made the difference between life and death – or at least, serious injury – in the blackout. Petrol rationing too brought hilarious suggestions as to how to make the fuel last longer.

'I'm not putting moth-balls in my petrol tank,' Tovell declared. 'I've decided I'll only use the lorry for the furthest deliveries – Yarmouth and Norwich – but for North Walsham and Stalham and the like, I've done up Uncle William's old cart. Good job I kept it after I got the motor. I had a long talk with Rajah Two this morning. I explained to him that I knew his social standing was far above that of a cart-horse but in war time we all have to do our bit.'

'And what did Rajah Two say?' asked Ted impishly.

'He agreed with everything I said,' replied Tovell. 'He nodded his head at my every word.'


Christmas was a rather bleak affair. Lizzie and baby Molly decided to stay for at least a week until New Year. Although they only lived next door the weather was so severe that they felt it made more sense to heat just the one house and they needed to stay indoors because the baby was unwell. It was necessary to summon "young" Dr Lambert to her on Christmas Eve because her fever was so high. The doctor was not unduly concerned and after advice and reassurances he expressed his relief at having to treat someone who had not either slipped on the ice or fallen off the edge of a kerb.

'Would you believe, Mrs Ellis,' he said to Lizzie, 'that the majority of my patients since the outbreak of war have been those who have suffered some injury, to a greater or lesser extent, as the result of the blackout? A former colleague, who has access to the statistics, tells me that four thousand deaths have occurred so far because of it – far more than caused by Hitler's bombs. At this rate he'll have no need to invade us – we'll finish ourselves off!' He laughed at his own joke and at once the assembled family was reminded of the doctor's jovial father. He was even developing a paunch which wobbled as he chuckled – just like Dr Lambert senior.

'Follow my instructions, keep the little one warm, give her plenty of liquids and she should be fine. I'll call again in a couple of days.' Without more ado, the doctor packed his medical bag and made for the back door, accompanied by Ginny. He paused on the step and called out, 'And a Merry Christmas to you all!'


They had just started to eat their Christmas dinner when the siren sounded. 'There she go – old Moaning Minnie! She don't half choose her moments!' Ted protested. Lizzie immediately announced that she was not going to go outside to the dug-out Tovell and Ted had already prepared. Even though Molly's breathing was so much better since inhaling the Friars Balsam, she would not risk taking the baby out into the bitter cold and would take her chances in the cupboard under the stairs. At this, Ted declared, 'Hitler int spoiling my Christmas dinner – no, that he int. That might be my last and I'm going to enjoy it while it's hot.' He promptly sat down at the table again and began eating.

Tovell looked at his wife. 'Ted's right,' said Ginny glancing anxiously in the direction of the tiny cupboard as her daughter, carrying her granddaughter, squeezed inside. 'This could be our last proper Christmas dinner. Reckon I'll finish my meal first.' With a smile, Tovell too walked back to his chair. At that moment, the all-clear sounded.

'Would you believe that!' exclaimed Ted. 'Bet some silly sod had had too much festive liquor and mistook our boys' planes for the Hun. And to think this food could have been wasted.'

At the end of their meal, they drank the health of their absent sons, Bobby and Alec, and son-in-law, Peter. At the mention of her husband's name, Lizzie could not prevent a tear from trickling down her cheek. She brushed it hastily away and forced herself to say cheerfully, 'I bet the three of them are getting drunk together in some pub.'

'Yes, let's hope they've been able to meet up,' said her mother. 'They might even be home next Christmas.'

This led to reminiscences about the first Christmas of the last war and inevitably, to recollections of friends and comrades who had not survived that conflict. Suddenly, Tovell realized the conversation was upsetting his wife and Lizzie. 'I think we boys ought to wash up for a change. C'mon, Ted! Let's head for the scullery.'


That night, when they were cuddled up in bed, Tovell's thoughts went back to the earlier discussion. 'Remember our first Christmas together, Ginny? Like I told you then, it was the happiest I'd ever known. The only thing that spoiled it was the thought that it might also be our last one together.'

'Yes, I was thinking the same thing,' Ginny replied. 'Knowing that you'd soon be in the trenches … We've been very lucky, haven't we?'

'We have, sweetheart. Since I came home in 1919 we've had twenty happy years together; seen the children reach adulthood and been allowed to grow old together.'

They were silent, lost in their thoughts, Ginny cradled against Tovell, his arm enfolding her, his knees tucked up beneath her legs. Then his hand left her waist, caressed her thigh and travelled down to the hem of her nightdress. 'And where does that hand think it's going?' she inquired archly. 'A moment ago it was leading me towards the churchyard.'

'Ah, well! I didn't mean we were old yet. I just meant we were lucky that we would be allowed to grow old together – in the future.'

'Hmm!' murmured Ginny, turning over so that she faced her husband and could put her arms round his neck. 'I have a feeling that old age is going to come and go at will as far as you're concerned. You're going to be a poor old codger whenever you're asked to do something you don't want to do, and a sprightly young cockerel whenever there's something you do want to do.'

'Are you going to keep nagging me, woman? Haven't you anything better to do on a Christmas night?'

# 1940

# I

The bad winter continued into the New Year but the freezing snow did not prevent the regulars from struggling to the *Admiral Lord Nelson* most evenings. There was a certain amount of gloating from those who had converted sheds and small barns into pigsties when rationing of bacon and ham, as well as butter and sugar, began on the eighth of January. But the main topic of conversation, apart from a continuing sympathy and admiration for the Finns who were holding out against the Russians, was condemnation of the newspaper reporters who were persisting in calling this a "phoney war". Those living along the Norfolk and Suffolk coasts, many with friends and relatives on both merchant and navy ships, were only too aware that the huge toll of vessels and crew, from the very first day, meant that the war at sea was far from phoney. There was general indignation later in January when, during one attack by German aircraft off Great Yarmouth, bombs were not only dropped on merchant ships but on a defenceless lightship. One Yarmouth man, out of a crew of eight, survived the ordeal.

Ted Carter had a moment of glory at the end of the month when the services of his Volunteer Life-saving Brigade were called upon after the Latvian steamer, *Tautmila,* was bombed a mile off shore and the burning vessel came aground on Walcott Beach just north of Haisbro. Ted's agonizing account of the Brigade's heroic efforts to haul the life-saving apparatus through the deep snow drifts to the stricken vessel earned him several free pints of beer as did his amusing conclusion to the story. 'That was dark time we got to her and the fire had died down. We climbed aboard and started to search for survivors. We only found one alive — barely — and he couldn't speak a word of English. That turned out that he'd been knocked unconscious and his mates thought he was a gonna. When the skipper called, "Abandon ship!" his pals left the poor bugger for dead. Cor blast, bor, if we hadn't struggled against the elements an' all to get to him when we did, he would have been a gonna. The Rocket

Brigade's gotta keep an eye on the ship 'til she can be towed away for repairs. I offered to take one of the night watches – o' course, you'd need a flask of rum with you to keep out the chill on that there beach – but they said I wasn't needed. Can't think why.'

Tovell returned from making deliveries one afternoon to find Ginny tearful. He had just missed her two brothers who had come to tell her that they had joined the Royal Naval Reserve. 'They say all fishing has been suspended for the duration of the war,' Ginny explained. 'They reckon they were lucky to be able to fish these last few months but the fleets have been attacked so much the government won't allow them to fish any more. They say most of the trawlers and drifters are being converted for minesweeping – just like last time – and anti-submarine duties. They decided they might as well stay with their boat.'

'All credit to them for volunteering. They're twenty five years older than the last time they volunteered,' said Tovell, solemnly.

'And there were three of them then. Three of them came to say goodbye to me but only two returned,' Ginny commented in little more than a whisper.

'I know,' said Tovell quietly, putting a comforting arm around his wife's shoulder. 'Poor young Ben - that was a tragedy.' Then he added, 'You went up to the cliff top after your brothers had visited you. Do you remember? That picture of you beneath Haisbro Lighthouse sustained me through all the long years which followed. Don't despair, little darling. They'll be back – I'm sure of it.'

Ginny stretched up on tiptoe and gave Tovell a peck on the chin before disentangling herself from his embrace. She began to set the table in a determined manner and said in matter-of-fact tones, 'I went to see Mary again this morning. She's had a visit from one of her son's friends - a survivor from the *Royal Oak*. He told her it all happened very quickly. Three torpedoes hit her simultaneously; she exploded, keeled over and sank within ten minutes. Most of the eight hundred odd who died would have been asleep below when the attack came. They were entombed. Mary said it was a comfort to think George didn't suffer for long. He joined the Navy when he was fifteen, you know. It was his whole life ... They've had to move the rest of the Home Fleet out of Scapa Flow now

– dispersed it whilst they make it more secure. They didn't think anything could get between the sunken block-ships; that it was a totally safe anchorage. Strange what one little U-boat can do …'

'Ginny, stop torturing yourself,' said Tovell. 'It's not going to be like last time. This attack was exceptional. Even Churchill in the House of Commons called it a remarkable exploit of skill and daring. Don't assume the U-boats are invincible and that the boys are in any more danger because of them. And while we're on the subject of not depressing yourself, stop listening to Lord Haw Haw's broadcasts.'

'But he gives more details than the BBC,' Ginny protested.

'What's the good of that if half the details are untrue? He's preaching German propaganda. He wants to demoralize us. Stick to the Home Service, sweetheart.'

But the news from the BBC Home Service was depressing over the next few weeks. Finland held out until the twelfth of March before succumbing to the Russians and signing an agreement giving Russia large areas of her territory. Events moved rapidly after that with Nazi Germany invading two neutral countries in early April – Denmark and Norway – and claiming that it was necessary in order to make them protectorates of the Reich in the face of aggression from the democracies! Denmark was occupied in one day with no resistance but the British Government promised Norway full aid and Mr Chamberlain announced that we had two strong fleets at sea. The press then forgot all about the phoney war and concentrated on the "Great Naval Battle" off Norway and published special editions to keep pace with the details as they were received. Excitement grew that at last the Hun were being sorted out and neighbours in the little Haisbro community stood outside to watch the planes crossing the coastline on their way to join in the fray.

Tovell was reluctant to start work before he had heard the eight o'clock news in the mornings; he endeavoured to be near a wireless set for the one o'clock bulletin and listening to the six o'clock and nine o'clock news was a nightly ritual for him and Ginny and the entire population. There was general praise for the BBC's service and all the details it gave. It was possible to keep a tally of the British and German ships and submarines lost and it seemed that Britain was losing considerably fewer than Germany. Delight over this was dampened by the thought that lives were nevertheless being sacrificed on both sides and some could belong to well-loved sons, brothers and husbands. Thankfully, no telegrams arrived for the Tovells or for their relatives and friends so they could rejoice that British soldiers were continuing to land in Norway. Hopes were raised that Hitler had been stopped but then came reports that he too was still landing forces in Norway: by air now that the Royal Navy was sinking his troopships. Soon there was deadlock and then, on the second of May, came Mr Chamberlain's statement that we were evacuating our forces from Norway. Worse was to come: by the tenth of May the Germans had skirted round north of the Maginot Line, France's white elephant of a defence system, to invade Belgium and Holland. On that same day, Chamberlain resigned and Winston Churchill took over as Prime Minister, with a mandate to form a Coalition Government. The war was far from over after all.

Ted Carter was, predictably, jubilant at the elevation of his hero. 'You'll see some action now, bor. Churchill's the man for the job. He'll soon sort that bloomin' Hitler out.'

Tovell had a soldier's view of the situation. 'It was inevitable that the Chamberlain Government would fall after the fiasco of the Norwegian campaign. No doubt, in years to come, we shall find out what went wrong. And I can't understand why the British Expeditionary Force hasn't budged from the Belgium frontier in the previous six months. We could have attacked whilst the Nazis were occupied elsewhere. Surely we didn't think, like the French, that the Maginot Line would hold them. Underground tunnels were a fine means of defence in the last war but things have moved on. And we shouldn't have assumed that the Ardennes forests were impassable to a modern day army. This is the age of mechanization. The tank, at least in German hands, has come a long way since the ones we knew and look how air warfare has advanced. We didn't have dive bombers then but look how successful they've been for Hitler. Our generals must be living in the past but Hitler isn't. He's employing the same *Blitzkrieg* tactics he used in Poland. Holland has fallen in only five days and now Belgium has surrendered. The French haven't counter-attacked either; they've been caught out by the speed of the Germans' assault. It looks to me like Hitler's trying to drive a wedge between us and the French. The British Expeditionary Force could be trapped; cut off from the Channel ports and if we lose all our men and equipment at this stage, we're done for.'

'We int done for,' Ted argued, 'not with Churchill at the helm.'

'You told me yourself, Tovell, after you'd read an account of Churchill's first speech to the Commons as Prime Minister, that he has said victory at all costs is our aim. And,' Ginny added, with a twinkle in her eyes, 'now that you're involved in our defence, victory is certain.'

'Alright, I admit I did get a bit excited when Anthony Eden made his broadcast that he was forming the Local Defence Volunteers.'

'A bit excited! Your shrieks of delight must have been heard by Hitler.'

'Well, everything so far has had an age restriction on it. This is the first force to state anyone from fifteen to sixty-five can join.'

'Do you know, Ted,' said Ginny, laughing, 'he was out of the back door and heading for the police station before the War Minister had finished his broadcast.'

'I wasn't the only one eager to do something. I read in the paper that most of the police stations in East Anglia had run out of enrolment forms in the first twenty four hours. Mind you, the emphasis Eden put on the fact that German paratroopers had played a key role in the defeat of Holland and Belgium and that they could also be used as part of an invasion here, must have influenced many people. But the part of his broadcast I really didn't like was when he said the only qualification for joining was that a person should be capable of free movement. Hell! I hope we'll be capable of a bit more than free movement!'

# II

Towards the end of June, Alec arrived home unexpectedly for a short spell of leave prior to being "re-assigned abroad". He had been with the Home Fleet off Norway until every available Royal Navy ship was diverted to the moles of Dunkirk and the neighbouring beaches to ferry away the beleaguered British Expeditionary Force and its French and Belgium allies. His mother, naturally, wanted to hear all his news but he would only relate to her what he had seen in general terms; leaving the detail to when he was alone with his father. When Tovell had a delivery of vegetables to make to Great Yarmouth, Alec accompanied him, seated beside him in the cab of the truck.

'Nothing prepares you for what you see, does it?'

'No,' replied Tovell. 'I was a lot younger than you when I was first in a battle. We were pinned down for days and when it was over I came across what remained of a pal of mine – a boy the same age as me. An old soldier had to drag me away.'

'A lot of the time you don't even know who it is. That's the trouble with high explosives – torpedoes, bombs, heavy artillery ... Sometimes all you can do is hose down the decks.'

'We went round to see Albert, Mary's remaining son, the other day,' said Tovell. 'He's been sent home on sick leave. Poor chap. He was in a terrible state. He's with the 2nd Battalion, Norfolk Regiment. They went to France at the start with the BEF. They'd had a terrible time getting to Dunkirk – repeated attacks by the Hun – and once there not many of his battalion got away. Albert says he can't remember much about their time on the beaches – I reckon his mind doesn't want to remember. All he can recall is the WVS ladies telling him he was home, spooning soup into him and dressing the sores on his feet. I bet that haunted look in his eyes will be a long time going. Mary had to tell him about his brother too – that he'd gone down with the *Royal Oak*. He was very upset about that, of course.'

'The soldiers were on the beaches for days,' said Alec. 'I think it took about nine days to get as many as we could off. The *Luftwaffe* was pounding them, and the rescue ships, constantly. The sea was full of floating bodies. We couldn't get that close to shore; it was the little ships which kept going backwards and forwards to the beaches. It was a hell of a sight, Father: pleasure steamers, yachts and I caught sight of the Gorleston lifeboat, the *Louise Stephens*. I didn't dare tell Mother but I also saw a lot of minesweeping trawlers and drifters. You could still make out the YH markings on several of them so they must have been Yarmouth fishing boats originally. A lot of minesweepers were sunk; I just hope her brothers weren't on any of them.'

'I should think we would have known by now. Their wives haven't had any telegrams, thank God. Changing the subject, the newspapers have been making the point that we've had to leave behind all our heavy equipment. It's going to be a battle in itself to replace all those tanks, heavy guns and vehicles. The Local Defence Volunteers won't be getting much in equipment 'til the main army has been re-stocked. Still, around here, most of us have our own guns anyway.'

'It was bad enough getting most of the men off. At least we still have an army – once thc poor devils recover – albeit a depleted one. I pity the ones left behind. They'll be in prison camps now – if they survived. The ones we got off were not just British: there were a lot of Frenchmen and Belgians amongst them. The Belgians were cursing their king for surrendering to the Nazis. They'd disowned him. No doubt the French will be feeling the same about their government now that they've agreed an armistice with the Germans.'

'Churchill tried to dissuade them but at least he's made it clear **we** shall never surrender,' said Tovell. 'Old Ted's right – he's the man for the job. He's an experienced soldier – served in India, the Sudan and South Africa when he was younger – and when he rejoined the Army in the last war he didn't go for a desk job, y'know, he went over the top with his men umpteen times before he was recalled to government. He believes in leading from the front and of course, no-one could make more inspiring speeches. I just hope boasting morale will be enough now that we're standing alone against Hitler.'

'But we're not quite alone,' Alec pointed out. 'King Haakon ordered the Norwegian Navy and their Merchant Navy to come over to us before we evacuated him. Queen Wilhelmina brought the Dutch Navy with her when we evacuated her last month and now General De Gaulle is here, although whether the French Navy will come over to us is debatable. One thing's for sure: London is going to be the seat of a lot of governments-in-exile until this is over. Czechs, Poles – in fact, men from every country which has been invaded are flocking here to join us so we're not totally alone. I've met Canadians, Australians and New Zealanders too.'

'Yes, the Commonwealth and Empire are coming to our support just like they did last time,' his father agreed, 'but have we enough equipment to defend ourselves? Eden's speech, which was on the nine o'clock news after the Dunkirk evacuation, was relayed to America too. He praised the way that four-fifths of the BEF had been saved but also emphasized the vast quantity of stores that had been lost in Flanders and appealed for tanks, planes and ammunition. We must pray America will respond. Everyone is certain Hitler will invade us now that he's conquered Europe. I'm training the local members of the LDV every evening and weekend – the press are calling us the Anti-Parachutists Volunteers – but whether we'll be ready in time is another matter. There's an agreement that the church bells won't be rung for services; they'll only be rung as a warning if there's an invasion or paratroopers landing. That's ominous, isn't it? There've been plenty of air raids on the county so far but nothing intense enough to herald an invasion. The ARP wardens are asking people to leave buckets of water at their front gates for them to use on fires. We haven't had any in our area yet, thank God.'

They had to stop talking as they approached yet another road block and had to show their identity cards. The soldiers who made a cursory search of their truck had their bayonets fixed. Tovell nudged Alec when he noticed that on the side of the road, close at hand, was a rubber mat embedded with spikes. They were not delayed for long: Alec's uniform, his father's Local Defence Volunteer armband and a wagon loaded with vegetables ensured they were soon on their way again. 'Good job we weren't in a hurry to get away,' Tovell commented. 'As soon as I'd have turned on the engine that mat of spikes would have been under the rear wheel.'

'They're certainly prepared for trouble. I haven't seen a single signpost since we left home. They must have taken them all down. And come to think of it, there don't seem to be any milestones either,' Alec remarked.

'When we get towards Great Yarmouth you'll see that every road into the town is barricaded. They're mining bridges in some places, so I'm told and painting out the names of towns on hoardings and on vans and lorries. What a state to be in! But then, we're so close to the Continent here: Holland is only ninety miles away. And you won't see many children in Yarmouth: most of them were evacuated to the Midlands on the second of June with their teachers. The schools here have been closed.'

'I'm not so sure an invasion is imminent,' Alec stated. 'I don't think Hitler is strong enough to invade yet. He's had huge losses too whilst he's been charging across Europe and Scandinavia. And I doubt his Navy is in a position to support an invasion. We destroyed and damaged a lot of his battleships off Norway and our submarines were more successful than his U-boats. Though the campaign to save Norway was a failure, it might have helped to save us.'

As they approached the town along the Caister Road, they were stopped a number of times at barricades manned by the military. At one point, Tovell commented on the trench at the side of the road. 'There are trenches all around the town and along the coastline as far as Lowestoft. Just think of all that digging! It certainly takes me back a few years. I always said I'd never want to dig again once I left the Army, but look at me now – a smallholder digging somewhere most days of the year.' They reached the Market Place eventually but before they got out of the cab, Tovell announced, 'Better move Blackie Two outside to the rear of the truck. She's supposed to be a working dog guarding the produce.'

Alec laughed. 'A working dog!' he scoffed. 'She's been curled up asleep between us for most of the journey.'

The Labrador did not take kindly to being woken up – she gave a pitiful little whine as Tovell dragged her off the padded seat, lowered the board at the rear of the open wagon and urged her to climb inside. She made at once for an old jacket of Tovell's, which was her bed whenever she was "on duty", gave a sigh and flopped down. She watched as the two men began to unload crates of produce and carry them to the stall-holders. When Tovell and his son returned from one such delivery, they found a policeman standing beside their vehicle.

'Is this your animal?' asked the officer. When Tovell nodded, he continued, 'You know you're not supposed to keep pets.'

'She's not a pet; she's my guard dog.'

'How can she be a guard dog when she's half-asleep?' asked the constable.

'She's a guard dog alright,' Tovell insisted. 'I had to get her so that she could patrol my smallholding. We've had a lot of thieves operating in our area stealing produce and poultry to sell on the black market in the cities.'

'Oh, I'm not disputing your need for a guard dog, just whether this one really is a guard dog.'

'Make out you're going to try to take one of the crates,' Tovell suggested. 'But be careful! Move your hand very slowly towards one of them.'

Alec had watched this interchange with interest. Whilst his father had been talking, he had seen him go to the cab, open the driver's door and put his hand under the dashboard. When he had withdrawn from the cab and approached the policeman, Alec was aware that he had something behind his back. Now, as the officer tentatively stretched out his hand towards a crate, Tovell stood behind him and extended his own arm so that whatever he was holding would appear, to the dog, to be something that the policeman was brandishing in his other hand. At once, Blackie Two went berserk: jumping to her feet, baring her teeth, growling, barking and snarling alternatively. The constable leaped backwards in alarm and would have knocked Tovell over had not the latter been on his way back to his cab to restore the cause of the commotion to its hiding place.

'Alright! Alright!' yelled the policeman. 'She's a guard dog. I believe you!'

As the man left, somewhat shaken and red-faced, Tovell made a fuss of Blackie Two, patting and stroking her. 'Good girl! Well done! Good girl!' he murmured repeatedly.

'How did you teach her to do that?' asked Alec.

'I didn't teach her. She's just a clever girl,' replied his father. Alec looked unconvinced. 'Okay! Look in the compartment under the dashboard – but don't let her see you. I keep the leash in there which she was chained up with. Her previous master used to beat her with it – or so we think. Anyway, it does the trick every time. Let's get the rest of the unloading done quickly in case he comes back with his pals; then we'll call on the Westgates before we go home.'

They were stopped once more as they approached the seafront. This road block was also the site of an anti-aircraft gun but as soon as Tovell explained that they were taking supplies to their friends, the Westgates, around the corner on North Drive they were ushered through enthusiastically. Tovell commented on this strange state of affairs as soon as they were inside the Westgates' large imposing house. 'Of course they were pleased to let you through once you mentioned foodstuff,' said Bill Westgate. Pointing at his wife, he added, 'This old softy treats them all like her grandchildren. She spends half her day cooking for them. She's always taking them hot food and drinks.'

Gladys Westgate interrupted her husband. 'Be fair, Bill. They bring us lots of rations from their depot.'

'Yes, well, they're not daft are they? And when she's not fussing over them she's up at the WVS HQ organizing heaven knows what!'

Tovell laughed. 'Do I detect a note of resentment? Are you feeling neglected, Bill?'

'Oh, he's always saying he's neglected,' replied Mrs Westgate, looking fondly at her husband. 'But I can't be idle. They closed down all our entertainment businesses last August, just before they declared war, and the hotels and guest houses have been taken over by the Army and the Navy. I'm used to helping with a busy holiday season and visitors staying virtually all year round; now all that's gone for the duration. I'm happy I've been able to fill the gap. He's just annoyed because no-one will let him do very much.'

'They keep telling me I'm too old,' Bill protested. 'I tried to join the Air Raid Precautions people but they said I was over the age to be a warden. I tried the Auxiliary Fire Service but they called me unfit as well as too old. I've managed to get into the new Local Defence Volunteers but only by making a fuss; telling them that they need my experience as a veteran. Even so, they say I can't fight – only man a desk.'

'I know how you feel,' said Tovell. 'I'm not so many years younger than you, Bill, so I've had the same trouble. But they've let me join the LDV, thanks goodness, and I'm training a lot of the men locally. I suppose you can understand that they don't want you to take any risks - and administration is just as vital as fighting.'

'Stuff and nonsense! The Somme was a long time ago and I've managed perfectly well with one kidney ever since. Look what I've done here. Ever since the war ended and we settled in Yarmouth, I've gone from a boxing booth on the pier to owning half the town and that wasn't from sitting on my backside at a desk. It's taken long hours and hard work – '

'And our son, Sam, and all his hard work,' said Mrs Westgate, interrupting.

'Yes, Sam, of course,' agreed her husband. 'I wasn't trying to belittle Sam's contribution; just trying to point out that I'm not an invalid, never have been and shouldn't be treated as such.'

'He's also a bit niggled that they welcomed Sam with open arms and made matters worse by saying they wanted his experience as a veteran. They've even made him an officer in the LDV but of course, as I keep telling my old darling here, Sam's a generation younger.' As she spoke, Gladys Westgate perched herself on the arm of her husband's enormous armchair and squeezed his hand affectionately. Then, looking at Alec, she said, 'But what really bothers me is what might happen to all you young people. I bet your mother's worried sick about you - and Bobby and Lizzie's Peter. I know I wake up in the middle of the night worrying about my grandchildren.'

'Yes, I think it's harder for parents – and wives - left behind,' Alec agreed. 'Mother's worried and so is my sister. They both think the best thing is to keep busy.'

'That reminds me,' said Tovell. 'I have a message for you from Mary. She said to say sorry she hasn't written for ages but she's got Albert at home with her now. He's on sick leave – trying to get over what happened to him at Dunkirk. He's in a bad way.'

'Oh, poor Mary,' exclaimed Gladys. 'I thought it was odd that I hadn't heard from her. I was going to write to your Ginny to ask how she was – knowing she must be suffering after George's loss on the *Royal Oak*. Mary was so kind when Bill was billeted with her at the Coastguard Station. Do you remember, you all spent the first Christmas of the last war there – before you went to the trenches? And she invited me to spend Christmas there too – to be with Bill. Her letters were such a comfort when he was wounded and during that long, long spell when he was recovering. I'll write to her and see if she thinks it would help if she and Albert came to stay with us for a while – to recuperate.'

'Poor George,' said Bill sadly. 'He was such a lovely boy; so was Albert. And Rachel was the sweetest little girl imaginable. Of course, she's your daughter-in-law, isn't she? She's Bobby's wife. All three of them were lovely children and great company to be with. Yes, Gladys is right, Alec. Instead of feeling sorry for ourselves because they won't let us oldies have a go at the Hun, we should be feeling sorry for you young ones and what awaits you.'

'Don't feel sorry for me, Uncle Bill,' Alec answered, deliberately sounding cheerful. 'You and Father and your generation did your duty and now it's up to my generation. We're all aware of that.'

'Yes, and you sound just like our grandchildren, doesn't he, Gladys?'

'They're happily working out when they'll be old enough to be called up,' replied Mrs Westgate, adding ruefully, 'I don't think they'll find it quite as much fun as they think.'

Remembering the conversation he'd had with Alec earlier, Tovell changed the subject to something less personal. 'I could see as we drew up in front of your house that you have a battery north of you.'

'Yes, it's got two six inch guns. The search lights keep us awake at night. We should keep the blackout blinds right down,' replied Bill. 'Mustn't complain though: it needs to be there. There's another at the Harbour's Mouth and an even bigger one on the other side of the river on Gorleston Cliffs. We've got anti-aircraft guns like the one round the corner, all over the town. A few years back when the number of visitors to the Norfolk Broads was increasing, we invested in some holiday cruisers, didn't we, Gladys? But they've been requisitioned too along with a lot of boats from other hire firms. The Navy's using them to patrol the Broads and the connecting rivers.'

Tovell nodded. 'A shopkeeper I was delivering to in Stalham yesterday told me they've moored boats in a line across Hickling Broad to stop the Hun from landing sea planes there. With all this preparation for an invasion, are you sorry you settled here instead of staying in Birmingham after the last war?'

'No, we've no regrets, have we, Gladys?' asked Bill. His wife smiled and shook her head. 'We've been very happy here and, of course, we've prospered in a way we never would have had we stayed in Birmingham.

I know that makes us in the front line now but you have to take the rough with the smooth in this life. Anyway, who's to say Hitler will only bombard the coastline before he tries to invade? He could bomb the cities as well. A lot of people we know have gone to stay with relatives inland – and you'll have heard the Yarmouth schools have been evacuated to the Midlands – but we've talked about it and we've decided to stay put, haven't we, Gladys?'

'Yes. From our bedroom window we can see across the seafront to the beach so we'll know straightaway if Jerry lands here. Bill's already put his guns and ammunition, which he uses for game shooting, in the ottoman. He's shown me how to load his rifles so we shall be a two people militia.'

Alec laughed politely but he was not certain that his hostess was joking. 'Don't mention the beach,' said Bill suddenly. 'That's a sore subject. I used to walk the dogs on our lovely beach every morning – it put me in a good humour for the day. Just look at it now – ruined because of Hitler. It's all barbed wire, mines and tank traps. It's the same with our back gardens: we've had to dig them up to put in Anderson shelters and throw out the flowers and shrubs to make way for vegetables. And think of all the hours we've spent covering the windows with Cellophane and strips of sticky paper. What a state to be in. Still, mustn't moan. Alec and his young pals risking their lives for us are the only ones entitled to moan. I expect you'll be stationed off the coast, Alec, ready to attack their troopships?'

'I think you can be certain a lot of our Home Fleet will be off here ready to thwart Hitler's invasion plans but, as it happens, I'm on a few days leave before going abroad. The rumour that's been flying around is that we're headed for the Mediterranean. Now Mussolini's joined forces with Hitler and Italy's declared war on us, we've got to defend the Suez Canal.'

# III

Ginny seemed to take comfort from the fact that Alec was on his way to the Mediterranean and Tovell decided not to point out to her that there was no logic behind her assumption that he would be in less danger there than in patrolling the North Sea. He felt she had quite enough to worry about anyway: she didn't know the whereabouts of either Bobby or Peter and the constant speculation in the press and in the news broadcasts about the imminent invasion, was enough to put more white streaks in her once luxuriant auburn hair. Rumour was rife: Hitler would be in London by August; he would invade next week; he was postponing the invasion; he would invade at the next full moon. But what was fact and not speculation was the increase in air raids and that, everyone agreed, was a preliminary to the invasion.

The bombing of Norwich on the ninth of July made particularly distressing reading because of the number of young girls killed as they were leaving the Colman's mustard factory at the end of their working day. Two days later, there were more civilian deaths in Great Yarmouth. In a flurry of activity, pill boxes went up everywhere and those left from the last war were hastily repaired.

The most cheering thing which happened in July was Churchill's decision to change the title of the Local Defence Volunteers to a more appropriate one – the Home Guard. Instructions came to the newly renamed force that in view of the scarcity of conventional weapons they should try making one which the Finns had invented and had used successfully a few months previously when they had been invaded by the Russians – the Molotov cocktail.

Rationing spread to include tea and cooking fat, and income tax went up again in the third War Budget as did the duty on beer and tobacco. And there was a new purchase tax. 'What the bloomin' heck is that?' asked Ted.

'It's a tax on any non-essential goods you may buy,' Tovell explained.

'Non-essential? Everything I buy is essential,' Ted maintained. 'I int giving the government any more of my money.'

'That's not very patriotic of you, Ted,' said Tovell, jokingly. 'This war's got to be paid for.'

'There's no-one more patriotic than Ted Carter, that there int. I'll just have to drink more beer so they get the tax on that. I'm as willing as the next man to do my bit.'

As the summer progressed the air raids increased; so did the numbers of planes involved in the attacks. The Tovells would stand outside their home watching the squadrons of bombers and fighters – too numerous to count – heading out towards the North Sea from their Norfolk airfields. Sometimes the *Luftwaffe* had left their bases so early that there were dogfights over the coastline. Ginny could not bear to watch these and always retreated to the shelter to join Lizzie and Molly, leaving her husband to root for the RAF. As he explained to Blackie Two, who was always reluctant to leave her saviour's side, 'We've lost the battle for France, girl; let's hope those youngsters up there can win the battle for Britain.'

By the beginning of September the raids on London became nightly, sometimes with daylight attacks too. The situation became so bad that fire engines had to be summoned from as far away as Ipswich in Suffolk. Children who had been evacuated from London a year ago but who had returned home when it seemed we were involved in a phoney war, were rushed away from the capital once more. Although most local children had been evacuated from the port and from the city, the rest of Norfolk was deemed still to be safe for incoming evacuees. Tovell chanced to be in North Walsham Market Place one day after a group of children from London had been gathered there. All were being ushered away to their new homes except for three who were huddled together in front of the Market Cross, their gas-mask boxes strung around their necks. One was a girl of about eight years old and she had her arms around two little boys, hugging them closely to her. She was glaring defiantly at anyone who went near the little group.

'Won't anyone take those three?' Tovell asked the owner of the shop where he had just delivered produce.

'No, no-one wants all three of them,' replied the greengrocer. 'She's a spunky little girl. She keeps telling everyone that she promised her mum that she'd take care of her little brothers. She says rather than be split up she'll walk back to London with them. I'd take them myself but the wife's sister turned up last week with her brood. She says she can't stand the bombing in Yarmouth and is going to stay with us for the duration. Cor, blast, that Hitler's got a lot to answer for!'

Tovell wrote out a Delivery Note for the man and then wandered over to the Market Cross. The little group was a sorry spectacle – dirty and bedraggled. Tovell could even smell them from a distance. The boys – one about seven and the other about four – had clearly been sick and their cheeks were tear-stained. Their sister's eyes blazed and she challenged Tovell as soon as he was within earshot. 'We're staying together, mister. We ain't stopping. We're going back home.'

'Yes, so I've been told,' Tovell replied genially. 'That's why I've come over. I thought I might help you with that. I've marched hundreds of miles in my time, across the continents of India and Africa, and I can tell you that in your present state you won't make it to London.'

The little girl looked at him quizzically. 'Why not?' she demanded.

'Because you're scrawny,' replied Tovell. 'I've seen scrawny men fall by the wayside many a time. They never made it home.'

'What's "scrawny"?' asked the elder of the two boys.

'I'll show you,' said Tovell. 'Push your sleeve up a bit above your wrist.' When the child had done as he was asked, Tovell pinched a little bit of the exposed flesh between his thumb and finger. 'That's "scrawny". Now look at the thickness when I pinch my arm.' So saying, he nipped a generous wedge of his own forearm. 'It's lucky for you I came along when I did. My wife's a very good cook and she'll soon build you up. When you're no longer scrawny you can set off back to London. And whilst she's fattening you up, I can teach you all the other things you'll need to know if you're to survive such a long march.'

'What other things?' asked the little girl, looking at Tovell suspiciously.

'Well, for one thing, I don't suppose you know how to forage - to live off the land.' The boys both shook their heads. 'On a long march you've got to find food and know what's safe to eat and what isn't. And then you've got to be able to recognize danger and know how to avoid it. There's a lot to learn before you start a long march.' He looked at his watch. 'If we leave now we'll get home just in time for dinner. What do you say?'

The two little boys looked up at their sister. 'I'm hungry,' said the younger one.

His brother nodded his agreement vigorously. 'Let's go with the man, Peggy.'

'Alright! But only until we're not scrawny any more. I want to go home.'

Tovell smiled. 'That's agreed then.' He looked behind him and, as expected, a WVS lady was standing there. She had been listening to the proceedings. 'Do I have to sign something, ma'am?' he asked.

'You do,' replied the woman. 'I'll go and get the form for you. Thank you so much. The billeting officer will be so relieved. He was beginning to think he'd have to take them home himself.'

'I ought to explain that I only live a mile or two from the coast. Will that be all right? Will it be regarded as safe?'

'I think the billeting officer will be happy to bend the rules slightly - in the circumstances,' said the volunteer as she hurried away.

Tovell turned his attention to the children. 'That's my horse and cart over there. We might as well load your luggage into it whilst we're waiting.' The little girl looked sheepish and hugged her brothers closer to her, eyes downcast. 'Does that mean you haven't got any luggage?' Tovell asked gently.

The child nodded. 'Our dad didn't want us to go. It was our mum who wanted us to be safe but he said, "no". She had to get us up in the middle of the night and out of the house while he was asleep. She said if we stopped to get things he might wake up.'

'Well, never mind. Let's get you in the cart.' Blackie Two was asleep on the seat. Tovell fondled her head. 'C'mon, girl. Wake up! You'll have to go in the back. We've got some company and they'll want to sit up front with me.'

'Can I go in the back with the dog, mister?' asked the older boy

'Of course,' replied Tovell. 'She won't hurt you. You like dogs, do you?'

His sister answered for him. 'He's always liked dogs but we hadn't the room. Dad says they eat too much anyway.'

'She hasn't been with us long. I found her. You two can be each other's special friend,' said Tovell.


Tovell came into the scullery and closed the back door behind him. Ginny was at the big stone sink rinsing some clothes. She half turned and smiled at him over her shoulder. He came up behind her and put both arms around her tiny waist and kissed the side of her neck.

'It's no good you getting amorous – I'm about to dish up the dinner.'

'Can't I give my wife a little kiss without being accused –'

He got no further because Ginny interrupted him. 'You smell horrible!' she exclaimed as she turned round to face him, drying her hands on her apron as she did so. 'And you're looking guilty. What have you been up to?'

'There you go again – accusing me.'

'You've brought Ted Carter home with you again, haven't you? Oh, Tovell, I feel sorry for him too since his wife died but he eats so much. He's only a little shrimp but he puts away enough for three.'

'No, it's not Ted – but you got the number right. Take a look outside.' Taking her hand, he dragged her to the back door and opened it. The three children, Blackie Two beside them, were standing as they had at the Market Cross, the little girl with her arms enfolding her brothers protectively.

Ginny was speechless, open-mouthed at the woeful sight. The girl, expecting trouble, hastily explained. 'We ain't staying, missus. The nice man said you'd feed us up so we could march back home.'

'Oh, did he now?' said Ginny, in amused tones.

'No-one else would have them,' whispered Tovell in his wife's ear.

'I'm not surprised. Look at the state of them. Why ever didn't the WVS ladies clean them up and make them change their clothes?' There was a strained silence. Ginny herself provided the answer. 'They haven't got a change of clothes, have they?'

'It's a long story,' said Tovell.

'Well, there's nothing else for it. The nice man will have to climb up into the loft and rake through those boxes of clothes he said only a sentimental old fool like me would keep, and find something to fit you all.'


Later that afternoon, Lizzie came in the back door. Her mother was slicing bread. 'Has Molly been a good girl?' she asked.

'Good as gold,' replied Ginny. 'She had a long sleep late morning but she's been awake ever since.' As Lizzie moved to go through into the living-room, Ginny stopped her. 'Before you open that door, I'd better explain that Father came home with more waifs and strays today.'

'Oh, no! Not Blackie Three and Blackie Four,' said Lizzie, laughing. 'He'll never convince anyone he needs more guard dogs.'

'No, they're not guard dogs,' replied her mother. 'Take a look round the door.'

Lizzie's reaction was the same as her mother's had been: she stopped in the doorway open-mouthed when she saw the latest additions to the household. Peggy was in one armchair cuddling baby Molly whilst her two brothers were kneeling on the floor playing with a wooden fort and soldiers under the watchful eye of Tovell who was seated in the other armchair. The children were clean, bright eyed and smiling. Tovell looked up and grinned as the women entered the room. He was clearly enjoying himself. Nodding in the direction of the little girl, Lizzie said, 'That dress looks familiar.'

'It should be,' replied her mother. 'It's yours.'

Hearing this, Peggy called across the room at once, 'You can have it back, miss. We're not stopping.'

'No, it's too small for me now. You keep it. You look very pretty in it,' said Lizzie. 'I'm glad you like my baby and I can see she likes you.'

'Oh, is Molly your baby? She's lovely. I love babies. I wish we hadn't had to leave our babies behind. I wanted them to come with us,' Peggy confided, tears glistening in her eyes.

'Babies? I thought it was just the three of you in the family,' Ginny exclaimed.

'No, we've got two little brothers. They're twins - ten months old.'

'But they could have come too – with your mother. Children under five are accompanied by their mothers, or so I understand,' explained Ginny.

Peggy shook her head sadly. 'Dad would never let them come. He didn't want us to come. He said Mum's first duty was to look after him.'

'What is your father's line of work?' asked Tovell.

'He unloads ships at the docks,' replied the little girl.

'That probably counts as essential work which means he won't be called up,' said Tovell, looking at his wife.

'Well, that doesn't stop me from writing to your mother and telling her that she and the littl'uns are welcome here,' said Ginny.

'He won't let her come. He says she's gotta see to his needs,' Peggy said sadly.

Ginny exchanged glances with her husband before adding, 'When you write to her on Sunday, you can tell her about us and I'll give you a little note from me to include in the letter.'

The older boy, Roger, looked up from his game. 'Mum said not to write.'

Peggy nodded her agreement. 'She said Dad would tear up our letters so she wouldn't know the address to come to us and, he might even come after us himself if he knew where we were.'

Ginny was visibly upset at these revelations and Lizzie quickly intervened. 'Your mother will be distraught without you and needs to know that you're alright. There is a way to contact her without your father knowing – through the WVS. Because of the bombing, they've set up information centres so people will know what's happened to their relatives and friends. We'll give your letters to our ladies here and they'll pass them on so that their volunteers in London can get them to your mother – during the day when your father's at work.'

'I don't like the idea of deceiving a father, but in the circumstances, I don't see what else we can do,' said her mother.

Lizzie realized it was time to return to more cheerful matters. 'I can see you boys are going to enjoy playing with that fort.' The children looked at her and beamed.

'We've never had a fort and soldiers,' Roger confided.

'I shall have to do some repairs on the structure and a few of the soldiers are looking decidedly worse for the wear,' said Tovell.

'That's because it was Bobby's favourite toy and Alec loved it just as much,' Lizzie pointed out. 'It's a miracle it's still intact with all the hours and hours of use it's had.'

'That's because it was so well made in the first place,' said Ginny, looking at Tovell fondly. 'Father spent hours working on it for Bobby. It was for Christmas 1914.'

'And he made me a Hindu bride doll and crib,' said Lizzie, beaming at Tovell affectionately. 'How I loved that doll and how my friends envied me. No-one else had a doll like it. I've wrapped it up carefully for when

Molly is older. But if you kept the fort perhaps you kept other toys these children would like.'

'Father's already said he'll search the attic again in the morning: mustn't take any chances with the blackout. We can't risk a light showing through a loose tile.'

# IV

The children settled into their new environment with varying degrees of success. Peggy missed her little brothers but found comfort from "adopting" baby Molly. Lizzie had contacted the County Education authorities on reading of the problems arising from male teachers leaving for the armed services. The resulting shortage of teaching staff was made worse by the influx of evacuees into the county, all of whom had had to be absorbed into local schools. Her offer to return to the profession for which she had been trained was welcomed and, with her mother's agreement, she left straight after breakfast each day to cycle the four miles to her school. She would return in time for tea, leaving Ginny to take Molly in her pram onto their land whilst she worked — just as she had Alec when he was a baby. Before she went to school and as soon as she returned, Peggy would assume responsibility for the baby who, now that she could toddle around, needed plenty of attention. And when Lizzie was there to take over the care of her daughter, the little girl would happily help Ginny with the cooking and the housework.

Roger too, settled in well. His affinity with animals wasn't confined to Blackie Two. He fussed over the cats and rabbits; he gladly fed the hens and collected the eggs; he helped Tovell to care for Rajah Two and even enjoyed preparing the swill for the newly-installed pigs and assumed responsibility for their welfare. Only the youngest child, Will, remained a sad little boy. Ginny had wisely allowed the three siblings to continue to sleep together in one bed, as they had been used to doing at home, but Will's constant bed-wetting was a problem. Tovell, eventually, made up a camp bed for Roger in the same room; but Peggy said she must stay sleeping beside Will so that she could comfort him after his constant nightmares woke him up. Ginny tried to find a solution: she read every advice leaflet the WVS had issued on the subject — bed-wetting being all too common amongst disturbed children only recently plucked from the London blitz and from their mothers' care — and gladly accepted the special mattresses that those helpful volunteers provided. The nightmares receded somewhat and the bed-wetting improved once contact had been established with the children's mother via the WVS rest centre close to their East End home, but neither problem disappeared entirely.

All three children, however, enjoyed foraging expeditions into the countryside and Tovell probably enjoyed them even more than his young troop. But even on these innocent outings the war was never far away. They were searching the hedgerows near heath land one Saturday when Peggy said, 'That's a funny place to put washing lines. The mums have to come a long way to hang their washing out: there aren't any houses near here.'

Tovell looked across to where the little girl was pointing. 'No, Peggy, they're not washing lines. If you look closely, it's wire not linen line which is strung across the poles and there are ditches between the rows of poles. They're there to stop enemy gliders and planes from landing here. We've had to put them on any open land like this – even golf courses and recreation grounds – to stop an invasion. But don't you worry about it: our airmen are winning the battle for us.'

'And Uncle Tovell's Home Guard will soon sort out any who slip through,' Roger assured his sister.

Lizzie caught sight of the little band marching along as she and Molly returned from visiting a friend. 'Father's in his element with those littl'uns,' she commented to her mother as she entered the scullery.

'Yes,' Ginny agreed, 'He's shed twenty five years since they arrived. He admits it's like having you and Bobby young again.'

'We loved our walks with him; especially if we could get him talking about his life in foreign lands. Roger loves animals so I bet he's been told all about the exotic birds and wildlife.'

'I think he's been told more of Father's old tales than that. I heard him and young Will playing a game the other day where they were saying they were outnumbered by hordes of Dervishes!'

'Oh, dear!' Lizzie laughed. 'That means another generation of schoolchildren are going to be entertained in the playground by heroic but entirely fictitious yarns.'

At that moment, the children, accompanied by Blackie Two, ran noisily into the scullery. 'Look what we've got, Auntie Ginny,' they called out, almost in unison. They clustered excitedly around her and opened their hands to reveal pennies which had been clasped so tightly that they had made imprints in their red and sweaty palms.

'The lady gave us a penny halfpenny each for the rosehips we'd gathered,' said Roger.

'And threepence for the blackberries,' added Peggy, proudly.

'How was Mrs Brewster?' asked Ginny, looking at her husband.

'The best I've seen her in years,' Tovell replied. 'She's got her Women's Institute ladies involved in all sorts of work. At least this war's done some good: it's made people like Mrs B – and me for that matter – feel useful again.'

Ginny smiled affectionately at him. She then bent down and put her arm around the shoulder of the youngest child as he stood in silence with his hand outstretched. 'How much did you earn today, Will?'

'I got a penny halfpenny too,' he replied shyly. 'And Peggy says I can have a penny of the other money.'

'Well, you did your bit and you deserve to be paid,' said Ginny kindly. 'Those rosehips you gathered will be made into syrup which will be very good for babies like your little brothers. I expect you've kept some back for me so that I can make rosehip syrup for you and Molly - and Roger and Peggy. Now go you off and put your earnings into your money boxes then wash your hands so we can have tea.'

# V

Autumn 1940 saw the Norfolk countryside change even more as the need to protect its profusion of airfields – both fighter and bomber bases – became a critical factor in Britain's defence. Dummy airfields were hastily constructed – some with shacks and wooden planes; others with only landing lights which were switched on at night – to act as decoys to lure the enemy to drop their bombs on them instead of the real bases. A number of airmen frequented the *Admiral Lord Nelson* in their off-duty periods so the locals had soon got to know when the fighter squadrons had been moved south during August and September. When they came back to their Norfolk bases in late autumn and Churchill announced that the Battle of Britain had been won, he did not need to tell the locals how much they owed to "so few". It was obvious from the number of familiar faces which did not return to the public bar that robbing Hitler of his plan for air supremacy had been achieved at great cost in human life. Invasion no longer seemed imminent but the fear was still there that it had merely been postponed

The enemy's bombing campaign now spread to other cities as well, even further from the East Coast, to Liverpool and to Coventry which had 1,000 casualties. After that, Birmingham, Manchester, Bristol and Southampton were also targeted. The government asked factories to ensure that their chimneys made as much smoke as possible to hinder the view of the attacking *Luftwaffe* pilots. And the War Savings scheme alone was not considered sufficient, so War Weapons Weeks were introduced to raise money for armaments.

Norwich held such a fund-raising week in October and, incredibly, netted a million pounds – the record for any urban area of similar size in England. Many East Anglian towns reached their targets and were rewarded by having their names emblazoned on the military craft which they had "bought". Smaller communities were determined not to be outdone and, although a Spitfire at £6,000 was outside their range, they pinned lists up in their village halls and set their sights upon more modest targets such as a magnetic compass at £150, a pair of binoculars at £17, or a square yard of deck at £3.

In October, the village of Haisbro itself had its first air raid and low flying enemy aircraft took to machine-gunning any groups of people they spied. The Land Army girls were ordered to wear their tin hats when working in the fields and Ted was caught trying to fashion a helmet for his horse, Bessie, out of a large tin bowl. Tovell had never allowed his young evacuees to walk to and from school alone – something Bobby, Lizzie and Alec had always done – and when he heard that a group of schoolchildren on their way home down a country lane on the outskirts of Norwich had been strafed by machine-gun fire from an enemy plane, he stopped transporting them by horse and cart which he felt would make them an easier target. Instead, he arranged his working day so that he could walk with them and order them to take cover under the hedgerows at the first sound of an aircraft in the distance.

Ginny was glad she had the company of the three children since she saw less and less of Tovell as the year progressed. She knew his role as sergeant in the Home Guard meant he was responsible for training his unit and expected him to be absent several evenings a week and part of every Sunday; but as time went by he was rarely at home any evening and frequently away for the entire weekend on training exercises. When he was at home, he seemed strangely quiet and preoccupied and often appeared physically exhausted. One morning, he said to her, 'Ginny, I think you should keep a case packed with essentials – and one for the little ones – in case we're invaded.'

'But everyone thinks Hitler has postponed the invasion now he's lost the air battle,' she protested.

'But it could happen at any time. He's not going to warn us in advance. You should be prepared,' Tovell argued.

'But why? Where would we go and surely the Germans, even if they did invade, wouldn't be concerned about one little old family like us?'

'Please, Ginny, just do as I say. I'll feel happier if I know you and the little ones are ready to leave at a moment's notice. You could go to David and Lily's farm at Fakenham. If I'm not here you could hitch Rajah Two to the cart. It'd take you a few hours to get there using the back lanes but you'd be safe. You'd just look like another refugee family.'

'But if you were not here we'd wait for you.'

'No!' shouted Tovell in alarm. 'Promise me you wouldn't wait for me. I couldn't go with you anyway. Remember, the Home Guard was formed as a militia, specifically to fight the enemy if they invaded. Now promise, Ginny, that as soon as the church bell sounded you wouldn't wait. You'd collect the children and go at once.'

Tovell's tone of voice and expression were so earnest that Ginny could not help being concerned. 'You're scaring me,' she exclaimed. 'Is there something you're not telling me?'

'Sorry, I don't mean to scare you, sweetheart.' He drew her to him and struggled to reply calmly. 'I've seen what invading forces can do to civilian populations; I just don't want you to risk hanging around to find out how Jerry will behave. I couldn't bear anything to happen to you, my little darling, so please, just promise you'll do as I say.'

The second Christmas of the war approached and it became clear that once more none of the boys would be home. Letters had arrived from Bobby, Peter and Alec but they were posted at intervals, indicating that all three spent most of their time at sea, and censorship prevented them from giving much information away. Reading between the lines, however, it was obvious that both Bobby and Peter, who had joined the Royal Navy at fifteen and after years of service were petty officers, were on the North Atlantic convoys. Alec's letters hinted that the rumour had been correct and that he was in the Mediterranean. His promise that he had lots to tell his father about an exciting encounter led Tovell to believe that Alec might have taken part in November in the attack at Taranto, when as Churchill had jubilantly announced, a "crippling blow" had been struck against the Italian Navy.

Ginny decided that they must make the best of things and try to ensure that the children enjoyed Christmas. Tovell took his little troop of evacuees in search of holly and mistletoe just as he had Bobby, Lizzie and Alec in years gone by. The Christmas tree was one growing on their own land and the newcomers enjoyed digging it up, dragging it indoors and decorating it as much as their predecessors had done.

Ginny knew that the children were still missing their mother and little brothers and she repeated her offer to have the rest of the family come to

Norfolk. As before, their mother declined the offer, fearing her husband would be so angry he would track them down and force all of them, including Peggy, Roger and Will, to return to the dangers of London with him. Realizing how distraught their mother must be and anxious to bring her some comfort by seeing for herself that her offspring were thriving, Ginny arranged for a photographic session one Saturday in North Walsham. She kept one picture of the two boys and Peggy, with Molly on her knee, for herself and displayed it in her front parlour as part of her huge collection of mementoes. A large photograph of the three siblings in a cardboard folder plus a postcard size picture of them, she dispatched in a parcel together with hand-knitted jumpers and rag soldier dolls for the infants. Under Ginny's direction, the children had all written loving messages to their mother on the back of the postcard which they had then enclosed inside a Christmas card made by Peggy. A few days later Ginny collected a reply from the WVS organizer in the village. The sight of the card which their mother had sent, a ten shilling note inside it for them, reduced the children to tears since it meant she would definitely not be joining them for Christmas. Ginny, tearful herself, felt obliged to explain to them that it was because their mother loved them so much that she had made the sacrifice of sending them to Norfolk to be safe.

Peggy was mystified about the ten shilling note. 'I don't know how Mum managed to save so much,' she confessed to Ginny. 'Dad don't give her much money and she has to spend most of it on him. We don't have meat and puddings at home like you give us – only Dad has that. He says he's the one who puts the bread on the table and he's the one who does the heavy work at the docks, so he needs the meat. Mum and me and the boys mostly have bread and dripping and soup when she can get a knuckle end to boil. That's why we were scrawny when Uncle Tovell found us. I don't think we ought to spend the ten shillings. We ought to save it 'til we see Mum again.'

'If your poor mother scrimped and saved to get that money for you – and she must have been putting something aside every week from the time you left home – it was because she wanted you and the boys to have something from her for Christmas - since she can't be with you yourself. I think she'd like to know that the three of you bought something that you'll really enjoy. That way she'll be comforted to think that stinting herself has been worthwhile.'

That night when she was curled up in bed beside Tovell, Ginny suddenly said, 'Do you think it's possible to hate someone you've never met? If so, then I hate Peggy's father with a passion.'

On Christmas Day the family attended the traditional Morning Service, holding hands and singing carols as they made their way along the country lanes to Haisbro. They stopped at the cottage belonging to Bobby and Rachel and the latter happily joined them. A few doors further on and Mary, Rachel's mother, was waiting on her doorstep to accompany them. Her son had recovered sufficiently to rejoin his regiment and so it had been agreed that she, as well as Ted, should join the Tovells for Christmas Day. The service itself seemed strange compared with other years because it was held in the Church Room, St Mary's being boarded up since the October air-raid which had blown out the windows on the south side and damaged all the rest. Ginny found comfort, nonetheless, in being able to pray for the safekeeping of her sons, Bobby and Alec, and her son-in-law, Peter.

She contrived to walk alongside Mary on the homeward journey knowing that her friend was still grieving for her elder son who would share no more Christmases with them. They happily reminisced about the many Christmas Day parties they had enjoyed in Mrs Brewster's parlour when her husband had been Station Officer and of their years as neighbours at the Coastguard Station. When Rachel, Lizzie, Tovell and the children hurried off down a side track to collect Ted from his cottage, Mary confided her latest worry to her friend. 'That int right, Ginny, the way she's carrying on. No married woman should behave like that when her husband's away at sea.'

'Mary, you don't know that she's doing anything she shouldn't,' said Ginny soothingly.

'Maybe not, but why doesn't she want to move in with her mother when we only live a few doors away from each other and are both on our own?' Mary argued. 'And it would save on the fuel.'

'Perhaps she wants to keep the house aired and be there if Bobby comes home unexpectedly,' replied Ginny.

'Be there! She's never hardly there,' Mary scoffed. 'She's in Norwich most days, on duty – or so she say. Why she had to join the Norwich branch of the Women's Voluntary Service instead of our own branch, I don't know. I reckon she wanted an excuse to be where I couldn't keep an eye on her. She may be my daughter – and God knows she was the apple of her father's eye though she was only a toddler when he was killed – but there's no getting round the fact that my Rachel's always been flighty.'

Ginny smiled. 'I can picture her now following my Bobby around the Station. I once heard him turn round and tell her he didn't want a tiny girl getting in his way. He made her cry and I told him off, but it didn't deter her. She told me once that she'd made up her mind when she was four that she was going to marry him.'

'Yes, and I told her off for the brazen way she pursued him,' said Mary sternly.

'Don't be too hard on her. They've been very happy together I'm sure. And as for joining the Norwich WVS, Rachel explained to me that it was because they had established War Nurseries there to look after the children whilst their mothers worked in the factories. With so many men gone to the armed forces, those nurseries couldn't be more necessary and Rachel is very good with children.'

'Yes, I grant you that, Ginny. Rachel is very good with children and that's a pity she has none of her own. Things might be different then. Look at your Lizzie - there's no chance she'd ever go off the rails. But I think it's the night life in Norwich that's the attraction: the picture places and the dance halls – and, of course, the servicemen.'

'She's young: she's still in her twenties. Bobby is a lot older. It's only natural she should enjoy films and dances and she goes with her girlfriends – she's told me. Anyway, everywhere closes at half past nine because of the air raids.'

'That's right,' Mary agreed. 'But that's so people can get home before the bombing starts. Trouble is, Rachel int always coming home. I knocked on her door early one morning last week and she wasn't there. She said she was working late at the nursery because they'd taken in families who'd been bombed out and she stayed there overnight to be on duty early again next morning.'

'Well, that sounds right to me,' said Ginny.

'I hope so, gal. The last thing we want with all that's happened is a cuckoo in the nest.'

Ginny looked sharply at her friend. Was this something she should be concerned about or was Mary still distraught at the death of her eldest child? Was she trying to find something to occupy her mind rather than worry about what could still befall her remaining son? She remembered how stoical Mary had been after the death of her husband in the last war and how she had been such a tower of strength when bringing up her three children alone. Was she afraid she would not be so strong this time? Exaggerating and inventing problems with her daughter might be her way of coping; safe ground because there was really nothing to be anxious about. Ginny decided there was no need to tell Tovell about this: it was probably all in Mary's mind.

1941

# I

The winter of 1940/41 was the coldest for forty years with Norfolk and Suffolk experiencing twelve degrees of frost on occasions and easterly gales from the North Sea blowing the snow into drifts. The one advantage of this was that during January 1941 both sides had to suspend air raids. By February, however, temperatures had risen and with an end to blizzards the bombing resumed and the blitz on London, industrial cities and key towns continued until May. The threat of invasion did not go away either so the need to train and equip the Home Guard units – the first line of defence – continued to be of the utmost importance. Shortages in the wake of Dunkirk were gradually overcome, particularly after America responded to Eden's cry for help by finding ways to send old weapons from the last war without violating her neutrality. By early 1941 all Norfolk Home Guard units had rifles and ammunition, the latter albeit in short supply, grenades and machine guns. Everyone had a uniform and boots – second hand, of course, since the Home Guard were reservists – so Tovell retrieved his old army boots from the loft and was cheered to find that they were still comfortable. Ginny took to teasing him, as she had done years before, for the meticulous care he took of both clothing and rifle, even polishing boots and buttons straight away after returning home from a route march or exercise. As the year progressed and the men became more proficient they were required to assist the regular armed forces by manning anti-aircraft guns along the Norfolk coast and by providing security at the many aerodromes which littered the countryside, sharing guard duties and patrols. There was even a hint that they might soon be issued with newly developed anti-tank weapons, an advance on their home-made Molotov cocktails.

Alec arrived home in February without any prior warning. He explained to his delighted parents that he was on his way to the Coastal Forces training base in Scotland. 'I applied for a transfer to motor gunboats and motor torpedo boats last December,' he explained. 'I'd seen them in action at Dunkirk and been impressed, but after Taranto I was convinced that MGBs and MTBs were for me. I don't know how much detail was released about Taranto but it must be the first time a battle fleet has been destroyed without the opposing battle fleet firing a shot. It was torpedo bombers from the air which crippled the Italian ships – the Fleet Air Arm's Fairey Swordfish launched from the carrier, *Illustrious* – and it convinced me that great sea battles between huge warships are a thing of the past. I think the aircraft carrier is the only big ship that will make a difference in the future. If I fancied being a pilot that's what I'd go for but I don't think flying is for me. But I still like the idea of being in command myself and like I say, I saw the gunboats doing a fine job at Dunkirk and I saw them in action again in the Med. They're fast and manoeuvrable: they dart in, stab at the enemy and dart away again. We're increasing our numbers of them because of the Germans' high-speed E-boats which are attacking our convoys. The Navy wants young men with experience of handling small boats – weekend yachtsmen even – to skipper our MGBs and MTBs. That's how I came to apply for a transfer.'

'So you want to be the naval version of a knight on a charger,' said Tovell with a smile. 'Is that all there is to it? I had wondered how you would fit in on a warship. Of course, you've been to university so that would have helped.'

'It didn't help much. I didn't really fit in,' Alec replied candidly. 'And you're right: that is the other reason I've opted for the gunboats. I didn't think I had much of a regional accent until my fellow officers started making fun of me in the wardroom. I suppose I should have grown a thicker skin. One senior officer – an older man out of retirement – told me something on the quiet. He'd read that, apparently, Lord Nelson had the same problem: he had such a broad Norfolk accent that his officers couldn't always understand him. He declared publicly that he was a Norfolk man and proud of it, so I'm in good company. But I still think I'll be better off and might command more respect, if I'm in a small gunboat.'

'I hope you're right, Alec,' said his mother anxiously. 'But even on a gunboat won't the officers still be a class apart?'

'It won't be like that, Mother,' Alec assured her. 'There isn't any real segregation: the boats are too small for that; a lot of the space is taken up by the powerful engines and the fuel to run them. Officers' quarters and crew's quarters are within feet of one another and we all eat the same food. I like that idea. There are only three officers anyway, two petty officers and a crew of about thirty ratings. I'm an old hand now: I've been in the service for nearly two years. As a full lieutenant and provided I don't muck things up during the training at Fort William, I'll be given my own boat.'

'I wonder where you'll be stationed. Hopefully, it won't be too far from here,' said Ginny.

'The chances are I'll be based at Great Yarmouth. They're calling the stretch of water between Haisbro Sands and Yarmouth, E-boat Alley because of all the attacks made on the convoys in this area. That's the reason Coastal Forces set up HMS *Midge* at Yarmouth in January. With luck, I'll join the flotillas there and if so, I'll be able to cycle home from time to time – so that you can cook me a decent meal,' he added with a grin.

On the eleventh of March came the welcome news that Congress had passed the Lease and Lend Bill enabling the President to sell, exchange, transfer, lease or lend war materials to any country whose defence he considered essential to the defence of the United States of America. Britain had been grateful for America's support since the outbreak of war but she was running out of options for ways to pay: she had leased air and naval bases in Newfoundland and Bermuda to America the previous September, "freely and without consideration"; then a further six bases in the Caribbean in exchange for fifty old destroyers from the United States Navy; also her supply of dollars was fast disappearing. As the press pointed out, it was an enormous relief to know that from now on Britain could have food and war materials on credit. This was not the time to worry about how great the debt would be or how long it would take to repay that debt in the future. All that mattered was the present: the threat of invasion, occupation and subjugation

April brought unwelcome news: on the sixth, Germany had declared war on Yugoslavia and on Greece which had been successfully repelling the Italian invasion; taxation went up, the meat ration went down and other food became subject to rationing; worst of all, air-raids increased and intensified. London, Coventry and the other big cities suffered but so did towns on the East Coast. Ipswich to the south and Kings Lynn to the north were targeted but it was Great Yarmouth which took the heaviest pounding. The worst of the bombing came on the nights of the seventh and twenty-fourth of April and on both occasions, Tovell was on duty with the Home Guard. He was thankful for this because he viewed the night sky with his fellow soldiers and not with Ginny, whom he hoped was asleep and could not see the glow from thousands of incendiary bombs which lit up the sky above Great Yarmouth. Had she been with him he knew she would have been fretting that Alec, newly stationed in the town as skipper of his own gunboat, was caught up in the inferno. Tovell, therefore, was able to comfort himself with the thought that their son would not have been in port but would have been out in the North Sea hunting the enemy intent upon attacking the convoys.

There were nights when the bombs fell in the open countryside and on the twenty-sixth an inn at Horning took a direct hit at closing time. A rescue party had to be sent from North Walsham but so great was the devastation that the number of dead could not be established until next day. This particular raid prompted the locals to speculate that the *Luftwaffe* had really been after the boatyards at Wroxham and Potter Heigham. There the boat builders who had previously constructed pleasure cruisers for the holidaymakers on the Norfolk Broads had turned their skills to producing high speed launches for the Navy and the R.A.F. In general, however, this increase in bombing raids seemed to point to only one thing: that they were the forerunner to the invasion.

# II

Trawlers were leaving Yarmouth Harbour as the motor launches returned to port from their stint as convoy escorts. Several of the ratings on the motor gunboats and motor torpedo boats raised a hand to the men on the converted trawlers as they passed on their daily mission to sweep the convoy route for mines and unexploded torpedoes. The men knew one another and many were drinking companions in the Yarmouth hostelries since HMS *Midge* and HMS *Miranda* - the base for the minesweeping trawlers and drifters - shared the Fishwharf, with the motor launches mooring at the southern end. Alec strained to see if he could spy his uncles but the atmosphere was too murky. Instead, he looked at the skyline and tried to identify which buildings had been hit the previous night from the location of the smoke clouds still hovering over them.

Once they had entered harbour and passed the Brush Quay bend in the River Yare, Alec looked beyond the Lifeboat Station to where the RAF had its Air Sea Rescue base at Baker Street on the Gorleston side of the river. He was looking for one particular launch and a familiar face. The launch was moored but he could see no sign of his friend. Soon they were alongside the Fishwharf and the Wren technicians were waiting to come aboard. The young sailors, like their predecessors down the centuries, were reluctant to pass up an opportunity to chat to the fairer sex and they hung around to exchange pleasantries with the girls. Eventually, the Leading Wren snapped at the men, 'Clear off you lot and let us do our job. Yours isn't the only boat we've got to give a turnround to this morning.'

As Alec prepared to leave he realized that his coxswain was also loitering, pretending to be busy. Alec grinned and nodded in the direction of the Leading Wren. 'Best of luck!' he whispered.

'I'll need it, sir,' muttered Petty Officer Marshall. 'The only things she's enthusiastic about are the bloody engines. She's not interested in anything else.'

'Maybe she's playing hard to get,' Alec replied.

Alec collected his bicycle from its hiding place in one of the Navy warehouses and rode across the South Denes towards the seafront. He made a slight southerly detour so that he could cycle past Nelson's Column. He looked up and gave the statue of Britannia, hundreds of feet above him, a jaunty salute. Once on South Beach Parade he sighed at the sight of the bomb-damaged Scenic Railway, his favourite ride at the Pleasure Beach on visits to Great Yarmouth throughout his childhood. When he came close to Shadingfield Lodge, the Officers' Mess, he drew alongside the kerb so that he could call out to two other gunboat skippers who were about to enter the grounds of the building. They chatted together for a few minutes, comparing their recent hunting successes with much good-humoured banter, before Alec continued on his way. He rode the length of the seafront past bomb-damaged hotels until Marine Parade gave way to North Drive and he arrived at the Westgates' home. He noticed that another bicycle was propped against the kitchen wall. He knocked loudly on the back door before entering, calling out as he did so, 'Morning, Auntie Gladys!'

'Morning, Alec!' replied Mrs Westgate. 'Arthur's beaten you to it today,' she added, indicated the young man in RAF uniform who was already seated at the table, hungrily eating his breakfast. 'Here's your food. I've been keeping it warm for you.'

'Thanks, Auntie Gladys,' said Alec as he sat down. Looking across at his companion, he quipped, 'I saw your boat had docked but there was no sign of you. Not surprising – the RAF doesn't put in the same hours as the Navy.'

'I got here first because I pedalled like the devil,' Arthur Gillings replied good-humouredly. 'I can't help it if the Navy is full of lazy slow-coaches.'

'No fighting at the breakfast table, boys. Eat your food,' Mrs Westgate commanded. 'My, my, this takes me back. You two were always squabbling at the table when you were little and used to visit us for your summer holiday.'

'That's because he was bigger and older than me and used to lord it over me,' said Alec, laughing.

'Lord it over you? Fat chance!' scoffed Arthur. 'You might have been younger than me but you could punch and kick as soon as you could walk.'

'You were both such lovely little boys,' mused Gladys Westgate. 'You were only a tiny baby, Arthur, when we spent that first Christmas of the war at the Coastguard Station. And Lily, your mother, looked little more than a child herself. It was August 1918 when we saw you for the first time, Alec. You sat on your mother's lap when we had our reunion at Mary's. It was a few years before you were both old enough to come to us on holiday. I've got some photographs of you both from that first holiday somewhere. I'll just go and find them.'

'Now look what you've done,' Alec whispered to Arthur as Mrs Westgate hurried out of the kitchen. At that moment another visitor arrived and both young men hastily stood up and competed to assist her as she flopped down on a chair at the table. 'Never mind the photographs, Auntie Gladys,' Alec called out. 'Margaret's here and she's starving.'

Mrs Westgate rushed back into the kitchen. She leaned over her granddaughter and gave her a quick kiss on the side of her cheek. 'I was worried about you. I expected you earlier than this. Your breakfast's ready. I'll get it.'

'It's been a long night, Nan,' replied Margaret. 'One air-raid warning after another – but you know that, of course. Plenty of casualties and lots of damage too, I'm afraid. Thank goodness I'm not on duty tonight.'

'You'll be able to catch up on your sleep,' said her grandmother.

Margaret laughed. 'I meant I'll be free to go dancing – if certain dashing young men care to escort me.'

Both of the dashing young men nearly choked in their eagerness to respond to this invitation. Mrs Westgate shook her head. 'You're a little minx, Margaret. Put these poor boys out of their misery and choose which one you want to go out with.'

'You're a spoilsport, Nan. I like having them fight over me - always have. They can both take me to the dance.'

'Actually, I can't,' said Alec regretfully. 'I'm at sea again tonight but I'll let you know next time I'm free.'

'Hmm, you might be throwing away your last chance,' replied Margaret. 'I told you I had to register in March – all women aged nineteen to forty had to – so that we could be directed into essential work. I've decided not to wait to be told what I've got to do; I'm going to join one of the Forces now so that I have a choice.'

'But you're doing Civil Defence work now; that's essential,' her grandmother protested. 'You don't want to join the armed forces.'

'Oh, I don't know – I might like it. Khaki isn't really my colour,' Margaret said, flippantly. 'The Wrens have the most stylish uniform but I quite fancy air-force blue as well.'

'Pay no attention to her boys: she's just teasing,' said Gladys Westgate with a hint of exasperation in her voice.

'Don't worry, Auntie Gladys. We know her of old,' replied Alec reassuringly. 'She's a bright girl and she'll choose whichever service can make best use of her skills.'

# III

The news of British successes in Egypt against Italian forces cheered Tovell but then Hitler sent Field Marshal Rommel to North Africa to help his ally. When the Fuhrer also sent troops to Greece in support of the Italians, Churchill withdrew troops from Egypt to help the Greeks. By the end of April, those troops had been evacuated, the Greek army had surrendered and their King had retreated to Crete, supported by some of the evacuated British and Commonwealth forces. Germany launched an airborne invasion against Crete and won; again the Allies withdrew. The press, to Tovell's despair, nicknamed the British Expeditionary Force the Back Every Fortnight!

There was a different story to grab the headlines and dominate the wireless bulletins when Hitler's deputy, Rudolph Hess, baled out of a Messerschmitt and landed in Scotland on the tenth of May. Speculation as to whether he had come to offer peace terms or was just another refugee continued for days. Then it was announced on the nine o'clock news on the twenty-fourth that the battle cruiser *Hood* had been sunk off Greenland and later, the grievous information that of a crew of over 1400, there were only three survivors. Ginny convinced herself that Bobby and Peter must have been on the *Hood* and that telegrams would arrive at any moment. After three days, when no such missives had arrived, and the nation had been informed that the *Hood's* attacker, the *Bismarck,* the pride of the German Navy, had been sunk herself, Ginny stopped worrying about her boys and reverted to her usual concern – the imminent invasion of Britain. On the twenty-second of June, Tovell was able to convince her that the invasion was now weeks away because Hitler, according to the news bulletin that morning, had decided to invade Russia instead.

'He can't invade two countries – one in the east and one in the west – simultaneously, can he? He won't have the men or the resources. With luck, Russia will be able to hang out for a month or two and he'll be too busy with them to think of invading us. I'm looking forward to seeing how the newspapers will manage to wriggle around this one. Up until yesterday, Russia was our enemy and has been ever since she signed that non-aggression pact with Germany in August 1939. And think what she did to Poland soon afterwards. Now she's our ally. We shouldn't be surprised, I suppose: Bolsheviks and Fascists made strange partners. Anyway, Churchill has made it plain in his broadcast that we are to give all help possible to Russia, the latest victim, as he put it, of German aggression.'

The other "good" thing about Hitler's latest attack was that, towards the end of July, Bobby and Peter arrived home for a few days leave prior to joining ships on a new convoy route – through the Arctic Ocean to Russia. Mary was alarmed when she opened her front door to find Bobby standing there asking whether his wife was at her house. She was further agitated when, on being told that Rachel worked for the Norwich WVS, Bobby declared that he would go into the city to meet her. Mary managed to convince her son-in-law that such action might mean they passed each other on the journey to and from Haisbro, and rather than waste any of his precious leave he should go to his parents' home. Whilst he spent time with them, she would contact the local WVS leader who had a telephone and could get a message to the Norwich nursery and rest centre where Rachel was a volunteer.

Ginny had just come in from working on the smallholding to start preparing the evening meal when Peter walked into the scullery. Ginny wept tears of joy and relief as she embraced him, quickly explaining that Tovell had gone to meet the three evacuees from school and that Lizzie usually arrived home from her teaching post only a few minutes later.

'That's all right, Mother,' Peter replied. 'I'm going to give this little lady a cuddle while we wait.' So saying, Peter walked past his mother-in-law and lifted Molly out of her high chair where she had been sitting, banging the tray with a wooden spoon whilst she watched her grandmother peeling potatoes at the draining board. 'I can't believe how she's grown and how heavy she is,' Peter exclaimed as he sat on a wooden chair nearby and stood the toddler up on his lap facing him. 'But then, she'll be two next month, won't she? Look at the expression on her face. She can't make me out. I reckon she's wondering who this funny looking bloke is,' said Peter, laughing.

Ginny turned around and smiled at the pair. 'That's your father, Molly.' Then to Peter she added, 'She isn't crying even though you're a stranger to her. Perhaps she knows instinctively who you are.'

'I hope so,' Peter replied. 'That's the trouble with being at sea – you miss so much ...' His words tailed away as the sound of a bicycle bell ringing loudly in the yard outside made Molly start to jump up and down and chatter excitedly.

'Yes, that's her! That's your mother,' Ginny said. 'She's early today. That's lucky. Go you outside and surprise her.' As Peter got up, carrying Molly, Ginny opened the back door for them and then closed it behind them so that she would not be a witness to the reunion. It was several minutes before the door opened and Peter re-entered the scullery, one arm still holding Molly and the other arm around his wife. Lizzie, like her mother before her, had been crying. 'Sit you down in the living room,' said Ginny, 'and I'll bring you both a cup of tea. Father and the littl'uns will be home soon so make the most of the peace and quiet.'

A few minutes later, Tovell and the children arrived; Bobby was with them. Ginny was reduced to tears once more as she hugged her son. Then, practicalities took over and she shooed him into the living room to be with his sister and brother-in-law whilst she, with Peggy's help, hastily prepared more food. Once they were seated around the large living room table, Bobby pointed out something that all of them had missed: that Peter had, as was obvious from his uniform, been promoted to Chief Petty Officer. 'Oh, that was ages ago,' said Peter, dismissing the congratulations. 'There were more important things to talk about in my letters home.'

The family spent the next hour happily exchanging news as they ate. Both Bobby and Peter were convinced that they had not been immediately dispatched on a return trip to America when their North Atlantic convoy had docked because they were destined for Russia. 'That'll be tanks and guns for Archangel or Murmansk,' said Bobby.

'And planes too,' added Peter. 'Air support is all important these days. The longer the Russians can hold out the longer the heat's off us. But I'm not looking forward to it. The conditions in the North Atlantic are bad enough but the Arctic route must be a lot worse.'

'Maybe we won't have so many U-boat wolf packs in the Arctic as in the Atlantic,' said Bobby. 'The nearness of the French ports they operate from to the Western Approaches and the North Atlantic has made our convoys very vulnerable. But the Germans may have established U-boat bases in occupied Norway, of course.'

'They'll certainly have air-bases there,' added Peter.

Ginny and Lizzie were looking decidedly distressed by this point in the discussion and were very glad when Rachel, smart in her dark green WVS uniform, came dashing into the room. Cheeks flushed with hurrying, she was clearly as pleased to see Bobby as Lizzie had been to see her husband. She quickly refused her mother-in-law's offer of food – claiming she had already eaten – and had eyes only for Bobby. He, for his part, had leapt to his feet to embrace her as soon as she had entered and no one was surprised when he said they had better be getting home. Peter made a similar announcement and within minutes, Ginny, Tovell and the children had been deserted.

'Wonder why they're all in such a hurry to get home,' Tovell commented with a gleam in his eyes.

His wit was wasted on Ginny who had not even heard the remark: she was thinking of something quite different. 'Perhaps we could get a message to Alec that the boys are home; then they could have their photograph taken together. And snapshots with the girls and little Molly, of course.' Then, with a faraway look in her eyes, she added, 'Wars must be good for the photography trade.'

# IV

Ted Carter had taken to the three young Londoners straight away and the feelings were reciprocated. Whenever Tovell was too busy with his Home Guard duties, Ted took it upon himself to involve them in the joys of the countryside. On government orders the schools had asked the parents of the older boys to allow their sons to work at gathering in the harvest and although these evacuees were too young to be enrolled, Ted saw no reason why they should not take part. The young master had long since abandoned all attempts to direct Ted's working day and so he did as much – or as little – on the farm as he liked and chose the jobs he preferred and left the rest. These were often allocated to an increasing number of Land Army girls and they treated the old man with the same affectionate indulgence as the boss.

Peggy, Roger and Will thoroughly enjoyed helping with the harvest and once it was over they embraced the "Dig for Victory" campaign and when they were not helping the Tovells on the smallholding they assisted Lydia Brewster – who had also become very fond of them – to convert her elegant gardens to vegetable patches. Some afternoons, by prior arrangement with the Tovells, she would collect them from the village school, give them their tea, potter in the garden with them and then hear their reading before Ginny came to collect them.

'I was at the school one day last week – I help out sometimes when they are short staffed, you know – and their teachers were glowing in their praise,' Mrs Brewster told Ginny one evening. 'They've caught up wonderfully with the local children and are better than some of them now at most subjects. They're a credit to you, and to Mr Tovell and Lizzie.'

'I've never been one for school work,' Ginny admitted. 'But Tovell has spent a lot of time with them with their books, and Lizzie too, but not so much lately. Tovell's always doing something with the Home Guard and, with Lizzie going back to teaching, she likes to spend time with Molly when she gets home, naturally. It's only fair to say that the time you are putting in on their education is what's making the difference.'

'Well, I hope that's helping,' replied Lydia bashfully. 'All those years I spent training to be a teacher only to have to give it up when I married … Such a pity we have to have a war before we can use our skills again.'

'You used them for Alec,' Ginny reminded her. 'I'll always be grateful for that and so will he.'

'Ah, Alec!' said Lydia. 'I think of Alec whenever my room is suddenly illuminated by the glow from the lighthouse. I know it's rather naughty but I always pull up my blackout blind when I go to bed: I like the first rays of dawn to wake me. Trinity House has given the elderly lighthouse keeper an assistant. I suppose they had to now that the shutters have to be hauled back from the light whenever a convoy is due to pass by. Yes, I always think of Alec when the light shines and wonder if he's out there chasing off the E-boats before they can attack our ships. It's lovely having him based so near by, isn't it?'

'Yes it is,' Ginny agreed. 'But I'm afraid it doesn't stop me worrying about him just as I always have.'

'Of course it doesn't. We worry about them from the day they're born. We wouldn't deserve to be mothers if we didn't.' Then, turning to the children who had followed the adults down the front path, Lydia asked, 'Have you got your bags and all your school books? I'll see you again next week. Thank you very much for all your hard work. We shall soon have a garden as good as the one at the lighthouse.' Pointing across the track which was Beach Road and in the direction of Haisbro Lighthouse, she explained to Ginny, 'The old lady who tends the ground around the lighthouse is doing such a splendid job that she inspired me to emulate her. But who am I to be calling someone, "old lady"? I'm one myself!' she admitted with a laugh. 'I'm so busy with all the war efforts around here that I forget that fact sometimes.'

It was August too – early morning of the sixth – that Ted and his friends in the Volunteer Life-saving Brigade received the call to be on standby in case their help was needed. In spite of the beam from the lighthouse flashing its warning of the presence of the treacherous Haisbro Sands, six ships from a convoy had run aground on the sandbanks during the night. In the event, the Haisbro men were not needed but they met in the *Admiral Lord Nelson* that night and were pleased to be joined later by a friend of one of the crew of the *Bailey*, the Cromer lifeboat which had rescued most of the survivors of the disaster. The Navy had called upon several lifeboats along the coast for help, but the main Cromer boat had reached the scene first to find a destroyer and its whaler trying to help the stricken steamers, floundering in the stormy seas, most with their backs broken and many of their crewmen already dead. The Cromer coxswain, Henry Blogg, had wasted no time, twice taking his boat up onto the deck of the sinking steamers to rescue desperate men clinging to the funnel. The second, smaller, Cromer lifeboat made a similar rescue as did the Great Yarmouth and Gorleston lifeboat, the *Louise Stephens.* In all, 119 rescued seamen were transferred to the waiting destroyers, with the Sheringham and Lowestoft lifeboats standing by.

August 1941 was also the month when the first small convoy of merchant ships and their Royal Navy escort vessels, having assembled at Hvalfiordur in Iceland, left for Russia and by November, the convoy system was well established. For Bobby and Peter there was no hope of being home for Christmas. At home, preparations for the festive season were hampered by shortages. The Tovells tried to buy a few toys for the children in North Walsham and Stalham. Although some cut-out toys and books were still available cars and trains, which Tovell had wanted to give to the boys, were nowhere to be found. 'It's because they're made of metal,' said Alec on one of his brief visits. 'I'll look for you in Yarmouth when I'm off-duty but I don't hold out much hope. You don't see a metal railing anywhere these days – they've all been taken down for making into ships and planes – and they dismantled the Revolving Tower on the seafront a few months ago so they could re-use the metal, although I think they suspected it was also a landmark for enemy bombers. You'd better give me some fabric bags to hide the stuff in – if I'm lucky enough to find any toys – because the shops have been banned from using wrapping paper.'

Rachel viewed Christmas as a time when she wanted to look her best – in case Bobby came home – and how was she to do that when she had already used up most of her clothing coupons? 'For heavens sake, girl!' exclaimed her mother. 'How can you be almost out of coupons already? We've only had clothes rationing since Whit Sunday. Sixty-six points a year for an adult seems plenty to me. Anyway, you've lots of clothes in your wardrobe I'm sure. You've been spending far too much on fripperies for years. Make do and mend, my girl, like everybody else.'

'Oh, well, I'll ask mother-in-law if she can spare any of her coupons,' said Rachel.

'No, you will not,' Mary retorted. 'Knowing Ginny, she'll have been using her allowance for the littl'uns – seeing how fast they grow. Oh, well, you'd better take some of mine, I suppose. I've no-one to dress up for, more's the pity.'


Thoughts of Christmas were temporarily put on hold with the momentous announcement on the nine o'clock news on the seventh of December that Japan had bombed the American base at Pearl Harbor in the Hawaiian Islands and then Manila in the Philippines. By the next day it emerged that at the same time as those bombings, the Japanese had also landed in Thailand, Malaya and several Pacific islands. Japan then declared war on Britain and America and the nine o'clock news on the eighth included Roosevelt's declaration of war, relayed from Washington, followed by Churchill's declaration. Two days later came the bad news that the Japanese had sunk two of our warships, the *Prince of Wales* and the *Repulse* off the coast of Malaya by attacks from the air. Next day, Germany and Italy declared war on America and a little later, America reciprocated by declaring war on them.

When Alec cycled home on a brief visit to hand over the few presents he had been able to purchase in Great Yarmouth, he had his own opinion of recent events.

'I bet the Japs studied what we did to the Italian Fleet at Taranto last year. Like I told you, it was all down to attack from the air – dive bombers from aircraft carriers. From what we've heard, the Japanese did exactly the same thing. They obviously had no intentions of negotiating with the Americans – that was just a ploy – because to launch all those attacks in different areas simultaneously must have taken weeks, if not months of planning. I don't expect it's been broadcast, but we're rushing the Australians home in case Japan attacks them next. Things have escalated very suddenly, haven't they?'

'But one good thing has come out of it,' observed his father,

'America is participating fully now. It made all the difference last time, so let's hope it will again.'

'It seems the whole world is at war,' Ginny murmured. 'However did we get into such a state?'

'Ask Herr Hitler,' replied Tovell.

# V

Bobby spent Christmas Eve watching cargo being unloaded at the docks in Murmansk. He was joined by his boss, the convoy's commodore, a jovial retired rear-admiral, who was happy to admit that he had been, "dug out of mothballs, like many of our ships". News of Pearl Harbor and America's declaration of war had reached them before the convoy had set out, but having spent the last ten days battling the elements in the Arctic Circle, they had only given a few passing thoughts to what was happening in the Far East. More relevant to them was the good news that the German advance had been halted at Moscow. Perhaps the Russian winter was going to do to Hitler what it had previously done to Napoleon. But the only thing the men of the merchant ships and their escorts had to look forward to was a bleak Christmas followed by many days waiting for the convoy's cargoes to be discharged and new cargoes, if any, loaded before the hazardous return journey.

'Look on the bright side, Adams,' said the admiral as they stood on the bridge surveying the quayside below them. 'We've been very lucky these last few trips that the Hun hasn't harassed us with anything like the force we'd expected. Maybe they haven't realized what we're up to yet. Perhaps they think we're only supplying the Russians via the overland route from Persia and that the warships their reconnaissance planes have sighted are just sizing up the situation ready for an invasion of Norway. It can't last, you know. They're bound to realize sooner or later and throw everything they've got against us.'

'If they've anything to spare, sir, after what they're doing to us in the Atlantic,' replied Bobby with feeling.

'My God, there he goes again,' exclaimed the commodore, pointing to a young seaman hurrying down the gangway, past the Russian guard and slipping and sliding across the icy cobbles in the direction of the anti-aircraft battery on the dockside. 'That lad deserves a medal for persistence,' he continued. 'I've watched him every day we've been here go over to

76

those women soldiers on the guns and offer them … goodness knows what. Black market stuff, I suppose. And every time they ignore him or gesture to him to be off. But he keeps on trying. Hope springs eternal, they say. Now when I was his age any kind of gift worked wonders in any part of the world.'

'Perhaps you always spoke the language, sir,' replied Bobby.

'Language? Never learnt a foreign language in my life. It isn't what you say it's the tone of your voice and the expression on your face when you offer the gifts that counts. No, I'm afraid our young cockerel won't get anywhere because the hens have been warned off fraternizing with us. You'd think we were the enemy not the ally.'

'Oh, no! Not another strike,' exclaimed Bobby as at that moment, the Russian men and women unloading the cargo suddenly walked away from the ship and sat down in a huddle on the quayside.

'Now that really is a language problem,' said the admiral. 'The First Mate hasn't a hope of getting them back to work.'

'Excuse me a moment, sir. If we don't do something we're never going to leave here.' So saying, Bobby yelled down to the radio room below the bridge, summoning one of his team of operators. The man responded at once, pulled on his great coat, left the ship and approached the group of Russian dockers. With much gesticulating and yelling, indecipherable to those watching from the bridge, the man harassed the workers until they got up and went back to work.

'Miracle, absolute miracle!' exclaimed the admiral.

Bobby laughed. 'He went to a special kind of language school, sir. I heard him arguing with some Russians on the quayside a couple of days ago and he told me his first job on leaving school was as a docker on Great Yarmouth quayside - unloading the timber boats from Russia. It seems the crews took to him and taught him their language – and "dialect"! Of course, even familiar curses and swear words are useless without the right tone of voice and facial expression, sir.'

'Alright, you've made your point, Chief Yeoman!' replied the commodore amiably. 'The shows over so you and I had better be getting to that official reception the Soviets have invited us to. What a way to spend Christmas Eve.'

# VI

Bobby and his brother-in-law, Peter, met up later on Christmas Day and walked to the Hall of Culture together. They tramped through the snow along Stalin Street, bending forward against the bitter wind. They were flanked by bombed-out buildings, evidence of the air attacks, still continuing, which Murmansk had suffered.

'How much longer do you think we'll be here?' asked Peter.

'Days yet,' replied Bobby. 'There aren't enough cranes, they haven't repaired the quayside which has been bombed so you can't stack heavy armaments there and the railway can't cope with the numbers of tanks we've brought. Our seamen are working flat out to empty the holds but that alone isn't enough. The Russians have got to cooperate. They're eager enough to constantly ask to see our papers and be as awkward and obstructive as possible. Pity they can't get there priorities right and realize we're here to help them.'

'We can't leave soon enough for me,' Peter asserted. 'All the boys on the escort ships are fed up with the waiting. You can only de-ice and clear up the ship so many times.'

'Yes, and that's another thing,' said Bobby. 'You've got plenty of men for jobs like that. The owners of the merchant ships only take on the minimum crew: they're only interested in profit. On the voyage here the blokes on our ship were on deck for hours at a time trying to keep down the ice. I bet that didn't happen on your destroyer.'

'I think they were limited to one hour outside before they were relieved, whatever the duty,' said Peter.

'You see? That's what I mean. The difference between the Royal Navy and the Merchant Navy has to be seen to be believed. Being a commodore's yeoman, as you know, I've been on plenty of merchant ships – in the North Atlantic before we started Arctic convoys. The commodore chooses the best ship for his means so sometimes we've been on quite grand stuff but often they're little better than tramp steamers. Whatever the state of the ship the poor ruddy hands get a measly wage, rotten food and inadequate clothing for the conditions. Do you know what our blokes got today for Christmas Day? One tot of rum! That was it; that was all the owner had provided as a celebration. And if the poor buggers get shipwrecked, no matter that they've been torpedoed or bombed through no fault of their own, their measly pay instantly stops. They survive or die unemployed and penniless.'

'Yes, I've heard that one,' said Peter. 'I agree it's scandalous. That'll have to be put right. Without the merchantmen there are no convoys.'

'I tell you, Peter, it's enough to make you turn Communist,' said Bobby, adding with a wry smile, 'or at least it would be if you hadn't seen at first hand that these poor sods are no better off.'

Peter, nodding in the direction of a group of men and women filling in a bomb crater in the road, agreed. 'I know what you mean. I bet they thought the Revolution was going to mean an end to poverty: no more Czars living in luxury whilst they starved. Now it's the political chiefs and party members living in luxury whilst the ordinary people still starve and live in poverty. And, to make matters worse, they have to contend with the secret police as well now – the NKVD. You have to feel sorry for them.'

'Yes, I do. Theirs must be a miserable existence anyway with this constant numbing cold.' As Bobby spoke, they came upon the grandly named Hall of Culture, a massive statue of Lenin standing in front. Alongside the statue the Soviets had put a war trophy on display – a shot down Messerschmitt. The only sign of grandeur was in the name of the building; inside it wreaked of neglect. It was dimly lit by single electric bulbs, their hanging flex pendants well spaced. Other sailors were there, sitting or standing in groups, but the atmosphere at that stage of the evening was not particularly animated. Peter and Bobby sat down at a table and ordered beer. They were charged four roubles for half a pint which they considered extortionate – especially once they had established that the predominant flavour of the beer was suspiciously like onions.

'Well, I think I shall give up Russian beer,' Bobby announced. 'It gets worse every voyage. They must be making it with onions now. I'm going to stick to vodka in future. At least they know how to make that properly.'

'According to our surgeon, vodka's very bad for you,' said Peter. 'He claims it makes you depressed.'

Bobby laughed. 'We're depressed anyway so what's the difference?'

At that moment Peter sighted a man he knew, a fellow Chief Petty Officer, and hailed him. The man came over and Peter introduced him to his brother-in-law. 'Tom here is from HMS *Norfolk*.'

'In that case I'm very pleased to meet you,' said Bobby. 'I'm always heartened whenever I catch sight of your cruiser. You're a reminder of our home county.' The man sat down with them, accepted a vodka and entertained them with the account of the famous hunt last May when *Norfolk* had been the first ship to sight the *Bismarck*. He described how, after being joined by HMS *Suffolk*, they had shadowed the great German battleship for four days and had eventually joined in the fray to deliver the final blows.

'That really pleased us,' said the man, 'being in at the kill. Not only had we avenged our mates on the *Hood,* but we'd stopped the *Bismarck* from breaking out into the North Atlantic. Think what havoc and carnage she'd have caused amongst our convoys'.

That statement deserved more vodkas and it was only after the arrival of more sailors from the *Norfolk* that the man left the table. No sooner had he joined his shipmates than another acquaintance of Peter's sat down with the two brothers-in-law. He too was feeling depressed. On his journey there he had passed the cook of a merchant vessel, clearly low on stores, haggling over a yak carcass with a Russian family. By the look of them, they needed the meat themselves. Next he'd sighted what passed for a funeral cortege: a small group of sad women huddled against the cold and pushing an old perambulator with a small wooden coffin perched on top.

'That really upset me,' explained the man. 'It reminded me of all the bodies I'd seen a few days ago. This Polish vessel got bombed as we came within range of the German airfields in Norway. We were the first escort to board her – not that there was much we could do. Most of the poor devils were already dead. We went down this alleyway and they were lying everywhere. The walls were covered in red lettering. One of our officers – a New Zealander – spoke a little Polish and he knew what they said – "Long Live Poland". Can you believe that? With their last breath they'd scrawled "Long Live Poland" on the walls in their own blood. I shall never forget that - never.'

'You'd better have another drink,' said Peter, breaking the strained silence. Then, glancing across the room, he added, 'Look, there are Poles over there, in that big group: Poles, Norwegians, Dutch and Free French.

No wonder they stick together – they've a lot in common. All exiles; their homelands occupied. We've a lot to be thankful for really. At least we're still free.'

There was another pause for reflection before Bobby broke the silence with a remark which made his companions laugh out loud at its incongruity. 'I wonder what the heads are like here. Ours were frozen up most of the time. Risky business taking your trousers down in this climate and squatting over a bucket of snow on deck.'

'Well, this is a rum old do!' exclaimed Peter. 'All we've got to cheer ourselves up with on a Christmas afternoon is a discussion about lavatories!'

'This may be called the Hall of Culture but I don't think we can expect much culture – or entertainment of any kind for that matter,' said Bobby.

'I don't know about that,' announced Peter's friend. 'I've been watching that middle-aged Russian over there – moving from table to table. She's coming our way.' The man smiled at the woman and she at once gave him her full attention, chattering to him non-stop. 'I think that must be Russian for, "Hello, sailor, want to come home with me?"' he said to Bobby and Peter. 'I might as well. I need cheering up.'

'Look at the state of her,' Peter exclaimed. 'She'll probably leave you with gonorrhea.'

'Oh, well, it'll give the surgeon something to do. He was moaning the other day that his services won't be needed. In these temperatures, he said, it would be nothing short of a miracle if anyone managed to catch something.'

'It's also an offence,' Bobby reminded him.

'I was only joking,' replied the man, patting his back trouser pocket. 'I'm always prepared.' Without further ado he got up and steered the woman towards the door, accompanied it seemed, by the cheers and bawdy words of encouragement of most of the men in the room.

'He's welcome,' said Peter. 'The only good looking – and clean – females around here are the ones in the Russian Army or Navy and they're scared stiff of giving us a second glance. We're the wicked imperialists, I suppose. But why their invasions of Poland and Finland didn't make them imperialists too, I don't know.'

Bobby was still thinking about the woman who had been so

desperate to find a client. 'I bet she's only trying to make some money to feed her littl'uns,' he commented. 'Her husband's probably fighting at the Front or already dead. There's an old woman who haunts our stretch of the docks every night. She takes her customers behind the stacks of timber. She's always in heavy boots and layers of scarves and coats. Don't know how she manages it in all that gear. The younger men won't go near her – too dirty, I reckon – but the older ones are not so choosey. It's probably her only source of income. What a life this is.'

'You're making yourself miserable again,' said Peter. 'And I think we may have been wrong – the Soviets are laying on some cultural entertainment. Look at that crowd of Russian sailors who've just come in and are lining up over there.'

Bobby turned around in his seat. 'Yes, I think you're right. They must be a naval choir.' The Hall of Culture resounded to the beautiful voices for the next hour and so moving was the performance that many a hardened seafarer was reduced to tears: an outpouring of emotion exacerbated by the effects of the vodka which had been consumed. When the concert was over, Peter and Bobby slumped across the table, laid their befuddled heads on their forearms and let their thoughts travel two thousands miles and more to Haisbro, Norfolk: Bobby seeing his beautiful Rachel in his mind's eye and Peter seeing his darling Lizzie and tiny Molly.

1942

# I

The year had ended badly with another bomb attack on Haisbro – more casualties and more homes damaged – and Christmas Day itself had been blighted by the announcement that Hong Kong had surrendered to the Japanese. The appalling weather continued into 1942 with snow and ice making the roads and lanes treacherous for weeks on end. In February, on Friday the thirteenth fittingly, the BBC Home Service announced that the German battle-cruiser *Scharnhorst,* which had been trapped in Brest, had managed to escape. 'That means she's free again to terrorize our convoys,' Ginny moaned, thinking of her boys. That same weekend, on the Sunday, came the even more shocking news that Singapore had fallen and that thousands of Allied troops and civilians were now prisoners of the Japanese. Churchill spoke on the nine o'clock bulletin explaining that Singapore had been ordered to surrender to save unnecessary loss of life. He urged the nation to take heart from the fact that America was now in the fight and that the Russians were taking on the Germans. But the news was received particularly badly in Norfolk once it was known that the 4th, 5th and 6th Battalions of the Norfolk Regiment had been hastily transferred from the Middle East to defend Singapore and were now amongst those captured.

'Thank the Lord my Albert's with the 2nd Battalion,' exclaimed Mary. 'He came so close to being captured by the Hun - and he's still not properly recovered from Dunkirk - that I don't know how he would have fared if he'd been taken prisoner by the Japanese. But you feel for all those poor men who've been captured – and for their wives and mothers. At least they're still alive because we surrendered.'

'I doubt the Australians are happy we capitulated so quickly,' commented Tovell ruefully. 'They were probably counting on us holding out. Now the Japs could invade them.' A few days later it appeared that such a catastrophe might be about to happen. The Japanese bombed the naval port and airbase of Darwin on the northern coast of Australia on the nineteenth of February – using a greater number of bombs than they had dropped on Pearl Harbor.

Soon there were more immediate things to worry about. Bad flying conditions in January had reduced the number of aircraft in the skies but with the weather improving, air-raids were resumed by both Britain and Germany. A warning against leaving lights on in shop windows as dusk approached resulted from a bad raid on Lowestoft one Saturday afternoon before blackout. 'Jerry must have something against Marks and Spencer and Boots,' Tovell told Ginny. 'A chap I met when I was delivering this morning told me that both their stores in Lowestoft were bombed out at the weekend, just as the Yarmouth branches were last April. But I mustn't joke. Apparently a lot of people were killed including Navy men in a café which took a direct hit.'

'All this bombing,' cried Ginny despairingly, 'it's wicked. Innocent little children being killed …'

'There's nothing one-sided about it, sweetheart,' Tovell said gently. 'You only have to look up at night to see not just the fighter planes but the bombers taking off from our airfields to know we're doing the same to them. When it's all over, someone will start adding up the scores and we'll probably find we've dropped more bombs on them than they have on us.'

This argument did not stop Ginny being incensed after one radio broadcast towards the end of April and she was still seething when Tovell came home. 'They said on the wireless today that the Germans have announced that they're going to target our towns which have historic buildings because we bombed their churches at somewhere called Rostock. The blasted cheek of it when you think of all the bombing they did of historic places before they invaded Poland and Holland and Belgium and everywhere. It said they're going to bomb three star towns listed in a guidebook for tourists called Baedeker.'

'I think they've already started,' Tovell replied. 'The sky towards Norwich was lit up last night and the reports we got at the Home Guard unit was that it was the worst raid on Norwich so far. Even the Teachers Training College got it this time.'

'Lizzie will be sorry – she has such fond memories of her time there,' said Ginny.

'I just hope Rachel's all right,' replied Tovell. 'I'm sure her rest centre was kept very busy last night and I doubt she'll be able to get home anyway. People have taken to trekking out of the city at night now for some time to avoid the bombings – you see them on the roads just pushing prams loaded with children and blankets - and I should think the buses and trains will be packed today with those trying to escape to stay with relatives in the country.'

The bombing raids continued to June and July and the Home Guard helped with the unenviable task of digging through the rubble in several towns on the Norfolk coast – King's Lynn, Sheringham and Cromer. But it was the attack on the night of the twenty-fifth of June which caused Ginny the most upset. She was late going to bed that night and had gone outside when she had heard one of the cats crying. The sight which met her when she looked south made her call her husband who, for once, was not on duty.

'Oh, no! They must have dropped thousands of incendiary bombs on Yarmouth to make a glow as enormous as that,' said Tovell sadly.

'But what about Alec?' cried Ginny.

'He's probably at sea,' replied Tovell, trying to sound confident.

'And what about the Westgates? And Lily's boy, Arthur?'

'Come inside, love. There's nothing we can do.'

But Ginny would not be comforted and by next morning she was convinced that her son and the entire Westgate family must have perished in the inferno. He had not intended to take produce to Great Yarmouth that day but by breakfast time it was clear to Tovell that he had no other alternative but to make that journey.

A pall of smoke hung over Great Yarmouth as Tovell drove towards it in his wagon. In the town itself some fires were still burning; other buildings were smoldering. The acrid smell was overpowering. Firemen, fire-engines, policemen and servicemen were everywhere. The ground was crisscrossed with hose-pipes. When he eventually arrived in the Market Place he saw that St Nicholas Church had been reduced to a burnt out shell. As he brought his vehicle to a halt, he heard one man call out to another that part of the brewery on North Quay had been destroyed. Dare he tell old Ted that bit of news? He was in a quandary as to what to do first but then, deciding that the priority was to find out if Alec was safe, he decided to make his way to the Fishwharf. He was stopped several times and had to show his identity card and getting onto the dockside proved even more difficult than usual. It looked as though his plea that he was delivering supplies to the naval stores was not going to work when one of the guards recognized him from previous occasions when he had given Alec a lift back to base, his bicycle in the back of the truck.

Once on the Fishwharf, Tovell looked at the numbers on the MTBs and MGBs moored there. He could not see Alec's boat amongst them. There were plenty of Wrens about, swarming over the boats which were docked. He considered asking one of them about Alec's boat but they were all so absorbed in what they were doing and working at such speed that he hesitated to interrupt such a hive of activity. His problem was solved when a cheerful girl, driving a tractor dragging a truck loaded with torpedoes, recognized him and called out to him.

'Looking for your son? They've been gone two days and we're not expecting them back in port just yet.' Tovell, relieved, thanked her and asked if she had been affected by the previous night's raid. The girl laughed. 'We're used to being shot at and bombed. We've survived so far. Fingers crossed!'

Remembering that he had also been instructed to check on Arthur Gillings's safety, Tovell drove along the quay until he was opposite the RAF's Air Sea Rescue Base on the Gorleston side of the river. He could see Arthur's launch, apparently intact, and as he watched he was sure that it was Arthur himself who climbed onto the quayside and walked away towards the wooden huts which Tovell knew were used by the stand-by crews. Satisfied that he had the right answer to give Ginny, he left the riverside. As he drove away he thought about the cheerful Wren. He wondered how many other pretty girls were Alec's close friends. He had implied to his father that off duty he was having a good time. Tovell believed him. He was shaken from this happy reverie when he came across closed roads. A policeman approached the lorry and spoke to Tovell. 'Sorry, you can't go through here. This whole area between South Quay and King Street is so badly damaged that the military has taken it over as a training ground. It prepares the men for the kind of fighting they'll be doing when they go oversees.'

Once more, Tovell gave his thanks and cut through onto the seafront.

More checkpoints and more smoldering buildings and he reached the Westgates' home. Miraculously, it was undamaged. Gladys was delighted to see him. In answer to his questions she assured him that they were all well. 'Bill and our son, Sam, were on duty with the Home Guard all night and I was at the WVS Rest Centre caring for the poor souls who were left homeless. In fact, the only one of us who came close to being bombed was Christopher, our youngest grandson. He was on fire-watching duties, the poor lad, along with the rest of his pals from the Boys Brigade. Of all the places they could have been stationed, where do you think they were? On top of St Nicholas Church! Obviously, there was nothing they could do except get out fast. Just as well they did before the spire fell on them! Christopher brought some of them to me at the centre for a bit of first aid treatment. None of the lads I saw was badly burned, thank God, but all of them were blackened from the smoke and very shocked. Strong sweet tea was all they needed; then we sent them home. What a lucky escape.'

'Margaret wasn't home on leave, was she?' asked Tovell anxiously.

'No, thank goodness. She's stationed at some airfield in Suffolk at the moment. I should think she's safer there than here. Young Arthur cycled over earlier to make sure we were alright. He asked about Margaret too. I think he's rather sweet on her.'

## II

The discussion Bobby had had with his commodore, about German attacks on Arctic convoys being less ferocious than expected, turned out to be premature. As 1942 progressed, the combined might of the U-boats, the surface ships of the *Kriegsmarine* and the dive-bombers of the *Luftwaffe*, once the convoys were within range of the airfields of occupied Norway and of Finland, made every voyage a nightmare. Even without the efforts of the enemy, the arrival of each convoy at Murmansk or Archangel was nothing short of a miracle, given the conditions against which each vessel and its crew had battled to get there. Four months of perpetual night through the Arctic winter, when the ice was so thick on the decks and the armaments that its weight threatened to capsize the ship, had given way to the Arctic summer and the promise of perpetual day – and the certainty of being seen by enemy aircraft patrolling from hostile coastlines or surface carriers.

Bobby had been with his commodore when he had addressed the assembled skippers of the merchant vessels, and their radio officers, before the latest convoy had left Iceland. As always, the admiral had explained the formation the convoy would take, how many columns it would have and the number each boat had been assigned. He had given them details of the signal codes to be used, the need to maintain radio silence except in dire emergencies for fear the short wave transmissions would be picked up by enemy aircraft, the rallying points in case they became dispersed, information about "friendly minefields" and of rumoured danger areas. He had appointed a vice-commodore to take over the command of the convoy if he was to be sunk and a rear-commodore in case the vice-commodore was sunk.

He had also emphasized that merchant ships were not to stop to take on survivors during an attack. This was the job of the corvettes and the destroyers – once they had beaten off the enemy – which would form part of the accompanying cover force of Royal Navy ships. These escorts would join them once they were at sea, taking up positions ahead, astern and on either side of the convoy. And, he was happy to announce, the plea for a rescue ship equipped with a sick bay had also been answered this time and that ship too would search for survivors. The Sunderland flying boats and the Catalinas of Coastal Command, based in Iceland, excellent aircraft for finding and attacking enemy submarines, would patrol around the convoy as far out into the ocean as possible. But for those who had never sailed in the Arctic before – since January the convoys had been joined by American ships and crews - he had a word of caution. He told of that phenomenon unique to those climes: sea-smoke or Arctic fog which formed suddenly when cold air condensed as it passed over the surface of a sea which was slightly warmer and how they must trail fog buoys behind their vessels or they would never be able to keep in formation. He had warned too of the added danger that their masts might protrude above the fog and be seen by enemy planes patrolling the clear skies above them.

The voyage had been fraught: there had not been so many U-boats shadowing them since in daylight it was easier for look-outs to see their conning towers peeping through the waves, but there had been so many attacks from torpedo-carrying dive bombers that they had suspected the enemy had an aircraft carrier in the area. The threat that the *Scharnhorst* was on the loose and the possibility that the battleship *Tirpitz,* which had already sneaked up on and sunk a straggler from an earlier convoy, might also have escaped from her fiord, had made it a harrowing time.

It was with great relief, therefore, that they at last approached Russian waters and were met by Soviet fighter planes – Hurricanes with red stars painted on their wings – forming an umbrella overhead, sharing the skies with the ever welcome land birds. Minesweepers and icebreakers also came out to meet them. The merchant ships formed into line ahead after Russian pilots had come aboard their vessels and, preceded by ice breakers, they entered the estuary of Kola Inlet. During their painfully slow progress to Murmansk they were vulnerable to air attacks from the Finnish and Norwegian airfields occupied by the Germans. Frequently, the air was filled with wailing sirens as enemy Dorniers dived upon the column. Many of the merchantmen had no ammunition left but the ack-ack batteries on the quayside went into action and the destroyers following the convoy joined in to repel the attacks every time.

At last they moored against the bomb-damaged docks - debris and all manner of filth, even human excrement, was scattered everywhere - and the lengthy process of unloading their cargoes began. One vessel, having offloaded its crates of ammunition, needed to cross to the opposite bank to discharge its other cargo. She moved slowly under the direction of the Russian pilot but when she was mid-stream she struck a magnetic mine and began to sink. The skipper of the vessel ran up and down yelling to shore through a megaphone. His pleas for help were met by indifferent stares from Russians standing on opposite quays surveying the scene. At last a tug left its mooring and came over but by then it was too late and nothing could be done to save the vessel. Her crew abandoned ship in their lifeboats and her cargo of brand new tanks and trucks sank to the river bed to form yet another obstruction.

This episode was quickly relayed by word of mouth to the other merchant ships and if that tale was not depressing enough, matters were made worse the next day when a young radio officer decided to take a walk into the countryside. He had wanted to mourn in peace the loss of his brother who had been killed on the outward voyage. He had returned to his ship in great distress having come across a ploughed field full of tanks where they had been deposited unceremoniously from an earlier convoy - broken, rusted and unusable. Another group of shipmates came across an airfield with brand new Hurricanes apparently abandoned and unused because, or so it appeared, the planes had been damaged by rough handling. This group was on its way to visit wounded comrades in hospital at Vaenga. They found their friends desperate to be taken back to their ships for the ward was full of injured Russian soldiers – the Front Line was only twenty five miles away – so beds had to be shared, there was no anaesthetic, few medicines, inedible food and everywhere was filthy.

These stories did nothing to lift morale and nor did the fact that the local population had no respect for anyone who was not in uniform – and amongst the merchant seamen only the officers wore uniform. Guards and petty officials continued to delight in obstructing everyone's progress by constant demands to see papers. Insult was added to injury when the victims of this bureaucracy realized their inquisitors were so ignorant that they often inspected their documents by holding them upside down. In short, the return convoy could not depart soon enough.

Bobby had only one opportunity to meet Peter because the stay in port was not as long as on previous occasions. This was because there were plenty of stragglers from earlier convoys waiting for an escort home and it was agreed that they would depart as soon as most of the current vessels had been unloaded. This meant that ships which were not yet unloaded would be left behind and would become, in their turn, stragglers but so miserable had the stay in Murmansk been, that the fortunate leavers gave them scarcely a thought. Bobby was not sorry to depart early since he had been troubled by a sense of foreboding as soon as they had docked in war-ravaged Murmansk. Like generations of mariners before him he was of a superstitious nature and he had come to see the escort cruiser HMS *Norfolk* as a talisman. It was customary for convoys to divide in Russian waters and half to proceed to the White Sea and Archangel. This port was further from the border with Norway and therefore safer from enemy air attack. On this occasion, *Norfolk* had been one of the Royal Navy ships which had gone with the Archangel contingent; for some reason, this had upset Bobby.

As the days had passed, other incidents had depressed him further. He was used to seeing people scrambling over the ice to salvage what they could whenever a ship's cook threw a bucket of waste over the side, but even this took on a new dimension when German prisoners, working on the dockside, joined in the struggle for rotting food. The Russian guards used their rifle butts on their prisoners with alacrity and when one man escaped from them and ran a short distance away, gnawing ravenously on his find, they shot him dead and left his bleeding body where it lay on the ice for all to see.

Bobby had watched this scene in horror, unaware that the commodore was standing behind him. 'Don't judge them too harshly,' he had said quietly. 'The stories that are emerging of the atrocities the Germans are committing against Russians are going to make them vicious. And from what I hear, the Soviets are just as ruthless with their own people. I was told a tale last night about a Red Navy officer who got drunk at a reception aboard one of our destroyers. Apparently he said something disrespectful about our King. Next day, the man was marched under escort to the quayside and made a formal apology to the captain of our destroyer. Our man said he accepted the apology, realize no insult was intended – that it was the drink talking – and that he was welcome to come aboard again anytime. The Soviets then marched the man away and, to the amazement of our ship's company, stood him against a wall and executed him by firing squad. Clearly, these are not a people to trifle with.'

With the approach of summer, the ice pack was retreating and breaking up allowing this homeward convoy to plot a more northerly course, away from the enemy airfields of Norway and Finland. They were to sail north north east into the Barents Sea towards Novaya Zemlya, then west between Bear Island and Spitzbergen and finally south west back to Iceland. This passage, in effect a northerly detour, meant they would skirt the summer icepack and, with luck, avoid being caught by the *Luftwaffe*. After a few hours at sea they were joined by the Archangel contingent and the rest of the Royal Navy escort – including, to Bobby's relief, HMS *Norfolk*. As soon as they were clear of Russian waters the anti-submarine trawlers and the three minesweepers which had preceded the convoy, left the formation to return to their base on the Kola Peninsula. Bobby was sorry to see them go.

At first the convoy was beset by gales and with most of the merchant ships not carrying cargo but only ballast, they were tossed around like flotsam. Progress through the rough seas was slow and sitting down to eat a meal at a table impossible, if not from the constant lurching and crashing of the ship then from the misery of seasickness. Nowhere could the sorry mariners find respite from their suffering: above deck they still faced bitter cold; below deck they endured the oozing damp as every bulkhead, as always, streamed with condensation. Mercifully, the weather changed and the storms died away and for the next few days the fog concealed them, but this made an astronomical fix on their position impossible. It was necessary for every ship to trail its fog buoy: a piece of wood on a towline which had a copper hood capable of raising a visible wake as high as five feet above the surface of the sea. By following the plume of spray created by the vessel in front, the ships could play "follow-my-leader". At times the fog was so dense that even the plumes could not be seen so ships had to use their foghorns as well.

When they neared the icepack, progress was even slower for they were hampered by floebergs – fragments detached from the main ice formations – and by "growlers", the dangerous iceblocks broken off from floebergs and icebergs, which have only a small area of their actual size showing above the water. The necessity to manoeuvre the vessels around these obstructions, together with the sudden arrival of blankets of fog, made it impossible for every ship in the convoy to stay on exact course all of the time.

'Thank God we've no reports at the present time of U-boats in the vicinity,' the commodore said to his yeoman one evening as they stood together on the bridge. 'If I had to order you to signal the convoy to zigzag to avoid the enemy, half of them would probably crash into the ice or into each other. Ah, well, I think I'll try to snatch an hour's sleep while I've got the chance.'

'Are there any changes of orders you want signalled, sir?' asked Bobby.

'No, the original orders stand and we did all the knuckle-rapping about making too much smoke the last time the fog lifted. There's no point in telling them to stay on course better – the poor devils are doing their best anyway. Wake me if anything changes.' So saying, the admiral retired to the chart house and curled up on a camp bed, fully clothed. He fell into an exhausted sleep within seconds. Bobby meanwhile went to check on his team of signalling ratings, men engaged for "hostilities only", not regular Navy men like him. They had, however, been together for some time, setting up home on whichever ship the commodore chose to fly his flag, along with the tools of their trade: semaphore flags, telescopes, Aldis lamps and the all-important code-books. It was whilst they were talking together that the vessel shook violently from the shock of an explosion and began to list to starboard. By the time Bobby got to the bridge the commodore was already there. The captain of the vessel was desperately trying to ascertain the extent of the damage.

'We must have struck a mine. You've had no reports of the enemy in this area so we can't have been hit by a torpedo.' As the captain spoke, geysers shot up out of the water close to other merchant vessels sailing nearby. At once the commodore gave orders to change course but by the time the signal had been hoisted on the masthead, more waterspouts were spurting up beneath the hulls of vessels. The roar of explosions came from all directions. Many merchant ships were firing their guns in panic, not knowing what they were firing at or the nature of their attacker, but assuming that either U-boats had penetrated inside the columns of the convoy or they were being fired on by the enemy's distant surface warships. All around, vessels were listing; some were already sinking.

'Signal to the escort commander that I'm passing command of the convoy to the vice-commodore,' shouted the admiral. 'We must have strayed into a minefield.' Before Bobby could respond, another explosion rocked the ship. He was thrown against the bulkhead and knocked unconscious. At the same time he was hit by jagged metal: part of the floor which had erupted as the detonation from the mine had torn through the ship, killing the signallers in the radio room where Bobby had been a few minutes before and ripping through the metal plating into the bridge. At once the vessel began to list even more dangerously and the captain gave the order to abandon ship. He hurried to his cabin and grabbed his confidential papers whilst the commodore descended the steps to the shattered radio room and with a despairing look at what was left of his team, collected together the blood-spattered code books. He ditched them over the side in a weighted sack before returning to the bridge.

At that moment, two of the crew appeared to collect any wounded for the lifeboats. One addressed the commodore. 'Hurry, sir, she's sinking fast. You need to get in a lifeboat. Not many places left. One boat has already capsized as we were lowering it.'

'Take my yeoman,' ordered the admiral, pointing to where Bobby lay.

The man went over and looked at the prostrate figure. 'No point in taking him, sir. He's got no chance. His guts are hanging out.'

'Then stuff 'em back in,' barked the admiral. 'He's still a young man. He deserves a chance. He can have my place. Now bugger off and let this old sea-dog die the kind of death he's always wanted.'


Hours later in the lifeboat, Bobby regained consciousness briefly. He asked after the commodore but fell back into unconsciousness before he had comprehended the reply. He was also unaware when a rescue ship – a specially converted former coastal passenger ship - came alongside his lifeboat and the other rafts from the commodore's flagship. The survivors, who were able, began to hoist themselves up the scrambling nets slung along the hull but many found their hands were numb and lifeless from the cold. They tried hauling themselves up by slotting their elbows into the large open mesh but they did not have the strength and found it impossible to respond to the exhortations of the rescuers leaning over the side of the ship. Those same sailors then climbed over the rail and down the netting and helped the exhausted men up onto the deck. They also threw lines to the pitiable men who, in their eagerness to be saved, had slipped off the rafts into the water. But most of them were unable to grasp these life-lines because they had no use in their frost-bitten hands. To the distress of the onlookers, these men sank beneath the icy waves. The severely wounded, like Bobby, were luckier: they were brought aboard in baskets attached to a small crane. He did not come round for several hours and by that time the Royal Navy surgeon and his medical team had taken him into their small operating theatre and saved his life. Four days later the rescue ship was struck by torpedoes and sank.

# III

Once more Bobby found himself in a lifeboat. The sick berth attendants had bundled him, and the other men recovering from their wounds in the sick bay, into warm clothing courtesy of the American War Relief Society. They had then fitted them with life jackets and a one-piece rubber life-saving suit. Somehow, they had manhandled them up on deck and into lifeboats. Bobby was lucky: he and two other sick men had the advantage of being in the same boat as the very competent Leading Sick Berth Attendant, Charlie Bennett. They were in the Third Mate's boat. This young officer decided their best chance was to wait to be picked up by the Royal Navy escort ships once they returned after chasing away the enemy. He, therefore, ordered the sea anchor to be streamed to ensure that they did not drift too much.

Charlie Bennett was kept busy from the outset. Two stokers were among the thirty survivors in the boat and both had been dragged from the burning bowels of their vessel after the torpedoes had hit. There had been no opportunity to grab their life-saving suits or their life-jackets and they were clad only in dungarees and singlets. Bennett put blankets around them which he had had the foresight to stuff into a kitbag along with medical supplies before abandoning ship and he rubbed whale oil into their frozen hands and feet. It was to no avail and both men died within minutes of one another. Bennett removed the blankets before easing their bodies, with the help of their shipmates, into the water. He turned his attention next to those men who had been thrown by the blast into the sea. Some of them were burned also and in every case their wet clothing had begun to freeze on them. He distributed the blankets and attended to the burns victims as best he could, in the knowledge that most of them were beyond his help.

After a few hours the Third Mate ordered flares to be let off at intervals in the hope that one of the escort ships would see them. By then the fog had descended and once it had cleared, several hours later, no other lifeboat or raft was in sight – they were completely alone in the Arctic Ocean. Anxious to reassure his men that all was not lost, the young officer told them that he was certain he knew exactly where they were. 'We're between Bear Island and Spitzbergen but we're closer to Bear Island.'

Bobby felt sure he knew what the Third Mate was going to propose next so he interrupted. 'Mr Holden, it might be helpful if I told you we've picked up radio signals from Bear Island but we're certain they're from an automated station not a manned one. On the other hand, we know there are people on Spitzbergen. A pal of mine was on one of the ships which evacuated the Russian coal miners last summer – the Canadians took off the Norwegian settlers - and he's taken supplies to the Free Norwegians who man the garrison and weather station which is there now - at Barentsburg. The Navy escort ships also use the island to refuel – the fiords are a safe bunkering place.'

'Thank you for that information,' said the Third Mate. 'Clearly, there's a very good chance of shelter and rescue at Spitzbergen. We'll set sail north.'

Charlie Bennett squatted down beside Bobby. 'That was very tactfully put - for a Royal Navy man. I thought all you Royal Navy officers and NCOs despised Merchant Navy officers.'

'Don't tar me with that brush. I've nothing but respect for the Merchant Navy,' replied Bobby with feeling. 'Anyway, you're Royal Navy yourself – '

'Ah, but, my old man and my brothers are not. They're all on merchantmen in the Atlantic and I know what good seamen they are.'

'Well, don't let on to Mr Holden but I've omitted one bit of information,' Bobby confided. 'We've also picked up signals which make us think the Germans might also be using Spitzbergen – as a weather station and a safe haven to bunker. It's a bloomin' big island; desolate and uninhabited except for the settlement at Barentsburg, so they could have set up a base there without the Norwegians knowing. Let's hope Mr Holden's reckoning lands us in the right camp.'

The man lying next to Bobby, another patient from the sick bay, opened his eyes and said, 'I heard that. We shouldn't be going there if there's a chance of Fritz capturing us. I don't want to be a prisoner of war.'

'You keep your voice down, Blakely,' hissed Bennett. 'We don't want to add to these men's worries. Morale is everything when you're shipwrecked. I should know: this isn't the first time I've had a ship sink under me. And you can take my word for it that if we're at sea for any length of time we won't care if we do end up as POWs.'


The men were cheered once the lifeboat's sails were hoisted: they knew where they were going; they had a purpose; the chances of soon being safe were high. The next day the wind died down and they were becalmed; the Third Mate ordered them to row instead. The weather changed again the day after and the gale which beset them was so ferocious that they had to heave to and put out their sea-anchor again. Now, the huge seas washed over into their small boat and the effort of baling out the water when they were already exhausted and frozen was agonizing. The violent movement of the little vessel as it was tossed about brought seasickness to many. The third man from the sick bay, who had woken from the anaesthetic after his operation to find himself in the lifeboat, was the worst affected. He was laying the other side of Bobby and his constant retching was pitiful to hear. Bennett did his best to calm the man, but he continued to vomit bile. When at last he was still, the sick berth attendant felt inside the hood of the man's one-piece suit, searching for a pulse in his neck. 'He's gone, poor chap,' said Bennett. 'He probably burst open his stitches and bled to death. It's a merciful release.'

Once the gale had abated, Bennett went to check on the other men in the bow of the lifeboat who had been a cause of concern for him from the beginning. These men had been caught in an oil slick. The oil had burnt their eyes, they had swallowed it and in some cases it had gone down into their lungs. They too had retched uncontrollably during the storm. Two of them, as Bennett had feared, were dead. He called for volunteers to help him heave the three bodies into the water. This in itself was no easy task for men plagued by frostbite, fatigue and depression. Then as the ocean became calm so the arctic sea-smoke returned. One man, peering into the ghostly mist, suddenly shrieked, 'What the hell is that coming towards us!' Everyone who was able turned and looked in the direction he was pointing. Orange buoys, or so it seemed from a distance, ten or even twenty of them, were floating relentlessly in the direction of their lifeboat.

Bennett was the first to realize what it was that was bearing down on them. 'They're corpses,' he said sadly. 'They're wearing the same orange life-saving suits that we're wearing. Their life-jackets are keeping them upright.'

'They're coming for us!' screamed the man who had first sighted them. 'They want to take us with them.'

'They've been caught in a current; it's the current which is carrying them along,' said the Third Mate. 'That's all it is. Take the oars and push them aside if any come too close. We don't want them to capsize us.' Most of the men were too mesmerized by the spectacle to move; they just watched as the school of dead men came nearer. It was Bennett and some of the Polish deckhands who carried out the Third Mate's order and deflected the corpses which threatened the safety of the boat. These dead men floated around the hull, joined up with their comrades again and continued on their southward journey.

Bennett could see how much this episode, coming close upon the hasty burial of their own dead, had upset the men. He began to chastise them for not having completed the ritual which he had instigated of rubbing whale oil into their frozen hands and feet every few hours. 'Do as our medical man says,' the Third Mate ordered. 'It makes sense. We need our hands to row and set the sails.' Seeing only lethargy and despair, Mr Holden sought to raise their spirits. 'I think we could risk using the engine for a while. We only have a small stock of fuel but we might be able to run for an hour. It will give us all a chance to rest too,' he added wearily. The action of travelling under power did indeed raise morale and after an hour they were out of the fog and in cold clear air. The man who had sighted the corpses started yelling again. This time he swore he had seen a ship.

At this news Bobby, whose abdomen was crisscrossed with scars and stitches, hauled himself up, wincing with pain and peered over the gunwale. 'I don't see anything,' he muttered to Bennett. 'Perhaps it's a mirage.'

'Oh, God!' exclaimed Blakely. 'He's going nuts. This isn't the desert – it's the ruddy Arctic Ocean.'

'I'm not going nuts,' Bobby replied calmly. 'You get mirages in the Arctic too. They're caused by temperature inversions. They give you extreme visibility too, so if there is something out there it could be miles away.'

Bennett stood up. 'Yes, I can see something,' he exclaimed. 'Mr Holden has some glasses.'

The man next to the Third Mate called out, 'He's asleep but here are the glasses.'

Bennett took the case which the man proffered and focused on the horizon. 'He's right!' he yelled excitedly. 'It is a ship. Mr Holden, wake up!'

'Let him sleep,' said Bobby. 'Look and see what we have left – flares or smoke candles – anything so that she sees us.'

At first, it seemed that all their efforts to attract attention had failed, but just as their engine spluttered its last, having guzzled all the available fuel, the ship appeared to turn in their direction. It was much further away than they had thought and seemed to take hours to come close to them. There was insufficient wind for the sails so those who could muster enough energy took to the oars again. 'There's no sign of any other ship. This one must have been a straggler from an outward going convoy. She must have left Iceland a few days ago and got separated from the others. Engine trouble perhaps. Anyway, whatever it was, it's lucky for us,' Bennett commented. But once it was possible to make out the ship's name, there was a commotion in the lifeboat as the Polish seamen began to shout and gesticulate; a few started to undo their life-saving suits. Bennett called out to one deckhand whom he knew spoke good English, asking the man what was upsetting his fellow countrymen.

'She's a Russian vessel,' the man, known to his shipmates as Waldy, replied. 'We would rather die than board a Russian ship.'

'Why? We'll be safe!' shouted Blakely, the man lying next to Bobby.

'No! You do not know what the Russians did to our people when they invaded our country; what they did to our families in Warsaw.' There were tears in Waldy's eyes as he spoke.

'I'd better wake Mr Holden,' said Bennett, making his way forward. He shook the Third Mate gently then, getting no response, felt for a pulse in the officer's neck. Grim faced, the sick berth attendant returned to Bobby's side. 'He's dead, poor little blighter. He didn't have an ounce of fat on him so I suppose it's a miracle he's lasted this long. Well, Petty Officer Adams, you're the only one left with any kind of rank – that makes you in charge.'

'I've no authority over Merchant Navy men,' Bobby stated.

'I don't think that will bother them,' said Charlie Bennett. 'They just want a leader: someone to tell them what to do.'

The Polish seaman nodded his head vigorously. 'Yes, he's right. But don't let the Russians get us. We would rather take off our suits and lifejackets and jump in the sea …'

'I know, I know. Long live Poland,' muttered Bobby, remembering the tale he had been told at the Hall of Culture last Christmas. 'I won't make you board her.'

'Never mind the Poles,' Blakely protested. 'What about the rest of us? We want to be rescued.'

'That must mean you're not suffering from frostbite,' said Bennett archly.

'What are you talking about? Of course I'm suffering from frostbite – we all are,' shrieked Blakely.

'Then if you've any sense you won't board the Russian,' stated Bennett. 'I've seen what Russian doctors – no, butchers - do to frostbite victims. Whenever we've taken on board any of our men they've treated, our surgeon has spent the entire homeward voyage trying to repair the damage they've done: reform the stumps, cover exposed bones … Last time, we had one poor beggar who'd had frostbite in all four limbs. The Russians had chopped them all off. So if anyone wants to spend the rest of his life needing someone else to help him eat, drink, shit and piss then go ahead – board the Russian. And as for you, Blakely, you've got a broken leg already; they'll have that off in no time!'

'But he has a point,' said Bobby and raising his voice, he announced, 'If any of you men want to be taken on board the Russian vessel just say so and we'll go alongside.'

There was silence and then one man commented, 'We're probably as safe as we can be here: at least no-one's going to waste a torpedo on a little lifeboat.'

There were a few murmurs of agreement before Bobby asked Bennett about the badly burned men. He replied, 'They're unlikely to last anyway so they might as well stay with us and die among friends.'

'That's settled then,' Bobby decided. 'Wave them our thanks and then set the sails. There's a bit of breeze now.'

'Thank you. Thank you,' said Waldy. He returned to the other Poles and told them the decision. Once they had done up their suits again they happily carried out the orders. They waved jubilantly to the Russian crew, watching incredulously from the ship's rail, as they sailed the lifeboat around the stern of the would-be rescuer. The Russian vessel then set off to resume its former course and when it was out of sight, Bennett and the Poles eased the Third Mate's body into the sea. As they were doing so, six enemy aircraft – Junkers Ju88s - flew low over their heads and roared off in the direction the Russian vessel had taken. The men watched as the bombers climbed high into the clear sky then broke formation before diving individually out of sight. Seconds later, they heard the faint sounds of explosions in the distance and saw twists of black smoke curl upwards along a line on the horizon.

'Someone's copped a packet,' Blakely muttered.

'They must have found the whole damn convoy,' Bennett said bitterly. Half an hour later he had further cause to curse when a U-boat suddenly surfaced beside them. 'And they must have told these bastards where we were. Keep calm boys: they only take officers and we haven't got any – now.' One of the sailors who emerged from the conning tower was carrying a camera and he proceeded to photograph the hapless survivors in the lifeboat. 'Smile nicely boys,' said Bennett sarcastically. 'We're the stars of the latest newsreel, soon to be showing nightly in Fritz's picture palaces.'

A German officer leaned over the guard rail and shouted in English, 'Are you Bolsheviks? Are you Communists?'

'No!' Bennett yelled back.

'Then why are you helping the Russians?'

'We're just deckhands; we take cargo where we're told,' replied Bennett.

The German obviously accepted this answer because he then demanded, 'Give us your captain.'

'He's not in this boat. We have no officers here,' said Bennett. The German conveyed this information to the man standing beside him who was obviously the commanding officer of the submarine. After a hurried discussion, a sailor was dispatched inside the vessel. 'He'll have been sent to get us some supplies. A U-boat came up alongside us the last time I was shipwrecked,' Bennett whispered to Bobby.

'Ask him for a compass,' Bobby urged.

This request was duly passed on and after further discussion a compass, along with bread, water and schnapps, was handed over to the stricken men. They thanked the German officer for his kindness and he, as a parting shot, told them to turn their little boat round. 'You are sailing in the wrong direction. If you head that way,' he said pointing, 'you will reach Norway and for you the war will be over.'

They watched in silence as the enemy retreated inside their submarine and submerged. When they could no longer see even the periscope, Bobby commented, 'If you think we're going to sail and row four hundred and fifty miles to Norway, you're mistaken, mate. We stick to Mr Holden's plan and make for Spitzbergen. We've a compass now, though from what I've heard from standing on the bridge, it can be as much as eight degrees out in the Arctic – the earth's magnetic pole pulls it down. But at least we can be sure we're going north. Let's just hope we don't miss the bloody island altogether.'

'We'll know if we go too far north: the drinking water will freeze solid even though it's the so-called summer,' Bennett observed. He had carefully rationed the emergency stores which the lifeboat carried, knowing they could be at sea for many days, but now he recommended that they eat most of the bread they had been given and that they wash it down with more generous amounts of water than he had been able to allow them previously. He cautioned that they drink only enough of the schnapps to cheer them but not enough to depress them! No one disputed what he said: as far as the sorry crew was concerned, he spoke with the authority of a doctor.

Once more they were alone on this vast ocean; surrounded by such a huge expanse of water that it seemed impossible that they could ever reach landfall. Days passed although how many exactly was open to argument. Confined in a small open boat with nothing to do - unless it was their turn to sail or row the vessel, if they were able – the men struggled to keep their minds from dwelling on the constant pain they were in, the gnawing hunger and the relentless cold. Perpetual daylight only added to their suffering. There was some degree of twilight at what would have been midnight but even this proved disorientating and the men longed for the comfort of real darkness. As it was, they felt totally exhausted as one twenty-four hour spell of continuous light merged into another. A sense of abandonment and hopelessness descended upon them all to a greater or lesser extent. As the badly burned men, one by one, succumbed, glad to be released from their agony at last, their weakened and despairing shipmates found it more and more difficult to heave the bodies over the side into the bleak ocean; eventually they did not have the strength to try and left their dead comrades where they lay. Bennett did all he could to raise spirits and when the men would no longer make the effort to rub the whale oil into their limbs, which he told them continuously was a life-saver, he did the job for them.

Bennett went to Bobby when he saw the latter struggling to undo the top of his one-piece suit. 'I shouldn't do that, Petty Officer,' he said quietly. 'You'll let in the freezing cold.' Bobby had been suffering from a fever for a couple of days and when Bennett felt his forehead he could tell that his temperature was getting higher.

'I want to look at the photos of my wife,' Bobby replied weakly. 'I've never thanked you for saving them for me.'

'Ah, I knew you'd want them,' replied Bennett as he reached inside the suit and retrieved the photographs. 'If I had a pretty wife like yours I know I wouldn't want to be parted from them. We had to cut what was left of your clothes from you but fortunately these were untouched.'

'This one was taken on our wedding day at St Mary's Church in Haisbro. Yes, Haisbro ... Shall I ever see that place again – or stand beside my Rachel in the church and sing the Haisbro hymn?' Bobby was still for a while and then he began to recite the first verse of the hymn. Several other men joined in the words: *God moves in a mysterious way His wonders to perform; He plants His footsteps in the sea and rides upon the storm.*' Everyone was quiet, each man lost in his own thoughts, many of them silently praying. Bobby gazed lovingly for several more moments at Rachel's photographs and then replaced them inside his suit with Bennett's assistance. Suddenly, Bobby struggled to sit up and Bennett helped him. Bobby was lying against the port side of the boat; facing the starboard side. He began to point ahead of him in an easterly direction. 'Follow the footsteps!' he said excitedly. 'Follow the footsteps!' Then he slumped back and drifted into semi-consciousness.

As Bennett eased his arm out from under Bobby's limp form and stood up, Blakely muttered, 'He's really gone nuts this time. He's delirious. He won't last much longer. Follow the footsteps! He's crackers.'

'No, he isn't. I can see what he was pointing at,' said Bennett. 'He meant us to follow the patches of sea-smoke. It's clear all around us here where the sea is icy, but over there it's misty and the fog is clumping together; shaped like footsteps.'

'So what?' moaned Blakely.

'You get a smoking sea when cold air condenses as it travels over a slightly warmer surface of the ocean. But land can give off heat too and merge with the icy temperatures to form mist – sea-smoke. He meant follow the footsteps to find land.'

'You're as nuts as he is,' Blakely snapped.

Waldy joined in. 'What have we to lose? Might as well follow the mist.'

'I agree. I'll take another oar,' said Bennett. 'We need more rowers. Come on, boys, we've got to try whilst we've still got some strength left.'

Days exposed to the bitter cold with little nourishment had taken their toll: dulled brains meant slow responses, weakened and uncoordinated muscles meant pulling on an oar was excruciatingly painful. Bennett, constantly exhorting them to take heart, organized a rota so that no man reached the point of collapse before a shipmate took his place at the oar. The exhausted men made little progress but after two hours of painful endeavour they were rewarded when Waldy sighted land through a clearing in the mist. They even managed a little cheer before Bennett urged them to greater efforts. As they approached the shore their little boat fell foul of reefs so Waldy leaned over the bow and guided them through the rocks. In spite of this the lifeboat eventually hit a submerged outcrop and overturned, throwing them into the icy surf close to the shingle beach. Most of them were unable to walk and crawled on all fours through the shallows. Bennett and the Polish seamen managed to carry the wounded and the unconscious men to safety between them; the bodies they left to float away to a watery grave. All of them lie panting on the shore for several minutes before Bennett looked up and saw to his amazement two wooden shacks only yards from them.

'Look, boys, someone's been good to us! Huts – over there! They must be for whalers or seal-hunters. They'll be supplies as well as shelter there. C'mon, just a bit more effort and we'll be alright.'

Once more they crawled and dragged themselves along until they reached the first of the wooden huts, Bennett and the Poles carrying the sick. Inside they found a stove with kindling and logs beside it, tinned food and basic cooking utensils. Most of the men collapsed on the floor and fell asleep immediately but Bennett, with the help of the Polish crewmen, managed to get the fire going in the stove and heat up a big saucepan of soup. They woke their comrades when the simple meal was ready and those who were not as severely frostbitten held the tin cups of soup to the lips of their shipmates who no longer had any feeling left in their hands.

Bennett went over to Bobby and helped him to sit up and drink the soup. 'We followed your footsteps and look where they've brought us. We'll rest for a few hours, eat and get our strength up and then some of us will go and search for help. Let's just pray we've landed somewhere that's inhabited.'

'You've done well, Bennett,' said Bobby weakly. 'But you mustn't go for help yourself: we need you here.' He pushed the tin cup aside. 'Sorry, can't take any more ... making me feel sick. I'm burning up ... are my wounds infected?'

'Could be,' replied Bennett calmly, adding cheerfully, 'We don't usually recommend getting shipwrecked as a means of recuperation after hours on the operating table.'

'You're almost safe now ...' said Bobby, his voice drifting away. Making a big effort, he continued, 'One more thing: let my Rachel know I was thinking of her – that I love her. Please.'

'Tell her yourself! You'll be back in a sick bay or hospital soon. I'm just sorry all my medical supplies have run out, but once you get the attention you need you'll be fine.'

Bobby smiled as he shut his eyes and lay back. 'Bet you got full marks for "positive bedside manner". Just tell my Rachel ... Must sleep now.'

'Here, Mr Adams,' said Bennett, alarmed. 'Don't give up! We're almost home and dry. If you snuff it, I'll be in charge and I don't want that.'

Without opening his eyes, Bobby muttered, 'Who are you kidding? You've been in charge since the beginning.'


A few hours later, Waldy and one of his fellow countrymen set out to try to find help. They were eventually driven back by a blizzard without having made any human contact. They had, however, come across wild ducks and managed to kill three of them: enough to feed the remaining twelve survivors. They returned to a hut reeking with the stench of decaying flesh and the moans of men tormented by the effect of warmth upon frostbitten faces, hands and feet. The heat from the stove had lifted morale for a while, dried their wet clothes and penetrated their chilled bodies, but it had also thawed their frozen limbs leaving them in agony and, in many cases, with the onset of gangrene. The Polish deckhands plucked and chopped up the duck carcasses and boiled them on the stove, adding tinned vegetables Bennett had found in the second hut during their absence. This time, Bennett fed Bobby only the liquid from the pot. 'Here's some duck gruel for you, Petty Officer. Just like they make at the Ritz.'

Bobby managed to keep some of the soup down. It revived him enough to say in a whisper, 'Pity they couldn't find any people today.'

'They'll try again when the weather eases,' Bennett assured him. 'They'll have to before the bears find us! The stink from this hut will be carried on the wind for miles. I've never had much luck attracting women and I certainly don't want to attract any man-eating bears!'

A few hours later, with the blizzard abated, Waldy set out again with another of the Polish deckhands. They were gone for two days and in that time three more men died – of gangrenous septicaemia. They managed to drag the bodies to the adjacent hut but no one had the strength to bury them. The survivors left behind began to fear that Waldy and his companion were dead too. Bennett was also worried: the supplies were running out, he knew no-one had the strength to go searching for more food – even scavenging for birds' eggs would be too much for them – many were totally demoralized after their harrowing ordeal and the remorseless suffering meant they were almost at the end of their tether. He knew that for some reason he was in a fitter condition than anyone and even though he hated to leave them with no medical assistance whatsoever, he resolved that he must be the next person to try to find help. The remaining Polish sailors took it in turns to leave the hut to see if they could spy their comrades. When at last one of them returned, shouting excitedly, Bennett went to the door and looked outside himself.

'I can see them!' he yelled. 'They're in sledges pulled by soldiers on skis – in white battledress. There are other soldiers too with rifles on their backs and other sledges.'

'They've brought the bloody Germans. Damn the Poles,' screamed Blakely.

The noise roused Bobby from his semi-conscious state. 'They've done the right thing,' he said weakly. 'We wouldn't have lasted another day.'

Moments later, Waldy and his friend hurried into the hut. Immediately, Blakely hurled abuse at them for bringing the enemy. 'No! No!' cried Waldy. 'This is Spitzbergen. They're not German - they're Norwegian!'

# IV

As summer progressed so did the need to make sacrifices for the war effort. The petrol ration had been halved for months and pleasure motoring was banned altogether from the first of July. No-one was surprised: it was obvious that fuel was needed for planes when the sky was full of aircraft, night after night, joining the 1,000 bomber raids on the industrial areas of the Ruhr and the Rhineland. You could not travel far in Norfolk or Suffolk without coming upon an airfield and these numbers were significantly increased when the 2nd Air Division of the 8th United States Army Air Forces arrived in East Anglia. Now the *Admiral Lord Nelson*, already a favourite haunt for many an exiled serviceman, whether Norwegian, Pole, Dutch or Czech, and for Commonwealth airmen from Canada, South Africa, Australia and New Zealand, became a second home for Americans too – once they had stopped complaining about and become accustomed to, warm beer! 'What about their lovely uniforms?' Rachel enthused to Lizzie. 'They all look like officers in them.'

Paper was another commodity in short supply and Tovell, that avid reader of newspapers, was sorry when their size was compulsorily cut. Ted had his own opinion on the situation which he voiced when he came round one afternoon to find the three children sitting at the table busily cutting old newspaper into small neat rectangles and threading the sheets onto string. 'You're making a fine job o' that, littl'uns,' he said. 'And you want to add all them bloomin' old forms the government keeps issuing. What a waste o' paper that is – as though we need telling how to do this, that and the other. They must think we're all loopy. Still their forms make good bum-fodder – that they do.' The children giggled and Ginny frowned disapprovingly at Ted. 'What's the matter with you, gal? What's wrong with saying "bum"? We've all got one and that'd be a rum old do if we hadn't.' He grinned impishly at her as the three youngsters laughed out loud; Ginny could not help smiling herself as she shook her head. 'You've finished that now. Go you hang 'em up in the privy and then old

Ted will take you down the farmyard so you can see all the new babies.'

'What new babies, Uncle Ted?' asked Roger eagerly.

'Well now, let me see,' mused Ted. 'The calves, the ducklings and the goslings are a week older than when you saw them last Saturday but you haven't seen the new little foal we had on Monday. Oh, and that master fine chicken house the young master was having built is finished and boxes of little chicks arrived yesterday.'

Roger beamed. 'Hurry up!' he called to his brother and sister. 'Don't be so slow.'

'What can we take them to eat?' asked Peggy. 'They'll take a lot of feeding, won't they? We're very good at salvaging – and at sorting it, aren't we, Auntie Ginny? We could keep some of our salvage for your new babies.'

'Don't talk to me about the salvaging campaign. I can never remember which week they're going to collect what. I put out the rubbish and it's the salvage week. Now I put out the lot in different bins and let 'em take their pick.'

'Would your babies like our camphorated oil?' asked Will, hopefully. 'Auntie Ginny won't need it to rub on our chests when we go down the air-raid shelter, cos it's summer.'

Ted glanced at a smiling Ginny. 'So you're not keen on camphorated oil, eh? That don't half stink I know, bor,' Ted agreed. 'But come the autumn you're going to need it again to ward off the chills in that there damp old shelter. No, you'd best keep it, Will. Come you on, littl'uns. Don't keep Bessie waiting. She's standing outside ready to take you in her cart. She int a very patient old girl, y'know. She's just as likely to go off home without us – 'specially if she's hungry.'


Lizzie was overjoyed when Peter arrived home for a few days leave. He bore signs of being in battle – his face was cut and bruised and bandages covered burns on his hands – but he said the reason for his unexpected leave was that his destroyer had suffered damage and was taking longer to repair at a Scottish shipyard than had been expected. He looked haggard and years older than he was but he explained that being at action stations for more than twenty four hours at a time had taken its toll and all he needed was to catch up on his rest. He was obviously delighted to be with his wife and little daughter again but Tovell detected that he seemed ill at ease whenever he was at his in-laws' house. When Peter proposed a trip to the *Admiral Lord Nelson* one evening, Tovell was not surprised. The walk there was somewhat strained as Peter kept the conversation strictly to general family and work matters. Once there, and with Tovell carrying both pint tankards, Peter chose a small table near the inglenook fireplace – as far away from the crowd at the bar as possible.

Tovell decided to bring matters to a head. 'You haven't told us how you got injured,' he said as soon as they were seated.

'It was a bad voyage,' answered Peter. 'A lot of men got hurt. You do what you can but it's never enough. I kept thinking of my father: what it must have been like for him when the *Hawke* was torpedoed in 1914. He returned to duty here at the Coastguard Station but those burns tormented him 'til the day he died.' Then Peter blurted out, 'I think Bobby's dead.'

Tovell sighed. 'I knew something was bothering you and I had a nasty feeling that that was what it was.'

'I don't know for sure and Rachel hasn't had a telegram, but that doesn't mean a lot. When convoys get into trouble no-one knows for ages what's happened to survivors.' Peter's bandaged hands shook as he lifted his tankard. 'We were on the return trip – from Russia to Iceland – and the weather had been atrocious. You can go for days without being able to get a fix on your position by the stars because of the dense fog or because of snowstorms. Compasses don't always work accurately in the Arctic either – something to do with the earth's magnetic pole - so it's not that surprising that some of the merchant ships strayed into a minefield. We know for certain that the commodore's flagship went down but some lifeboats got away. Whether Bobby was in one of them, I don't know. They were picked up by a rescue ship and I only know that because I saw it with my own eyes. I'm up on deck all the time, being in charge of the four-barelled Pom Pom, and because we had charts showing where the mines were – the poor old merchantmen didn't have that information – we were able to go in and help with the rescue. Again, I've no idea whether Bobby got on the rescue vessel but I do know that ship was sunk a few days later. Usually, the Germans don't sink rescue ships but something must have gone wrong because she was torpedoed. I heard about that when we got to Reykjavik from a pal on a corvette who'd seen it go down. U-boats had managed to get inside the convoy and several merchantmen were hit. There were lifeboats and rafts everywhere but we, as the escort, had to go after the enemy first. The U-boats cleared off eventually, probably because they realized the new convoy which had left Iceland for Russia a few days before was in the vicinity. That convoy would have meant richer pickings: the ships would have been full of tanks and planes. By the time we got back, a lot of the lifeboats had dispersed and I'm sure some of them were never recovered. If Bobby was on one of them he might still have got away and might still be alive. Survivors in lifeboats have been known to last for days …'

Peter's voice trailed away. Tovell had heard his story in silence but now he said, 'But in those temperatures, the chances are not good, are they?' Peter shook his head. 'Poor Rachel,' Tovell continued, 'and it's just as well Ginny has our three evacuees to fuss over.'

There was no further opportunity to continue their conversation for a big red-faced farmer ambled over. 'Ah, Tovell! Just the man. I was hoping I'd bump into you. You've got stables, haven't you?'

Tovell glanced at Peter, who was clearly still upset, before he replied. 'Yes, but I've only got two and one of them's occupied by my horse, Rajah Two.'

'That's all right: I only need one,' the man replied. 'You know that hush-hush place the RAF's got near White's Farm – they've been putting up more buildings the last few months and bringing in more women to work there. Most of the girls have been billeted together in one big house, but one of them brought her bloomin' horse with her and she got landed on us. She's a right little madam and such a pain in the backside that my missus says she's got to go. Either that or the wife says she's moving back with her mother and I can look after myself - and Miss Nasty. Trouble is the damn girl will only move to somewhere that's got a stable.'

'I'd like to help you out,' replied Tovell, 'but Ginny's got enough to do looking after the extra three we've got already.' At that point, Peter looked up and nodded at Tovell. 'Ah, yes! On second thoughts, maybe another person to fuss over would be good for Ginny. She's never been afraid to speak her mind, so I'm sure she'll soon sort out your Miss Nasty.'

Ginny was not enthusiastic about the new arrangement and told her husband so in no uncertain terms. She ended her lengthy tirade with a home truth. 'Your trouble is you can never say "no" to people. Everyone puts on you – and on me at the same time since everything you get into means more work for me. And where in heavens name are we going to put her? She's not having Lizzie's room: that's for her and Molly when they want to sleep here and Peter's away. Alec still uses his room when he's off duty long enough to get home and the littl'uns are in Bobby's old room. Perhaps you'd like her to have our room?'

'Well,' began Tovell sheepishly, 'I thought perhaps she could have your Auntie May and Uncle William's room.'

'You know I've never let anyone use that room,' snapped Ginny.

'Yes, I know. But you can't keep it as a shrine to them forever. They wouldn't have wanted that,' added Tovell gently. 'And it is wartime. We have to do whatever we can to help.'

Ginny did not reply to these arguments but instead tried a different tack. 'And what about Rajah Two? Did you think about him and how he would feel about another horse being here?'

'It's true he's never had to share his quarters before but I had a long conversation with him when I fed him this morning. I explained the situation to him in great detail and he appreciated that I'd had no choice but to agree. He neighed his agreement several times.'

'Oh, you! He was neighing for his fodder,' said Ginny, laughing as she slapped Tovell on his chest. He grabbed her wrist and pulled her close to him. With his arms around her he promised, 'I won't let her be a nuisance to you. I'll speak to her if she shows any signs of taking liberties.'

'No, you will not,' Ginny retorted. 'I'm quite capable of fighting my own battles, thank you. If she wants to live in our house she'll obey the same rules as everybody else.'

Next morning a horsebox arrived containing a mare, her owner and assorted trappings belonging to the two of them. Tovell went to assist but was pushed aside by Miss Nasty. 'I'm the only one who ever handles her. She'd be frightened if you touch her. Where's your animal?'

'He's outside. We have a small paddock,' replied Tovell.

'That's good. She likes being out in the fresh air. I hope your horse is a gelding.'

'He is,' Tovell answered, smiling to himself. 'Follow me, miss. I don't know how Rajah Two will react. He isn't used to company.'

'Rajah Two?'

'The first Rajah was my mount in South Africa – during the Boer War. I bought this horse because he reminded me of him so, of course, I called him Rajah Two.'

Miss Nasty, to Tovell's surprise, grinned and said confidently, 'I'm sure the two of them will get along fine.' They had reached the paddock and Tovell unlatched the gate. Miss Nasty pushed her horse forward. 'Off you go, girl. Say "hello" to Rajah Two.'

Tovell closed the gate behind the horse and watched with some trepidation as Rajah Two, who had been grazing on the far side of the paddock, let out a whinny and came galloping over at such speed that it seemed he was intent upon attacking the intruder. The newcomer whinnied in reply and to Tovell's relief, Rajah Two stopped as soon as he had reached her and began to nuzzle her head.

'I'll stay here awhile – so she doesn't think I've deserted her,' Miss Nasty announced.

'Then I'll get on with unloading your kit,' said Tovell. 'By the way, I don't think I know your name.'

'It's Claire.'

'Very well, Miss Claire, I'll leave you to it.' Tovell glanced back on his way to the horsebox and saw that their new lodger had gone inside the paddock and was fondling the heads of both horses. When Ginny came out of the scullery door to help with the luggage, he was anxious to reassure her, 'You needn't have worried about Rajah Two: the way he's reacted I think the old boy must have been feeling lonely. He seems delighted to have company. He's making a great fuss of that mare. And as for Miss Nasty – her name's Miss Claire – she's obviously good with animals. Rajah Two likes her and if he likes her she must be alright.'

Only minutes after meeting Miss Claire, Ginny decided she did not share Rajah Two's opinion of her. They were standing in the bedroom of Ginny's late aunt and uncle and the new lodger had shown her disapproval of her proposed billet by wrinkling up her nose in disgust. 'This room hasn't been used for years,' Ginny explained. 'I've had the window open since I knew you were coming but it might take a day or two for the mustiness to clear.'

'A day or two! I should think it will take years. And it's not just musty – it's dreary.'

'It's the only bedroom we've got spare and if I'd had anything to do with it, you wouldn't be standing here now. It was never my intention to let the room but, we all have to make sacrifices in wartime, I suppose.'

'Oh, well, it will have to do. You'd better show me my sitting room now.'

'Your sitting room! Tovell didn't say anything about a sitting room.'

'Tovell? You call your husband by his surname?'

Ginny smiled, 'Yes, I know that seems strange but he wouldn't have it any other way. When he was billeted with me and the children at the Coastguard Station, at the beginning of the last war, he said he had joined the Army as a boy and ever since officers and men had called him Tovell. He said that was what he'd always been used to answering to; not to his Christian name, which is Alec.'

'So his name is Alec. That's interesting. Well, I'm sorry if you have been incorrectly informed but I must have a sitting room to myself. You could hardly expect me to spend my off-duty hours in this bedroom.'

'Well, the only other room is on the ground floor - the front parlour. I only open that if we have company.'

'So it's as damp and musty as this room.'

'No, I have a fire in there regularly to air the room, but if you were to use it all the time that would be a problem. We keep a fire in our large living room because I cook on the range in there, but we couldn't afford to have a second fire going in the parlour every day.'

'I'll pay you extra – whatever you ask – but I must be on my own. I really don't like company.'

'It's not just the money. We're not supposed to waste fuel because of the war. We're supposed to live in one room.'

'In that case I'll move into the stables with the horses.'

The last remark made Ginny soften her approach a little. 'Yes, I gather you're happy with animals.'

'Animals are fine; humans are the problem.'

'Come you on downstairs then and I'll show you the parlour. But you've got to understand this is not a hotel – it's a family home – and you can't expect, and you certainly won't get, the services of a hotel.'

As they descended the narrow staircase to the living room and crossed to the door of the parlour, Miss Claire said, 'Don't worry: I'm under no illusion that this is a hotel. You won't need to wait on me. I'll collect my food and take it to my room myself.'

When they were standing in the centre of the bleak room, surrounded entirely by the heavy dark furniture which had belonged to her uncle and aunt, Ginny could almost hear Miss Claire groaning. For the first time, Ginny was aware of how dismal the place was and when she thought back she could remember only a few occasions when her uncle and aunt had used the room. Perhaps they had not liked it either. In a sudden attempt to make amends, she hurried over to the huge sideboard. The top was covered entirely by framed photographs. 'I'll remove all of these so you can put your own things here,' she announced. 'You'll feel more at home then.'

'Don't bother: I haven't got anything much to display,' Miss Claire replied, somewhat wistfully. At that moment Molly, who had been dozing on the couch in the living room, woke up and began to cry. Ginny went to fetch her and returned with the toddler in her arms. She found her lodger over by the sideboard looking at the photographs. 'Are these all of your family?' she asked. She picked up a picture of Bobby in his naval uniform. 'Is this your son?'

'Yes,' replied Ginny proudly, 'Bobby, my elder son. And this is my younger son – Alec. He's with Bobby and my daughter's husband, Peter. It was taken the last time they were all on leave together.'

Miss Claire took the second photograph from Ginny's hand. Alec was wearing a thick white polo-neck sweater under his naval jacket and his cap was set at a jaunty angle. He had adopted a roguish grin for the picture. Miss Claire pointed to his image. 'Handsome devil, isn't he?' she commented. 'And he knows it – I've no doubt. You can leave them all. They won't bother me. Oh, and this is your husband, isn't it?'

'Yes, that's Tovell. He was Regimental Sergeant Major. It was taken in August 1919 in Cambrai. It was the day he finally left the Army. He's standing beside his commanding officer – Lieutenant Colonel Bradshaw. The other man is the colonel's batman – Walters, I think his name was.'

'Williams – his name was Williams.'

'You know him?'

'Yes. He only died a couple of years ago. I was quite fond of him. He was so good with animals.'

'Well, what a coincidence. Tovell will be pleased to hear you knew Mr Williams. He liked him very much.'

'He might not be so pleased to learn I also know the other man in the picture. He's my father. He's Brigadier Bradshaw now.'

'But your name's Claire.'

'Claire is my Christian name. My full name is Claire Bradshaw.'


Tovell was delighted at the news and wanted to know all that had happened to his former commanding officer in the intervening years. His daughter, however, made it clear that she was not keen to talk about her father so Tovell did not press her but asked her to give him his regards when next she wrote home. 'I don't have very much contact with the family,' said Miss Bradshaw, somewhat curtly, indicating that the discussion was at an end.

When Tovell collected the three children from school later that afternoon, Miss Bradshaw had been returning from exercising her horse. The sight of her, a stranger riding into their yard, brought their exuberant antics to a sudden halt. 'I didn't realize you had a young family as well,' she said harshly.

'This is Peggy, and Roger, and Will,' replied Tovell, indicating the youngsters in turn and ignoring the implied criticism in her voice. 'They're our young friends from London. They've been staying with us the last two years. Say "hello" to Miss Bradshaw, littl'uns. She's going to be staying with us too now – and her horse.'

The mention of another animal to look after cheered Roger up at once. He approached the newcomers and stroked the mare's nose gently. 'I help Uncle Tovell to look after Rajah Two,' he confided. 'I hope the two of them will be friends.'

Miss Bradshaw's expression softened as she replied, 'They're friends already. Come and help me unsaddle her and put her in the paddock. You'll see how much she and Rajah Two like playing together.'


Miss Bradshaw kept her word and came out of the parlour to collect her supper tray. Tovell had already eaten and departed for Home Guard duties but Lizzie was at the table with Molly and the other children. Peter was sitting there too with dressings, smaller now after Doctor Lambert's ministrations, still on his hands. Ginny introduced her daughter and son-in-law. There was a polite but brief exchange of pleasantries and Miss Bradshaw withdrew to her own sitting room. She emerged three hours later saying she must go to bed as she was on duty at the RAF Station at six. By that time the Ellis family had gone back to their house next door, the three children were in bed and Ginny was sitting in her armchair darning socks. Miss Bradshaw seemed mildly surprised and even a little grateful when Ginny said she would wake her at five with a cup of tea.

Will's sleep had not been disturbed so much of late but perhaps the presence of a stranger upsetting his routine had had a detrimental effect because that night he woke up screaming. Peggy did her best to console him but he would not be comforted. The noise woke both Ginny and Miss Bradshaw. The latter flew into the children's room in a rage. 'I'm on duty in a few hours. How am I supposed to sleep with this racket going on?'

'Sorry, miss,' said Peggy. 'He hasn't had a nightmare like this for ages. I'll try and keep him quiet.'

'Nightmare? What kind of nightmare?' asked Miss Bradshaw.

'He thinks the hands are after him,' replied Roger, propping himself up on his camp bed.

'Hands? What hands?'

'The dead ones,' Peggy explained. 'When we were at home Mum, Will and the twins used to walk part of the way to school with Roger and me in the mornings. We'd see the men collecting the bits of bodies - from the previous night's bombing. They'd put them in sacks but one morning a sack fell off the cart as we were passing. The bits fell out and one of the hands landed on his foot ...' Peggy stopped as Will shrieked and buried his head in her chest. Miss Bradshaw stared at the pair in silence; then left abruptly. Peggy called after her, 'I'll keep him quiet, miss.'

A few moments later, Miss Bradshaw returned. She was holding a small calico animal in her hand. 'Here you are, Matey,' she said to Will. 'This is Tiger. He'll protect you. My nanny made him for me when my parents sent me away to a dreadful place called boarding school. You'll have to tuck him into your nightshirt for tonight but tomorrow evening I'll make you a pocket for him. My nanny used to sew pockets inside my nightdresses so that Tiger could hide there without the other girls seeing him.' Will stopped sobbing and looked up at Miss Bradshaw. Tentatively, he took the scruffy soft toy she offered. 'Now there's a rhyme you have to say each evening before you go to bed. "Tiger, Tiger, hold me tight. Keep me safe throughout the night." Do you think you can say that, Matey?' The little boy nodded and repeated the rhyme with her. 'Now back to sleep. You won't have any more nightmares now that Tiger is with you. I'll see you when I get back from the station tomorrow.'

As Miss Bradshaw returned to her room she did not see Ginny watching from her own door which was slightly ajar. 'That will be something to tell Tovell tomorrow,' Ginny whispered to herself as she climbed back into bed.

## V

A week later a telegram arrived – for Peter. It gave him fresh orders: he was to report to Chatham docks and a new ship. 'They can't have finished the repairs on my old ship,' he said to Tovell. 'I'm not complaining though. I've no wish to return to the Arctic just yet.'

'Maybe they're sending you to the tropics this time. Then you'll say you're too hot,' commented his father-in-law as they walked back from the pub.

'No, I wouldn't moan about that. In fact, the only thing I'm moaning about is leaving Lizzie and little Molly again. When you're bored to death, waiting around for something to happen, they're all I think about.'

'I know what you mean,' Tovell agreed. 'All I ever thought about in the trenches was Ginny and the children. And how I resented not seeing them growing up.'

'Yes, I suppose I've been lucky to get some brief spells of leave. I have seen Molly go from baby to toddler. A lot of blokes haven't been home since the war started. I'm still going to miss them though.'

Two weeks after Peter left, Alec arrived home. When he put his bicycle in the shed he saw that there was a new ladies' model resting against the wall. On leaving the shed he noticed that there was another horse in the paddock. He called out as he strode through the scullery into the living room, 'That mare with Rajah Two looks familiar – '

'She should - it's Bella,' said Claire Bradshaw who was sitting at the table, Will on her lap, hunched over a reading book.

'Podge!' exclaimed Alec. 'What are you doing here?'

'I could ask you the same thing, Sailor.'

'I live here,' Alec retorted.

'So do I. I'm the latest waif and stray your parents have adopted.'

Tovell and Ginny had watched this exchange in astonishment. 'How come you two know each other?' asked Tovell at last.

'We've known each other for years,' replied Alec. 'I'm sure I've told you about Podge – the girl I used to meet on the beach and the cliffs in the school holidays. That reminds me: why aren't you staying with Nanny Barker?'

'She died last year - unfortunately,' Claire answered sadly.

'I'm sorry. I know how much she meant to you,' said Alec quietly.

Tovell broke the silence that followed. 'Why on earth didn't you tell us that your friend was my CO's daughter?'

It was Alec's turn to look surprised. 'I didn't know that she was.'

'Bradshaw's not such a common name. If you'd just said Bradshaw –
'

'But I didn't know that. In fact, come to think of it, we never told each other our full names. Mainly, we used our nicknames.'

'That's true,' Claire admitted. 'I didn't know Alec's surname was Tovell until I saw his photograph in your parlour.'

At that point, Ginny interrupted. 'Claire, look at the time.'

The young woman glanced up at the clock on the chimney breast over the cooking range. 'Got to be going, Matey. Duty calls,' she said to Will, gently lifting him off her lap. 'We'll finish this story tomorrow evening.' As she spoke, the little boy went behind her and undid the ribbon of her overall at the back of her neck. As she stood up, the cover-all smock slipped down revealing her RAF uniform.

'So, you didn't join the Army,' commented Alec.

'I told you I wouldn't – to spite Grandfather and Father.'

'Don't listen to her,' said Tovell. 'She joined the RAF because they let her play with all the fancy equipment they've got.'

Claire scowled at Tovell playfully as she made for the door, Will clinging to her jacket like a shadow. They heard her ringing her bicycle bell as she left the yard. Will came back indoors sorrowfully and went to Ginny to be comforted. 'Never mind, Will,' said Ginny, giving him a hug. 'Her watch will be over before you leave for school in the morning. You'll see her again then.'


Ginny noticed that Alec made a point of getting up next morning so that he could have breakfast with the children and Claire when she returned from duty. After the youngsters had left for school, Alec suggested they exercise the horses and Claire readily agreed. She was, therefore, later going to sleep than she would have been normally. The whole performance was repeated again next morning before Alec had to return to duty himself at Great Yarmouth.

When Ginny joined Tovell on the smallholding after Alec's departure, she commented, 'Those two seemed to get along fine, although they do argue a bit.'

'That's because they've been friends for a long time,' her husband replied. 'It's just banter. It shows how used they are to one another's company.'

'Hmmm,' murmured Ginny.

Tovell looked at her and laughed. 'I'm not sure I like the sound of that. I hope you're not getting any ideas. They see each other as pals and enjoy one another's company as such. Just as well that they do. I know Claire has settled in well and seems like one of the family now, thanks to Will – and there's no swank with the girl – but you can't get away from the fact that she's not one of us. Her father's a general for one thing and if I remember correctly, Williams once told me that the wife – her mother – is from a titled family. They're very wealthy too. So, my little darling, if there are any matchmaking thoughts in that lovely head of yours, forget them. Claire is way out of Alec's league. Just let them enjoy being pals.'

'Hmmm,' Ginny murmured again.


Three weeks after Peter's departure for Chatham docks, a second telegram arrived – for Rachel. She found it on her doormat late one night when she returned from Norwich. She ran to her mother's cottage in hysterics and together they both hurried to the Tovell's house and banged repeatedly on the door. Tovell and Ginny knew at once from the state their visitors were in what must be the matter. The stark words on the telegram, "lost at sea, presumed dead", were, therefore, no surprise. Lizzie had heard the commotion as Rachel and Mary had tried to wake the household next door and she rushed over to join the family, cradling a sleepy Molly in her arms. Claire and the children had been roused too but as soon as the young woman realized what had happened she ushered Peggy, Roger and Will upstairs and stayed with them until they went back to sleep.

Downstairs, Ginny sat rigid in her armchair by the cooking range saying nothing, staring ahead of her, traumatized by the news she had dreaded for so long. Rachel was inconsolable and when Lizzie tried to comfort her she snapped, 'It's alright for you: at least you've got something to show for your marriage – you've got Molly. What have I got? Nothing! It isn't fair.'

No-one knew what to respond to this so Tovell tried introducing a little hope into the gathering. 'We mustn't despair totally. Peter told me that it's chaos when ships go down in the Arctic. No-one knows for months which men have survived. Sometimes a lifeboat reaches land – a small island or even occupied Norway. If they end up in a prison camp the news wouldn't filter through for ages.'

Rachel would have none of this. 'He's dead. I know he's dead. Why did he have to go to sea? Why didn't he want to stay here with me?'

Mary intervened. 'I know you're upset, girl, and understandably so. But now you're talking squit. Bobby's been in the Navy since he was a boy. He was in it when you were chasing after him and when you married him. That's a bit late to moan now because you fell for a sailor. The Navy was his life just as it was for your brother.' She turned away from her daughter and addressed Ginny. 'I know what you're feeling. George was my first-born too. I'm truly sorry. The only comfort I could find in what happened to him was that if he had to die, I'm glad it was quick and that it was with the Navy which he loved so much. Reckon it's the same with your Bobby. I'm going to take Rachel home now so that you can mourn in peace, Ginny. God bless you.' With that Mary went over to where her friend was sitting and squeezed her hand. When Ginny looked up there were tears in her eyes.

In the weeks that followed, Rachel's grief manifested itself in anger and bitterness. At times, the resentment she felt towards Bobby for deserting her became almost vitriolic and her mother lost patience with her. Mary also condemned the way her daughter threw herself into a social whirl, never declining an invitation to a party or a dance, befriending any serviceman who gave her a second glance. 'That int right,' she confided to Ginny. 'No woman recently widowed should behave like that.'

'Don't be too hard on her, Mary. She's hurting inside – we both know that,' said Ginny, soothingly. 'I reckon she's afraid of being alone because then she'd have to face up to what she's lost. Anyway, I reckon we should keep this to ourselves – the way Rachel's behaving; going off the rails. I don't think we should tell Lizzie or Tovell about it. She may only be going through a phase and once she comes to terms with things she may settle down again.'

'Settle down? When has she ever settled down?' demanded Mary.

Ginny could not think of a suitable reply to that question so instead she voiced her own personal hope. 'Bobby may not be lost. He may come back in a few months time and we wouldn't want him to hear bad things about Rachel, would we?'

'I think you're clutching at straws, Ginny. But I'll go along with your wishes. We'll only talk about this between ourselves.'

Ginny herself was having difficulty in facing up to what she had lost. She was glad she had the three children, Claire and Tovell to look after as well as the smallholding, because it meant that most of her days were filled with responsibilities and duties. There was little time to dwell too much during those hours but at night, especially when Tovell was on Home Guard duty, she would lay awake for hours thinking back over the years and picturing Bobby growing up. Sometimes when Tovell was there beside her she would awake to find herself weeping and he, half asleep and without saying a word, would put a comforting arm around her.


Alec too, made the effort to console his mother by cycling home much more often than he might have done otherwise. One morning he reported for the usual debriefing, collected his bicycle and joined the queue waiting to leave by the barrier at the Fishwharf. He was looking straight ahead, wondering how long it would take to get through the military checkpoint, when a seductive voice said, 'Hello, sailor! Want to come home with me? Very cheap rates!'

Alec looked to his left, ready to make a sharp retort, but what he saw made him laugh instead. Claire was draped in a theatrical pose across the bonnet of an RAF jeep, grinning at him. 'What the hell are you doing here, Podge?' he asked.

Claire stood upright and snapped at him. 'Don't call me that! I'm not a child any more. I'm a big girl now.'

'Yeah, I'd noticed,' replied Alec, a mischievous gleam in his eyes as he looked pointedly at her jacket where the buttons were threatening to pop under the strain of covering her ample bosom.

'Do you want a lift home or not?' she demanded, but there was laughter in her voice. 'I've just wasted half an hour hanging around for you. I wish I hadn't bothered when all I get in return are insults. Throw your bike in the back and let's get going.'

Once they were seated in the vehicle and had been allowed to leave the quayside by the soldiers, Alec asked again what Claire had been doing inside the Navy base. 'Liaison work,' was her clipped reply. 'I saw you had docked when I'd finished my official business so I waited in case you had long enough between voyages to come home. It's to do with radiolocation – the reason I'm here, I mean. It works on the principle of an ether radio wave hitting an interposed object and being reflected back to the transmitter.'

'All sounds very clever,' Alec quipped.

'Don't be patronizing,' Claire retorted. 'It is very clever. The boffins at Bawdsey developed it before the war. There are stations all round the coast like the one where I work at Haisbro. You must have seen the masts. It was our secret device – radiolocation or RDF, as it's called. People are starting to use another name now – radar. My money's on that one. It sounds just right to me. The point I'm trying to make is that this secret weapon of ours saved us in the Battle of Britain. That device guided our Hurricanes and Spitfires towards the enemy fighters and bombers.'

'I wasn't trying to be patronizing,' Alec assured her. 'I know the Navy has high hopes of it too. All we had during the Norwegian campaign was star shells and snowflakes to light up the area to give us a chance of spotting the conning towers of U-boats. But there's asdic now, isn't there?'

'Yes, but that's a form of sonar: an anti-submarine device. It's only useful if the enemy is submerged because it works on the principle of echo location. But the beauty of radar is that it can detect surface U-boats regardless of the conditions – never mind if it's pitch dark or there's dense fog – and, of course, it can "see" any warship or aircraft approaching. It's in a lot of your ships already – particularly the corvettes - and the way it's being developed and the pace at which it's being developed, could solve your convoy problems both in the North Atlantic and the Arctic.'

'That should please my brother-in-law,' Alec commented. 'But you still haven't explained what you're doing here.'

'Give me a chance,' Claire replied testily as they stopped at another check point on the Caister Road. Once they were on their way again and had left Great Yarmouth behind, Claire continued. 'You have a form of detection equipment on your boats now, but as I said, the technology is moving fast; your existing MTBs and MGBs are gradually having the latest version installed and your new Dog Boats will come with the up-to-date radar fitted. Radar mechanics like me have been asked to help out – with the training. Inter-service cooperation and liaison, and all that stuff.'

'So if the system fails whilst we're at sea, the operator should be able to get it going again?'

'That's the idea,' answered Claire.

'Sounds all right to me. Funny you should mention the new Dog Boats – I've asked to transfer to one. They're heavily armed, powerful – four huge supercharged engines – though still not as fast as the E-boats unfortunately. They can carry out long-range missions and stay at sea independently for long periods. One of those would suit me fine.'

'You boys and your toys,' said Claire, grinning.

'Look who's talking! You're besotted with your radar.'

'No, I'm not. I'm keen on other things too.'

'Like what? I'll grant you that you care about Bella and you quite like the children – young Will especially.'

'Of course I care about them. Anyway, children are little animals really. They're only a nuisance when they grow up. And I am interested in lots of things besides my work.'

'No, you're like our Leading Wren who brings her girls to service our boat whenever we dock. My coxswain lusts after her but he says she's only interested in the engines.'

'He can't be sure of that. Perhaps she thinks that's all he's interested in. He should ask her out.'

'That all sounds too complicated.'

'You would say that – you're a man.'

The news from abroad had been depressing throughout the summer months: Commonwealth forces had been defeated in Libya in late June and Tobruk had surrendered. By July we were retreating in Egypt too and by mid-July the broadcasters were telling of the very grave situation in Russia with the Germans attacking on a 650-mile front and Stalingrad likely to fall. August brought more disheartening news with the announcement that a reconnaissance raid on Dieppe had failed, resulting in heavy losses amongst Canadian troops and many taken prisoner. The King declared Thursday the third of September a day of prayer and even factories stopped work for fifteen minutes for a broadcast service. Ginny and Mary, along with many others, attended the service at the parish church in Haisbro as the fourth year of the war opened. Their prayers were personal: Mary praying for the safety of her remaining son, Albert; Ginny for Alec and Peter and also for Bobby to miraculously come home.

As September ended there were tales of desperate scenes in Stalingrad with hand-to-hand fighting in the streets, but still the Soviets were holding out. October saw the Allies launch an offensive in Egypt and on the twenty-third of that month Montgomery proved that we did, after all, have a general to match Rommel. Churchill spoke of the victory at El Alamein as a turning point - the end of the beginning - and the church bells rang out in celebration. Still there was heavy fighting in and around Stalingrad but November brought hope for Russia that the opening of another front – the invasion of Vichy French North Africa – would force Hitler to divert troops. Lizzie was convinced that her Peter was with the Royal Navy escort protecting the thousands of Allied soldiers, mostly American, led by General Eisenhower, landing on the coasts of Algeria and Morocco.

December arrived and Ginny began to dread Christmas – the first since Bobby was lost at sea. Mary was bothered too when it was announced on the nineteenth that British troops had moved into Burma against the Japanese. She had soon convinced herself that her son was amongst them and that she would never see him again – until a Christmas card arrived from Albert posted in this country.

Alec had been a frequent visitor – since Claire's arrival, as Ginny was quick to point out to Tovell – even though he had never been able to stay for more than a few hours. Ginny was hopeful, therefore, that he would want to be with them at the festive season. But Alec told his parents that he had to stay at his base, HMS *Midge,* over Christmas because it was traditional for officers and NCOs to serve the Christmas dinner to the men. Claire then said the same tradition applied at her station so even though she was not on watch, she must remain there. It was, therefore, an effort to make Christmas Day a cheerful event for the children. Tovell, fortunately, was not on duty and he did his best to amuse Peggy, Roger, Will and little Molly and play festive games with them. Ted, too, was happy to be invited as usual and even happier in the afternoon once he was full of traditional Christmas food and drink. Mary, Ginny and Lizzie were subdued but content just to watch the little ones enjoying themselves. It was late in the afternoon when a sudden draught made Ginny look in the direction of the door to the scullery. What she saw made her gasp.

Mary heard her and looked up. Seeing that Ginny was ashen-faced and open-mouthed, she exclaimed, 'What is it? You look like you've seen a ghost.'

'I have,' whispered Ginny. 'I can see Bobby.'

'I'm not a ghost, Mother,' said a low voice. 'I very nearly was – but not quite.'

The children watched, bewildered, as the adults jumped up and surrounded the newcomer, hugging him and bombarding him with questions. He would answer none of them: he had only one thing on his mind. 'Where's Rachel?' he demanded. 'I went home first, then to mother-in-law's house. I realized after that you would all have gathered here. Where is she?'

Mary was at a loss for words but Ginny came up with an answer which satisfied her son. 'When we were told you were lost at sea and presumed dead, Rachel was distraught – as we all were. She said she could not bring herself to celebrate Christmas so she volunteered to be on duty. Jerry doesn't stop the bombing just because it's Christmas.'

1943

# I

It was as though Bobby's homecoming was the signal for better times ahead. January 1943 saw the Russians surround the German army at Stalingrad and lift the siege of Leningrad. Things were going so well in North Africa that Churchill and Roosevelt met there at Casablanca and at a press conference on the twenty-fourth the President was confident enough to declare that the Allies' aim was nothing short of "unconditional surrender" by the enemy. The general feeling was that this could not come soon enough as more evidence emerged about the Nazis' persecution of the Jews: ration books taken away from Czech Jews, 6,000 Jews a day still being executed in Poland, the Jewish ghetto in Warsaw empty, no more Jews to be left in Berlin or Bohemia by the end of February. Such atrocities were remembered as people watched the bombers depart on their nightly raids to Nazi Germany.

Bobby read the newspapers and listened to the wireless broadcasts as he recuperated, but he said very little - about current affairs and the war news or about his ordeal. Frostbite had claimed one finger from his right hand and two from his left; his face was scarred in places; his hair was totally grey and he looked ten years older. Mentally, he was withdrawn and morose – a shadow of his former self. His family had prised out of him over a period of time that the Free Norwegian soldiers had transported him and the remaining survivors to Barentsburg by sledge. There they had been cared for by the doctor whose patients were normally the soldiers who manned the garrison and weather station. A Royal Navy cruiser, which had come with supplies for the Norwegians, eventually embarked them and brought them back to Loch Ewe in Scotland. Bobby admitted that he owed his life to the Navy surgeon who had first operated on him aboard the rescue ship, to the Norwegian doctor at Barentsburg who had had to operate on Bobby again as a result of the infection which he had suffered during his time in the lifeboat and, to Charlie Bennett whose tireless efforts to keep his charges alive had continued at Barentsburg whilst they waited months for a passage home. Tovell, however, sensed that there was some underlying misery gnawing at Bobby which was hindering his recovery. Rachel had requested and been granted leave from her WVS duties to care for her husband but one evening, when Tovell himself was not on watch, he called at their home in the village and suggested that Bobby might like to accompany him to the *Admiral Lord Nelson*. It did not escape Tovell's notice that both Rachel and Bobby seemed relieved by this invitation.

They sat at the same table by the inglenook fireplace that Peter had chosen when he too had been weighed down by a secret. The drinks and the convivial atmosphere began to loosen Bobby's tongue and he talked in glowing terms about Charlie Bennett and how he had written to the authorities about him and how the other survivors had endorsed his remarks. 'I hope they agree to decorate him. If any man deserves a medal, he does.'

Tovell was encouraged by Bobby's enthusiasm, the first he had shown about anything since his return, to inquire how he had got on at the medical assessment he had attended in Norwich that afternoon. 'The surgeon said he would gladly give me a medical discharge,' Bobby replied, 'but that's the last thing I want and I told him so. I know I can't go to sea again: not just because I've lost fingers but because I've lost so much of my guts. I was lucky I didn't end up with a bag – I know some blokes who've had their innards blown away do end up with a colostomy. Reckon I have the skill of both the surgeons who operated on me to thank for that. Trouble is, since I've lost so much of my intestine, everything goes through me so quickly that I couldn't stay on the bridge with a commodore a full watch. I have to be near the heads and go straightaway. And I have to be careful what I eat and you can't be that choosey on board ship. You eat what the cooks dish up or starve!'

'So you've asked for a shore job?'

'Yes. I've said I'll do anything, just so long as I can stay in the Navy.'

'What about your general health? Did the doctor say you were fit enough to work? You certainly don't look very fit to me.'

Bobby was silent for a while, staring intently at his tankard of beer before he replied. 'I think the fact I look unwell is more a state of mind. I've got to get away. I know that sounds crazy when all I wanted was to get home but I just can't stand it.' He looked up at Tovell with desperation in his eyes. 'The fact is I've got to get away from Rachel. That's the craziest part of all. When I was in the lifeboat, the thing that kept me from giving up – and believe me I wanted the blessed relief of death – was the wanting to be with my Rachel again. I know it's good of her to stay at home to take care of me but it's suffocating me and worse still, all the time she's making plans for us. She can't seem to settle and just be glad I'm home. And she keeps wanting us to go places and I don't have the energy or the inclination.'

Tovell smiled. 'Remember that doe we had once? She wouldn't settle and kept kicking the side out of her hutch. Ted brought his young buck round to meet her – he said that would solve her restlessness. He was right: she was fine once she had young. Did your sister tell you that that was one of the things that upset Rachel after she got the telegram – that you two hadn't had any children?'

'Yes, Lizzie told me.'

'Then,' said Tovell gently, 'is that the answer?'

Once more, Bobby looked down and was silent. When he looked up again his eyes had a haunted expression. 'Yes, it is but I can't oblige. The Norwegian doctor told me that he'd been able to join up my guts just as the Navy surgeon had done but he couldn't join up some other tubes – I can't remember their name – because they were missing – blown away. The upshot was I'd never father a child.'

'Does Rachel know?'

Bobby shook his head. 'I daren't tell her. I think she'd leave me and if she did that my life wouldn't be worth living. I would wish that I'd died in the Arctic. You know how you feel about Mother – well, that's how I feel about Rachel.'

'I'm sorry Bobby - really sorry.'

'The funny thing is I think I've always been a disappointment to Rachel. I've never been able to live up to her expectations of me. Trouble is I think she'd created this image of me when she was small but it was only ever in her mind – it wasn't really me. I'll always be a disappointment to her now. I'll never be her hero now.'

Both men were silent for several moments and Tovell's gaze fell upon the men who were drinking at the bar. As usual, there were servicemen in a variety of uniforms but predominantly they were American airmen from the many airfields in the district. Tovell looked at Bobby – in his distress he had his hand covering his eyes – and said quietly, 'There are a lot of young bucks around here at the moment and the beauty of it is they are only staying for the duration.'

Bobby looked up slowly and shook his head. 'I couldn't do that: I couldn't love another man's child. I couldn't treat the child right – knowing it wasn't mine.'

Tovell sighed. 'So that means you think I didn't make a very good job of it.'

Bobby looked at Tovell stunned for a moment before he exclaimed, 'I'm sorry. I didn't realize what I was saying. I just never think of you as not being my real father – and nor does Lizzie. You were a wonderful father to us both and still are.'

'I can assure you, Bobby, that never once has it made any difference to me that you and Lizzie were not my flesh and blood,' said Tovell earnestly. 'I could not have loved you any more if you had been mine. So think about what I've said. If you love Rachel as much as I love your mother – and you say that you do – then you'll do anything to keep her and make her happy. Just be certain you choose a buck who looks like you!'

Three weeks later, Bobby got the shore job he wanted: he was put in charge of supplies to HMS *Watchful* – the Great Yarmouth base under the command of an admiral who directed all naval operations in the town including those of HMS *Midge* and its flotillas of MTBs and MGBs and of HMS *Miranda* and its fleet of minesweepers. Bobby was given an office in one of the largest warehouses on the Fishwharf - with a lavatory right next door. A promotion to Chief Petty Officer went with the job. Alec was delighted and promised his mother that he would keep an eye on his half-brother and ensure that he was soon restored to his old self.

Alec was also pleased that the flotillas of new Dog Boats – the Fairmile D class motor torpedo boats and motor gunboats – had begun to arrive in Great Yarmouth during January and February. He was now the proud commanding officer of one recently commissioned boat. They took her out to sea on trials and her performance was everything that Alec could have wished. He was happy as they returned to port; he was amused too when he detected a slight stammer in the voice of his burly coxswain when the latter gave the call for harbour stations. A flurry of feet and a swish of bell-bottomed trousers and the deck was lined with not only the usual ratings but also the Wren technicians who would service the new vessel. The Leading Wren so admired by the coxswain, was amongst them. The sailors themselves were delighted to be standing shoulder to shoulder with the girls, feet spread, hands behind their backs, chests out, heads held high, knowing that the crews of all the other boats moored in the harbour would be watching.

Trials over, these new Coastal Forces Dog Boats took their turn at defensive and offensive work. They patrolled E-boat Alley, the stretch of water between Yarmouth and Haisbro notorious for the many attacks made there by the enemy on British convoys sailing the East Coast Route from the Thames to the Firth of Forth. Since the previous year, policy had changed and the MTBs and MGBs now defended the "Z line", an imaginary line eight miles to the east of the convoy route, intercepting any E-boats intent upon attacking the merchantmen and any other enemy vessels planning to lay mines in the convoy "corridor". Many nights, however, their roles were reversed and they went on offensive missions off the Dutch coast, seeking out the enemy's convoys which were always heavily defended by German Naval escorts. From March onwards, there was an increase in the number of offensive operations allocated to them and a decrease in their convoy protection role which now went largely to the C class boats which they had manned previously, a fact which cheered all the young men of the Dog Boat crews who eagerly anticipated the prospect of exciting actions against the enemy.

Just such a night was the seventeenth of March when units of motor gunboats and motor torpedo boats had set out on a joint mission. Alec's gunboat was part of a three boat unit whose senior officer was a Canadian. When they came upon their quarry - an enemy convoy sighted earlier in the day by a reconnaissance aircraft – they crept in quietly and unseen. When they were close enough, the Senior Officer gave the executive signal and all three boats turned in and attacked the escort vessels line abreast, enabling the torpedo boats to go on and attack the merchant vessels in the convoy. In the ensuing chaos, both the MGBs and MTBs were lucky to escape the wrath of the escorts virtually unscathed. They were, therefore, in jocular mood as they headed for home in the early hours of the eighteenth of March.

'Have you asked that Leading Wren out yet?' asked Alec as he stood beside his coxswain.

'No, sir,' replied Petty Officer Marshall.

'Why not?'

'Well, sir, she might say "no".'

Alec looked at his coxswain - a big man as tall as Alec himself but much broader and with a luxuriant growth of beard – and he laughed. 'What a funny lot we are: not afraid to face the enemy but terrified of being rejected by a girl.' Marshall agreed and chuckled himself. 'Have you at least found out her name?'

'Yes, sir. It's Dorothy.'

'Well, that's some progress I suppose.' Then, returning to naval matters, Alec said, 'We're not far from port. Better get the men to fall in on the foc'sle.'

'Yes, sir,' said the coxswain. 'No trouble getting them to do that these days, however cold, wet and exhausted they are, not since the Army decided to put ATS plotters on the gun battery at the end of the South Pier! They're convinced the girls are peeping at them from under their camouflage nets as we enter harbour.'

As the men lined up on deck at the bow of the boat, Alec scanned the shoreline and his smile faded. 'Looks like the *Luftwaffe* were extra busy last night,' he commented as he put his field glasses to his eyes, surveying the pall of smoke which hung over a number of buildings. 'I think they've got the Shadingfield – the Officers' Mess.' He handed the glasses to his coxswain.

'No, sir,' replied Marshall. 'I can see the Shadingfield; it's still intact. That smoke is coming from behind it. Oh, God, I hope it isn't coming from the Wrens' hostel.'

Alec took the glasses back and looked again. He nodded and as they entered harbour said, 'We'll be docked in a few minutes. We'll know then.'

They looked anxiously along the quayside as they made their way up river to the Fishwharf and their berth. The usual Wren teams servicing the minesweepers and the rescue tugs were nowhere to be seen. No–one was waiting for them either as they docked. Alec saw Bobby hurrying towards the returning vessels and called out to him.

'The Wrens' quarters have taken a direct hit,' Bobby yelled back. 'It's just a pile of rubble. Can you release any of your crew to help dig out the survivors?'

'Certainly!' Alec shouted in response. He turned to his coxswain. 'Take as many of the men as you like. I'll join you once I've been to de-briefing with the SO.'

When Alec arrived at the corner of Queen's Road and Nelson Road South, he found that the building where the Wrens had been billeted had indeed been reduced to a massive pile of rubble. The scene was one of frantic activity: everywhere people were trying to shift the masonry, using their bare hands if they had no other implement. Policemen were there, Air Raid Precaution wardens – many of them women - firemen, Home Guard volunteers and predominantly, sailors. As Alec approached, one young rating picked up a Wren's cap, the headband emblazoned with the same motif as the cap he was wearing – HMS *Midge*. He looked at it for a second then cast it aside, and began digging even more furiously than before. Fires had broken out and there was only one fire engine to tackle them – other engines must have been deployed at bomb sites elsewhere in the town. Alec saw that a group of Wrens, their faces and pyjamas smeared with brick dust and plaster, many wearing borrowed sweaters in the chill morning air, had formed a human chain and were passing buckets of water to the firemen from a standpipe in the adjacent road. In that same street he could see two ambulances and a WVS van, the ladies handing out mugs of tea to survivors and helpers alike. He caught sight of Aunt Gladys comforting a young girl who clearly had just been rescued, tucking a blanket around her shoulders.

Alec went over to join Petty Officer Marshall. 'Is she safe?' he asked.

The coxswain shook his head. 'We haven't found her yet. I checked over there when I first arrived,' he said, nodding in the direction of an undamaged stretch of pavement where bodies covered by blankets had been laid out. 'She wasn't amongst them, thank God. The bomb dropped three hours ago when most of the girls were still in their bunks. They've been trapped a long time now. I hope there's still enough air for them to breathe.'

'There'll be pockets of it,' Alec replied.

At that moment, a sailor cried out, 'I can see fingers. There's someone over there.' At once he and his comrades began to claw away the debris and after a few minutes they were able to drag out a young girl, dirty, cold and with blood trickling from numerous small cuts where a window had probably crashed down on her. Sobbing with relief, she cried, 'We knew you boys would dig us out.'

'Are the Leading Wrens with you?' Marshall demanded.

'No,' replied the girl. 'Their cabin was further down the corridor from ours.'

'Where? Show me where,' cried the coxswain in desperation.

The young Wren was still dazed and her eyes were not accustomed to the bright light after her dark tomb. After a few moments trying to get her bearings she pointed and declared, 'There! Their cabin would have been there.'

Marshall thanked her. Two of the sailors carried her over the rubble and gave her into the care of the WVS ladies, then returned to pull out more survivors trapped in the same spot as the girl. Marshall, Alec and several policemen moved to the area a short distance away and began to dig where the girl had indicated. After some twenty minutes of determined effort they heard muffled voices crying, 'We're here!' They pulled out two girls before they were able to rescue the object of the coxswain's affection. Alec and Marshall between them carried her across to the street and set her down on the pavement.

'Are you alright? Are you hurt?' asked the coxswain anxiously as he knelt beside her.

'I think I'm alright. Just give me a minute,' said Dorothy, pushing the hair out of her eyes with a shaky hand.

'I'll go and get her a blanket and some tea,' said Alec. Before he moved away he mouthed the words, 'Speak to her. Tell her,' and nodded encouragingly at Marshall.

The coxswain took off his jacket and put it around the girl's shoulders. He gently brushed cement dust from the back of her head. Tentatively he said, 'We were so worried about you. We thought we'd never find you.'

Dorothy looked up and half smiled. She had begun to shake quite violently now and she pulled the collar of the jacket more tightly around her neck. Marshall did not know what to say to her. Out of the corner of his eye he could see his commanding officer returning. Suddenly, he blurted out, 'There's something I've wanted to ask you for ages.'

'What is it?'

Again Marshall was at a loss for words then he managed to stumble out the question, 'Would you come to the pictures with me?'

The girl stared at him for what seemed an age and then she began to laugh: softly at first but then hysterically. Marshall looked at Alec, holding the mug of tea and the blanket, as the latter squatted down beside the pair. 'You see, sir? I knew she'd think going out with me was ridiculous.'

'She's in shock,' replied Alec who, seeing the distress in his coxswain's eyes, was wishing he had minded his own business.

'No, No!' said Dorothy, wiping away the tears which were making little rivulets through the grime on her cheeks. 'I'm laughing because it has just occurred to me that if a bomb has to drop on me before you ask me out, what has to happen before you ask me to marry you?'

It was Marshall's turn to stare in shock before he too began to laugh – with relief at first and then with joy. He leant forward, folded his arms around her and hugged her to his ample chest. 'Hey! You're squashing me – and I've had enough of that for one day,' Dorothy protested. Then seeing the look on his face, she tweaked his bushy beard and added, 'And don't you go lovey-dovey on me. We've got work to do. There are still plenty more of my shipmates trapped.'

There was a memorial service for the dead Wrens a few days later. Replacements quickly arrived for them and for the more badly injured of the 40 survivors. Most girls went back to work straight away, in spite of their cuts and bruises, so that there was scarcely any hiccup in the operations of Coastal Forces from Great Yarmouth. Following the principle of making the best of things, they even rejoiced in their new hastily-found accommodation which had to be in the same area as their original quarters so that they were within easy marching distance of the Fishwharf. Those girls who found themselves on the seafront itself, billeted in a hotel previously a favourite with holidaymakers, declared themselves to be particularly fortunate. Thus, mourning for their comrades was pushed to the back of their minds and they got on with the job.

A couple of weeks later, Alec re-boarded his boat after he had been to a debriefing and was met by the comforting sight of female ordnance artificers checking the guns on deck and the cheerful sound of girl technicians quizzing the Petty Officer Motor Mechanic on the performance of the engines below deck. The coxswain greeted him on the bridge with the information that Miss Bradshaw was below in the radio room. She had been sent in response to the problems their operator had been having with the new radiolocation system.

'By the way, sir,' said Marshall, 'we've set a date for the wedding. We'd be honoured if you would attend.' Seeing Claire appear as she climbed back to the bridge, he added, 'and, of course, we'd be pleased if your young lady would come too.'

'My young lady? Oh, you mean Miss Bradshaw,' replied Alec. 'Miss Bradshaw isn't my girlfriend. We've known each other since childhood. She's more like my sister.'

Claire scowled at Alec before turning to speak to Marshall. 'I'd be delighted to come to your wedding provided I'm not on watch. I'll check and let you know.' Addressing Alec, she said, 'If you want to sleep at home tonight you'd better come now. I'm not hanging around for you – brother!' As they made their way down the gangplank to the quayside, Marshall, who had been joined by his fellow petty officer from the engine room, heard her snarl, 'You're a cheeky blighter, Alec Tovell!'

'She's going to give him hell for that remark,' the coxswain commented with a laugh.

'"She's more like my sister",' muttered the mechanic. 'What a load of old eyewash. Sister - my ass! Who does he think he's kidding?'

Once Alec had returned to base, Claire wasted no time in complaining about him to his mother. 'It was really humiliating – and in front of his men too.'

'What you really mean is, you're disappointed that he still views you as that little girl he used to play with on the beach every summer.'

'Yes, you're right. But how can I change that? Once a man thinks of you as a friend – a pal – how can you make him see you in any other way?'

'You must make him jealous. You must make him see that other men don't view you as a pal; then he'll see you with their eyes.'

'But how am I going to do that?'

'You'll think of a way. An opportunity will present itself and you'll seize it. Instinct – just rely on your instinct.'

'And if that plan doesn't work, is there another plan?'

'Of course there is,' replied Ginny with a twinkle in her eyes. 'But let's give the jealousy plan a chance first.'

The very next time Claire was at the port and Alec's boat had docked, his two petty officers viewed the scene on the quayside from the bridge. Claire was by then such a familiar visitor to the base that she was allowed to drive her small jeep onto the Fishwharf without any hindrance from the soldiers on guard duty at the gates.

'Well, the Royal Air Force is here again,' commented Marshall. 'The skipper must be forgiven.'

'And here comes his brother with the bike,' said the mechanic, indicating the figure of Bobby wheeling the cycle towards the jeep, accompanied by an American serviceman. 'And the American Army Air Force is here too. Wonder what that's all about.' The two men watched as Bobby introduced his visitor to Claire. All three chatted for a few minutes and then Bobby waved and left to return to his warehouse. They saw the American place the bicycle on the back of the vehicle and continue to talk animatedly to Claire. The mechanic, with a roguish wink to the coxswain, called out, 'Hey, skipper! Better hurry up, sir. There's a big Yank chatting up your … er … sister.' They were then rewarded with the sight of their commanding officer rushing down the gangplank just as the newcomer was getting into the passenger seat of the jeep and Claire was climbing into the driver's side. 'That's the quickest he's ever left the ship,' said the mechanic with a chuckle.

Claire saw Alec coming and stuck her head out of her door. 'Your bike's on the back. Get in quickly, please. Your brother has asked me to give Dwight here a lift back to his base.'

The American interrupted. 'I ought to go in the back so your boyfriend can sit beside you.'

'Oh, he's not my boyfriend,' said Claire in as offhand a tone as she could muster. 'We're childhood friends. He's more like my brother, aren't you, Alec? You stay where you are. Alec will be happy to go in the back, won't you, Alec?'

Alec muttered something through gritted teeth as he climbed into the rear of the small vehicle. The American turned in his seat and greeted him warmly, offering his hand and introducing himself. 'Dwight Cobalt, 2nd Air Division. Pleased to meet you, Alec.'

Alec managed to return the greeting whilst Claire, glancing at him in the rear view mirror, enthused, 'Dwight is a pilot. He had to ditch his plane in the drink last week and one of your other boats picked him and his crew up.'

'Yeah, that's right. We took a lot of flak leaving Berlin. We were lucky we made it as far as the North Sea. We were mighty glad to see your boys. Had to bring them a few bottles by way of thanks. The guard on the gate said to give them in at the Base Victualling Office. Your brother said he would pass them on to the crew which saved us. Then the engine wouldn't start when I got back in my jeep so he's going to get that fixed too.'

It was not necessary for Alec to say very much on the journey to

Haisbro. Claire flirted outrageously with the American and he, clearly, was lapping up the attention. Then he said something as they approached the smallholding which made Alec sit up and take notice. 'There's a dance at our airbase tonight and your brother has asked me to take his wife along.'

'What? Bobby wants you to take Rachel to a dance? That hardly seems likely.'

The American did not appear to notice that he was being accused of lying and taking a piece of paper out of his pocket, replied affably, 'Your brother has written down her name and address.' Turning to Claire, he said, 'Perhaps you wouldn't mind showing me where this is.'

Claire drove the jeep into the yard and as she brought it to a halt the Tovells came hurrying to greet their visitors. Ginny went round to the passenger door exclaiming, 'Bobby as well as Alec. That's lovely.' She stopped abruptly when she saw her mistake. 'I'm sorry,' she said to Dwight, 'but you looked just like my son, Bobby - from a distance and through the windscreen. Actually, you look the way he used to look years ago before he was wounded so badly.'

Dwight got out of the jeep and so did Claire. She made the introductions once more and then, in reply to Ginny's invitation, explained that they did not have time to stop for tea because she had to take Dwight to Rachel's house before they continued on to his air base.

'Bobby's asked Dwight to take Rachel to a dance tonight,' explained Alec.

'What! That hardly seems right,' exclaimed his mother.

'That's what I said,' muttered Alec.

Tovell's response was not what Ginny or Alec had expected. 'I think that's an excellent idea. Bobby's still recuperating and hasn't got Rachel's energy. It will do her good to have a night out and she's always loved dancing.'

Ginny looked at her husband in astonishment but said nothing further. Dwight then turned to Claire and said, 'Sorry, ma'am, I should have asked if you'd like to come too. If I walk into that dance hall with a lady on each arm, I'll be the envy of the entire base.'

Before Claire could respond Alec said enthusiastically, 'Yes, that's the answer. Rachel's such a pretty little thing and with all those men ogling her – no offence Dwight. But if Claire's there to take care of her – '

Alec got no further before a red-faced Claire interrupted him. 'Rachel can take care of herself. She doesn't need me as a chaperone. I'm on watch tonight anyway, so sorry I can't accept your kind invitation, Dwight.' Glowering at Alec, she added, 'Some of us have to work, you know.' She got back into the driver's seat, slammed the door and started the engine up straightaway. Dwight got into the passenger seat hurriedly and they roared out of the yard back onto the road.

The men followed Ginny into the scullery where she turned on them with eyes blazing. 'Whatever were you thinking of? You're both as bad as one another.'

Alec looked at his father quizzically. 'What have we done wrong?' he asked his mother.

'What have you done wrong? Well, for one thing you've offended Claire and really hurt her.'

'How?' Alec inquired innocently. 'What did I do?'

'You implied that she was not pretty and that she did not need protecting because no man would be looking at her.'

'I didn't say that, did I, Father?'

Tovell felt it was wiser to keep silent and clearly his wife did not expect him to reply because she continued to rant. 'Not in so many words but that was what you meant.'

'But Claire doesn't need protecting. She's perfectly capable of defending herself. She weighs half as much again as Rachel and I bet she still packs one hell of a punch. I felt her fist enough times when we were young. So I was only telling the truth. I don't see what she's got to be offended about.'

'Pah!' snorted Ginny. 'As for you, Tovell,' she said, turning her attention to her husband, 'I think you must have taken leave of your senses encouraging Rachel to go cavorting with an American serviceman. And Bobby, well, I can only think poor Bobby is more sick than we realized.'

'Perhaps he just wants to make her happy,' suggested Tovell quietly.

Ginny looked at him in exasperation for a moment then said, 'Get out of my scullery the pair of you and let me get the tea in peace. Go you in the living room and play with the children. They've got more common sense between them than you two; perhaps some of it will rub off.' Minutes later, the unmistakable strains of "Run Rabbit Run" filtered through the closed door. She pushed it slightly ajar and saw Alec sitting cross-legged on the hearth rug beside Will, Roger and Peggy standing up and acting out the words of the song and Tovell conducting the proceedings from his armchair. She smiled indulgently at the happy scene, shook her head and went back to the sink.


Next morning, after she had spent the night on duty, Claire was still seething. 'Well, so much for the jealousy plan,' she declared.

'I grant you that things didn't work out as we'd hoped,' said Ginny, adding diplomatically, 'but the circumstances were exceptional yesterday.'

'You mean that Alec insulting me was exceptional,' scoffed Claire.

'No, no, I mean we didn't expect Bobby to have asked that Dwight to take Rachel to the dance. And as for Alec, I tackled him about what he'd said and he couldn't see what he'd done wrong. He genuinely couldn't understand how he'd offended you, so I think you can take it that he definitely wasn't being offensive. He was just worried about what could happen to his brother's wife. It didn't occur to him how it might sound to you. He left this morning just before you got home. He was his usual cheerful self; blithely unaware that he was at fault. I reckon he thinks I was the one at fault for making a fuss about nothing.'

'Mmm, well, I'm still angry and upset.'

'I know, Claire. I would have been too in your shoes. But give him another chance, please. I'm sure the jealousy plan can still work – given the right circumstances.'

'And if it doesn't, what's your back-up plan called?'

'I suppose you'd call it, "being creative",' Ginny replied.

# III

Peter came home briefly between voyages and again he had the fact that his ship was in dock for repairs to thank for his few days with the family. He had not seen his brother-in-law since just before he had embarked on that fateful return convoy and the voyage during which he had been shipwrecked not once, but twice. Peter had no intentions of returning to his ship without spending a few hours with Bobby.

They met in a dockside pub near Yarmouth Fishwharf; the place was crammed with uniformed servicemen. Bobby was delighted to see Peter and to have the chance to talk about the Arctic with him. That particular theatre of war was so unique that many men who experienced it found it impossible to talk about it with anyone who had not been there. At first they talked of the ordeal which had befallen Bobby. He was open about his recovery and the limitations his health now imposed upon his career prospects, but he omitted to mention to Peter what he had confessed only to his step father: that he could not give Rachel the child she wanted.

Peter then mentioned the convoy which had set out for Russia after he had been sent to Chatham and whilst Bobby was still stranded at Barentsburg – the convoy whose fate had been raised in Parliament and was now the subject of an inquiry. 'I was damn lucky my ship was so badly damaged I had to be reassigned,' said Peter with feeling. 'But for that I might have been part of the escort for PQ17 – the massacred convoy, as everyone calls it. No-one dares admit they were on guard duty on that voyage: it could get you lynched in a dockside pub – especially if there are any American merchant seamen about!'

'You can hardly blame them,' said Bobby. 'As far as they were concerned we limeys ran away and left them to their fate. We even heard that one in a Yarmouth pub.'

'I'll never understand how the Admiralty got it so wrong. You never withdraw the escort and tell a convoy to scatter and make its own way. The Admiralty must have been certain the *Tirpitz* and other big battleships were about to attack the convoy or they would never have ordered the Royal Navy escorts to leave the merchant ships and seek out the enemy. Cruisers, destroyers, all of their crews expecting they were about to be part of a great naval battle and what happens? Bugger all! Hours, days, they must have spent at action stations and not a sign of an enemy warship. Meantime, the merchantmen saw the enemy alright: U-boats and German aircraft sunk twenty four of thirty six of them – mostly American. What a disaster! We're never going to live that one down.'

'Mother said questions were asked in Parliament; it was in the papers. Of course, we knew nothing about it until the Navy cruiser took us off Spitzbergen,' Bobby explained. 'The men said the next convoy came under heavy attack too so we stopped the convoys and after that just sent through individual merchant ships – poor devils. I reckon the theory was that it would be safer once summer was over: perpetual winter darkness makes it difficult for aircraft to attack.'

'I bet that was what we told the Soviet Union but I think the fact that we were massing ships to transport and escort forces to open a new front in North Africa had more to do with it,' Peter asserted. 'As soon as we heard Montgomery had managed to stop Rommel at El Alamein, I was sure that was why we had suspended Arctic convoys – to mass an invasion fleet. I was there, Bobby; it was a sight to see. There must have been five hundred merchantmen full of troops – mostly American – headed for Vichy French North Africa. Protecting them had to be the priority. But we re-started the Arctic convoys in December so one minute I was sweating off North Africa and the next I was freezing off North Russia. That's the Navy for you!'

'Are things any better in the Soviet Union for the merchant seamen?' asked Bobby.

'Slightly better,' Peter replied. 'They don't get their pay stopped now if they're shipwrecked which has to be a good thing and they're allowed to spend time in the International Clubs – the Interclubs – at Murmansk and Archangel. They can't go in the Intourist Hotels – they're still for officers only – but there isn't any form of entertainment for anyone at the other ports. Mind you, "entertainment" is hardly the right word anyway, is it? They're pretty bleak establishments, aren't they? The hostesses the Soviets provide to dance with the men daren't even smile for fear they'll be accused of fraternizing with us. Twenty girls mysteriously disappeared a few months ago, so I was told. Secret police had a hand in that, no doubt. There's still a thriving black market – chocolates and cigarettes continue to be the main currency and the Russian children are still the go-betweens as they were when you were there.'

'Never could understand where all the roubles came from,' Bobby mused. 'Someone was giving it to the children to buy stuff with. Whoever it was had put the fear of God into them: you never saw a littl'un touch a chocolate or a cigarette himself.'

'Oh, and you'd laugh if you saw the kind of things the ships' captains have been thinking up to keep the men out of trouble and to relieve the boredom: sports days and regatta races – in those temperatures! The Russians think we're mad!'

'Yes, all in all, I can't say I'm sorry to be done with Arctic convoys. But I am sorry that I'm never likely to go to sea again,' Bobby added sadly.

Peter remembered something he had read in the morning paper: Germany had stated that it had come across the fact that Russia had massacred 10,000 Polish officers when it had invaded Poland in 1940. The Poles had asked the Red Cross to investigate. 'What do you think?' Peter asked. 'Are the Soviets capable of an atrocity like that?'

'You saw how ruthless the top people – the party officials - were. The ordinary Russians lived in fear of their lives, didn't they, the poor devils? And if you asked any of the Polish seamen I came across, they'd be in no doubt. They'd answer a resounding "yes".'


May brought an increase in raids by low-flying aircraft all along the East Coast. The planes came out of the sea with no warning, dropped their bombs and were gone. The result was many deaths and much destruction in East Anglian counties. As Alec said to Claire, 'Your radiolocation - your radar - can't seem to pick them up.' She replied that it was because they flew below the radio waves but the system was being perfected all the time. Barrage balloons, a familiar sight already in many areas, were installed by Air Raid Precautions in parks and recreation grounds in Yarmouth and Gorleston to discourage the low-level attacks but they did not prevent them entirely. Alec and his crew became used to ducking behind a bulkhead whenever a lone raider flew into harbour and zoomed along the

150

length of the river, strafing the multitude of ships moored on either quay in defiance of the hail of flak from the Bofors guns which greeted him. On one such occasion, on the eleventh, they could hear other planes bombing the north of the town. On being told later that North Drive had been one of the roads which had suffered, Alec cycled there to see if the Westgates were safe. He was relieved to find their house undamaged but Bill was sitting at the kitchen table in some distress. He had helped with the rescue operation; there had been many dead and injured but what had upset him most of all was the fact that yet another hostel for servicewomen had been hit.

'They were laid out on the Wellesley Recreation Ground,' he said sadly. 'Twenty-six ATS girls. I know we shouldn't feel any different – all deaths are to be regretted – but somehow it seems that much worse when it's young girls. I just pray this war will come to an end soon.'

A couple of days later it seemed that hope had been brought a step closer. The wireless broadcasts and the newspapers had been full of the Allies progress in North Africa against the Axis powers. The British 8th Army had advanced from the east and had joined up with the mainly American forces advancing from the west. Now came the news that the German forces were trapped in the middle. They surrendered on the thirteenth of May. Churchill had spoken of using Africa as a springboard to attack the soft underbelly of Europe. When, the very next day, there were air attacks and sea bombardments upon towns in Italy, it was assumed that his planned offensive had begun. In many workplaces and public houses, people began to make bets with one another as to when the war would end.

Churchill also made a broadcast from America on the fourteenth because it was the third anniversary of the formation of what had become the Home Guard. His message was that as the Army was deployed more and more abroad, the defence of Britain was increasingly in the hands of the Home Guard. Sunday the sixteenth of May was an opportunity to celebrate the anniversary and to display the skills of the Home Guard to the public with parades and demonstrations of street fighting in towns and cities. Ginny decided at the last moment to take the three children to see the parade in North Walsham and she hitched Rajah Two to the cart.

Claire was on watch and Tovell had been with his unit since the previous evening so there was no obligation to stay at home to feed either of them. The four of them in fact regarded the outing as a little holiday. They enjoyed the parade except that the person they had come to see particularly – Tovell – did not appear to be there.

'Perhaps he was marching on the other side of the road from where we were standing and we didn't notice him,' Roger suggested. Ginny was not content with this possible explanation and when she caught sight of some Haisbro men after the parade she asked them about her husband. They looked at her blankly and said that no-one of that name was with their unit. Another man joined them and said that Tovell had been with them at the beginning and had done much of their initial training but he had not been part of the unit for some time. Ginny by then was becoming increasingly upset and next challenged an officer who had the misfortune to be walking past. He was at first thrown off balance by the onslaught of her questioning but quickly regained his composure. He replied diplomatically that a number of men with particular skills or previous military experience had been creamed off and transferred to specialist units; he felt sure that this was what must have happened to her husband. As to why the latter had not thought to mention this not insignificant fact to his wife, he could not hazard a guess. The journey home to the smallholding was not, therefore, the happy carefree ride that the morning's outing had been.

Ginny waited up for Tovell that night and when he came home, visibly weary, she let him eat his supper but as soon as he had slumped into his armchair she told him about their expedition to watch the Home Guard parade. Unperturbed and with eyes half-closed, he asked, 'Did the children enjoy it?' When she mentioned that they had not seen him, he replied, 'Didn't you?' and promptly fell asleep.

The next day, after Tovell had gone to deliver produce in Stalham, Ginny went into their bedroom and sat on the bed staring at his chest-of-drawers. After a few minutes struggling with her conscience, she got up and made abruptly for the door. There, she hesitated and turned round towards the bed again. The photograph on the small bedside cabinet caught her eye and she came back, sat down and picked up the picture. It had been taken during the previous war and showed four soldiers – Tovell and her three brothers. It had sat beside her bed ever since she had received it and was the last photograph she had of her youngest brother, Ben. She gazed at it for several moments before replacing it, with a sigh, in its usual place on the little cabinet. Then, because the images had evoked other memories from the past, she opened the drawer where she kept a box of treasured letters. She took out the pile which was secured inside a different colour ribbon from the rest, undid the bow and began to read her favourite letter – one she had read hundreds of times since Tovell had sent it to her from the Front, recalling the day he had seen her standing in front of the lighthouse on Haisbro Cliffs. *Do you remember, my little darling, that I compared you to the poppies? I said I thought they were lovely because they were bright, cheerful and colourful – like you. The red poppy grows wild here too, Ginny. The fields are full of them – just like they are at home. So you see, sweetheart, I have in front of me a constant reminder of you. The sight of all these flowers gives me hope – hope that one day I'll be back in our own Poppyland with you, my only love.*

The words comforted Ginny. How foolish she had been to lie awake last night tormented by thoughts of where her husband might have been yesterday. The officer was probably right: Tovell must have been transferred to some other unit and he had not wanted to worry her with the details. She put the letter back in its pile, retied the ribbon and returned the missives to their box before replacing it in the cabinet. She got up from the bed, crossed the room in a determined manner, but hesitated again once she had reached the doorway. She wanted to continue down the stairs but she could not stop herself from turning around once more and rushing back to Tovell's chest-of-drawers. Then, hesitantly at first, she began to search it drawer by drawer. When Claire, who had come home after a double watch, went looking for her she found her sitting on the bed with snapshots in her hand and tears rolling down her face.

'Whatever is the matter?' Claire asked anxiously, coming into the room.

Ginny looked up at her. 'Tovell wasn't at the Home Guard parade yesterday. The other men in the unit he'd told me he was with, hadn't heard of him. I know I shouldn't have gone through his things but I had a dread that he was up to something. Now I'm certain: I found these hidden at the back of a drawer.'

Ginny handed Claire the photographs. 'But these are all pictures of you and your children.'

Ginny nodded. 'He's always carried them with him; always kept them next to his heart – or so he used to say. Why would he stop doing that? Why would he hide them at the back of that drawer? It must be because he didn't want certain people to know he had a family. He's up to his old tricks again – that's what it is.'

Ginny dissolved into tears once more and as she hid her face in her handkerchief Claire looked more closely into the drawer she had indicated. She had caught sight of something else at the back and now she pulled it out. The title on the cover of the book was, "The 1938 Norfolk Calendar." Curious, she opened the book and saw at once that it was not a calendar. She snapped it shut and put it back where it had been concealed. She turned to Ginny and said, 'I don't know what you mean by, "his old tricks".'

'Women! He's always attracted women,' replied Ginny. 'Many of the ones he used to consort with still live round here. They're middle aged now but they still fancy him. I can tell by the way they look at him whenever we meet them at church or at a market. He can still draw them. He's an attractive man, isn't he? I bet he's got some woman somewhere away and he doesn't want her to know he's married; that's why he doesn't carry our pictures with him any more.'

'I'm sure that isn't the reason,' said Claire. 'Yes, he's still attractive in a rugged outdoor sort of way but he's definitely working with the Home Guard. I agree that it's not with this local unit but it's with some other unit – several nights a week, at weekends and on training exercises. I expect those photographs are so precious to him that he doesn't want to risk losing them or getting them spoiled. As for other women, you did say ones he **used** to consort with. I think that's the key word. I'm sure he's never consorted with another woman since he married you.'

Ginny looked up at Claire. 'Well, he's always been very loving towards me – I'll grant you that. I've never suspected anything like this before – not 'til now.'

'There you are then,' said Claire, smiling. 'I should put those photographs back and not give it another thought. You're very lucky, you know. I've never come across a kinder man than your husband.'

Ginny smiled too. 'Funny you should say that. I thought the same thing when I first met Tovell. Kindness is so important; in fact, I think it's the most important thing in a person.'

'And, I've seen the way he looks at you. He can't be cheating on you when he looks at you the way he does. You mean everything to him. I'd think myself very fortunate indeed if a man ever looked at me the way he looks at you.'


The boys in navy who manned the boats on the Yarmouth side of the River Yare were popular with the girls but so too were the boys in airforce blue who manned the boats on the Gorleston side of the same river. They were regarded as equally dashing in their fast Crash Boats – their high speed launches – and Number 24 Air Sea Rescue Unit had the advantage of being more easily accessible than the Royal Navy units on the Fishwharf. Admittedly, the junction of Baker Street and Riverside Road had a barrier of sorts: weighted barrels place on the highway as an obstruction which forced vehicles to reduce their speed almost to a standstill to manoeuvre around them. But there was nothing to stop the young ladies of the locality from walking along the cobbled quayside or from chatting to the young men in their white roll-necked sweaters as they maintained their boats after a launch. They had no WAAF technicians waiting for them to return to port as their Navy counterparts across the river had Wrens – they had to do their own maintenance work. But, nonetheless, there was no shortage of female company and Arthur Gillings frequently had a WAAF waiting upon his return – Margaret Westgate. Since being reassigned from her Suffolk base, she had worked at the far end of Gorleston Cliffs but she would often cycle to the quayside during a break from duty in the hope of seeing Arthur.

The RAF Marine Branch had built wooden barrack-type huts just across the road from where the rescue launches of Number 24 Unit moored. These were crew-ready rooms for the men waiting a call-out. The rear of the buildings also provided shelter and a measure of privacy for a young couple like Arthur and Margaret wanting a quick cuddle before returning to duty. The huts were situated on land which in peacetime had been a drying area for the nets of the fishing boats which had plied their trade from the harbour. The land beyond the wire fence which surrounded the huts was an open grassed area; on this particular day, it was swarming with children recently out of school. Some were intent upon their carefree games, others were searching for anything interesting which might have been dropped from a plane or blown there after an air raid, several were making a fuss of the goats tethered there to graze and a few were staring at the young couple with more than a passing curiosity.

'Stop it, Arthur. The children are watching us,' said Margaret.

Arthur, who had his back to the young voyeurs, glanced behind him. 'They're all supposed to be evacuated,' he replied.

'Some have come back home – the unhappy ones, I suppose,' said Margaret.

'Don't expect we're the first courting couple they've seen,' Arthur added casually.

'Well, it bothers me even if it doesn't bother you,' Margaret retorted. 'And I can hear your mates chatting in the duty room. These walls are only timber.'

'Let's go across the road then,' Arthur suggested with a sigh.

They duly trotted to the other side of Baker Street and Arthur ushered Margaret to a secluded spot behind the gutting sheds which had previously been used by the girls who cleaned the catch of the fleets which moored on the Gorleston side of the river. Arthur was just getting back to where he had left off when Margaret protested again. 'I can't stand this smell. It reeks of fish.'

'What smell? They haven't landed herring here since the government banned all fishing at the end of the 1939 season.'

'It still stinks of herring. Anyway, I've got to get to Gorleston Station to meet Claire.'

Arthur took Margaret's hand and began to walk with her away from the gutting sheds. 'Might as well go and give the horses a kiss seeing as you're not interested,' he grumbled. They wandered towards Bells Marsh Road and Arthur leaned over a fence and rubbed the noses of two old cart horses which were having a rest from their early morning rounds pulling bread delivery wagons. This was a favourite spot with Arthur: it reminded him of the farm near Fakenham where he had grown up and it restored his good humour.

'You haven't forgotten about tonight, have you?' asked Margaret. 'And you have remembered to tell Alec to meet us outside the Floral Hall?'

'No, I haven't forgotten and yes, I have remembered to tell Alec,' replied Arthur, grinning. 'I'm not a complete idiot.'

Margaret did not bother to respond to the last remark; instead, she continued with her own line of thought. 'I still can't get over the coincidence. I've been friends with Claire ever since we did our training together and our first posting was to the same aerodrome. Then, to find out last week when we were arranging for her to come down and visit me that she knew Alec ..., well, it was just amazing.'

'Yes, but when he used to tell us about this girl he always played with on Haisbro beach during the school holidays, he didn't tell us her name was Claire. He used to call her Fatty, or something like that.'

'He called her Podge, but don't you dare call her that, Arthur. She hates that nickname and it will ruin her stay if it's mentioned.'

'I'll be on my best behaviour – promise!' This prompted Arthur to voice a concern of his own. 'Talking of behaviour, I hope your friend's visit isn't going to spoil our usual after-dance session.'

'Trust you to think of that,' replied Margaret, hugging his arm more tightly. 'No, it won't spoil that: Alec can walk Claire back to my billet. But I'm not sneaking past the soldiers guarding the pier. I told you last week that I'm never going in the Cosies on the pier with you again. Sitting amongst that crisscross of open timbers was quite unnerving. I could hear the waves crashing only inches away from my bottom. It put me right off!'

'Oh, well, we wouldn't want anything to put you off, would we?' said Arthur, grinning impishly.


The Floral Hall was packed with dancers. All the men and, a large number of the women too, were in uniform. Margaret was in her element and enthused to the other three about the joys of this very modern circular building. 'It's only four year's old,' she informed her companions. 'I was here at the Grand Opening – just before the war. The hall was full of flowers and those floor-length windows which are blacked-out now were open to the lido outside. People were swimming or sunning themselves on the lawns. I can still smell the roses. I came here to dances lots of times in those early weeks. There was floodlit bathing and you could climb the outside staircases to the roof balconies. The intersecting walls protected you from the wind. The views over the beach and the harbour were wonderful. The balconies had soft lighting too. It was **so** romantic.'

Margaret regretted her last comment when she saw the frown on Arthur's face. The four of them were standing together on the raised area surrounding the huge circular dance floor. 'C'mon, let's dance!' she called out to her companions as she darted to the nearest steps and ran lightly down them onto the maple dance floor below. Arthur dashed after her immediately and had soon whirled her into the crowd; Alec and Claire followed at a more leisurely pace. The proximity of the other couples forced them to dance closely together but in spite of the enforced nearness, Claire felt Alec was not really with her. He spent most of his time, in fact, looking around him as they danced and responding to the greetings of all the girls who called out, 'Hello, Alec!' as they passed him. Twice they retreated to the tables on the raised balconies surrounding the dance floor and sipped drinks: soft drinks because no alcohol was being served. They were joined by Arthur and Margaret but conversation was difficult above the strains of the orchestra and each time they soon returned to dance under the glass domed ceiling.

The orchestra played many popular Glen Miller numbers which must have been particularly pleasing to the ears of the American servicemen on the dance floor. At one point Claire thought she had even caught sight of Dwight, a young woman entwined around him with her head buried in his chest. The woman looked up at him briefly and smiled. She reminded Claire of Rachel. The lights had been dimmed for the smoochy dance so Claire could not be sure of the identity of the partners; she forgot about them instantly. She was much more concerned that her own partner was not holding her as tenderly as she would have wished and was somewhat irritated that he persisted in chatting into her ear about mundane things instead of letting the romantic tunes work their magic.

All too soon it was the last dance – the significance of which was lost on Alec. He waltzed Claire around the ballroom as cheerfully as ever and did not appear to notice that everyone else seemed to be locked in a slow passionate embrace. Once outside the Floral Hall, Arthur whispered something in Alec's ear. All Claire heard was their final exchange when Arthur said, 'You know where the WAAFs are billeted, don't you?' Alec replied, grinning, that of course he knew.

Claire, through gritted teeth, muttered, 'You would!'

Arthur then shouted to Claire, 'Alec is going to see you back to Margaret's digs.' With a wave, Arthur and Margaret, arms around each other's waists, hurried off and were soon disappearing up the cliff side steps.

'Where are they off to?' asked Claire.

'Arthur lives up there,' Alec replied. 'The Air Sea Rescue boys used to be billeted in private homes, but now they're all together at the Cliff Hotel.'

'You don't mean he's risking taking Margaret to his quarters?'

'No, he's not that stupid. He's taking her to one of the shelters built into the cliff side. You must have seen them when Nanny Barker brought you to Gorleston on day trips. We always call them the Roman shelters because they're ornate and supported by pillars.'

'Of course I know where you mean but surely the lower parade is out of bounds? The military must patrol it, and the cliff top, in case the enemy lands on the beach. And the Links Battery has searchlights.'

Alec nodded. 'That's why they're going up the Cliff Hotel steps. They'll sneak along the cliff side making sure the soldiers don't see them and come down into one of the shelters. They'd better get a move-on though. Those shelters are very popular at this time of night.'

'How do you know?' Claire demanded.

'How do you think?' Alec answered mischievously.

'So if Arthur's taking Margaret to the Roman shelters, where are you taking me?'

'To the NAAFI,' replied Alec.

'The NAAFI!' exclaimed Claire, horrified. 'Why?'

'Because I'm hungry. It isn't far. It's over there, just around the corner, down Beach Road. It's great. They have everything.'

'I know what a NAAFI's like!' Claire snarled as Alec dashed off ahead of her. She drew an imaginary pistol from her hip and fired at his retreating back; at the same time emitting a loud 'Pow!'

He turned round at the noise and laughed. 'I can't waste time playing cowboys and Indians. I'm starving. Hurry up!'

Seeing it was useless to feel offended when clearly he did not even realize he had given offence, Claire ran after him and tucked her arm into his. They entered the canteen laughing; looking to the service men and women already seated at the tables, every bit like a couple.

The truce did not last long because once he was full Alec confessed that he had taken the decision the previous year not to pursue Margaret himself. 'That was very magnanimous of you,' Claire commented. Her sarcastic tone was lost on Alec.

'Yes, I could see he was serious about her. It wasn't just a bit of fun anymore as far as he was concerned. We'd been fighting over her since we were little.'

'Fighting over her?' Claire's hackles were up at this revelation. 'So although you'd known her since you were young and played with her just as you did me, you didn't regard her as a sister?'

'Of course not! She was such a pretty little thing I never thought of her as a sister; nor did Arthur. We both used to vow we were going to marry her when we grew up.'

Claire felt her cheeks getting hotter and redder. 'So, because she was a pretty little thing you never saw her as a sister?'

Warning bells sounded in Alec's head. What was that telling off he had had from his mother? 'You've always had a pretty face, Claire. I've always thought how pretty it was. But you were not exactly little, were you? You were a big sturdy tomboy who could look after yourself and – '

'Don't say any more, Alec,' Claire hissed menacingly. 'That hole you're digging for yourself is getting deeper.' Claire wanted to throw back her chair and flounce out of the building. The thought that she did not know how to reach her billet from the canteen and that the blackout would make it doubly difficult to find her way, kept her seated at the table. Another serviceman, unwittingly, came to her rescue. The man was from Coltishall aerodrome and he had visited the Haisbro station on several occasions as a specialist controller, directing Spitfires to their enemy targets with the help of the Haisbro radiolocation screens. He was clearly delighted to see Claire and she made the most of the opportunity, inviting him to sit down and introducing him to Alec – her childhood friend. When he had left, Claire said casually that the man had asked her out a couple of times. Alec did not respond to this information in the way she had hoped.

'I'm sure you had a good time,' was Alec's reaction. 'He seemed a nice bloke.' Claire did not reveal that she had turned the invitation down on both occasions.


At the first opportunity on returning home, Claire recounted the entire sorry tale to Ginny. 'Clearly, the plan to make Alec jealous is a wash-out! You're going to have to tell me about this "being creative".'

'I will,' Ginny agreed. 'I'll tell you about it the next time we know Alec is getting some leave.'

'It would help if I looked delicate; vulnerable – as though I needed looking after. Alec's always been one for wanting to mend broken wings –.'

'Don't remind me!' Ginny interrupted, laughing. 'Sometimes you couldn't move here for injured animals and birds in assorted boxes and cages. He should have been a vet.'

'You know, what I really need,' said Claire 'is a plan that will let me lose twelve inches in height and three stone in weight. The trouble with your Alec is that all his life he's been surrounded by small slender girls – you, Lizzie, Rachel and Margaret. He thinks that's normal. I don't think he's capable of finding any other type of woman attractive - never mind loving them. They say a man always looks for his mother when he's searching for a prospective wife. The only thing I have in common with you is the colour of my hair.'

'No,' said Ginny after reflection. 'We don't have just red hair in common: we have the same temperament – fiery!'

# IV

Alec did not get any leave for some time. Events had moved quickly and Sicily was attacked, as the first section of the soft underbelly to which Churchill had referred, on the tenth of July. Reports spoke of 3,000 ships being involved in the invasion which led the Tovell family to assume – correctly as they learned later – that Peter might once more have been transferred to the Mediterranean to assist with this operation. There were repercussions also for the flotillas of motor gunboats and motor torpedo boats around the eastern and southern coasts of Britain. Although none were transferred from Great Yarmouth in the run-up to the invasion, many other ports saw their flotillas depleted, so there was added work for those remaining.

Bombing raids on the German industrial regions had also increased through the spring and summer; some, such as the breaching of dams on the Ruhr, led to speculation that Jerry's production of armaments and other war supplies must be seriously affected, making an end to the conflict that much closer. The intensity of the bombing raids – by the USAAF during the day and by the RAF by night - led to a change in procedure for the flotillas necessitated by the large number of aircrews who ended up in the North Sea. Although the cold was not as intense as that which awaited shipwrecked men and ditched airmen in the Arctic Ocean, the chill of the North Sea could still kill in a remarkably short time. Joint operations were, therefore, instigated between the Royal Navy and the Royal Air Force Marine Branch. It was decided that gunboats and high speed launches should position themselves on the flight paths of returning bombers ready to pick up the crews of any planes which had to ditch in the North Sea. Thus, rescue times were considerably reduced and, consequently, so were the chances of men dying from hypothermia.

Alec and Arthur found themselves on the same joint operation on a number of occasions throughout the summer. Frequently, the men they saved from the sea were Americans who flew in the B17 Flying Fortresses and the B24 Liberator bombers of the 2nd Air Division of the 8th Air Force from airfields in Norfolk and Suffolk. One of the crews which Alec's boat picked up off Cromer at this time included Dwight who had suffered his second ducking in the North Sea but who, once again, had survived uninjured. They rescued men from a number of different Allied air forces and navies but also German survivors from the *Kriegsmarine* and the *Luftwaffe*. Part of the duties of both the Royal Navy and the RAF Marine Branch was to make regular visits to check whether any one had taken refuge on a "Cuckoo": life-rafts permanently moored at intervals in the North Sea and modelled on the "Lobster Pots" which the Germans had anchored in their waters.

An incident involving the crew of a ditched German fighter was one Arthur could not get out of his mind. It had been the turn of his launch to service the "Cuckoos" anchored off the coast of East Anglia. The men Arthur and his shipmates found on one of the floats looked no different to any other group of survivors – bedraggled, miserable and in some cases, wounded – but they were German airmen who knew that, although saved, they would become prisoners for the duration of the war. As they were entering harbour, one young man huddled with his comrades, tried to attract Arthur's attention as he passed. He held out a scrap of paper to Arthur on which he had scribbled a note. As he handed it over he spoke what were clearly the only two words of English he knew – 'Red Cross.' As Arthur glanced at the few lines which, naturally, made no sense to him, the man undid his wrist watch. He turned the watch over and pressed the back of it to his lips before passing it to Arthur. He pointed to the note and once more repeated the words, 'Red Cross'. Arthur knew the pleading in the man's eyes would haunt him. He looked at the watch which the man had handed to him face down and saw two letters – intertwined initials – had been engraved on the back casing. At once he handed it back to the man. The latter, alarmed, tried to press the timepiece into Arthur's palm. 'No,' Arthur shook his head. 'You keep it.' Then, holding up the note, he nodded repeatedly as he placed it inside his pocket, assuring the man with the words, 'Red Cross. I'll give it to the Red Cross.'

Later, as he walked along Marine Parade to the big isolated house at the end where Margaret worked, he kept reliving the scene and especially the moment when the man had kissed the engraving on the back of his watch. He was sitting on the low wall at the front of the house, gazing across the open grassed expanse of the cliff top towards the sea, lost in thought, when Margaret tapped him on the shoulder.

'You're a nice surprise,' she said cheerfully as she leaned forward and gave him a peck on the side of the cheek. 'I wasn't expecting you. When did you dock?'

'Oh, two or three hours ago. We had to hang around for the Army to come and collect some prisoners of war we'd picked up. I went to your billet first and your landlady told me what time you'd be off duty. I told her not to cook for you: that I'd be taking you for a meal.'

'That's good. Where shall we go?'

'Leave it to you.'

'The canteen in the High Street, then. I love their rice pudding: it's almost as good as Nan's.'

'It'll take us a while to get there. If you're hungry –'

'It'll only take half an hour. The walk will do me good: I've been sitting for hours. But if you haven't had any sleep – '

'I'm fine. I don't want to sleep. I want to be with you.' Arthur's tone was so serious that Margaret glanced at him anxiously. She was about to question him when she was hailed by a group of soldiers walking along the cliff top opposite. She waved back to them. 'They all seem to know you,' Arthur commented petulantly.

'Of course they do,' Margaret replied, unperturbed. 'Because the Links Battery isn't far from us, the soldiers on the guns know all the girls who work at Struan House.'

'Hmm. Yes, you're all girls there, aren't you? What exactly do you do?'

Margaret put her finger to her lips. 'You know I can't tell you. All strictly hush-hush.'

'Oh, come on. You're always saying that. It's a listening post, isn't it? Or, since you trained with Claire, is it the same sort of place as her station?'

'My lips are sealed,' Margaret replied dramatically. 'I've signed the Official Secrets Act. Do you want me to be shot at dawn as a traitor?' Then, changing the subject and with a mischievous gleam in her eyes, she added, 'If you don't want me to walk home along Marine Parade I could always cut into Bridge Road and go along Victoria Road instead.'

'You mean so you could bump into all those hundreds of soldiers billeted at Gorleston Super Holiday Camp?' Arthur grinned at Margaret, placed an arm around her shoulder and hugged her to him. 'You're a proper little minx – but remember you're my little minx; no-one else's.' But Arthur's good humour soon faded and as they walked along he related the sad tale about the prisoner. 'You could see how upset the man was at the prospect of not seeing his wife again.'

'It needn't have been his wife. Perhaps it was his girlfriend he was upset about.'

'No, it was his wife. I couldn't understand what he'd written to her but I saw that it was addressed to a "Frau" somebody. I'm sure "Frau" means "Mrs". I expect he wanted her to know he was still alive so she'd wait for him.'

Alec said very little more until they had reached the canteen half way along the High Street and were sitting at a table with trays in front of them. The place was quite crowded and they had had to search before they found a small table where they could sit alone. There were a number of mothers there with small children and toddlers, urging their offspring to eat. Even this scene appeared to depress Alec further and towards the end of their meal he said something which indicated what was bothering him.

'It could happen to me, you know.'

'What?' asked Margaret, startled after the long period of silence which had preceded this comment.

'I could be taken prisoner. Our boat could be attacked and sunk; we could be rescued and taken prisoner by the Germans. It happened to one of the Gorleston launch crews a couple of years ago.'

'I should think they were grateful to be saved. They were still alive even if they were captured.'

'Would you wait for me – if I were taken prisoner, I mean?'

'You daft old thing – of course I would.'

Arthur considered this reply for a moment and then said, 'It would be better if we were married.'

Margaret stared at him. 'That's a shocking way to propose to a person. You'll have to do better than that, Arthur Gillings.' She immediately got to her feet and made for the door with Arthur hurrying to catch up with her. Looking over her shoulder at him, she said, 'I'll excuse you because you're tired. I bet you didn't get much sleep when you were at sea. I'll walk with you back to the Cliff Hotel and you can have an early night. You don't have to walk me to my billet: it's not far from your quarters.'

'No, Margaret. Stop rushing off. I'm not tired; I want to be with you. Let's go to the pictures. They'll have changed the programme today. One of the crew said he saw the trailers and they both looked good pictures.'

'Hah! That's a laugh. When did it matter to you what kind of picture was showing? You never watch the screen anyway. You don't take me to the pictures to watch the picture, do you? What man does?'

Arthur caught up with Margaret and took her arm. Once they reached the bottom end of the High Street, and ignoring her remarks, he propelled her across the road and into the foyer of the Coliseum. They settled into their seats in the back row and as soon as the lights dimmed, Arthur put his arm around Margaret and after a few kisses began to chew her ear. Before long the chewing stopped and quiet snoring began. Gently, she removed his arm from around her back and edged herself away from him slightly so that his head fell onto her shoulder. There it rested for the next two and a half hours whilst she enjoyed the films. The newsreel had almost finished when a message flashed across the screen calling all Air Sea Rescue crews back to base immediately. The lights went up in the cinema as Margaret roused Arthur from his slumbers. Looking down the length of the auditorium, scarcely a man stood up in response to the appeal; but on the back two rows there was a hullabaloo as crew men gave their girlfriends a hasty peck then stumbled over one another as they struggled to free themselves from the confines of the seating.

Margaret ran with Arthur down the wide sloping corridor to the foyer and the exit out into the street. Once there, the klaxon could be heard calling the men to their boats. Arthur, swept up in a crowd of his comrades, dashed across to the junction and disappeared around the corner of the public house into Baker Street. A fellow WAAF, who had been waving goodbye to her own boyfriend, came and stood beside Margaret. 'It's just like being on an airfield again and watching their response when they get the call to scramble,' she commented. 'Why on earth do they have to race one another to be the first one away?'

The pair were about to walk off when Arthur re-appeared. To Margaret's amazement, he ran back across the High Street and grabbed her hand. 'You didn't give me your answer,' he said.

'No, I didn't because it wasn't romantic.'

'I've come back, haven't I? I've ruined my crew's chances of being the first boat away; they're going to kill me. Isn't that romantic enough?'

'No, it isn't!'


Four mornings later, Margaret was rudely awakened by the other two girls in her room. They dragged her, protesting, from her bed and forced her to look out of the window. A large banner was suspended between two trees in the garden and emblazoned upon it were the words, "I love you Margaret Westgate. Please marry me".

# V

The summer progressed happily for the children. They spent hours playing out in the sunshine and needed no encouragement to carry on the little jobs around the smallholding which had become second nature to them. They continued to go on foraging expeditions which, in accordance with the government's many campaigns, they now referred to as salvaging expeditions. They not only searched for fruit in season but acorns, pine cones, nettles and medicinal herbs for the collecting centres. Their friend, Mrs Brewster, seemed to be the organizer and coordinator for absolutely everything so their efforts meant plenty of visits to her cliff top home and home-made cakes and fruit cordial in her front garden beneath the watchful eye of the lighthouse.

The children were approaching the third anniversary of their arrival at Haisbro and memories of their lives before that had begun to fade. It seemed to them that they had always lived with the Tovells and been part of the convivial atmosphere of their home – until a chance remark at the dinner table changed all that for Will. Ginny had prepared a rabbit pie after Ted had shot one on the nearby farmland. It was a favourite dish with all of them; fortunately, the children never associated such treats with their own dear pet rabbits! Will had been eating heartily when Tovell said to Ginny, 'It's lovely to see how they've grown. You're not the scrawny little things you were when you first arrived, are you?' Roger and Peggy just nodded and carried on with their meal; but Will stopped eating at once and stared at Tovell wide-eyed. Thinking the child must have misheard him, Tovell reiterated, 'I said you're not scrawny any more, Will.'

The little boy pushed his plate away. 'Not hungry,' he mumbled.

'But you love that pie,' said Ginny in astonishment.

Tovell then made matters worse by stating, 'Eat up! You don't want to be scrawny again, Will.'

'Yes, I do!' yelled Will as he pushed his chair aside, ran out of the living room, dashed through the scullery and out into the yard.

The adults looked at one another, stunned. It was Claire who said, 'I'll go.' She immediately got up and followed the child outside. By then he was nowhere to be seen. She found him eventually curled up in the straw in Bella's stable. 'Good job I gave the horses clean bedding once they went out in the paddock or you would be a very smelly young man by now,' she said kindly. Will did not reply. 'What's up, Matey?' she asked.

At first the little boy did not respond; then he muttered, 'Want to be scrawny again.'

Claire considered this response and the remarks which Tovell had made at the table. 'So you were scrawny when Uncle Tovell found you. What did he say to you then?' she asked intuitively.

After another silence, Will mumbled, his head still half buried in his arm, 'Uncle Tovell said we were too scrawny to march back home to London. He said Auntie Ginny would fatten us up first.'

Claire smiled. 'Ah, I see. Well, that was a long time ago and I don't think Uncle Tovell and Auntie Ginny could spare you now. They need you here to help them.' Will looked up at her hopefully. 'Come on, Matey. Let's go back inside so Uncle Tovell can tell you himself.' Claire bent down and effortlessly lifted the little boy to his feet. 'Race you back to the house, Matey!'

The pair re-entered the living room hand-in-hand. Claire guided Will to his chair and pushed his plate back in front of him. Winking at Tovell, she said cheerfully, 'I've just been telling Will how you couldn't possibly let him go back to London now he's big and strong. You need him here to help you on the land, don't you?'

Realization dawned; Tovell smacked his forehead with the palm of his hand. 'I'm an idiot, Will! I forgot to tell you all the plans we've got for utilizing any little pockets of land which are left for vegetables. It's everyone's duty to help with the 'Dig for Victory' campaign, you know. Our local Agriculture Committee must have already ploughed up any remaining open spaces. I bet there isn't a village green or park anywhere in Norfolk that isn't cultivated and doing its bit to feed the hungry. That's a very important job. And Auntie Lizzie was only saying last night that she thought she should have a chicken run in her back garden. We're lucky here: the government lets us keep so many of the eggs our hens lay according to how many of us live here, but in most places, people have forgotten what a real egg tastes like – they only have dried egg powder.

Roger has his work cut out every morning getting round feeding all the hens and other animals we have, so if there's to be more chickens next door you'll have to give your brother a hand. Can you do that, Will?' The little boy nodded his head; his eyes were shining with enthusiasm. 'In that case, you'd better eat up. You're going to need all your strength for the extra work.'

Shortly after this, Ginny received a letter from the children's mother via, as usual, their own personal postal service – the WVS. It contained momentous news: the children's father had been killed during a daylight raid when bombs had fallen on the dock where he was working. Although the letter was short and there was no direct appeal for help, it was clear that the rest of the family would like to be invited to move to Haisbro.

Ginny was in a dilemma and decided not to tell the children straightaway what had happened: she felt she needed to discuss with Tovell first what they could do - if anything. The children were at Lydia Brewster's when Tovell arrived home; he had Ted Carter with him. 'I know I should feel sorry about the father but I don't,' Ginny declared. 'The problem is I don't see how we could accommodate three more people here. When I first encouraged them to come here we didn't have Claire with us and the twins were only little babies. Then there's having two women in the scullery and the fact that the littl'uns regard us as their parents now …' Ginny's voice trailed away.

'The government is still encouraging people to move to safer areas away from the bombing. The council will find them somewhere to live,' Tovell assured his wife.

'But all the places that are left are awful – falling down and empty for years. We're always hearing about evacuee families going back home. They say they'd rather take their chances on being bombed than suffer the damp and cold of derelict hovels miles from anywhere down muddy tracks.'

'Don't you fret now, gal,' said Ted. 'They can all come and live along o' me.'

Both Ginny and Tovell looked at Ted in astonishment. 'But you live in a tithe cottage, Ted. It's just meant for farm workers and their families,' Tovell argued.

'You just leave it to me. All I've gotta do is have a word with the young master. His father was a good old boy and so is he. There won't be no problem, that there won't. And,' Ted added perceptively, 'there'll be no other woman for their mother to squabble with and no one for the littl'uns to run to if she won't let 'em do something you've been letting them do.'

Ted departed immediately on his mission to convince the farmer that, suddenly, it had become that man's duty to do his bit for the war effort by housing a family of six. Ginny still had her reservations. 'Ted's place isn't big enough for all of them – even supposing the farmer agrees. They'll be so cramped together and it will be dirty and –'

Tovell interrupted her. 'Ginny, it will be fine. They're not used to a palace. They live in a city slum – just like the one I grew up in. It will be less cramped for them here than the home they've got now. At least Ted's place has got water laid on inside the scullery - just as we have. I bet that poor woman has to rely on a tap outside in the yard shared by umpteen other families – and a shared privy. Mind you, I don't doubt the place is dirty. Ted probably hasn't done any cleaning since his wife died.'

Ginny cheered up at the thought of a problem which she could solve. 'Oh, that's nothing to worry about. If we all work together we can have it ship-shape in no time. You'll probably have to white-wash straight through once we've cleared the muck out and Ted won't have enough furniture for them all. I'm sure we can find some bits we don't really need and some spare bed-linen. Lizzie's probably got some stuff too - and Rachel. What we haven't got I'll ask the WVS for: they've been kitting out homeless people ever since the bombing started. Yes, I'd better make a list right now of what they'll need - whilst it's all fresh in my mind.'

Tovell smiled at his wife affectionately as she chattered on, completely absorbed by her practical and technical plans. 'Come here, woman,' he said, pulling her gently towards him. 'I'd better grab a kiss now whilst I've got the chance. I can see you're not going to have any spare time left over to give your poor old man any attention.'

Ginny stretched up on tiptoe in response but only managed to make contact with her spouse's chin. 'Off you go! This woman's busy,' she replied as he bent down and claimed his kiss. Once he had left, another thought occurred to her: how would Claire react to this development?

'I'll be sad to see them go,' Claire said when Ginny told her the news, 'but perhaps it's for the best. I've got very fond of young Will but I'm not his mother.'

The young master did not put up much of a fight; Ted won easily. He then had to suffer half the neighbourhood descending upon his property with buckets and brooms followed by paint, curtains, furniture and what seemed a never ending traffic of bits and pieces. His horse and cart were then purloined as a taxi. Soon the three children he already knew from previous visits to the farmyard were tumbling from his vehicle with assorted pets and possessions together with two even younger siblings and a rather tired-looking woman. The entire brood was ushered into the little cottage by his elderly farm hand who had never looked happier. But life was to cheer up for the farmer too – a bachelor whose experience of living with his dominating mother had left him so traumatized that on her death he had vowed never to allow any woman into either his house or his life. Firstly, the government had been prepared to pay him rent for housing evacuees; secondly, with extra cash in his pocket he could afford to pay the mother of his lodgers to improve his dreary lot. She cleaned his ramshackle farmhouse, did his washing whilst he was out working and left him a cooked meal on the steamer for whatever time he came home. Thirdly, he did not feel so lonely when he heard the childish laughter and saw the little ones scampering around his domain.

The one downside to the new arrangement was that old Ted started work later than before and put in even fewer hours than he had done previously. 'Bessie and me has gotta take the littl'uns to school in the morning and collect 'em again in the afternoon.' The farmer pointed out that their new home was only a little over a half a mile from their village school. 'Ah, but, you gotta think o' the Hun! You never know when they're going to invade.' The farmer was a reasonable sort of chap and he also had the more reliable services of the Land Army to call upon so he did not pursue the matter any further.

Tovell found he had to reorganize his day too with the departure of the evacuees. He had always arranged his working hours around the need to escort them along the much longer route from the smallholding to their school ever since low-flying enemy aircraft had been known to strafe country lanes.

Ginny missed them too and the scene which she had witnessed at Stalham Station when she, Tovell and the three older children had met the rest of the family off the train would remain with her always. Their mother had been quite overcome when they had met. Unable to speak, she had hugged the offspring she had not seen for three years to her and wept. They, for their part, had been rather bewildered and Roger and Peggy had even seemed a little embarrassed at this display of emotion, standing there on the public platform. The twins had looked so glum and undernourished that they had reminded Ginny of the little waifs who had stood outside her scullery door. They were the most confused of all since they did not even remember they had a sister and brothers: they had been mere babes in arms when their mother had secreted their elders away to safety. Claire, who had not been on duty that day, had pretended that she was so that she would not have to say her farewells to young Will. But after a few days they had all settled in to their new surroundings and once their mother was no longer a stranger to them, the older ones had begun to talk to her about the life they had been leading. She realized how much the Tovells, Lizzie and little Molly and in particular, Claire, had meant to them and regular visits back and forth were soon instigated. One other innovation which she had to adjust to was sweet indeed – for the first time in her life she had her own money which she herself had earned.

One aspect of the new arrangement bothered Ginny: what would happen when the war was over and the government ceased to pay out money to support evacuees? They would all be expected to return home then. Better not to think about it, Ginny concluded. You should take one day at a time. What else could you do in wartime?

# VI

During the summer, a gunboat collided with Alec's boat during the height of an attack on an enemy convoy off the Dutch coast. Both vessels managed to get back to Great Yarmouth but then needed to proceed to a boatyard for repairs. The crews enjoyed a pleasant couple of days taking their vessels the scenic route up river, through Breydon Water to Reedham, along the Haddiscoe Cut to the River Waveney and so into Oulton Broad. They had moored overnight at a riverside pub owned, so they had been told by crews whose boats had already made the same voyage for refits, by a landlord who felt his contribution to the war effort lay in ignoring licensing hours for members of the armed services. By the time they reached the boatyard which was to carry out the repairs, they were all in a merry mood and looking forward to a stay, however brief, in the congenial surroundings of Oulton Broad. A message awaited them however: the Captain was to return with all speed to HMS *Midge* leaving his vessel in the hands of his First Lieutenant. He was to bring his coxswain with him. No more meandering along sunlit waterways, Alec and Marshall caught the train and returned to Great Yarmouth across the same lush countryside but via a more direct and, therefore, much quicker route.

Their Commander explained to them that they were to replace a captain and coxswain who had both succumbed to a debilitating illness after eating at a local hostelry. Their boat had to sail that night regardless, because it was on a pre-arranged assignment. Clandestine operations were not unusual; Alec had been on several as had Arthur. The Navy's motor boats and the RAF's launches were both ideal for such work since they were speedy, had a reasonably shallow draft and could be manoeuvred near to the enemy coast, and their low silhouettes were not easily discernible by shore batteries.

The two men quickly went aboard their temporary charge. The First Lieutenant, who as in all the boats acted as Gunnery Officer, was well known to them but the other officer, who would act as Pilot and be responsible for their navigation, was straight from training. He introduced himself as Sub-Lieutenant Michael Gibbs. In reply to Alec's questions, he admitted that this would be his first voyage and that he was nineteen years old.

They approached the Dutch coast without mishap, landed their agents, rendezvoused with the other agents whom they were to bring home, and embarked them and their equipment, all according to plan. It was still dark although the low heavy cloud had shifted somewhat and the moon was threatening to peep through. Nevertheless, they had every hope of leaving German patrolled waters undetected. Intelligence reports had informed them of likely minefields and although E-boats were patrolling the area they were confident that they could avoid contact with the help of their relocation system. Once the agents were aboard, Alec gave the order to wait in silence with the engines cut for several more minutes. The crew strained to hear the noise of an engine: a sign of any E-boat which might be in the vicinity. All was quiet and with dawn approaching, Alec gave the order to start up their engines and head west – for home. Suddenly, the night was illuminated by a burst of star-shells. One landed on deck and fire broke out. The sailors rushed to douse the flames, knowing the danger they were in, given that the hull of their vessel was made of ply-wood. Simultaneously, the E-boat closed in on them from the north and opened fire. In that first barrage, their Vickers machine-guns were disabled, gun crews wounded and an Oerlikon gunner killed. Then a shell hit the bridge ripping off a section of the armour plating and knocking Alec and the First Lieutenant flying. The coxswain called out to Sub-Lieutenant Gibbs. The young man got to the bridge and seeing the captain and his second-in-command sprawled motionless, he froze – but only momentarily.

Petty Officer Marshall had glimpsed that fleeting look of panic in the officer's eyes and called out, 'Make smoke, sir?'

'Make smoke!' yelled the sub-lieutenant as he rushed to the controls and frantically cranked the handle on the telegraph to show on the speed indicator in the engine room below that he wanted maximum revolutions. In spite of damage to one engine, the mechanics managed to get up sufficient speed for the Dog Boat to escape into the night trailing its curtain of smoke. Miraculously, the E-boat did not turn and pursue them, its captain confident perhaps that he had done enough to sink them. Once the immediate danger was over, the wounded were carried below to the mess deck and the young officer called for a damage report. The burst of speed which had been necessary to enable them to escape had put too much strain on the damaged engine and it had failed. The chief motor mechanic also reported that a second engine was giving trouble and that before long he feared they would be running on only two engines.

As daylight arrived, the sailors on deck scanned the skies for enemy aircraft. Thankfully, they saw none but half an hour later they were sighted by a RAF Halifax bomber which flew low assessing their damage. Shortly afterwards, Alec appeared on the bridge, a dressing on his forehead and others covering minor shrapnel wounds. 'I've had a damage report,' he told the sub-lieutenant, 'and I know we've one dead and six wounded. But did you engage the enemy?' he asked the anxiously.

'No, I did not, sir,' replied the young officer.

'Thank God for that!' exclaimed Alec.

The sub-lieutenant grinned. 'I knew the score, sir. The First Lieutenant had briefed me whilst we were waiting for you and Mr Marshall to arrive. He suspected we were about to embark on a "cloak and dagger" mission. He told me how we must avoid firing at the enemy because if we lost and were captured, we would be taken as prisoners of war but our passengers would be executed as spies. They might also reveal under torture the details of the operation and the network of people supporting them. For the same reason, I did not break radio silence in spite of our plight, sir. Didn't want to bring U-boats or E-boats to our position.'

'Well done, Mr Gibbs,' Alec said warmly. 'You'll not forget your first voyage in a hurry.'

'We've got company, sir!' the coxswain called out. As he spoke, a cheer went up from the sailors on deck. Speeding towards them was a launch from the Gorleston Air Sea Rescue Unit and following behind that they could see Gorleston Lifeboat, the *Louise Stephens*.

All the casualties were taken to the Royal Naval Hospital at Great Yarmouth which was only a short ambulance drive from where the boats had docked. Alec was not kept there for long but was allowed a spell of rest and recuperation at his Haisbro home. He still had two days leave left when his mother observed that he seemed to have recovered fully from his injuries. 'Now's your chance,' she said to Claire. 'You're not on duty 'til tonight. Why don't you suggest to Alec that you take the horses out for some exercise? You know this district well. You must know somewhere secluded where you can be alone.'

Claire nodded. 'Are you sure being creative, as you put it, will work? Have you ever tried it?'

'Yes. Once,' replied Ginny, eyes twinkling.

'Who with?'

'Tovell, of course.'

'Not with your first husband?'

'He didn't need any encouragement,' Ginny replied, bitterness plain to hear in her voice. Then she continued, evenly, 'I know men like to think they're taking the lead but sometimes you have to do that for them. Give them that bit of confidence, so to speak.'



The August sky was blue and cloudless, there was scarcely a breeze and it was cool amongst the trees. Bella and Rajah Two had clearly enjoyed having a longer outing than normal and grazed contentedly when their riders dismounted and tethered them to nearby bushes. Claire spread out the blanket on the grass and unpacked the bag of food Ginny had prepared for them. 'It was kind of your mother to make us a picnic, wasn't it?' she said.

'Yes, it was,' agreed Alec. 'Now, what shall I have for a start?' As he rummaged around peeping inside the sandwiches, Claire reflected that they had not fallen out once since they had left home. Ought she to risk spoiling this harmonious atmosphere? Perhaps she should be content to enjoy this beautiful day and hope that the memory of it, remembered in retrospect, would do the trick and lead Alec to have more romantic thoughts about her. On the other hand, she had not seen him for weeks and, as several other flotillas had been sent abroad recently, what guarantee was there that she would see him again any time soon? No, she could not waste this opportunity: there might not be another. And she had rehearsed her plan over and over again: what she would do and say to him; what he would do and say to her. She stood up and quickly undid the buttons of her blouse and then the top of her slacks. Alec looked up in alarm and mumbled through his half-chewed sandwich, 'What the hell are you doing?'

'Getting undressed. It's hot and I've got my swimming costume on. I thought we could go for a swim in the river later. Pity you can't get on the beach these days – all mines and barbed wire. It's years now since we've taken a dip together.' As she spoke, Claire slipped off her blouse and stepped out of her slacks. Alec was careful not to look directly at her as she did so. She knelt down in front of him and reached forward towards the pile of sandwiches nearest to him. Her bare flesh was only inches from his nose; he had an unbroken view of her cleavage.

'You're falling out of that costume,' he muttered, trying to avert his gaze.

'I bought it years ago before the war,' she replied. 'You can't get them now. I wasn't what you might call fully developed then, so it's a bit tight.' After a little more jiggling about she found the sandwich with the filling she wanted and sat back on her heels. Alec was looking a bit flushed and both continued to eat in silence. He kept his eyes studiously lowered. Claire reflected ruefully that Alec had not said any of the things she had expected him to say. Perhaps she should have shown him the script.

'I'm not as hungry as I thought,' Alec announced suddenly. 'I've had enough.' He began to pack the precious muslin bags together and throw his bits of crust to the birds.

Things were not going well, Claire mused. 'How about that swim then?' she proposed hastily.

'I haven't got any swimming trunks with me,' Alec replied.

'So? You can swim in your pants, can't you? Or you could take them off too. I'll take my costume off as well if you do - so you won't be embarrassed. We can go skinny dipping like we did when we were little – before Nanny Barker found out!'

Alec immediately got to his feet. 'Claire, what's got into you? I don't think I like you like this. We're not children now.'

'No, we're not but you don't seem to realize that. I'm not a child any more, Alec. Why can't you treat me the same as you do all those other girls? You wouldn't be protesting if one of them was here with you now. We both know what you'd be doing to them.'

'Claire, stop it! You should be glad I treat you differently.'

'Why? This is wartime, Alec. Either one of us could be killed tomorrow. We have to make the most of the here and now. That's been your philosophy with those other girls, hasn't it? I don't want you to be a gentleman. I want you to be a man – my man. I've loved you since I was a little girl and I want to be able to look back and remember that this day you were my man – even if you never are again.'

Alec stared at her in disbelief. His only reaction was one of shock. The silence was palpable. Claire stared back at him for a few moments then she jumped up and dashed off into the trees. She ran as fast as she could, tearing the flesh on her arms and legs on the brambles, treading on stinging nettles with her bare feet. On and on she galloped, jumping over fallen branches, heart pounding, lungs bursting, tears streaming down her cheeks, anxious only to put as much distance as possible between her and the scene which she knew would mortify and haunt her for the rest of her life. She stopped running when she could go no further. She clung to a tree trunk, gasping for breath; only when she was calmer did she realize that she was not alone – ten yards from her lay another couple. They had not heard her approach because of the noise they were making as they did what she had planned she would be doing at this moment – copulating ecstatically. Suddenly, their gyrations brought them where she could see their faces – it was Rachel and Dwight who were locked together in that naked embrace. Instantly, she pulled back so that the trunk hid her. Simultaneously, she caught a glimpse of Alec through the trees, searching for her. Whatever else happened, she knew she could not let him see what she had just witnessed.

She ran back the way she had come, careful not to tread on any branches and betray her presence to the couple. She dashed past Alec without saying a word. She had made sure that he saw her, knowing that he would follow. Once she reached the clearing in the wood, she grabbed her clothes, jumped into her shoes, released Bella's reins and climbed into the saddle. She was riding away as Alec approached. Further on, she stopped behind a derelict cottage, dismounted and put on her slacks and blouse. She tidied her hair as she hid behind the flint wall. She watched Alec and Rajah Two ride by before she remounted. She arrived in the Tovell's yard only seconds behind him. Neither said a word as they unsaddled their horses and released them into the paddock. Claire ran ahead and entered the scullery first. One look at her face and Ginny did not need to be told that the plan had gone horribly wrong. Claire fled to her room; Alec packed his kitbag and was on his way back to base within half an hour. His mother was left bitterly regretting that she had broken that most important rule: never to interfere in her children's lives.

After what she felt was a decent interval, Ginny went upstairs and knocked gently on Claire's bedroom door. After a while, a muffled voice asked, 'Who is it?'

'It's only me,' Ginny answered. 'There's no one else here. Can I come in?'

'Might as well,' Claire mumbled.

When Ginny entered the room, closing the door behind her, she found Claire face down on her bed, her eyes red and swollen; her cheeks tear-stained. 'I'm so sorry. I should never have suggested anything,' Ginny began. 'I should have minded my own business.' Ginny had expected the girl to be furious with her but now that she had calmed down Claire was trying to be reasonable about the incident – although she still felt hugely embarrassed.

'Perhaps it was me,' she said, generously. 'I suppose I wasn't very subtle about it. Subtlety has never been one of my strong points. I'm more of a jump-in-with-both-feet type of girl. All I do know for sure is that I can't face Alec again. I'll have to move out.'

'Oh, please, Claire, don't do that,' Ginny pleaded. 'You're making me feel even worse now.'

'If I don't move out, Alec won't want to come home again; I know how much he means to you both.'

Claire had attended Petty Officer Marshall's wedding some weeks previously and had had an enjoyable time. She had been treated by all the crew as their skipper's lady and had allowed herself to think that it might not be too long before fiction became fact. She now faced the problem of how to get through the forthcoming wedding of Margaret and Arthur, knowing that Alec was a lifelong friend of both of them and would surely be invited. Margaret came to see her after Claire wrote to her saying she did not think she would be able to attend.

'I want you to be my bridesmaid. You know I do,' Margaret protested. 'Arthur has asked Alec to be his best man.'

'Oh, dear. That makes it even worse,' said Claire. 'You see, Alec and I have fallen out.'

'From what you've told me, you're always falling out. You're like an old married couple. You'll just have to make up before the wedding.'

'Not this time,' Claire replied sorrowfully. 'There'll be no making up this time. It will spoil your day if I'm there. You ought to ask one of the girls you're stationed with to be your bridesmaid.'

'But I want you.' A thought occurred to Margaret and she asked, 'You're not playing games with Alec, are you?'

'Games?' Claire's stomach seemed to turn over at the thought that Margaret might have heard something about that embarrassing episode. Had Alec told Arthur about what had taken place?

'Yes, you know what I mean, Claire. I tend to forget that you're upper crust; one of the landed aristocracy. I've met other girls from your class who've joined the services and they're all having a lovely war. They're thoroughly enjoying themselves with boys they wouldn't give the time of day to normally. Once the war is over they'll go back to their own kind and marry someone from their own class. Is that it? Have you fallen out because Alec realizes you're just playing games with him?'

'Class! Whatever is all this talk about class?' Claire demanded. 'That's all finished in this country. When the war is over the old class structure will be gone forever.'

Claire spoke so vehemently that Margaret believed her. 'There speaks one who has been to university,' she said, smiling ruefully. 'All that left-wing stuff has really rubbed off on you, hasn't it? But you're wrong. The class divide will still be there when the war ends. It's just been pushed aside for the moment because it's expedient to do so. But are you saying that you're not playing games with Alec; that you're not too high and mighty to marry him?'

'Me, high and mighty? That's not how I would describe myself; and nor would Alec – believe me! And just for the record, my mother didn't marry within what you would call her class. When she married my father she married beneath her according to her parents. My grandfather threatened to disown her; it was my grandmother who negotiated some kind of a peace.'

'But your father's a general,' said Margaret.

'He is now but at the time he was a humble lieutenant – and with very little family money behind him either. So don't accuse me of having a class-riddled background.'

Margaret laughed. 'Actually, I've always got the impression in the past that you were rather ashamed of your family – embarrassed by them anyway.'

Claire nodded. 'Yes, I suppose I am a sort of inverted snob.'

'But I'm relieved to hear you're not just playing with Alec: that you would marry him.'

'That's not going to happen, Margaret. He wouldn't marry me if I were the last woman left on earth. I told you we've fallen out – and it's permanent. You should ask one of your room-mates to be your bridesmaid because Alec will never agree to be Arthur's best man if he thinks there's a chance of me being there.' Then, anxious to change the subject, Claire asked, 'Are you still adamant that you want your grandfather to give you away?'

'Yes, I am,' replied Margaret. 'Nan and Granddad brought me up so he should give me away.'

'Didn't they bring you up because you refused to live with your father after he remarried?'

Margaret scowled. 'Yes, all right, I was the one who left home – he didn't throw me out. But he still did a dreadful thing: marrying again so soon after my mother died.'

'Well, I've never been in your situation, but I should think if someone's had a companion for years and then that companion dies, they would feel very lonely. Perhaps your father was so happy when he was married to your mother that he wanted his life to be like that again.'

'Oh, don't you start! All I get from Nan and Granddad is that I should use the wedding to "build bridges", as they keep saying. "He'll be so hurt if you don't let him give you away. He is your father." Why should I forgive him? Think how he's hurt me.'

'Does Arthur feel about his mother the way you feel about your father? After all, Arthur's mother remarried after his father was killed in the last war.'

'He adores his mother – and his step-father,' Margaret admitted grudgingly.


Claire was Margaret's bridesmaid in the end: it was Alec who could not attend the wedding. 'Something about being called to someone's deathbed, so he told Arthur,' said Margaret. 'One of Arthur's shipmates is going to stand in for Alec as best man so you can't get out of being my bridesmaid.'

'I won't have to wear a frilly dress, will I?' asked Claire, concern written all over her face.

'No, you won't have that excuse either,' replied Margaret. 'This is a wartime wedding and I think we should all be proud to wear our uniforms – girls as well as boys.'

'Thank heaven for that,' said her friend.

'Nan found some icing sugar at the back of her cupboard the other day so she's going to make me a wedding cake. I know she shouldn't – the government banned the icing of cakes last year – but those cardboard pretend wedding cakes look so silly. She bought the icing sugar in 1939. You don't think it will poison anyone, do you?'

The ceremony took place on Friday the third of September – the fourth anniversary of the outbreak of war. Claire had been able to "borrow" an RAF jeep and enough petrol to not only fill the jeep's tank but that of the car which the young master had been persuaded to lend to Ted. With two vehicles at their disposal a sizeable party left Haisbro for Gorleston that morning. Tovell refused to allow Ted to drive the farmer's very large and very ancient car so he sat in the back along with Mary and Ginny. Lydia Brewster sat in the front beside Tovell. Following them was Claire driving the jeep and with her the younger guests – Rachel, Lizzie and little Molly. Tovell spent the journey wondering whether, if he were challenged, going to a wedding would be regarded as the banned "pleasure motoring", but he was also a little mystified that Claire did not seem able to keep up with him. Several times he had looked in the rear view mirror and the jeep had not been there. Unbeknown to him and his passengers, this was because Claire had to make a number of unscheduled stops so that Rachel could be sick. Claire and Lizzie agreed to keep this bit of news to themselves.

Bobby was waiting for them when they arrived at St Andrew's Church in Gorleston. Everyone was pleased to see him since he did not seem to get home to Haisbro very often. Claire was worried that the church, which she knew was large for a parish church, would seem unwelcoming because it would be so empty. She had reckoned without the family and friends of the bride and groom. Margaret had been persuaded by her grandparents to make her peace with her father and allow him to give her away. He was there with his second wife, his parents,

Bill and Gladys Westgate, and as many of the bride's brothers, sisters and assorted relatives as the duties of war service would allow. Added to that, Margaret's WAAF colleagues who were not on watch were there and her landlady and her family.

Arthur's side of the church was full too. His mother, Lily, and stepfather, David, had travelled by train from Fakenham and brought some of Arthur's half-brothers and half-sisters, of varying ages, with them. And one of his stepfather's sisters, Annie, who had been Arthur's favourite aunt when he was a little boy, had journeyed with her husband from their smallholding at Winfarthing to see him wed. The Haisbro contingent was particularly pleased to see that David had at last agreed to be fitted with an artificial leg. Tovell and Bill Westgate, his former army comrades, congratulated him on how well he was walking: with scarcely a limp. 'Lily kept nagging me,' David admitted. 'She was forever on about how artificial limbs had improved and how much easier I'd find it to get around the farm. As far as I was concerned, Cambrai was a long time ago and I'd managed perfectly well ever since using my crutch. But you know what women are.' His male friends nodded their commiserations before allowing themselves to be ushered into the church by their wives.

The number of Arthur's supporters was also swelled by his RAF colleagues: it looked as though everyone who was not at sea or on board guarding a boat was there. This was not perhaps so surprising since the distance between the church and the quayside was only double the distance from the cinema to the boats and the klaxon calling the men to their base could be heard all over the town. Claire, who had dreaded the service, quite enjoyed it because, with so many people in the congregation, it was a cheerful gathering and everyone sang the hymns with gusto. They took photographs outside the church near the porch and showered the happy couple, not with confetti because of the paper shortage but with rice, as they ran down the long slope through the churchyard to the road.

Ginny was concerned that Gladys, who had insisted upon holding the reception at her house, would not be able to feed so many people, given the restrictions that rationing had brought. That problem was solved when the Service personnel, after offering their congratulations to bride and groom, set off on a pre-arranged tour of celebration. They headed for the quayside and beginning at the southern end, drank the health of the newlyweds in the *Belle Vue* to begin with, proceeded north to the *King William*, made a slight detour into Pier Walk to the *Lifeboat Tavern* and ended up at the *Dock Tavern* which was conveniently situated very close to the crews' wooden huts. They had restricted themselves to one drink at each venue, knowing they could be called out on a rescue mission at any time. The members of the crews on stand-by then bade their comrades farewell and retired to the wooden huts. The remainder, WAAFs still accompanying them, retraced their footsteps to Pier Walk, passed the bombed out Bethel Chapel – so beloved by generations of fishermen – and trudged up Cliff Hill to their quarters at the top. At the Cliff Hotel, the married men took their leave whilst the rest escorted their female companions to their billets unless, of course, they were able to persuade them to linger and take the sea air from vantage points in the Roman shelters dotted along the cliff side!

The wedding party at the Westgate household went well and Ginny marvelled that Gladys had managed to accumulate so much food. The Haisbro crowd soon congregated in one room along with Arthur's family from Fakenham and Winfarthing.

Lily announced that she would have been happy to make Margaret's wedding dress – in spite of the shortages – had this been a traditional wedding.

'You certainly worked miracles with the outfits for my wedding,' said Ginny, warmly.

Lily smiled. 'Only because Lady Meredith was kind enough to give us her dress to cut up.' Then she added sadly, 'Poor Lady Meredith. It must have been dreadful for her losing her sons – and in the final weeks of the war when she must have thought they were going to survive.'

'Yes,' Ginny agreed. 'She'd been a good employer to both of us – to all her staff – but those deaths seemed to break her spirit. Neither she nor Lord Meredith lived very long after the war ended, did they? We don't see much of their grandson around the village and he's never involved himself in public life the way his grandfather did.'

Tovell broke the silence which followed by asking cheerfully, 'Are we to understand then, Lily, that you're still dressmaking?'

'Oh yes,' Lily answered. 'Most of my trade now is in alterations: patching clothes people bought before the war so they'll last longer and, of course, trying to make those awful utility frocks look nicer.'

David intervened, 'I don't know how we'd manage if it wasn't for Lily. There are so many of us trying to get a living from the farm – my younger brothers too. And,' he added proudly, 'Lily's so clever, it'd be a shame to waste her skills.' The tender look that David gave to his wife at that moment was not lost on Tovell and he remarked to Ginny later that he had seen David give that same look to Lily on many occasions – twenty nine years previously.

The group was joined by Bill and Gladys Westgate. Reminiscences of when they had all been together at the Coastguard Station in Haisbro in 1914 flowed thick and fast. They spoke of departed friends and of comrades who had not survived the Great War; of how Arthur's grandmother, Mrs Gillings, would have loved to have seen him grow up and marry; they talked of what had become of their children and grandchildren in this war. Lydia Brewster, living as she did quite close to the Coastguard Station, spoke of the memories evoked in her whenever she looked out of her bedroom window and saw the present-day coastguards on patrol along the cliff top by the lighthouse.

'I'm reminded of you – Bill and Tovell and David – when I see them in their khaki battledress, rifles on their shoulders. They tell me their duties are the same as yours – still coast watching, still looking for mines, and for spies and saboteurs landing – or signs that they already have landed. Little has changed really except there are so many aeroplanes around which they have to be able to identify and I do pity them trying to rescue seafarers when they are obstructed by barbed wire and mines. I'll be glad when they get their navy uniforms back: it will mean the war is over at last. Yes, I shall never forget the day in 1914 Mr Collins arrived and told me he was taking over the running of the Station – in place of my husband.'

This led to a discussion about Mr Collins and why Alec had been called to the Collins's home. Claire, who had been sitting quietly in a corner, paid more attention at this change in the conversation. 'We had a letter from Mr Collins,' Tovell explained. 'He had enclosed a letter for Alec and said in our note that his wife was very ill and he would be grateful if we could get the letter to Alec as a matter of urgency. Naturally, I went down to Yarmouth Fishwharf straightaway and gave the envelope to Bobby to give to Alec as soon as he docked. We owe Mr Collins a great deal for what he did for Alec when he was younger. He would never have gone to university but for the Collinses, so it was the least I could do.

Bobby told me later that in the letter Mr Collins had begged Alec to try to get some leave so that he could visit. Mrs Collins wanted to see Alec desperately and her husband felt time was running out. Alec is there now otherwise he would have been here today – as Arthur's best man.'

'Didn't Mr Collins write to you too, Mrs Brewster?' asked Mary. 'I know you and Mr Brewster went to stay with the Collinses several times once your husband had retired. I thought your two families were close.'

'Yes, that is so,' replied Lydia Brewster. 'We didn't visit so much in later years because Harold was reluctant to leave his home, so they stayed with us a couple of times. But I didn't tell them when Harold was so ill at the end. I didn't feel I should be burdening someone else with my troubles. I didn't write to Mildred until after Harold's death. I expect Mr Collins feels the same way. If his wife was asking for Alec, then that's different. He couldn't ignore her last wish – if that's what it is.'

Tovell, fearing the conversation was getting too morbid for an occasion such as a wedding, asked how many of the guests had heard the morning news broadcasts. Every one had and then discussion revolved around the announcement that Montgomery's 8th Army, together with the Canadians, had landed at dawn on the toe of Italy. 'It's still the soft underbelly of Europe but nevertheless,' Tovell pointed out, 'it's the mainland, not an island.'

'Yes,' Bill agreed, 'you could call it Europe proper. It should all be over soon. There's been no mention of American forces taking part, has there? I expect that means that they're planning a surprise attack elsewhere.'

'I've had letters from Peter over recent weeks,' said Lizzie. 'And although he's banned from saying where he is exactly, he's mentioned repeatedly how hot the weather is. I reckon he's in the Mediterranean. The Home Service said a huge naval bombardment preceded the invasion.'

'The sooner it's over and all our boys come home, the better,' said Ginny.

'Amen to that,' said Mary and Gladys in unison.

# VII

Alec looked around the study, a room in which he had spent so many happy hours, dark and gloomy now with the curtains half closed. He walked around the walls, pausing now and then to touch a favourite book. Everywhere the shelves were straining under the weight of the volumes crammed upon them. He remembered how he had felt the first time he had entered this room. How old had he been? Twelve, perhaps. His stay had been arranged by his godmother, Lydia Brewster, and had been the first of many. How he had marvelled at this array of books – hundred upon hundred of them – and how many of them he had come to love. Richard Collins had retired from teaching at the nearby public school about a year before Alec's first visit. Although he had ended his career as headmaster, even in those later years he had ensured that he conducted some classes himself. He had told Alec how much he missed his pupils and how he felt his life had little purpose once he had left his profession. Alec never knew whether this was true or whether Mr Collins was just trying to make him feel more comfortable with the arrangement; to feel he was not accepting charity but rather that he was the one doing the favours by allowing himself to be taught. And Richard Collins was a brilliant teacher; Alec had felt inspired by his tuition. Mrs Collins too – or Aunt Mildred as she insisted Alec call her – tutored him as well. She had trained as a teacher before her marriage – as had his godmother – but was not allowed to continue once she was wed. She had told Alec on one occasion when her husband was out, how much she regretted leaving her profession and how much she enjoyed teaching him. He was sorry that she was gone.

There were voices in the hall; he heard Richard Collins thanking the doctor for coming; then the front door opened and closed. A couple of minutes passed before Richard Collins entered the study. He seemed to have aged considerably since Alec's last visit – an overnight stay on his way back to base from a naval training course at Portsmouth. The scars on his face – a legacy from Passchendaele – seemed deeper or perhaps his face was just thinner and his features more haggard. He was bent forward and his crippled left arm swung slightly in front of him as he shuffled towards his desk. Alec went forward and said, 'Why don't you sit down whilst I make us both a cup of tea.'

'Thank you, Alec. While you do that I'd better telephone the undertaker. The doctor has made out the death certificate so I can arrange for them to take Mildred … away.'

'I'm so sorry,' said Alec. 'I know you had been married a long time.'

'Yes, over forty years I believe. But the last few months have been very gruelling. I'm relieved they are over. No one should have to go on suffering pain …'

'I'll go and make that tea,' said Alec. He did not hurry in the kitchen, wanting to give his former tutor time to recover. When he returned to the study with the tea tray Richard Collins was replacing the telephone on its stand.

'They are going to arrange the funeral for next Friday.'

'Oh, I'm sorry,' said Alec, 'but I can't stay that long. They would only grant me seventy two hours leave.'

'That's alright. It doesn't matter. The important thing is that you got here while Mildred was alive. She wanted to see you very badly, Alec – to say goodbye. Did she ever tell you that she regarded you as the son she didn't have? I'm afraid she had a lot of regrets. But then, show me the person who says he has no regrets and I will show you a liar.'

'I can get a message to Mrs Brewster for you. I'm sure she would want to come to the funeral.'

Richard Collins looked up sharply. 'No! Please don't do that. I don't want Lydia here.' He continued in a quieter tone of voice. 'She buried her own spouse a few years back and told us afterwards. She obviously wanted to spare us the funeral. I'll write to her when it's all over. Don't worry: Mildred will have plenty of mourners. Old friends, former teachers will attend I'm sure and when I was a house master she took a great interest in the boys. They were an outlet for her maternal instincts, I suppose. There will be a few who regarded her as a surrogate mother who will want to attend – if this war hasn't already killed them all.'

'Will you stay here or will you sell the house and buy something smaller?' Alec asked gently.

Richard Collins smiled. 'I'm glad you asked that,' he said. 'I've something to show you.' He unlocked a drawer in his desk and handed a document to Alec. 'It's a copy of Mildred's will. Read it!'

'I'm not sure I should be looking at this. It's private; nothing to do with me.'

'It has everything to do with you. Read it!' Alec scanned the pages and when he looked up, speechless with shock, Richard Collins commented in amused tones, 'I told you she regarded you as a son.'

'But surely this house was owned by you both jointly?'

'No, I was always the poor relation. I came to the marriage with nothing so it is fitting that I leave it with nothing. My wife was from a wealthy family; they bought her this house as a wedding present when she married me.'

'I cannot believe that Aunt Mildred would leave you without a home. When did she make this will?'

'Yes, I must not be melodramatic. I don't think she intended to leave me without a roof over my head. She made that will some years ago when my health had deteriorated. We both expected me to go first: a logical conclusion given the various injuries I had sustained in the war. She expected to live for many years after I was gone. But she was anxious that if she then had an accident that the house should not be sold and that the proceeds, along with her personal wealth, should not be divided amongst her numerous relatives who had always ignored her. I think she then forgot that she had made the will.'

'But you had not forgotten. Why didn't you remind her about the will – especially when she became ill?'

'Ah, well, let's say I had my reasons.'

'It doesn't matter anyway. I don't want the house,' said Alec emphatically. 'And I don't want Aunt Mildred's money either.'

'You would rather her greedy relatives have it all?'

'Of course not. The house and the money belong to you, by rights.'

'Not according to this legal document, drawn up by her solicitor and witnessed by his clerk.'

'Then I'll have to have a solicitor draw up another document. Anyway, there's no guarantee I'm going to survive the war. The E-boats are still faster than the new Dog Boats; we often come off badly with heavy casualties. Whilst the details are being sorted out, promise me you'll go on living in the house as though nothing had happened.'

That October all the motor gunboats were converted to carry torpedoes in addition to their other armaments. When it was the turn of Alec's boat, the crew was given a few days leave. Alec had had no intention of spending the time at home, but Bobby had news which made him change his mind. 'Father came to see me whilst you were at sea. Lizzie has heard that Peter is a prisoner of war. She'd been getting increasingly worried when she didn't hear from him. Naturally, she's distraught and Father wants both of us to try to visit, if only for a short time.'

'How the hell did that happen?' Alec demanded.

'Well, we can only guess, of course,' replied his half-brother. 'He could have been captured at any time during the last months. The Navy was heavily involved in the invasions of both Sicily and Italy and we've had to keep the sea lanes open to Malta and the Middle East. I bet our boys were with the Yanks when they landed at Salerno and Anzio last month and obviously we would have had losses. Peter's ship could have been sunk and the survivors taken prisoner. According to Father, Lizzie's beside herself because she's feeling guilty about something or other; she thinks she's let Peter down.'

'The Navy transferred Dog Boats to the Med, though not from here, and from what we've heard they've done sterling work spying out the coastlines before the invasions. But at least one has been sunk by shore batteries and the survivors taken prisoner, so I suppose the same thing could have happened to Peter. Maybe he won't be a prisoner for long. The new Italian Government, which took over after Mussolini resigned, soon surrendered, didn't they? We're not fighting the Italians anymore, so as long as we get moving and drive the Germans out of Italy quickly, Peter could soon be free.'

'I can't see us driving them out quickly. Rommel is in command in the north and they're rushing reinforcements to Italy as fast as they can. But that's good news for the Russians: it takes some of the heat off them though from what they say in the papers, they're doing all right driving Jerry back anyway. But if Peter was taken weeks ago I shouldn't think he's still in Italy. He'll have been transferred to a prison camp in Germany by now.'

When Alec arrived home he tried to say all the comforting words which were expected of him to his mother and half-sister, but at the first opportunity, when he was in the scullery he asked, 'Where's Claire, Mother?'

'She isn't here, Alec,' replied Ginny, watching his reaction closely. 'The RAF has sent so many of the men abroad lately that they've had to increase the number of WAAFs stationed at Haisbro. They've been moved to larger accommodation at Bacton: the house where they were quartered in the village was far too small. Claire had to go with them. She should have been billeted with the others before. She stayed with us only because of Bella. Are you sorry she's gone?'

'No, Claire was always arguing.'

Ginny laughed. 'It takes two to argue, Alec.'

'Ok. So **we** were always arguing.'

'Your father and I are always arguing. It's normal.'

Alec stared at his mother for a moment and then said, 'No, it's you that's always arguing. Father never says much when you're carrying on about something. I was right in the first place: it doesn't take two to argue, it only takes one. You're an argumentative type and so is Claire.' Then, thinking he might have upset his mother, he said casually, 'I thought I saw Bella in the paddock.'

'Yes, she's stayed with us. I'm glad because at least we see something of Claire when she comes to exercise Bella. I miss Claire: she was good company. Your father misses her too. He says she reminds him of me.'

'She's not a bit like you,' said Alec, surprised.

'You just said we were both argumentative. Anyway, he doesn't mean in appearance but he says she's just like me in every other way – you know, in personality and outlook.'

'I don't know where he gets that one from – '

'Well he should know, Alec. You see me only as a mother; perhaps there are sides to me that only he has seen.'


Alec remembered what Bobby had said and he tried to find out what it was that Lizzie had on her conscience. She told him she was tormented by the fact that Peter, at the end of his last leave, had left behind a watch which he had always taken to sea with him. 'If I'd only found it straight away, I would have chased after him. But it was days later when I was tidying his drawers – putting away the clothes I'd laundered ready for his next leave – that I came across it. He would have been at sea by then.'

'You shouldn't feel bad about it, Lizzie. It wasn't your fault that Peter left it behind. And he didn't get captured just because he didn't have that particular watch on him,' said Alec, trying to sound reassuring. 'I expect he was just unlucky: in the wrong place at the wrong time.'

'There you are, you see. Even you think luck played a part in his capture,' Lizzie retorted. Alec cursed himself for his unfortunate choice of words as his half-sister continued. 'It was no ordinary watch: it was Sergeant Harris's gold watch and chain.'

'In that case, Peter probably decided to leave it at home for safety. No-one takes a gold watch and chain to sea. I'm amazed it never got stolen.'

Lizzie was not convinced by these remarks. 'You don't understand, Alec. You never knew Sergeant Harris. He was billeted with Peter and his mother. Peter was very fond of him: I can still remember how upset he was when he heard that the sergeant had died. He regarded that watch as a good luck charm – a talisman. Maybe he thought that whilst he had it on him, Sergeant Harris was watching over him. Bobby would understand: he told Peter once that he felt the same way about HMS *Norfolk*. That was his talisman.'

'It didn't do him much good in the Arctic, did it?' Alec commented.


Lizzie confessed to Lydia Brewster, in the end, what it was that was really troubling her. 'I feel so guilty about Peter. We could have had so much more time together but for me. Even when we were little, both growing up at the Coastguard Station, he was fond of me. George, Mary's elder son, was always teasing him about it. They were pals, if you remember, and almost the same age.' Lydia smiled and nodded her head as Lizzie continued. 'But the teasing made no difference to Peter. He kept asking me to marry him for years: every time he came home on leave he asked me. But I kept turning him down. It wasn't that I didn't want to marry him: it was because I didn't want to give up teaching.'

'I know, my dear,' replied Lydia. 'I was the one who encouraged you to train as a teacher. I knew you would be a very good one and you were – you are now. The fault lay with the system; not with you. It was wrong that we had to choose – teaching or marriage. We couldn't have both. Thousands, I'm sure, chose as you did to go on teaching. I remember saying to my daughter, Muriel, after the Great War ended what a pity it was that a generation of young men had been killed and that women like her would never know the joys of marriage and family. She said I was not to feel sorry for her because she doubted whether she could have sacrificed all those years of training and a profession which she loved, to get married. She also said that if she had wed and then had not been blessed with children, she would have felt that her life had been wasted. Of course, she has her friend Caroline. They both lecture at one of the women's colleges in Oxford. They share a house and Muriel says no husband could ever have been a more loving companion. They've even bought a burial plot to share. I think that's rather lovely, don't you?

But I digress. Let's hope this war brings more changes for the good. The last war brought us the vote – I think it was an acknowledgement of the wonderful work women had done during the war. Of course, when it was first granted in 1918 it was only for women over thirty who were either householders or the wives of householders. It wasn't until 1928, as you will remember, that it was extended to women over twenty one. Let's just hope the government appreciates what women have done in this war. Even around this district we have women serving in Civil Defence as Air Raid Wardens, Fire Watchers and the like. Only last April, women up to fifty-one were called-up to work in the Armed Services, the Land Army or in the factories. Now we have women auxiliaries in the Home Guard. If we're good enough to do all these things in wartime, we're good enough to work in industry or the professions in peacetime - without having to choose between that and marriage.'

'It's just that I feel so guilty at the way I've treated Peter – and not just because I kept putting off marrying him. You know how much he adores Molly. He's been saying for a long time that she needs a little brother or sister but I've argued against that. I kept telling him that it wasn't right to bring another child into the world as it is now. And I harped on the threat of invasion. The truth is I was so happy to be teaching again that I didn't want to give it up – not even to have another baby. Now he's been taken prisoner and could be locked up for years – he could even die in captivity. I feel so bad about not wanting to make him happy above everything else. He's always been so good and kind. I feel so guilty.'

'Lizzie dear, we are all of us racked with guilt. We all look back and are tormented by the things we've done.'

Lizzie smiled. 'Not you, Aunt Lydia. I'm sure you've never done a single thing in your life of which you're ashamed. You cannot possibly know what it is to feel guilty.'

'Oh, Lizzie, if only that were true. Believe me, dear, I've had plenty to feel guilty about. The only thing to do is reconcile yourself to it and try to make amends when you can.'


The stress and upset over Peter's capture was to some extent mitigated by a piece of good news in the family. Mary rushed round to tell Ginny as soon as she knew. 'Rachel's expecting. She's just told me and Doctor Lambert has confirmed what she'd suspected. I tell you, Ginny, this littl'un's come in the nick of time. The way she's been carrying on – well, I don't know how Bobby put up with it. The number of times that girl has told me she was staying late in Norwich to see *Gone with the Wind* when I know full well she was going dancing at the Samson and Hercules ballroom. I could see her evening shoes in her bag. Well, all that will have to stop now and so will all the presents that Dwight has been giving her – nylon stockings and chocolates, would you believe, Ginny? She'll have to go back to using gravy browning on her legs like all the other young women round here.'

'I wonder if Bobby knows,' said Ginny, deliberately interrupting her friend's tirade.

'Now that's a thought. He doesn't get home as much as I thought he would, being only a few miles down the coast. Still, it looks like he got home enough! I'll ask Rachel. Maybe she's written to him or perhaps she wants Tovell to give him a message. He gets to Yarmouth on business quite often, doesn't he?'


Tovell sat with Bobby in the pub near the docks. He gazed studiously down at his tankard of beer so that he would not have to look at his stepson's face as he read the letter. When Bobby had finished reading it he folded it up, put it back in its envelope and placed it in his inside pocket. He drank some more beer before saying in a trembling voice, 'It's happened. I don't know how I'm going to stomach this. All I can think of is that my Rachel's been with that bloody Yank.'

'But she's content now, Bobby. She told your mother and me that she hasn't been out dancing for weeks. And she's asked Dwight not to call for her anymore.'

Bobby looked up startled. 'Did she tell him she was expecting?'

'I don't think so. She said to us that the reason she doesn't want to go out is because she's ill. She hasn't been to the WVS in Norwich lately either and she's told the local WVS unit that when she feels better she will help out at their canteen in Haisbro. She's suffered with terrible sickness apparently – poor girl.'

'So long as he doesn't know or doesn't suspect …'

'It would help if you came home more – at least overnight even if you can't get leave. You need to be seen around with Rachel more and she would appreciate your support, I'm sure. Don't forget that this has happened because you love her and want her to be happy. Well, she is happy now in spite of being ill. You need to share that happiness with her and let her mother and everyone else see that.'


October was also the month that Mary's son, Albert, arrived home on a forty-eight hour pass. He was due to board a troopship in Liverpool and had been issued with tropical kit. He had been anxious to say goodbye to his sister, Rachel, and to his mother. The visit was strained and the farewells emotional. 'The way he hugged Rachel it was as though he was sure he'd never see her again,' Mary said to Ginny. Turning to Tovell, she asked, 'Where do you think he's headed?'

'I wouldn't be surprised if they were sailing for India,' Tovell replied. 'The Japs have made several attempts to invade India from Burma. I think we must be massing a bigger army there.'

'Last Christmas I'd convinced myself he was fighting the Japanese – until that Christmas card came,' Mary reflected ruefully. 'Now you're telling me he could really be fighting them this Christmas.'

'No, not that soon,' Tovell assured her. 'They've got to get there first and the voyage will take weeks; then they'll have to give them training in jungle warfare. You couldn't launch an attack on the Japs without special training first.'

'I suppose that's some comfort,' said Mary. 'But when you think that the Far East has been such a dreadful place for the Royal Norfolks – the

$4^{th}$, $5^{th}$ and $6^{th}$ Battalions have been prisoners of the Japanese since the fall of Singapore, haven't they? Why do they have to send the $2^{nd}$ Battalion there too? That seems downright cruel to me.'


The news that was released in October, which cheered the seafaring men of the family, was the announcement that towards the end of the previous month, midget submarines had dared to enter Altenfiord in occupied Norway and lay explosive charges beneath the hull of the *Tirpitz,* the *Kriegsmarine's* modern battleship. Bobby, Alec and Arthur celebrated the news in the Westgates' kitchen with Bill.

'It was the fear that the *Tirpitz* was on the prowl which led the Admiralty to scatter convoy PQ17 - with tragic results,' said Bobby with feeling. 'Although they didn't manage to sink the *Tirpitz,* they must have badly damaged her. The aerial photos showed her surrounded by small ships – repair boats, no doubt – and the oil slick was two miles long. Hopefully, she'll never leave that fiord again and be no more threat to our Arctic – or North Atlantic – convoys.'

'Yes, you've got to take your hats off to those boys in the midget subs,' said Bill. 'They must have had a hell of a job creeping through the minefields protecting her.'

'It's a miracle they got anywhere near her,' said Alec. 'She'd have had heavy anti-submarine netting just below the water all around her. The report said three of our midget subs were lost. It didn't say what had happened to the crews. Maybe some of them got to the surface and were rescued – taken prisoner.'

'It makes you think we might be that much closer to winning the war, doesn't it?' said Arthur. 'We're definitely winning the battle to get the convoys through – the food and the war supplies. I reckon this year has been the turning point. Do you realize that two convoys actually reached Britain from America without any losses at all - and they sank some U-boats on the way?'

'It's been the same with the Russian convoys,' said Bobby. 'They've been getting through with fewer losses, thank God.'

'Of course, we've got the air cover now – aircraft carriers and the very long range Liberator bombers Roosevelt loaned the RAF,' said Arthur. 'But I suppose we should acknowledge that it's the boffins who are really winning the war for us. Think how they've developed radar. The short wave one we use in our aircraft has made a huge difference to locating surface vessels and with most Navy escort vessels having radar and Huff-Duff on board, we're beating the U-boat wolf packs.'

'Claire would be pleased to hear you say that,' Alec exclaimed involuntarily. 'She's always singing the praises of radar.' Afterwards, Alec wondered whatever had put Claire into his mind. He had been trying so hard to make sure that thoughts of her did not enter his head.


Air raids continued throughout November, both sides attacking relentlessly. Ipswich suffered a particularly bad onslaught on the third when 1700 houses in the town suffered damage from incendiary bombs. On the sixth, the Chief of Bomber Command announced that his intention was to destroy every centre of production vital to the enemy's war effort. The sound of aircraft, day and night, leaving the airfields of Norfolk and Suffolk for Germany, bore out his pledge. The broadcasts and the newspaper reports also indicated heavy attacks on Berlin in December and the Thursday before Christmas a huge raid, the biggest so far, of 1300 bombers and fighters, mainly American but with British support, was made on military installations. The press, in spite of official refusals to identify these sites, insisted that they were secret rocket-gun installations. This news bothered Tovell. 'The Hun was always coming up with new ideas and weapons ahead of us in the last war – until we scored a first over the development of the tank. Hope they haven't got something nasty up their sleeves this time.'

Ginny, however, could not worry too much about speculation in the press: she had the Christmas arrangements and cooking to worry about. She had asked Claire to join them but she had said she must remain at the station. Alec said the same thing: he could not leave his base, HMS *Midge*. Lizzie would be with them and little Molly, but she knew her daughter's thoughts would be with her prisoner husband, Peter. Mary had agreed to spend Christmas Day with them, as usual, but Ginny knew that she too would be fretting – for her son, Albert. Rachel would be there but Bobby kept saying he was not sure whether he could get away from the base.

There was no doubt in Ginny's mind that Christmas would be a miserable affair unless Ted and the evacuee children were there to cheer everyone up. She was worried about the additional numbers to feed now that Peggy, Roger and Will's mother and little brothers had joined them but she invited them just the same. To her dismay, they refused because their mother felt she had to cook for her employer. The problem was only solved at the last moment when the young master, to Ted's astonishment, invited some of the Land Army girls who farmed his acres to have Christmas Dinner with him. 'He's never invited anyone to spend time with him in that there house since his mother died. That's a rum old do, bor,' Ted declared to his drinking companions in the *Admiral Lord Nelson*. 'Reckon he was thinking they'd do all the cooking. He int loopy.'

The decorations went up in the Tovell household and the goose went in the oven early on Christmas morning. The family walked to morning service at St Mary's, collected Rachel, Mary, Ted and the family on their way back and found Bobby waiting for them when they got home. As she embraced her son, Ginny reminded him that it was a year to the day that he had returned from the dead and how happy she was that he would be sitting down to dinner with them all that day.

The afternoon went well. They sang and played games with the children and even the youngest two boys, who were used to visiting the Tovells by then, joined in as though they had always spent Christmases at their home. The children's mother, Joan, was a little tearful at times, understandably, since this was the first Christmas Day her children had been all together since Christmas 1939. She did not mention her late husband and no one else mentioned him either. Everyone enjoyed the festive tea which Ginny had prepared as much as they had enjoyed their dinner, but as soon as the table had been cleared, Bobby announced that he must return to base. Rachel was very upset and pleaded with him to stay but he insisted that he had to leave. After his departure they tried playing more games but Rachel said she felt unwell. Tovell, in spite of the petrol restrictions, decided he had better give her and her mother a lift home in the lorry. On his return, he felt obliged to offer the same service to Ted and his adopted family.

'You won't believe this,' he told Ginny on his return, 'but the land girls were still at the farmhouse. You could hear the music and the laughter. Old Ted couldn't get over it. The young master must have discovered rather late in life the joys of female company.'

Ginny was too occupied with thoughts of her own to share Tovell's amusement. 'I wish Bobby hadn't left like that. Poor Rachel had been so pleased to see him. He was acting very strangely. The baby's showing a bit now but I noticed several times that it was as though he couldn't bear to look at her. And that decision to go back to base was very sudden. He hadn't mentioned it before.'

'Perhaps he thought it would upset Rachel – and you – and spoil the afternoon if he mentioned it earlier.'

'I don't know. Something is just not right between them. I don't know what it is but I hope they soon sort it out. This should be such a happy time for them both.'

Bobby spent the rest of Christmas Night sitting in his little office on Yarmouth Fishwharf with a bottle of rum for company. He fell into a tortured sleep – drowning in the Arctic one minute and fighting American airmen, one in particular, the next. He was still there next morning, a Sunday, but there were thankfully no emergencies. The unofficial Christmas truce must be holding, he thought. He switched on the wireless and heard that Eisenhower had been appointed on Christmas Day as Commander-in-Chief of all the forces on the Second Front. He switched the set off mumbling, 'Another American. Can't get away from them,' and promptly went back to sleep. More rum, more nightmares and then it was Monday and officially Boxing Day. He turned on the wireless again and this time the news jolted him out of his rum-befuddled slumbers. The *Scharnhorst*, the battle-cruiser which the previous year had humiliated the Royal Navy by escaping through the Straits of Dover to Germany, had been sunk before she could attack an Arctic convoy. What was more, the ship which had first sighted the *Scharnhorst* and had been the first to fire on her and damage her, had been Bobby's talisman, HMS *Norfolk*. He had always followed intently any news about Arctic convoys and had been delighted in November at the announcement that two of them had got through to Russia completely unscathed. Now this sinking must surely mean that, with *Tirpitz* severely damaged and still confined to her fiord for repairs, the danger to his former comrades on the Arctic route must be greatly diminished. The broadcaster was calling this confrontation between the *Scharnhorst* and the cruisers of the Royal Navy escort, the

Battle of the North Cape. Bobby liked the sound of that. He would get himself cleaned up and go and find his brother Alec. They must celebrate the Battle of the North Cape together. What a pity Peter was not here to share the celebration with them.

# 1944

# I

The conversation in the *Admiral Lord Nelson* was once more dominated by discussions about tides, the position of the moon and weather forecasts, as a likely indicator of when the invasion would be. This time the invasion they were speculating about was not the invasion of Britain by Germany but the invasion of occupied France by the Allies. Heavy bombing of the French coast, especially the Pas de Calais area, was assumed to be a preliminary bombardment as were the attacks on what the announcers on the wireless called "military installations." The news that Montgomery had been brought home from Italy and been put in charge of the British armies for the Second Front, together with letters from relatives living in ports like Felixstowe, stating that the town was jamb-packed with soldiers, made the invasion seem so imminent that bets were laid nightly as to the date.

Bobby, Alec and Arthur, conferring together at the Westgates at the end of March, were also convinced that the invasion must come soon. Bobby had recently had a drink with a former shipmate on leave in Great Yarmouth. 'He said the Russian convoys have been suspended already. They did that last summer again but that was because the passage was so dangerous once the ships were vulnerable to constant air attack in perpetual daylight. But to suspend them in early spring can only mean the Royal Navy escorts are needed for the invasion. He's heard they're withdrawing ships from the North Atlantic too. It seems like every ship of the Home Fleet is being taken out of northern waters.'

'It's the same with Coastal Forces,' said Alec. 'Some of our flotillas have already gone south and they've been replaced by flotillas from Scotland. One of them is manned totally by Norwegians. They've been operating in their own waters through the winter but it's too dangerous now with longer hours of daylight – same as in the Arctic. We've also been told that patrolling the Z line to protect our East Coast convoys against E-boat attacks has got to take priority, so we're not to go on so many attacking raids on Jerry's convoys off the Dutch coast. That can only mean that we can't afford to lose any of our supplies: they must be needed for the big day. Have you had any indicators, Arthur?'

'I know there's been a massive build up of American Air Force operations all this month. They've been flying constant bombing mission over Germany from the Suffolk and the Norfolk bases. We've had to be on station in case they ditch on the return flight. With so much going on we've had joint operations with the air sea rescue launches from Lowestoft and Felixstowe. It's a hell of a task. We're covering a ninety mile stretch along our coastline extending a hundred miles east to the Dutch coast. The sky between Felixstowe, Cromer and Holland must be the busiest for air traffic in Europe. Thank heavens there's an air sea rescue station at Wells-next-the-Sea now to cover the stretch north from The Wash. The raids must be in preparation for an invasion – can't be for anything else.

By the way, something strange happened yesterday. We picked up some Americans from a ditched Fortress. One of them was in a really bad way; I don't know if he made it. An ambulance was waiting when we docked at Gorleston. Anyway, what I wanted to tell you was, when he was aboard our launch, one of his mates realized he wanted to look at the photo he had of his girlfriend. This chap got the picture out of the man's wallet but as he went to hand it to the poor bloke he dropped it on the deck. I picked it up and – it was uncanny – the girl in the picture was the spitting image of your Rachel, Bobby.'

Mary was concerned in April when reports were made public about operations in the Burmese jungle by a force under Wingate. They had established an airfield 150 miles behind the Japanese lines and a large Commonwealth army had been flown there. 'I just know that's where my Albert is,' Mary told Ted as soon as he entered her living room. 'He's in Burma, in the jungle fighting the Japs. We've just been listening to the news, haven't we, Rachel?'

'Yes, we both think it's too much of a coincidence with father-in-law thinking he was being trained in jungle warfare,' said Rachel.

Ted muttered a few words of sympathy but he had called on them early that morning to tell them some news he had heard the previous night. It seemed, however, that no-one was particularly interested in what he had to say because he had only uttered a few words before Mary returned to her concerns about her son and Rachel got up and left the house. Ted abandoned his unreceptive audience and went about his business.


Four hours later, Ted was driving Bessie along a cart track between two fields when he realized that something was partly obstructing the path. 'Whoa, gal!' he called out to the mare, pulling on the reins. He dismounted and went to investigate. At first, what he saw shocked him into silence, then he exclaimed sadly, 'Oh, dearie, dearie me! Poor little old girl.' He hurried back to his wagon, climbed aboard and yelled and waved to two Land Army girls working in the field adjacent to the track. They looked up, recognized him, waved back and then went on working. In desperation, Ted grabbed his shotgun and fired two shots in the air. They looked round again, saw him waving the gun indicating that he needed them, and ran across the field to him. By the time they reached the cart he had climbed down again. He tried to stop the younger land girl, no more than seventeen, from going any further along the path but she looked over his shoulder and screamed so piercingly at what she saw that other women workers on the next field heard her and came running. Before they arrived on the scene, the older woman hit her young companion to stop her hysterics. Then she went over to the figure lying in the grass and felt for a pulse even though she did not expect to find one. Suddenly, she cried out, 'The baby's still alive. He just moved.' As she spoke, the other two women reached her. One of them, seeing the situation, immediately led the sobbing girl away and sat her down, shaking violently, where she could not hear what was being said.

The other woman went to help her friend. 'I've got some nail scissors in my pocket, Janet. What can we use for a clip?'

'Your hair slide will do if it's a tight fit,' the older woman replied. As she spoke, she peeled off her green jumper and held it out for her friend to place the baby in it and wrap the material around him. 'You go with Ted and take the littl'un to the doctor in the village. Better get the other two to go with you in the wagon. I'll stay here with this poor girl – 'til the police get here. You'll call at the constable's house too, won't you?'

The woman nodded. 'What about you, Janet? Are you going to be alright here with – this poor lass?'

'Yes, I'll be alright. You'd better hurry. He may not last long without help. It's a miracle he's still alive.'


An hour later, the village constable arrived with a man in civilian dress. They were both clearly upset by what they saw. 'What's your name, miss?' asked the plain clothes policeman, taking a notebook and pencil from his pocket.

'Janet Harding,' answered the Land Army woman. 'We didn't hear her. We were working on the far side of that field but we didn't hear her cry out or call to us. I'll never understand why we didn't hear her.'

The man nodded as he looked around and made notes in his book. 'I take it you haven't moved anything, miss? She was exactly like this when you found her, was she?'

The woman hesitated before she replied. 'I did move one thing – her frock. Her last thought must have been to save the baby. She'd dragged him onto her middle and pulled the skirt of her frock up around him – to try to keep him warm. I couldn't leave her like that – all exposed – so I pulled it back down.'

'Right, well, thank you, miss. You can go now if you like. The constable will stay with her until the ambulance arrives. There'll have to be a post mortem to establish the cause of death, although I don't think there's much doubt about that – clearly, the poor girl bled to death.' Turning to the uniformed policeman he said, 'When they've taken her away, you'd better do something about this mess. Don't want the public chancing upon it. Could give some old dear a heart attack. No downpour, however heavy, is going to wash this lot away. Probably best to set fire to the area.'

'Yes, sir,' replied the village constable. 'I'll close this path off; stop people from coming along here 'til then. Better wait for you to give me the all clear to start the fire, had I?'

'Yes, I'll let you know after the post mortem,' said his superior. 'But I can't think there'll be any suspicious circumstances. Just a pity the poor girl was out here alone when it happened.'

'What was her name? Are you trying to contact her husband?' asked Janet Harding.

'Yes,' replied the village constable. 'Ted Carter knew who she was – known her since childhood, so he said. Dreadfully upset is old Ted. And he knew where to contact her husband. Seems he isn't far away: he's stationed at Great Yarmouth. I've already spoken to the police there and someone's on their way to his base. What a terrible bit of news to have to give to a man. Her name was Rachel – Mrs Rachel Adams.'

# II

Tovell sat white-faced as Ginny told him what had happened. He had been out in his lorry making deliveries all day and had been totally shocked when he had come home and been told the news.

'Poor Mary,' said Ginny. 'She's already lost one son and now her daughter.'

'What about Bobby?' Tovell demanded. 'Has anyone seen Bobby?'

'No,' Ginny replied. 'The policemen who broke the news to him at the Fishwharf drove him straight to the Norfolk and Norwich Hospital. Apparently, when Ted and the Land Army girls got the baby to Doctor Lambert's house, the District Nurse happened to be there. She took care of the littl'un whilst the doctor drove his car and they went straight to Norwich with him. I was wondering, now you're home, as soon as you've had something to eat, could you drive Mary and me there?'

'I don't think I fancy anything to eat. Let me get cleaned up and then we'll go.'

'Tovell, I think I know now what was wrong – why Bobby was acting so strangely with Rachel last Christmas.'

Tovell glanced anxiously at his wife. 'What do you mean?' he asked sharply.

'Mary thinks Rachel must have been feeling ill and suddenly wanted some fresh air because she left the house abruptly whilst Ted was talking to Mary.'

'Ted? What was Ted doing there?'

'He was passing and just dropped off to tell them something he thought might interest them. He'd been drinking with some American airmen in the pub the night before and they'd told him that their plane had got badly mauled and they'd had to ditch. The Air Sea Rescue people picked them up. What Ted wanted to tell Mary and Rachel was that they'd said their friend Dwight – the Texan Claire brought here and who was a friend of Bobby and Rachel's – had been badly injured and they didn't think he would live. It was then that Rachel ran off. Mary didn't think anything of it and I'm certainly not going to point it out to her, but I think that news was what caused Rachel to have the baby like that.'

'Perhaps you're right,' Tovell muttered, trying to sound casual.

'Don't run off,' she said as Tovell moved back into the scullery to wash. 'The point I'm trying to make is, what if Dwight and Rachel did more than go dancing together? I know Bobby was the one who suggested that – I never could understand what had got into him – but what if he suspected that it was Dwight's baby and not his? That would explain why he didn't seem able to bring himself to look at Rachel when she was carrying.'

'You're right – whatever you do don't mention this to Mary. Let me get changed and we'll drive to Norwich. I think I've got enough petrol coupons left. Thank heaven we're running a business or we wouldn't have those.'


Mary, Ginny and Tovell gazed down at the tiny infant in his cot. He seemed to be sleeping peacefully enough and there was nothing laboured about his breathing. Ginny was struck by how like Bobby he was when he was a new baby and for a moment she wondered whether her suspicions about his parentage were unfounded. Then she recalled the occasion when Claire had driven into their yard and she had mistaken Dwight for Bobby. Mary bent over the cot and stroked the baby's head tenderly. Ginny knew her thoughts would be with her dead daughter so she nudged Tovell, gesturing towards the door. 'We'll leave you to have a few minutes alone with your grandchild,' she said gently. 'We'll be in the waiting room, Mary, when you're ready to leave.'

Bobby was sitting there bent forward, elbows resting on his knees, his head in his hands, when they entered the waiting room. Ginny took the seat beside him and placed her hand on his forearm in a comforting gesture. 'I'm so sorry, Bobby,' she whispered. He nodded, tight lipped, face screwed up, unable to reply. Tovell took the seat opposite; Ginny could feel his distress.

They sat in strained silence for several minutes before Bobby looked up at Ginny and, in a sudden outburst, exclaimed, 'Why the hell did she have to leave the house if she felt ill? Why didn't she stay with her mother?'

'Perhaps she thought she'd feel better if she had some fresh air,' Ginny replied, soothingly. Bobby shook his head despairingly, put his hands back over his eyes, and was silent once more. After a while, Ginny tentatively asked, 'Have you been to see the baby yet?' Bobby shook his head. 'Perhaps you should,' said his mother. 'It might help.'

Enraged by this, Bobby shouted, 'Why the hell should I want to see it? Rachel's dead because of it.'

Taken aback by the fury in her son's tone, Ginny said nervously, 'I didn't mean to upset you. I'll go back and join Mary.' With a worried glance at Tovell, she got up immediately and made for the door.

She was outside in the corridor and about to close the waiting room door when she heard Tovell speaking his own words of condolence. His voice was low so she could not hear exactly what he said but her son's response was loud and clear. 'You're sorry! Is that all you can say? You're sorry! This is all your fault. I'm going to regret all my life that I listened to you. She'd be alive now if it wasn't for you. You killed my Rachel.'


No-one spoke on the journey home. The three of them sat in silence in the cab of the wagon. Mary's face was a picture of misery and Ginny, sitting beside Tovell, could feel her husband's tension. Mary refused to stay the night at the Tovells saying she needed to be alone and so, with some trepidation as to whether it was wise for her to be on her own, they left her at her house. Ginny felt that some comforting word that there was still a future was a necessary precaution. Her parting comment, therefore, as they saw Mary into her cottage, was, 'He looked a sturdy little lad, Mary. I'm sure it won't be too long before they let you bring your grandchild home.'

Ginny was thankful that Lizzie did not appear as soon as they got indoors. Obviously, she had not heard the lorry come back or she and Molly would have been round asking after the baby. She made some tea and took the tray into the living room and set it down on the table. Tovell seemed unaware of her presence: he was sitting in his armchair staring at the embers in the grate of the cooking range. She poured the tea, placed his cup on the little table beside his chair and sat down in her own seat opposite him. After a few sips of tea, she said, 'I heard what Bobby said to you. I know you're in torment. You'd better tell me why he was blaming you for Rachel's death.'

Tovell looked up, seemingly as surprised to see his wife sitting there as he was at her words. It was several seconds before he replied, 'Bobby was right: it was my fault. I broke the cardinal rule – never interfere in other people's lives.'

'Aaah,' said Ginny with a wry smile. 'So that's what he was accusing you of. I know exactly how that feels. I'm sure you acted with the best of intentions. We all do – when we interfere.'

'This wasn't something minor: a bit of advice which didn't matter either way. This was major and it did lead to her death. He was right to say that.'

'Your tea is there beside you,' said Ginny quietly. 'Drink some while you decide whether you want to tell me what happened.'

'Whether I want to confess, you mean?' Now it was Tovell who smiled wryly. 'I seem to recall having a conversation like this before, only then I was the one telling you that confession was good for the soul.'

'And you were right. It did help me.' Then with a slight laugh, she added, 'Do you realize that was almost thirty years ago?'

'I do want to tell you because I hate to keep anything from you. But you must promise me that you won't mention it to anyone, not even to Bobby. He has cause to hate me now; he would never forgive me if he knew I had also betrayed his secret.'

'I promise – of course I do.'

'You were almost right in what you said this morning, except that there's no doubt about who the baby's father is – it's Dwight. The injuries Bobby got in the Arctic meant he would never father a child – the doctor told him that. He was distraught about it, naturally, because he knew how much Rachel wanted a family. He told me about it one night in the pub – I guess he had to tell some one. His fear was that Rachel would leave him if she knew. I don't think he ever had any other girlfriend, did he? She meant everything to him. That was when I put my nose in and suggested he find a look-alike from amongst our comrades from overseas. When Claire brought Dwight here and you mistook him for Bobby and he told us he'd been asked to take Rachel dancing, I knew Bobby had taken my advice. If I'd only kept my mouth shut Rachel would still be alive.'

'Perhaps not, dearest,' said Ginny kindly. 'Mary had been worried about Rachel for a long time – ever since she first went to Norwich to work for the WVS. She was off dancing and staying out all night; Mary was afraid they'd be a baby then. I kept that from you – well, I wasn't absolutely sure that Mary had got it right, of course. Strangely enough, when Rachel announced that she was expecting, it never occurred to Mary that it might not be Bobby's baby. Best to leave it that way, I reckon. And best not to tell Bobby how Rachel was behaving whilst he was at sea – and when she thought he was dead.'

'Yes, I agree. It would only make matters worse. We must let him have some happy memories of Rachel. I'm not sure all that information makes me feel any better though, sweetheart. I still shouldn't have interfered.'

'Oh, dear, Tovell. That means I have to confess something too. You're not the only one around here who is an interfering so-and-so. I put my oar in and ruined Alec and Claire's lives.'

Tovell looked at his wife quizzically. 'I know Alec and Claire fell out and haven't spoken to one another or been near one another since, but are you saying it's your fault?'

'Yes, I'm afraid it is. I meant well, as you did with Bobby and Rachel, but I should have minded my own business and let them sort their lives out themselves.'

'So what did you do that was so bad?' asked Tovell.

'Well, Claire has always adored Alec – from childhood, so she said. Alec, on the other hand, only saw her as a friend. With him, it was just the way you said it should be – pals. He was fond of her but not in the way she wanted. And yes, I know you said I shouldn't get ideas and that Alec wasn't in her class; but I thought they'd be a perfect match. Anyway, first of all I told her to make him jealous – so that he'd see her as other men saw her; not as a friend.'

'Didn't that work?' There was a hint of amusement in Tovell's voice.

'It was a total failure so I advised her to …, be creative.'

'Creative?'

'Yes, creative. You know …., give him a bit of encouragement.'

Tovell laughed out loud at that. 'Yes, I'm getting the message. You mean you encouraged her to be creative with Alec the way you were with me all those years ago?'

'Yes, that sort of thing,' replied Ginny sheepishly. 'Of course, I wasn't specific and I definitely didn't tell her what I did with you but she understood what I meant. Trouble is, it didn't work and Alec was so offended that, as you said, they haven't spoken since. I feel so bad about it. If I hadn't interfered, Alec would probably have worked it out for himself, in the course of time, that Claire was the girl for him.'

'There's time for him to do that yet, so don't feel too badly about what you did. They're both still alive so you haven't done the harm that I have to Bobby and Rachel,' said Tovell sadly. 'What I did can never be put right.'

# III

The days which followed Rachel's death were difficult for them all. Bobby had refused his mother's request to come home with her from the hospital, saying he must return to his base. His superiors must have decided that he was not in a fit state of mind to be on duty because next day he was sighted in Haisbro banging on the door of the village constable. A little later both men were seen by the Land Army girls in the field where Rachel had died. They saw the policemen indicate the spot, now reduced to scorched and blackened scrub, and then walk slowly away. 'That poor man,' said one of the girls. 'He must be the husband. Do you think we should go over and say something?'

'No, definitely not,' said Janet Harding firmly. 'He needs to be on his own. Other people butting in would just add to his distress at this moment.' Nevertheless, she kept a wary eye on the figure as he sat on the ground staring at the burned undergrowth. When, at last, he left the field she made an excuse to return to the farm and followed him at a discreet distance until she saw him enter his mother-in-law's house. She returned to her work after that.

Mary had no success in motivating Bobby to do anything and eventually she called upon Ginny to help her to make arrangements for the funeral. The day before the funeral the baby was allowed to come home. As she cradled him, Mary said to Ginny, 'This reminds me of the last war. We were all so upset at what had happened to the men – all those deaths so close together – but what made us keep going was the littl'uns. We had to bear up for them, didn't we? I reckon it will be the same now. This little mite will keep me going. I just hope he'll do the same for Bobby.'

'I'm sure he will – in time. But now that the baby's home, what about the funeral tomorrow?' asked Ginny. 'Shall I stay here and look after him – rather than take him with us?'

'No, you ought to be at the funeral. I'll ask that Janet Harding who stayed with my Rachel … She's popped in a couple of times on her way back from the fields to see if there's any news of the littl'un.'


Bobby endured the service, the internment and the formal tea at his mother-in-law's afterwards like a man in a trance. Once more he refused his mother's invitation to go home with her and departed for Great Yarmouth as soon as he had drunk a cup of tea. Janet Harding had handed over the baby and left as soon as the funeral party had entered the house. Mary had then endeavoured to persuade her son-in-law to sit down and hold the baby but he had declined. What was more, everyone could not help noticing that he had been reluctant to even look at the child. In the days which followed, he refused to go through Rachel's possessions and did not enter their house once she had died. It was Mary, assisted by Ginny, who eventually sorted her clothes and disposed of them.

'Everything is so scarce it would be a crime to just leave them here going to waste,' said Mary, even though the task almost reduced her to tears on several occasions. She was, however, determined not to break down and Ginny was reminded of how stoical her friend had been in the face of hardship, during the previous war. Ginny ensured that she opened each drawer and container ahead of Mary but the precaution proved unnecessary when nothing incriminating, linking Rachel with the Texan, came to light.

Weeks passed and Bobby did not visit or write to his mother-in-law. Family and friends, concerned that she was bearing the stresses and strains of a young baby on her own, gave what support and practical help they could. Lizzie and Molly were frequent visitors and were happy to baby sit to give Mary a break. Lydia Brewster too, gave her time as did Ginny. She suggested that Mary and her grandchild might like to move into the Tovell household for a few months so that the two women could share the inevitable sleepless nights, but the new grandmother would have none of it. 'I know my duty,' was her reply, 'and I won't shirk it. Anyway, that Janet helps me out when she can. There's something odd about her. She joined the Land Army in '42, when they were glad to take older women who were childless widows, into the Services – so she say. Widow she may be but I don't reckon she was always childless. Right from the first day she knew how to handle that little mite. She knew how to stand up with him and walk around with him, comforting him whenever he grizzled and you've gotta have had littl'uns of your own to know that. Yes, I reckon there's a sad story there.'

In the end, Ginny wrote to her son at his base and told him he should visit his mother-in-law. She pointed out that it was not fair that she was bearing the burden of her own grief for her daughter, plus the strain of coping with a young baby, without any comforting word from him. Ginny did not receive a reply to her letter and Mary did not get a visit. Tovell, whose sense of guilt had been increased when he had realized that he had deprived Ginny of the attention of her elder son, was the one who came to Bobby's defence. 'I wouldn't be surprised if all their leave has been stopped and they're confined to base. We haven't seen anything of Alec either, have we? He hasn't been home since the funeral. When I delivered to Norwich Market yesterday I was talking to a bloke from the Midlands. He said his part of the world was full of American soldiers and he'd passed convoys of trucks and tanks on the roads, all moving south. I saw the same thing in the Norwich area. And the Army is putting up direction signs on the roads - just arrows and initials which must mean something to them. It must be the Second Front, Ginny. Perhaps we're about to invade mainland Europe at last.'

'You could be right,' Ginny agreed. 'That soft underbelly Churchill was on about has proved to be a lot tougher than he thought. Still, at least we've got as far as Rome now. The Allies entered it last evening according to the wireless today.'

When the Tovells got up at six o'clock next morning there seemed plenty of aircraft about but since the skies above Norfolk were usually busy they were not sure if this was significant. They made certain they fed the livestock quickly and got back inside the house for the eight o'clock news bulletin on the Home Service. The announcer merely mentioned that we had informed the French that we could only give them a one hour warning of attacks on any of their towns and to get out into the countryside without delay. This was enough to make Tovell tune in to the English-speaking German broadcasts which he was always discouraging Ginny from following. Sure enough, the German announcer reported that paratroopers had landed in Normandy, that the Allies were bombing Calais, Dunkirk and Le Havre and that their *Kriegsmarine* were attacking Allied landing craft.

Tovell set off for North Walsham that morning reluctant to leave the wireless set. When he reached the greengrocer's shop in the Market Place he did not have to ask if there was any news: the owner was bursting with the information that the eleven o'clock bulletin had included a message from Eisenhower that D-Day had begun today, the sixth of June. The shopkeeper had also had a telephone call from his brother in Colchester, telling how they had been unable to sleep from about three o'clock that morning because of the thousands of aircraft droning overhead. 'That's why I've kept the wireless on,' he confided. 'I was sure this was going to be the day.'

Tovell made sure he was home for the one o'clock news and he and Ginny listened to it together. They heard that Mr Churchill had told the House of Commons that the commanders had reported that everything was going according to plan and that the vast operation was the most complicated and difficult ever undertaken. When the announcer went on to speak of it being the biggest landing of troops ever and that 4,000 ships and thousands of smaller craft had made up the invasion fleet, Ginny was near to tears.

'Peter would have been there if he hadn't been a prisoner. He'll be so sorry he missed that. I wonder whether Alec and Arthur took part.'

'Dog Boats and RAF Crash Boats will have been there, I'm sure,' replied Tovell. 'But I expect our two boys were out in the North Sea waiting to rescue ditched airmen and Alec will have been fighting off the attacking E-boats as well. They'll have plenty to tell us, no doubt.'

They were glued to their wireless set again in the evening, and this time Lizzie and a sleepy Molly joined them. They listened to war correspondents describing the scenes they had witnessed on the beaches; they learned that the Allies had landed on five separate beaches – the British and the Canadians on three of them and the Americans on the other two. The King spoke, asking for their prayers, and there was a short service broadcast from the studio. The family joined in and prayed for a speedy end to the war. Lizzie added her own prayer – for the safe and prompt return of prisoners of war.

Next day the news was released that the invasion should have taken place twenty four hours earlier but was postponed due to bad weather. Although it lifted long enough for the planes to fly, the wind and rain returned immediately. It was so cold that Ginny contemplated keeping a fire going even after she had finished the day's cooking. She dismissed the idea firstly, because of the chronic shortage of coal due to the miners striking and the priority needs of the military and industry; and secondly, because it would be unpatriotic to indulge in such comforts when our soldiers where digging in to chilly rain-soaked trenches. Prior to this week, the weather had been hot and there had been no proper rain for months; the land was parched and the Tovells had feared for their crop yields. Now the rain came down relentlessly and turned their smallholding into a quagmire. Ginny did not feel it would be unpatriotic to complain about that. Tovell was more philosophical. 'Don't fret, little darling,' he said. 'This is nothing. You should have seen the mud of Flanders: it swallowed men and horses alive.'

Ginny turned to him. He had a pained faraway look in his eyes. She went to him and hugged him. 'I'm so glad you're not there now – with our boys in France. You've done your bit and I couldn't bear it if you went away again.'

The elaborate deceptions which had been put in place in the run-up to D-Day to convince Hitler that the invasion would take place anywhere other than on the Normandy beaches had, against all reasonable odds, worked perfectly. Churchill, however, mindful of the euphoria which had gripped the nation after this historic landing, warned against over-optimism. This proved to be a timely word of caution when, in the ensuing days, it became clear that our advance inland had not been as speedy as had been hoped and that the Germans were putting up a fierce defence. Tovell, reading the newspaper at the breakfast table, commented to Ginny, 'I just hope this isn't going to deteriorate into a copy of the last war – both sides facing one another across miles of trenches.'

Worse was to come when, a few days later, the news was released that the Germans were retaliating against Britain by dispatching a new weapon, one which had been hinted at for some time – a pilotless aircraft. An announcement was made in Parliament; it was described as a winged bomb, smaller than a Spitfire and probably rocket-propelled. By night it could be detected by flames at the rear; by day by the trail of smoke which it left. It flew low and straight and when its roaring stopped, its light would go out and it would explode within five to fifteen seconds. The government was confident that our multitude of gun-batteries, assisted by our myriad of searchlights at night, would shoot the invaders down before they could do much harm. The press and the news announcers were unsure of what to call this new threat, Hitler's secret weapon, until the RAF came up with an appropriate nickname for it – the doodlebug.

# IV

Ginny had not seen Lydia Brewster for some time so she volunteered to escort Peggy, Roger and Will to the cliff top home of her son's godmother. Once the children were busily engaged on their allotted gardening tasks, the two women went into the kitchen. Ginny wanted to unpack the boxes of goods which she had brought for Lydia in her role as a Women's Institute organizer. 'I'm sorry I haven't been able to bring you any children's clothes but I've given the rest which Tovell found in the attic to Peggy's mother,' Ginny explained. 'But when Mary and I were sorting through poor Rachel's things we came across some items which would probably fit an older girl. She wasn't very big, was she?'

'No, she was quite petite,' Lydia agreed. 'That might well be the reason for her tragic death.'

'That thought torments Mary; and also that she wasn't with her when it happened and how terrified she must have been.'

'Poor Rachel – so young. And of course, there's all the other young people losing their lives long before their time,' said Lydia sadly. 'But these clothes will be gratefully received by some other mothers. Please thank Mary for me. We've set up exchanges in most towns now. With all the shortages, people are really grateful that they can exchange the clothes their children have grown out of for larger sizes and know that the things they've brought in will help some other family. That must be one of the only good things you can say about war – we get better at helping one another.'

Ginny nodded. 'I'm afraid I couldn't find you much for your book salvage drive. The children's books we give to Peggy's mother, of course; but there are a few novels here. Whether they're good enough to join the stock you send as replacements to bombed out libraries, I don't know.'

'Never mind if they're not. We're grateful for everything which people donate. The WVS likes to keep some books at their rest centres and we pass a lot on to the Forces.'

'As for crockery, I could only assemble this one box of oddments. I've wrapped newspaper around each item. There are a few cups, rather more saucers and five plates; all different patterns, I'm afraid.'

'That's fine, my dear. People will be really pleased to see a bit of pattern. It must be years now since the government said all new crockery made must be plain white. Quite right too, of course. We couldn't afford to waste our scarce labour and materials on mere decoration. This stuff will be very gratefully received. Have you looked in the Eastern Daily Press's advertisement section lately? It's still full of messages from people wanting to buy crockery and furniture. That's understandable, of course. You have to be newly married or bombed out before you qualify for a government permit to buy new furniture – and then there are only the utility brands available.'

'Yes, Arthur and Margaret were lucky when they got married that they didn't have to worry about setting up home straightaway,' said Ginny. 'I gather they felt it was pointless whilst the war was on and they are both in the Services. When they get leave or a sleeping-out pass, they have Margaret's large bed-sitting room at the Westgates as a retreat.'

'I'm sure they're just happy to be able to spend a few hours together. And as for the bombed out families, even though they can get the permits to buy new, a lot of the poor dears don't have the ready cash to buy replacements straight away; so anything the rest of us can spare is a lifeline.'

Lydia suddenly remembered she had made cakes and rushed to the oven. 'Thank goodness! Another minute and they would have been burnt,' she said. 'I always try to make a few buns for the children if I know they are coming, and a jug of fruit cordial. It's lovely having them around. I never saw much of my daughter Julia's children when they were young. They didn't come to stay with us very often although I used to go to King's Lynn to see them. Harold would never come with me – he preferred his own home – so as he got weaker I didn't dare to leave him; I had to stop visiting them too. Now, of course, they're grown up and in the Forces.'

Lydia left the kitchen and walked towards the front door. Ginny accompanied her. 'If it's alright with you, I'll go and see Mary for a little while and then come back to collect the children. I know Peggy and Roger are old enough to find their own way home but Ted worries about them – low flying aircraft and so on. His house is on my way home – well, there's only a slight diversion – so I might as well call for them.'

'That will suit me fine,' replied Lydia as she opened the front door. 'By the way, have I told you I've been asked to serve on the local Food Committee now? One of its more elderly members dropped dead last week, I'm afraid. You know, Ginny, I feel guilty when I realize that, in a way, I'll be sorry when the war ends. I hate all the killing and destruction and pray that it will end soon, but I have enjoyed being useful again. I suppose it has also made me see how empty my life has been since Harold died. Looking after him filled my day.'

'Tovell thinks this war has cost so much that we will take ages to recover from it,' Ginny said. 'He thinks there'll be shortages and rationing for years to come so you could be needed on WI services and the Food Committee for a long time yet.'

'I'd like that,' said Lydia, smiling. She leaned outside the front door and called out, 'Cordial and buns, children!'

The three youngsters ran into the hallway excitedly. Ginny shouted at them, 'Careful! Wipe your feet. You'll spoil Aunt Lydia's carpet.'

Lydia laughed. 'It's past spoiling, I'm afraid. I've had it years and it's quite threadbare in places now but it will have to last a bit longer. Even if you could get carpets – and they're very scarce, aren't they? – they cost about ten times what they did before the war. But we mustn't complain. All the factories have had to change over to war work, haven't they? Grouts silk factory in Yarmouth only makes material for parachutes and crepe bandages, so I'm told. But what does it matter if the hall carpet is threadbare? There's only me to see it most days.'

Ginny collected the children as she had promised and Lydia sat down in her living room and rested her feet on a footstool. She loved having company but sometimes it was quite a relief when they left. When she heard the bell jangle yet again she was a little irritated; but she got up out of her comfortable armchair and hurried along the hallway thinking one of the children must have left something behind. She opened her front door but no-one was there. Were some of the other village children playing tricks on her? She looked around the garden but there was no sign of any intruders. She began to wonder if she had been hearing things but as she was about to go back inside she happened to glance down and see a small book, a red rosebud enclosed within its pages, lying on the doorstep. She stared at it for a few moments and then, her hand trembling slightly, she bent down and retrieved the book. It was made of parchment, the poems within it had been hand-written in copperplate and each page had been beautifully illuminated like a manuscript created by a medieval monk. She opened the front of the book where the rosebud lay and read the dedication: *For sweet Lydia, the love of my life.*

She hugged the little book to her and once more looked around the garden. There was only one place where someone could remain concealed: a large tree near the gate. She walked towards it saying softly, 'Come out, Richard. We're too old to play hide and seek.'

'I give up. You've found me.' Richard Collins peeped out from behind the tree trunk. Then he stepped out onto the path and gazed at Lydia Brewster for several moments in silence before he spoke. 'Have pity on this wounded warrior, pretty lady - this poor, homeless, wounded warrior.'

Lydia laughed as she hugged him, her weariness gone. 'Wounded, yes, but you are neither poor nor homeless. Alec has told me the whole thing. He's already been to a solicitor.' They walked arm in arm into the cottage as Lydia asked, 'Why have you ignored my letters?'

'I did not dare to read them until yesterday. I feared that if I opened one and heard you speaking to me from the page, I would not be able to stop myself from rushing to your side. Having observed the correct decorum all these years, I had to wait an appropriate amount of time before coming to you.'

'Ten months might seem improper haste to some – '

'I made a slight adjustment to the proprieties to take account of our advancing years, my dearest. You said we were too old to play hide and seek; we are also too old to waste time. We have years to make up for and we may not have that much longer left.'

Lydia looked down at the volume of poetry she was still holding in her hand. 'Thank you for this. I shall always treasure it. You must have spent hours and hours making it for me – not just on the compositions but on the beautiful illuminations.'

'It was a labour of love. Over the years, whenever I've felt despairing, I've composed a poem to you. I've recited these offerings to myself in my darkest moments and found comfort in them because they brought you closer to me. I was not able to write them down, of course, until these last few months. I told myself then that I must be disciplined and not come to you until I could present them to you properly. They helped me to keep to my resolve to conform to the proprieties – to a certain extent anyway.'

'I shall enjoy reading them over and over again. I might even let you see what I've written about you over the years. My offerings have been in prose - I didn't have your poetic skills – but they tell of my love, nonetheless.' Lydia smiled, kissed Richard gently and then, changing her mood, said cheerfully, 'Come and sit down here on the settee and I'll make you some tea. When did you last eat?'

'How little has changed, my love: your main concern is still for my material welfare.'

'You've just had a long journey, so of course I'm concerned about whether you are hungry. And where is your luggage? Have you already booked into a hotel?'

'Questions, questions! No, I am not hungry - for food; only for you. My luggage, such as it is, is hidden behind that tree in your front garden. And no, I have not booked into a hotel: I was rather looking forward to living in sin with you.'

Lydia stared at him and then laughed. 'Richard, it's nearly thirty years since we last lived in sin.'

'Yes, I'm sorry to say it is and I'm not the young Lothario I was then, my sweet.'

'Richard dear, you were never a young Lothario. You were middle-aged, as I was. You were a very young fifty, as I recall.'

'Oh, dear! Nothing wrong with your memory, then. In that case you're going to have to make allowances for this aged Lothario. Forget the tea and come and sit by me on the settee.'

'One thing hasn't changed with the years: you still have the same rich, enticing voice, Richard.' Once they were seated, arms entwined, Lydia's head resting on his shoulder, she said, 'There's something I have to ask you straight away. It's been bothering me ever since Alec told me that Mildred had cut you out of her will. Was she punishing you? Had she guessed about us?'

'No, I don't think she had. It was as I told Alec: she thought I would die years before her. It was a reasonable assumption: my injuries have caused me a lot of problems, as you know. When I came back from the war I had changed – she commented on that fact – but she assumed it was because of what I had seen and done. The trenches changed most men.

226

No, I don't think she suspected. And you and I were very careful, whenever we met, never to let Mildred – or Harold – know that there was a bond between us. Mildred liked you.'

'I liked her. It was very difficult. Harold liked you; you always seemed to get on very well together.'

'We did. Ironic really. I was desperate for those short visits to continue; I lived for the next one. Just seeing you made me happy but at the same time I felt guilty.'

'When Alec told me you hadn't tried to persuade Mildred to change her will, I assumed that guilt was the reason.'

'Yes, it was.'

'We were only together a few months - precious though they were.'

'Betrayal is not confined to physical adultery. In my case the betrayal was life long because I never stopped loving you. You, not Mildred, possessed my heart, mind and soul, even if you never possessed me physically after those all too short months.'

'I assuaged my guilt by trying to be as kind as I possibly could to Harold. His health, as you know, deteriorated over the years. But although I lived with him, it was as you have said: he only had the outer shell; you had the inner me.'

They were silent for a few moments, content to hold one another; to be together. Then Richard said, 'Although Alec has transferred the deeds of the house and the money to me, I shall give them both back to him when the war ends. In case I do not survive that long – and now that at long last we are together, I pray that I shall last much longer than that – I have made a will leaving the house and money to him. I wouldn't want to live there anyway. It was Mildred's house and I would always associate it with her.'

'That's how I felt when Harold died. As you know, we had retired to that old house his parents had left him but I had never felt at home there. I was glad to sell it and buy this little cottage. I didn't like living away from the sea and the lighthouse either. I'm much happier here and now that you have joined me …'

'I hope that means you are willing to make an honest man of me at last, my sweet Lydia – woman-of-my-dreams.'

The news travelled fast amongst the former inhabitants of the Coastguard

Station. Mary had rushed to tell Ginny as soon as she had caught sight of Mr Collins shopping with Mrs Brewster in the village. When he was seen pottering in that same lady's front garden and, it was confirmed that he had not booked into the *Admiral Lord Nelson,* speculation was rife. Rumours were quashed when an engagement announcement appeared in the local newspaper and the happy couple made a formal visit to the homes of their friends.

'She was quite kittenish,' Ginny observed to Tovell after Richard Collins and Lydia Brewster had left. 'I've never seen her like that. What an amazing turn of events.'

'I suppose we shouldn't have been that surprised,' said Tovell. 'The two couples have been friends for years. It makes a lot of sense for the surviving partners to join forces. Mr Collins told me he has already made arrangements for Alec to have that big house back and to have the money Mrs Collins left him. That, in effect, makes the man homeless. He'll have his pension from teaching so he and Mrs Brewster should be able to live comfortably.'

'You make it sound so – ordinary,' Ginny protested, 'as though it's just a housekeeping arrangement. I think there's more to it than that. Like I say, she was kittenish and so happy. And the way he looked at her, as though he was very fond of her. I don't think this is just a case of sharing a house to make the money go further.'

'Well, I made a lot of wrong assumptions as far as Mr Collins was concerned, didn't I?' asked Tovell. Then, with a mischievous gleam in his eyes, he added, 'Perhaps he was interested in sharing more than just poetry readings with his landlady.'

'Oh, you! You would think of something like that,' said Ginny, laughing. But though she appeared to dismiss the idea, the thought which her husband had put into her head was still there when she went to bed. Tovell was just dozing off to sleep when she said, 'That can't be right: Mr Collins was such a gentleman.'

'Perhaps Mrs B got creative,' Tovell muttered sleepily. Ginny slapped him playfully for that remark and the action woke him fully. 'If there was something going on between them all those years ago,' he commented, 'they behaved very honourably, didn't they? They both stayed with their spouses until death. They did their duty by them, so they deserve to be together now and have a little happiness.'

Ginny turned over and snuggled up to Tovell. 'You're still an old romantic at heart, aren't you?' she said warmly. Then a few moments later she added, 'I wonder what I should wear for the wedding.' The only reply she got was a snore.

# V

The happy couple decided there was no point in delaying the ceremony and obtained a special licence so that they could marry as soon as Lydia's grandson could get leave to give her away. He arrived together with his brother, sister and widowed mother, Julia, from King's Lynn. The bride's other daughter, Muriel, together with her friend, Caroline, also made the journey from Oxford. Bobby was able to requisition a Royal Navy jeep on the pretext of picking up supplies, and he and his half-brother drove to St Mary's Church in Haisbro just in time for Alec to take his place at the altar, beside his former tutor, as his best man. Mary, the baby on her lap, hoped Bobby would sit next to her but instead he eased himself into the pew occupied by his sister Lizzie. After the brief service and whilst photographs were being taken outside, Mary tried to hand the baby to Bobby. He immediately walked away but his mother-in-law pursued him further into the churchyard.

'You've got to acknowledge this poor child sometime,' she persisted. 'It's not his fault – what happened.'

'Isn't it?' snapped Bobby.

'I know how much you grieve for her but you're not the only one. How do you think it is for me? I lost a husband in the Great War and a son and a daughter in this one – and God knows whether Albert will survive. But I'm not taking it out on this poor little mite. Think what he's lost? Rachel would have adored him and been a wonderful mother to him. But he's lost her – he's lost a mother's love. Stop feeling sorry for yourself, Bobby, and do your duty by him.'

'You don't understand,' Bobby muttered sheepishly.

Mary scarcely heard his response so intent was she on speaking her mind now that at last she had the opportunity. 'And we can't go on calling him "baby" forever. He has to have a name and he should have been christened before this. It's not so long ago that we all went to Arthur Gillings's wedding to Margaret. Now he was born just after his father died but that didn't stop his mother and grandmother knowing their duty and having him christened. That's only right and proper.'

Bobby, red-faced, was about to reply when he caught sight of someone standing behind a tombstone. 'Is that woman trying to attract your attention?'

Mary looked round and regaining her composure, replied, 'Yes, that's Janet Harding. She looked after the baby on the day of the funeral. She said she'd have him now so I could go to the wedding breakfast.'

'She's keen, isn't she?' commented Bobby sarcastically. 'Is she as keen to look after her own kids or is it only other people's she likes?'

Janet heard the remarks. The colour drained from her face and she swayed slightly and gripped the top of the tombstone to steady herself. Then she turned abruptly and ran out of the churchyard.

Mary was aghast and she turned on Bobby. 'That was a cruel thing to say. That poor woman lost her whole family in the Baedeker raids on Norwich – her husband and three little children. When you think how much you're suffering, spare a thought for her. You've got regrets; what about her regrets? They were all together in the communal air-raid shelter when her youngest started crying because she'd left the cuddly toy she slept with in their house. Janet went back for it and while she was fetching it the shelter took a direct hit. She's tortured herself ever since because she wasn't with her littl'uns when they died. For the last two years and more that's all she's wanted - to die so she could be with them. But last week she told me this little baby had made her realize that life was still worth living. If he can do that for her – a total stranger – he can do the same for you, if you only let him.' Bobby was looking somewhat shamefaced so she added, 'I know you didn't mean to be unkind: it's the drink talking. You stink of it, Bobby. And I know you're only trying to drown your sorrows but that's never worked for anyone and it won't work for you. Stop drinking and pull yourself together otherwise don't bother to come near us again. This little mite doesn't need a drunk for a father. The state you're in we're better off without you.'

Mary stormed off carrying the baby. As she passed the Tovells she called out to them. 'Please give my apologies. I can't come to the wedding breakfast: I must find Janet.'

'Well, I wonder what that was all about,' said Ginny. 'She was certainly giving Bobby a piece of her mind.'

'And I bet I know what about,' Lizzie stated grimly. 'He came and sat next to me and he reeked of booze. Mary will have been telling him that he had no right to be drunk in church and in front of his baby son.'

'He's been drinking for a long time – even before Rachel died,' said Alec. 'I've told him he's a fool. With his medical conditions his poor old guts won't take it; he'll end up drinking himself to death if he doesn't watch out.'

'He survived the Arctic because he had the will to live then: he wanted to get back to Rachel,' said Tovell, sadly. 'What's he got to live for now?'

'His little son,' Lizzie retorted. 'That poor baby has already lost his mother; it isn't right that he should lose his father too. If Mary's pep talk doesn't do the trick I'll have a go at him myself.'

'I doubt whether a sisterly telling off will even penetrate his dark moods,' said Alec. 'The Wrens who work in the torpedo rooms and the workshops say he often doesn't bother to go back to his quarters to sleep; he stays in that little office of his all night. They're frightened to go in there when they come on watch in the mornings in case they find him hanging.'

Ginny, fortunately, did not share this image because she already had a picture in her mind's eye. 'If he's drunk, he could have killed you both on the way here,' she said in alarm.

'Don't worry, Mother. I took the keys off him before we left the Fishwharf. I drove here and I shall drive back. By the look of him, he isn't feeling very well at this moment.' They all followed Alec's gaze and saw that Bobby had sat down on a grave and put his head between his knees. 'You had better go on to the wedding breakfast. Aunt Lydia will be wondering where you all are. We mustn't spoil their wedding day; they both looked so happy as they left the church. Tell them we're sorry to have to leave but we're back on duty this evening. I'll stay with Bobby until he feels well enough to travel; then we'll go back to Yarmouth.'

'Oh, dear, Alec,' said his mother, hugging him. 'What a pity Bobby's spoilt things for you. I know how fond of both of them you are.'

'I got to the wedding and did my best man bit – that's what counts. I won't be able to give the traditional speech but Father can do that for me, can't you?'

'But I haven't prepared anything. You've caught me on the hop,' protested Tovell.

'You made a beautiful speech at our wedding,' said Ginny. 'And as I recall, it was the only speech because your best man – Ted – wasn't in a fit state to deliver his.'

'I remember that,' said Lizzie, laughing.

They all embraced Alec. Ginny wanted to go over to her elder son to say goodbye but Alec discouraged her saying Bobby would be embarrassed at his mother seeing him in such a state. She took his advice and contented herself with waving in Bobby's direction before taking Tovell's arm. They walked behind Lizzie and Molly up the little hill from the church and round the corner into the forecourt of the *Admiral Lord Nelson.*

'I'm glad they decided to have their wedding breakfast here,' Ginny confided to her husband. 'I shall be thinking back to when we had our big day in that same room.'

'So I'm not the only one who is still a romantic at heart,' whispered Tovell.


A few days later, Tovell announced that he was going to try to see Bobby after he had made his deliveries in Great Yarmouth. 'The best person to help a drunk is another drunk – a reformed one,' he added hastily, seeing the alarm in Ginny's eyes. 'I'd have drunk myself to death years ago if it hadn't been for you. You were my incentive to control my drinking, sweetheart, but he has no-one in your place now that Rachel's gone.'

'He'll probably refuse to even see you,' Ginny said.

'Yes, I know. But I've got to try: if anything happens to Bobby that will be my fault too.'

Ginny followed Tovell out into the yard and hugged him before he climbed into the cab of the lorry. 'I hope he'll see you – and listen to you. This needs to work as much for you as for Bobby.'


Tovell had crates to deliver to the naval warehouses so had no difficulty in gaining access to the Fishwharf. He was pleasantly surprised when he went to visit Bobby to find him in an approachable mood. Not only was he willing to speak to Tovell but he suggested they find a meeting place outside the base; furthermore, he did not propose going to a public house.

'I'm off watch now. We could go into the Market Place and get a meal at the National Restaurant.'

Bobby even laughed on the journey back into town when they had a near miss with a double-decker bus. Tovell had taken his eyes off the road for a second when speaking to Bobby and had failed to halt at the correct point at a junction. The front of his lorry was a few inches into the main road. The bus driver first blasted him with her horn then opened her side window and told him in no uncertain terms what she thought of his driving skills. 'Can't call her a **lady** bus driver, can you?' Bobby quipped.

They parked the lorry and walked across the Market Place. 'There seem to be more children about,' Tovell commented, 'and more civilians. At one time the place appeared to be military personnel only. I had to be careful never to leave my Home Guard badge behind. I felt undressed if I wasn't wearing it.'

'Yes, the children are filtering back and several schools have reopened,' Bobby replied. 'Bill Westgate says when the schools were first evacuated the one not far from his place was allocated to the Home Guard; but they've been sharing it with the returning children for some time now. Of course, a lot more people moved back to Yarmouth once we invaded France. I reckon they feel it's safer here now.'

'Safer but not entirely safe. You're still getting some air raids, aren't you? And, of course, there are these damn doodlebugs.'

'Yes, the siren went last night as I was leaving the base. You don't get much warning – not like with aircraft. I saw the ruddy thing only about a minute later coming in over the sea. The search lights were circling and they found it straight away and all the batteries opened up hoping to explode it over the water. They all missed. I reckon it must be difficult to hit something small which is travelling so fast. And they have to get the warhead itself – nothing else is vulnerable. The bloomin' thing just kept coming right over my head. It was low and you could see the plume coming out of its exhaust. I turned round and watched it fly west. The buzzing sound of that engine is something I'll never forget. Then the noise stopped suddenly and the light in its tail went out. I heard a muffled explosion seconds later. I reckon it was over the marshes by then and probably didn't do much harm. The "raiders passed", the all clear, came a few minutes later. Jerry's been sending them over in huge numbers, hasn't he? Even Churchill's admitted that they've killed thousands.'

'According to the wireless, we're bombing their launch sites,' said Tovell.

'Yes, but Arthur's RAF mates across the river have heard the *Luftwaffe* are launching them from aircraft now – modified Heinkels. Our fighters are after them, of course. What's even more worrying is the rumour in the press that there's a V2 rocket which is far worse than the V1s, the doodlebugs.'


They crossed the road from the Market Place and walked along the pavement past several closed shops, towards the former Angel Hotel. As they entered the canteen, Bobby indicated a boarded-up jewellers shop nearby, commenting, 'Can't get the stock, I suppose.'

The place was crowded, mainly with people in uniform. Tovell looked around and despaired of finding an empty table. The last thing he wanted was to have to share with some one else. They queued up for their meal and, trays in their hands, looked around for somewhere to sit. At that moment, Tovell saw two soldiers get up from a small table in one corner and, calling to Bobby to follow, he made for it immediately. He just beat two ATS girls to the prize. He felt a little uncomfortable about banging his tray down on the table in such an impolite act of possession; but this was no time for chivalry.

'I'm going to miss spam fritters when the war is over,' Bobby quipped as he sat down and transferred his food from the tray to the table. 'What did you choose?'

'Corned beef cottage pie,' his stepfather replied.

'I've had enough corned beef to last me a lifetime,' Bobby commented. 'The Navy sails on corned beef, cocoa – and rum!'

At first, they continued to chat about the war: the failed assassination attempt on Hitler; the successes the Russians were having; the progress our armoured divisions were making in France – which set Tovell off reminiscing about the tanks used in the Great War. But as they finished eating, Tovell knew he could delay no longer in getting around to the purpose of his visit. 'Bobby, do you remember when you were a little boy and I was billeted with you?' he began. 'And do you recall how much I used to drink then?'

'What a surprise!' Bobby exclaimed, smiling. 'Yes, of course I remember.'

'It wasn't easy to curb my addiction,' his stepfather continued purposefully, 'and, trying to stop altogether was downright painful at first. But if I hadn't managed to cut down and eventually to control the urge to drink, I wouldn't be here now. Of course, I have your mother to thank.'

'It's alright, Father, you don't have to say anymore. Mother-in-law had a go at me at the wedding.'

'Yes,' said Tovell, grinning, 'we noticed her having words with you.'

'You could say that,' Bobby replied ruefully. 'But she was quite right: I am responsible for that baby even if not in the way that she thinks. I did engineer his conception. She doesn't know about that, of course, and I shall never tell her.'

'Of course not. There would be no point in telling her and it would do a lot of harm.'

'I started to cut down on the booze the next day, but as you say, once you've got used to it – and used to relying on it – it isn't easy. Mother was the reason you persevered and the boy has to be mine. I've already said to Alec that we'll borrow the jeep again as soon as we can both get time off together and come home – even if it's just for a few hours. I need to build bridges with Mary, and Alec has got something on his mind too – don't know what – but he wants to put that right.'


Ginny was overjoyed when Tovell arrived home that evening and related the day's events to her. He also told her that after he had given Bobby a lift back to his quarters, he had driven along the seafront to make a brief visit to the Westgates. Both Arthur and Margaret had been there with Bill, but Gladys had been at the WVS centre. Bill had been pleased to tell him that they had seen a lot of Alec over the last few weeks.

'He seems happy to spend an increasing amount of his off-duty time here. We play a lot of cards together,' Bill explained. 'He visits me at the Home Guard depot sometimes as well.'

When Bill left the room, Margaret could not resist disclosing more information. 'When you see that good looking son of yours,' she said to Tovell, teasingly, 'you can tell him that my girlfriends are missing him. They say the Floral Hall isn't the same without him. They want to know why he's suddenly gone… teetotal.'

When Tovell shared these revelations with his wife, her eyes lit up. 'Now don't jump to conclusions,' he cautioned her. 'There could be a lot of reasons why Alec has given up… partying.'

Ginny was excited at the prospect of seeing both her sons together in their former home again and when that day eventually arrived, she was particularly pleased that Bobby was looking better than he had at any time since his return from the Arctic.

'I'll be back for something to eat before we return to base, but I need to go and see mother-in-law now,' said Bobby. 'I've been giving some thought to what she said about having the christening. I've decided I'd like the baby to be called George, after her elder son who was killed on the *Royal Oak*.'

'That's a lovely idea,' Ginny agreed. 'Rachel would have liked her son to be named after her brother.'

Bobby paused and looked down, biting his lip, for a moment. When he looked up again his mother could see the sorrow in his eyes. 'And I have to apologize to Mary's friend – Janet, I think is her name. Did you hear about that?' His mother nodded. 'If she'll forgive me, I'm going to ask her to be George's godmother.'

'I'm sure she would love that,' said Ginny.

Alec spoke up then. 'While Bobby's at his mother-in-law's, I thought I'd just go and see Claire,' he said casually. 'Will she be at the station or at her quarters in Bacton? Do you know the times of her watches?'

'She isn't here any more,' Ginny replied. 'She was promoted to Flying Officer recently and she's due to get her own station.'

'They've been sending the men abroad in droves now that we have so many different theatres of war,' Tovell explained. 'Many of the radar stations are staffed solely by women now and there are plenty of women commanding officers. Claire's on a COs' training course at the moment and then she'll be sent to take charge of a station somewhere.'

The disappointment was plain to see on Alec's face so his mother hastily intervened. 'Claire said she'll let us know when she gets settled. Little Will was dreadfully upset when she came to say goodbye. She's promised to write to us, and to him, and to spend her leave here – when she gets some.'

'We've still got Bella with us,' his father added. 'Claire knows we'll take good care of her 'til she can make arrangements to have Bella with her at her new posting.'

'This is all a bit of a shock. It hadn't occurred to me that Claire might not be here,' said Alec. Ginny and Tovell exchanged glances but neither was sure what would be a fitting response. Alec solved the problem by suddenly making for the back door, saying, 'I suppose I might as well go and tell Bella what I was going to tell Claire.'

# VI

The fears that operations in France might deteriorate into trench warfare proved to be unfounded when the Allies managed to break the stalemate and start advancing again by the end of July.

August was a momentous time with news of another landing in force on the Riviera coast of France. Montgomery followed this by a broadcast on the Forces Service which heartened many a wife and mother at home: that the end of the war was in sight. This was followed by reports of uprisings in France and then the announcement that Paris had been liberated on the twenty-third. Churchill was pictured in the press walking down the Champs Elysees beside General de Gaulle, waving to the crowd. Ted was so pleased at this public recognition of his hero that he even brought his newspaper round to the Tovells in the unlikely event that they had not seen a copy that day.

Ginny, Lizzie and Molly, together with Mary, Janet and baby George, shared a pew at St Mary's on Sunday the third of September. The war had being going for five long years but this was the happiest anniversary service they had attended because everyone was convinced that they would not be gathering for another next September. As the month continued there was more evidence that the war was nearly over: Home Guard parades would not be compulsory after the eleventh; the blackout would become a dimout from the sixteenth although the relaxation would not apply to London and coastal towns; Russian successes at pushing back the enemy were continuing and the Soviets had occupied the Warsaw suburbs; the Americans had broken through the Seigfried Line along a nine mile front. Jubilation at all these events was dampened only by the fact that the flying bombs had not ceased their devastating missions. The Allies had captured the doodlebug coast but the V1s were still being launched from aircraft. Doodlebug raids on Ipswich and Norwich were nightly events. And the V2, for so long a nasty rumour, had become a hideous reality, flying at more than the speed of sound and delivering explosive loads ten times the strength of the V1s. News about the death and destruction they were causing was kept deliberately vague by the authorities; but anyone who had seen the huge craters which they created at the point of impact, was left in no doubt as to their power.

Flying bombs apart, there was much to give people hope. But just in case this led to carelessness or even extravagance, the wireless programmes and the articles in the press continued to urge restraint and economy with copious dollops of advice on how to "make do and mend", "waste not, want not" and "grow your own"!

Tovell, grooming Bella and Rajah Two on Sunday morning of the seventeenth of September, looked up when he realized that the droning noise in the sky above him was louder and more constant than usual. What he saw made him call Ginny from the scullery. Out in the North Sea, Alec on his Dog Boat, and Arthur on his Crash Boat, saw it too. Vessels from Great Yarmouth, Lowestoft and Felixstowe had already been dispatched on a joint RN and RAF operation to station themselves on the flight paths of thousands of aircraft – most of them towing gliders.

'Now we know why they've just formed a combined British and American Airborne Army, sir,' commented Marshall as he and Alec watched the fly past from their bridge.

'Yes, I think you're right,' Alec agreed. 'My brother says a Polish Parachute Brigade is part of them. He's been a great admirer of the Poles ever since he was with them in the Arctic. And by the look of it, they're taking plenty of equipment with them,' he said pointing to the Halifax aircraft then flying overhead towing tank-carrying gliders. 'They're headed for Holland but perhaps they're going further on towards Germany. Maybe this is a landing to outflank Jerry.'

There was little time to speculate once this airborne armada neared the Dutch coast. The German shore batteries opened fire and the *Luftwaffe* came to challenge the invaders; dogfights broke out high in the sky with the fighter escorts. Given the vast number of aircraft involved in the operation, it was no wonder some towropes failed and their gliders descended towards the waves. Once they hit the surface of the water the soldiers inside hastily scrambled out and into their dinghies, praying they would not be sitting ducks for too long. Soon the sea was dotted with them and the RAF air sea rescue boats and the Royal Navy rescue motor launches, their powerful engines roaring, dashed through the waves to the stricken men. In many a dinghy the arrival of high speed launches, ploughing through the water, creating plumes of spray, was greeted with cheers. Overhead, air sea rescue aircraft circled. They dropped smoke flares to aid the launches in their search for ditched gliders and planes and, if they saw men in the water, they dropped airborne lifeboats. They also gave early warning of the approach of E-boats or flak-ships so that the motor torpedo boats could break away and go to meet the enemy before they could attack the rescuers and the rescued.

Launches loaded with the soldiers and parachutists just saved from the sea sped back to the East Anglian coast and discharged their human cargo so that the men could join the queue again for the next flights out. The vessels then returned to their former stations off the Dutch coast. Some rescue launches limped back to their home bases rather than sped back because of the damage they had sustained. Antwerp, at the head of the Scheldt Estuary, had been taken by the Allies weeks before but the land on either side of the estuary itself had been left in enemy hands. Many crewmen had cause to curse this tactical oversight when repeatedly they had to enter the large expanse of the estuary to rescue ditched soldiers and found themselves coming under heavy fire from the inshore batteries.

The following day the sky was again filled with thousands of aircraft and gliders although fog over the Norfolk and Suffolk airfields delayed the take-off for three hours. Late that afternoon, Alec's boat picked up the crew of a Stirling which had been shot down by anti-aircraft fire as it left the Dutch coast for home. Mugs of kye – the Navy's favourite cocoa and condensed milk drink – and corned beef sandwiches soon restored the men's spirits. 'We did this same run yesterday,' the pilot told Alec. 'We dropped men at Nijmegen then and at Arnhem today.'

'So it's the Rhine we're after,' said Alec.

'Yes, I assume they're meant to secure the bridges.'

The rescue services remained on station for the next eight days; the weather was bad for seven of those days. Pilots they picked up spoke of heavy low cloud over the battle areas which made dropping supplies to the forces below very difficult and far from accurate. Conditions were so poor on the twenty-second and twenty-fourth that all air operations were suspended. The rescue vessels below in the North Sea remained on station and took turns to return to base to refuel. The motor torpedo boats, though slower that the air sea rescue launches, could stay at sea for longer and they rode rough seas better although seasickness, whilst standing by for hours or days on end, could inflict its misery on naval crews as well as air sea rescue crews.

On the last day of the joint operation, the Dog Boats, which normally worked in threes, had become separated because of the need to disperse and pick up ditched air crews spread over a wide area. Alec had been alerted that a Stirling aircraft had sighted Carley floats some distance out from the Dutch coast and he proceeded north in search of them, parallel to the coast but out of sight of the shore batteries. His radar operator alerted him to the approach of three vessels closing in fast just as a deckhand on watch yelled, 'Raiders on starboard bow!'

Alec peered through his binoculars and muttered, 'Three E-boats headed this way.' Then he called out, 'Action stations!' He was joined on the bridge by his newly-appointed second-in-command, First Lieutenant and Gunnery Officer, Michael Gibbs, who had been the third officer and pilot on the "cloak and dagger" mission the previous year. He handed the binoculars to the young officer and asked, 'What do you think, Mr Gibbs? I believe this situation calls for us to follow the Navy's best-loved signal.'

'You mean Lord Nelson's signal, sir?' asked the young man incredulously. 'England expects etcetera?'

'No, Mr Gibbs,' replied Alec with a grin, 'not that signal. I mean, "Engage the enemy more closely"!'

'Aye, aye and yippee to that, sir!'

'I've seen what can happen when three E-boats set upon a single MTB,' said Alec in more serious tones. 'They circled her and all fired broadsides. She was totally aflame in no time. We mustn't give them the chance to trap us in the middle. We can't outrun them – they're faster than we are – and it wouldn't be right anyway with ditched men in the vicinity. We must attack them. We'll zig-zag to confuse their gunners until we get closer and then we'll zoom straight towards them. Our narrow bow isn't going to present much of a target for them so we should be able to get between the boat on the extreme port side and the one in the middle. We must hit both E-boats simultaneously so you must arrange your guns so that some are firing on the port side and some on the starboard side. The gunners must commence firing just before we get there. We should be through and out the other side so fast that with a bit of luck they'll hit each other with their retaliatory fire. In the confusion, we'll circle back and again at speed come through between the middle boat and the third one, again with you having all guns blazing.'

'Sounds good to me, sir,' said the First Lieutenant enthusiastically.

'And to me – in theory. But just in case it doesn't work, we'll call up some air support anyway,' said Alec. He reached for the voice pipe as Mr Gibbs hurried off to instruct his gunners.

Minutes later, torpedoes just missed them as the Dog Boat zig-zagged. Plumes of water sprayed the deck as the enemy's cannons also missed their target and missiles fell in the water all around them. They sped towards the E-boats and passed between the first two boats as planned, pom-poms rattling, but unaware at the speed they were travelling of whether they had scored any hits. They slowed when they were astern of the vessels, turned and began their run back towards the E-boats. When they were almost on top of them and on course to pass between the middle boat and the remaining one on the flank, the stern of the one in the centre suddenly swerved round and in so doing struck the bow of Alec's Dog Boat. The motor torpedo boat was moving so fast that the blow had the effect of driving her towards the third E-boat. Seeing a collision of sorts was unavoidable, Alec made the most of his opportunity and rammed the vessel broadside. Miraculously, his boat was still able to depart from the scene. He shouted for smoke and depth charges as they made their escape. Looking back before the smoke screen obscured his view, he saw the centre boat turning in circles, her steering mechanism obviously disabled. Fires were breaking out on all three boats.

'I don't know if our shots did that damage or whether they hit one another,' he said to his coxswain.

'I don't think it matters, sir,' Marshall replied, laughing. 'We shall claim the hits and Jerry is unlikely to want to dispute that.' He looked up at two Spitfires overhead, flying in the direction of the burning E-boats. 'Here's your air support, sir. A bit late!'

First Lieutenant Gibbs joined them on the bridge. 'What's the damage?' asked Alec.

'Pretty bad, sir,' replied the young officer. 'We're taking in water on the port side and the starboard side.'

'To be expected, Mr Gibbs,' replied Alec. 'First we were rammed and then we rammed them. What about injuries?'

'Plenty of those but I don't think any are too serious. No one got hit: they're not shrapnel wounds but fractures, cuts and bruises as a result of being thrown about during the ramming.'

'Right. Do what you can for them and we'll call up some help before we sink. And we're hardly in a position to search for those Carley floats. We'd better request a Walrus to do that.'

As the officer hurried off, Alec went below to inspect the damage to the bow of the boat for himself as well as to instruct the radio operator. When he returned to the bridge Marshall commented, 'One good thing about all this: while the boat's in dry dock being repaired we should get a nice bit of R and R, sir.'

'Yes, you're right,' replied Alec. 'We can all do with some proper leave.'

'You might even have time to deliver that letter in person, sir,' said Marshall, grinning slightly but continuing to stare straight ahead.

'What letter?' Alec demanded.

'The one it's taken you all week to write, sir.'

'You're a nosy bugger, Marshall,' said Alec, good humouredly. 'I'll have you know I've only been able to write when it's been calm. The only stuff I write when it's rough is the kind I have to write - the official sort.'

'Yes, sir, of course.' Then, with a twinkle in his eye, the coxswain continued, 'You'll give my regards to Miss Bradshaw, won't you, sir? If you should happen to see her.'

'What makes you think I shall see her?'

'Educated guess, sir. And I'm sure she'll say "yes", sir.'

'What makes you think I've proposed to her?'

'Another educated guess, sir.' The two men looked at one another and started laughing. At that moment a Walrus sea-plane appeared. 'That's lucky,' Marshall commented. 'Must have been in the area.' The pilot flew low over them, clearly assessing their damage before departing on the hunt for the survivors in the Carley floats. At that point the Dog Boat was low in the water and moving very slowly whilst the sailors inside endeavoured to plug the holes in the wooden hull and pump out the water which had already flooded the forward mess deck and the galley. Some twenty minutes later, responding to a shout from the bow lookout, Marshall called out, 'The cavalry's here, sir.'


Air sea rescue crash boats took the crew off and a Royal Navy launch towed the sinking Dog Boat back to their home port of Great Yarmouth. Once they had arrived at the Fishwharf, Alec supervised the loading of the injured men into the waiting ambulances. As soon as he had seen them off to the Royal Naval Hospital, he took his action report straight to the Commander as his senior officer was still at sea. When he returned a little later he was able to tell his coxswain and the other uninjured members of his crew that their well-earned leave had been granted. Alec then went to find Bobby. After a quick reference to his recent exploits he asked his half-brother whether he had the address of Claire's new station.

'Sorry, Alec,' Bobby replied. 'Father hasn't left anything for you. Perhaps she hasn't told him where she is yet.'

'Then, can you do me a favour and finish this off when you know?' Alec handed an envelope to Bobby. 'As you will see, I've addressed it officially to Flying Officer Claire Bradshaw and then on the next line, put RAF. All you need to do is complete that line with the name of the station.'

'Certainly I can,' said Bobby. 'But I thought you said your boat was smashed up.'

'It is, but I've just had orders to ship out straight away. As you must know already, the Norwegian flotilla is returning to Lerwick in the Shetland Islands today: they can resume operations in their own waters now the winter darkness is closing in. Apparently, one of their skippers has been carted off to the Naval Hospital this morning with suspected appendicitis. I've got to take over his boat. I don't expect they'll let me come back until my boat is repaired.'


A few hours after Alec had left port, Tovell arrived at his stepson's little office. 'We heard from Claire today,' he began. 'I can't see Alec's boat at her usual mooring, so perhaps you'll pass the information on to him when he docks.'

'Sorry, Father; can't do that. Alec's boat is in for repair and he's been sent to Scotland as a replacement skipper,' Bobby explained. 'It doesn't matter though: he left a letter for Claire. I'll just have to finish addressing it for him. It's here somewhere.' Bobby started to search under the papers on his desk and then he caught sight of his empty out-tray. 'Damn! They must have collected the mail early when I wasn't here. I bet they saw that sealed letter and thought it had to go too. I'll pop over to the registry and see if it's still there. It would probably get to her anyway eventually – provided someone conscientious picks it up at the sorting office and checks where she's stationed.'

'Is Alec expected to be away long?' asked Tovell anxiously.

'No, not long,' Bobby replied. 'He can write her another letter when he gets back. I don't expect it was very important.'


The press was full of the fact that the failed mission to take the Rhine bridges had been the biggest airborne operation ever. They did not mention that had it succeeded the northern Netherlands might well have been liberated before winter. As it was, Arthur and 24 Air Sea Rescue Unit saw increased "cloak and dagger" missions to the Dutch coast to take off Allied soldiers who had managed to avoid being amongst the thousands taken prisoner by the Germans at Arnhem. These men had been sheltered by Dutch families in spite of the fact that the latter were enduring what they called the "Hungerwinter", which claimed thousands of lives, as well as the threat of execution if they were discovered aiding Allied servicemen. The Dutch Resistance organized escape routes and it was they who arranged for this stream of servicemen to be evacuated.

Alec, in the icy waters where the North Sea meets the Arctic Ocean, was also involved in clandestine missions – to the Norwegian coast. These usually entailed landing agents to set up wireless telegraphy posts or taking off agents whose positions had been compromised. Frequently, they took off civilians – sometimes whole families with children – whose lives were in danger having been betrayed for sheltering agents. These groups they took back to Lerwick which already had a very large Norwegian population. Many families had lived there in exile ever since they had escaped from the invading Nazis in the spring of 1940.

Alec did not remain skipper of the Norwegian boat for long: its own commanding officer was kept in Great Yarmouth – under observation at the Royal Naval Hospital – only until it was decided that he did not have appendicitis after all. He wanted to rejoin his crew and travelled north by train and then begged a passage from Aberdeen to Lerwick. Alec thought he would be able to return to his base by the same route but sickness, which affected another Dog Boat captain, scuppered this plan. The boat he took over had a crew of British and Commonwealth sailors. All were used to clandestine operations on the Brittany or Dutch coasts: ones which entailed landing agents or parties of commandos and taking off escaped prisoners of war passed down the line by the resistance fighters. They were not used to operating on the Norwegian coastline with its hazardous rocky approaches and fiord inlets.

Alec's first mission with his new crew was towards the end of October. They were to land two agents on the Norwegian coast and two tons of equipment which the agents would use to set up an observation post and wireless telegraphy station. They carried a Norwegian pilot who knew the particular stretch of coastline where they would make their landfall. The designated pin-point – the particular beach – would be difficult to reach and had been chosen for that very reason because its isolation made it safer. The deck of the motor torpedo boat was loaded with cans of petrol which would be needed for re-fuelling, given the distances involved and the length of time they would be at sea.

Alec called the crew together before they left port and explained the procedure they would follow. 'When we near the pin-point we shall get as close as we dare and then lower the surf boat, crewed by the First Lieutenant and two oarsmen, our passengers and their equipment. The voyage will have its hazards: we must cross an enemy convoy route as we approach Norway and cross it again on our way back; there is also an E-boat base at Egersund not far from our destination. We must wait offshore for the surf boat crew to unload the equipment – which could take one to two hours – and row back to us. For these reasons, as a precaution, you are to keep these leaflets on you.' Alec paused while the coxswain passed the papers around the crew. 'You will need these if something goes wrong, we have to abandon ship and you find yourselves on Norwegian soil. You will see that they are a list of questions and statements in Norwegian – the English translation is beside each one – which you may need to show to any local inhabitants you meet in the hope that they will help you. I want you also to look at this map. If you are stranded in occupied Norway your best bet is to make for the border into neutral Sweden. I would advise you to travel only in twos or threes: large groups would attract too much attention. One thought to keep in mind is that the war is nearly over so if you land up in a camp – whether it's a prisoner of war camp in Norway or Germany, or a refugee camp in Sweden – it won't be for long.'

The men did not have time to dwell on these sobering thoughts: a gale blew up soon after they left Lerwick and the passage to the Norwegian coast was a perilous one. In all Dog Boats the practice was for the sailors to remain on deck and only go below when absolutely necessary because of the ever-present fear of hitting a mine. Such an occurrence was bad enough for a large vessel but for a small motor torpedo boat it would be disastrous. Only the engine room workers, the radio and radar operators and the crew member who had been cajoled into the role of cook for the day, remained below deck. But even the icy blasts biting into the faces of the sailors on deck did not prevent them from succumbing to seasickness. The process of refuelling from the jerry cans, whilst their speed was reduced and only two engines were running at a time, would have been difficult enough in calm seas but with a heavy swell running it was a nightmare for the men. The process took an agonizing two hours to complete, they slipped on spillages and crashed into the freezing bulkheads; the fumes from the petrol increased their nausea and for some men made them vomit even more violently. Had they been capable then of thinking past the immediate miserable moment, the thought of an internment camp on a surface which did not move, would have been very welcome.

No sooner had they completed the refuelling process than they had to cease cruising altogether when their radar operator alerted them to the fact that there were ships passing ahead of them. Alec ordered power to be retained in case they needed to withdraw in a hurry. They watched in silence as a convoy, escorted by heavily armed trawlers, made its way parallel to the coast and moving south. The escort remained on station and fired no star shells in their direction. Alec heaved a sigh of relief that they had not been seen. Once he felt it was safe to do so, he ordered the engines restarted and they continued towards the coast and their objective travelling relatively slowly at eight knots. The Norwegian pilot identified the lighthouses they could see as the correct landmarks. They slowed down even more and Alec ordered the men to use lead lines at the bow and either side of the hull to ensure that they did not creep too close to the rocky shoreline and become impaled or stuck in the shallows. He had just decided not to press his luck any further when he was thrown off balance as suddenly, the boat lurched to one side and above the screech of the wind he heard the unmistakable sound of timber being ripped apart.

Alec regained his balance, hauled himself out onto the deck and stumbled past a sailor, lead line still in his hand and a look of disbelief on his face. He reached the bow of the boat in time to stop another man from turning on a flashlight. He grabbed it from him and lent over the rail and shielding the lamp with his body, switched the beam on for only a couple of seconds. 'I can make out the timbers of a boat just below the surface,' he said to the First Lieutenant who had hurried to join him. 'This beach must have been used as a pin-point before. They must have had to scuttle the surf boat for some reason and she got caught in the rocks. Damn it! Let's go below and see how bad it is.'

Water was already flooding the compartments below deck as the two men made their way forward. The straight bow of a clinker-built surf boat was protruding through the hull of their vessel. Jagged rocks had also penetrated in places and the seams of the Dog Boat were also leaking as a result of the impact. 'We've had it,' said the First Lieutenant. 'If we pushed her off the obstruction we'd never be able to patch a gaping hole this size.'

'Even if we did, it would never hold for long in this gale,' said Alec. 'She's taken a battering coming over as it is; we'd never make it back to port. We'll have to abandon ship. You've been with this crew a long time so we'll swap places. I'll go with the agents and you can stay with your men.'

'That's much appreciated, sir,' said the officer.

'I'll take the Norwegian pilot with me. The two of us can row – we won't need your two men."

'With all due respect, sir, I've been in a beach party several times before and you need a three man crew – two to row and one steering,' the First Lieutenant insisted. 'I've always been the one with the long sweep oar doing the steering.'

'Yes, I know,' Alec replied. 'Given the circumstances – and the conditions – I'd rather make do with just two of us this time. But before you leave the ship get the surf boat over the side and put the stores and the agents in it. The pilot too; he can stand by until I join them. He's going to have to find us a different landing place. This one's no good now. Our boat will probably get dashed to pieces in the storm tonight but there's always the chance that she might still be visible by daybreak and get seen by aircraft on a reconnaissance patrol. There's also the possibility that some of the men might get picked up and handed over to the SS – heaven forbid!'

As he spoke, Alec dashed into his tiny cabin and grabbed the confidential papers. Looking back over his shoulder he shouted to the First Lieutenant to get some men to come down to the galley and fill some sacks with tins of food. He then opened the door of the radio and radar room shouting, 'We're abandoning ship so follow the procedure for dumping the confidential code books.'

'Thank God for that, sir!' replied the radar operator, grinning. 'My feet were getting wet.'

The engine room too was awash and the mechanics were equally pleased to be leaving their posts. Back on deck, the lifeboats were already being lowered and Alec called the First Lieutenant and the two petty officers – the coxswain and the chief engineer – to him. 'You've a hell of a long walk across the southern tip of Norway and round to Sweden, gentlemen. Don't forget to split the men up into twos and threes once you reach the beach. Best of luck and see you when the war's over!'

Alec wished the rest of the men luck as they went over the side but his words were whipped away by the gale, so he patted each one of them on the back and they nodded their thanks. Once the lifeboats were safely away, the pilot brought the surf boat alongside and Alec climbed down the scrambling nets. Once aboard he looked at the two agents in the stern of the boat. Both were prostrate with seasickness. He climbed over the seating and the boxes of stores to take a closer look at them. Both of them were wet and shivering with cold. As he bent over them snow began to whirl around his head. He grabbed a tarpaulin and spread it over them before returning to take his place on the seat in front of the Norwegian. 'Hope you like rowing,' he shouted to the officer. 'I don't think we're going to get any help from those too.'

'No matter,' the pilot replied cheerfully. 'We go north?'

'Yes, the crew's going south so we'd better go north,' replied Alec.

Then, as he slotted his oars into the rubber lined rowlocks he added, 'I've never rowed one of these before. A double-ended boat, straight bow and stern, may be great for an easy turnround at a beach but I bet it's a bugger trying to make any progress in her – especially in rough waters.' As an afterthought, he shouted to the pilot, 'I shouldn't joke about those two: they're in a bad way. I just hope you can find us some shelter quickly or this will be a very brief mission.'

Doodlebugs continued to rain on Suffolk and Norfolk on a daily and nightly basis but the V2 faster-than-sound rockets seemed to be aimed only at the City of Norwich. Many people were injured but thankfully, no one was killed by them. There was also much in the news to celebrate: everyone rejoiced with the inhabitants of Dover and the other Channel ports when they decorated their streets with flags at the beginning of October on hearing that Calais and its environs had fallen to the Allies: no longer would they be the victims of its long-range guns. By the middle of the month, Athens had been liberated and southern Greece was in Allied hands. In the Pacific, the Americans landed 100,000 troops on Leyte Island in the Phillipines.

The news was not all good, however, and Bobby was particularly upset by the announcement that the Nazis were exterminating Poles, including the survivors of the Warsaw horrors, using gas chambers in one of the concentration camps. His depression over this was only lifted with the news that the *Tirpitz*, the indirect cause of so much death and destruction to convoy PQ17, and disabled and out of action since the midget submarines had damaged her in September of the previous year, had finally been sunk by Lancaster bombers at Tromso on the thirteenth of November. The Russians had also crossed the border into Norway just below the North Cape and had taken Kirkenes and Petsamo, the bases from which German aircraft had attacked the convoys and the Murmansk Bobby knew so well. His jubilation at these events led Ginny to comment to Tovell, 'I don't think Bobby will ever be able to get over the things that happened to him in the Arctic.'

Sunday the third of December was an important day for Tovell because the Home Guard was officially being stood down then, although not disbanded. Ginny was delighted because it was a further sign that the war was almost over and even happier that her husband would have no further excuse for wandering off somewhere on so many nights and weekends. When Tovell said he wanted to hear the Home Service's description of the march past in London, Ginny said she would listen to the programme with him. 'The King is going to take the salute; representatives from every unit in the country will be taking part,' Tovell said.

'Won't they have parades in every town today?' asked Ginny.

Tovell nodded. 'Yes, the nearest one to here is in North Walsham. They'll be reading out the King's message, thanking us all.'

'Won't you be marching?'

'No, it'll be the 5th Battalion on parade. I used to be with them at the beginning but then I got transferred to 202 Battalion.'

Ginny said nothing but she remembered how upset she had been when she had taken the children to North Walsham Market Place and Tovell had not been there. He was looking a little sad so she said sympathetically, 'I expect you'll be sorry to be stood down after all this time.'

'No, not really,' he responded. 'At least I'll have the time now to work on all those Christmas orders. Thank goodness Molly and Peggy haven't asked for ships and aeroplanes; but all four of the boys want them.'

Soon after this, Claire made a brief visit to Haisbro and stayed with the Tovells overnight. She had brought presents for all the children and left them with Ginny to be passed on to their mother. Her main reason was to visit Matey – young Will. She had been writing to him regularly ever since she had left the area and he had been replying - with a little help from Tovell - but she was anxious that they should spend some time together before Christmas. She did not ask after Alec and Ginny, following her vow not to interfere ever again, felt it was better not to raise the subject.


Just before Christmas there were slightly worrying bulletins about Hitler massing troops along a seventy mile front in the Ardennes region. This was followed by the news that the heaviest battle of the war in Europe was starting. After that, there was a clamp-down on all official announcements. Ginny decided she could not worry about what was probably just a hiccup – everyone said the war was ending – and she had more pressing worries with all the people to cater for on Christmas Day. Ted was bringing his adopted family and Mary had asked if Janet could be included. Ginny had agreed but was concerned that Bobby might be upset that his mother-in-law appeared to have adopted a substitute daughter so soon after Rachel's death the previous spring. When Bobby arrived in time for Christmas Dinner he did not seem to be at all offended; in fact he went out of his way to be sociable to Janet. Baby George was so happy with her it was as though he had adopted her too - as a substitute mother.

Bobby had brought presents for all the children and left them in the scullery until after they had eaten. He had something quite large for George and had managed to acquire enough brown paper to conceal the gift. Janet immediately sat the baby on the floor and Molly knelt down beside him to help him to unwrap his present. Little George was most appreciative of the brown paper and enjoyed discovering how to tear it up and make a scrunching noise by crushing the pieces between his tiny hands. He was not particularly interested in what had lain hidden beneath the paper - a beautifully carved wooden rocking horse - but the adults were most impressed.

'He'll enjoy playing with it when he's a bit older,' Mary said comfortingly to Bobby. 'I'm amazed you managed to get him something like this.' As she spoke, the other children were unwrapping their gifts. Every one was a toy carved from wood. 'I can't believe this. Where did you get them all from, Bobby?'

'Don't ask,' replied her son-in-law. 'Let's just say it's a miracle what you can pick up around the docks.' Bobby noticed Tovell smiling knowingly and when the two of them went out into the yard later for a quiet smoke, he mentioned the matter. 'I gather you've seen that kind of stuff before?'

Tovell nodded. 'And I think you were right to be so cagey about it in front of your mother-in-law.'

'Yes, she'd never let little George play with that rocking horse if she knew a German prisoner of war had made it,' said Bobby.

'You're right there,' agreed his stepfather. 'There was a group of prisoners with their guards at the Christmas service this morning. They were seated a couple of rows ahead of us. Mary was next to me and when we all stood up to sing and she noticed the coloured shapes sewn onto the backs of their jackets, I felt her stiffen. At the end of the service, I made sure we all remained in our pews until the group had left the church - in case she couldn't contain herself and said something nasty. You can't reason with her. She blames every single German for her son's death.'

'I don't expect those blokes you saw in church are any different from our Peter now he's a POW. All they'll be thinking about is getting home and being with ...' Bobby's voice trailed away. He looked down and with the sole of his shoe, ground the butt of his cigarette into the cobbles so hard that the paper disintegrated and the grains of tobacco flew out over several stones.

Tovell could feel his anguish. Clearly those wounds had not yet healed. A few moments passed in silence before Tovell felt he must break the tension. 'All the toys you brought today were beautifully made. You can just picture the men when they get back to camp, sitting in their Nissen huts whittling away at some piece of wood they've picked up whilst they were out on a working party. I know wood carving kept me from going crazy with boredom on many a long voyage on a troopship. With the shortages, I'm sure hand-crafted goods must fetch a good price.'

Regaining his composure, Bobby replied, 'They fetch a good price after they've changed hands a few times outside the POW camps; but the blokes who spent hours making them don't get much. I reckon the man who made that rocking horse only got a handful of cigarettes for it.'

'You're probably right,' agreed his stepfather. 'But now we'd better go back indoors before your mother sends one of the boys out to find us.'


As the year came to a close, Lizzie, of course, was sad that Peter was still not home. She was getting letters from him on a regular, though infrequent, basis from his prisoner of war camp through the Red Cross and she was writing to him even more frequently. At least she had the comfort of knowing he was alive and well. Mary was still concerned about her son, Albert, but she too had had a letter which had told her little except that it was very hot where he was and the insects were a menace. 'At least he's alive – or was when he wrote this,' she said stoically. Only Ginny was feeling disgruntled – and neglected. 'They must have the Forces postal service in the Shetlands. He could have sent us a card,' she complained to Tovell.

'You don't know if Alec was able to send a card. Maybe he was at sea and didn't dock until after the last Christmas post.'

'Hmm. But we've only had one letter from him since he went to the Shetlands and there was hardly any news in that. All he was concerned about was whether Claire had responded to his letter and had sent her reply here.'

1945

# I

Tovell listened intently to the snippets of information which filtered through in January about the German advances on the Belgium-Luxembourg border. The names he heard of towns, bridges and rivers were familiar ones to him: they had been battle areas in the Great War too. He watched the planes – Fortresses followed by Mustangs mostly, leaving the nearby airfields to support and supply the Allied armies – every day that the foggy weather allowed. Snow and ice still covered the Norfolk roads and he felt for the generation of soldiers who would be enduring the conditions he remembered so well. It was the end of January before the press and the radio broadcasts spoke of the enemy retreating after the failure of their "Ardennes bulge" but by then more personal issues were overwhelming the Tovells.

When the bell on the front door jangled loudly one evening, Ginny was startled. 'No-one ever comes to the front door,' she said as she got up from her chair and hurried into the parlour and through to the small entrance lobby. When she opened the door and found a policeman standing on the step, her heart missed a beat. 'Alec!' she exclaimed. 'You've come about my son, Alec.'

'No, madam,' the policeman replied. 'Are you Mrs Virginia Tovell?' When Ginny nodded, he continued. 'I've come about Flying Officer Bradshaw. I understand you are her next-of-kin.'

'Claire? What's happened to Claire?' Ginny demanded as she half-dragged the constable into the chilly front parlour.

'I'm afraid there's been an accident, madam,' the policeman answered. 'The officer has been transferred to the hospital at RAF Uxbridge but her condition is such that you are urged to go there straight away.'

When they were waiting to be seen outside the ward, Ginny wondered whether they should confess that they were not related to Claire. 'No, I don't think we should say anything at this stage,' Tovell answered. 'She must have had her reasons for putting us down as her next-of-kin.'

A sister arrived exuding brisk efficiency and immediately launched into an account of Claire's injuries. 'It was a very heavy fall from a great height, I'm afraid. She broke her back – '

'She's paralysed!' Ginny exclaimed in horror.

'At the moment, yes,' replied the sister. 'But we do not expect that to be permanent. Several vertebrae in her lower spine were damaged but we think the spinal cord is intact. Once the situation is stabilized and the accompanying severe bruising goes down, we expect the paralysis to gradually disappear. She has other injuries, however, which may cause longer term problems.'

'What other injuries?' asked Tovell with trepidation.

'Both her lower legs were shattered for one thing,' answered the sister in matter of fact tones. 'The surgeon did a fine job piecing them together but if the circulation does not return properly then amputation is the only solution. Even if she keeps her legs, she will always have mobility problems. Added to that she has various internal injuries and both wrists were damaged so she is completely helpless at the moment. Come this way, please.'

Glancing at one another nervously, Ginny and Tovell followed as the woman marched rapidly down a wide corridor, starched skirts swishing back and forth as she moved. 'She won't be able to talk much: she's heavily sedated. We don't usually have female officers. All these wards we're passing are for male officers, so she's been fortunate in that she has a room to herself.' They stopped outside a closed and curtained door. The sister tapped briefly and then entered the room. 'Visitors for you, ma'am,' she said before ushering the Tovells inside and closing the door as she left.

Ginny approached the bed where Claire lay. There was a cage over the lower half of her body to keep the bedclothes off her injured limbs. Both hands were bandaged to above the wrists; her face was swollen and her eyes blackened so that she was scarcely recognizable. A drip was attached to one arm and there were various tubes peeping from under the sheets and draining into bottles hung alongside the bed. 'Hello, Claire dear,' she said quietly. 'It's Ginny and Tovell.'

Claire opened her eyes and tried to smile. 'Hello. You've had a long journey,' she said weakly.

'Not that far but it wouldn't have mattered how far we had to travel, we wanted to see you, didn't we, Tovell?'

'That's right. We're really sorry you had this fall, Claire,' said Tovell.

'My own silly fault,' Claire muttered. 'Should have waited for daylight and the gale to drop.'

'Claire dear, I know you had some kind of disagreement with your parents a long time ago,' said Ginny gently, 'but I also know, as a mother, that they would want to be with you at this time.'

'You're here; that's what counts. Tell my parents if you must, but don't tell Alec. Couldn't bear it if Alec saw me like this.' Claire shut her eyes again. A tear trickled down her cheek and Ginny wiped it away for her.


The Tovells sat with Claire all afternoon, speaking to her encouragingly whenever she was awake. They left when the sister came to give her more injections. The journey home in the lorry took until midnight because of the absence of signposts and the need to drive slowly along the unfamiliar roads. Tovell was grateful that he had been permitted to use his sidelights since the previous September and the dimout which applied to inland towns meant that some built-up areas they passed through had starlight street lamps where the candle power was a tiny fraction of normal. Once they were within twenty five miles of the coast, such a luxury was not allowed as the blackout regulations continued to apply. There were still white lines running down the middle of the main roads — broken lines but continuous at bends - for which Tovell was thankful; but he felt exhausted by the strain of driving under such conditions and was relieved when at last he entered the yard of their smallholding. His ordeal, however, did not prevent him from setting out again next morning to find Clair's family home in North Norfolk.


The meeting was cordial if somewhat stilted. The general walked with Tovell to his wagon and shook hands with him. 'I'm grateful to you, Tovell, for letting me know. Can't think how this mix-up occurred but as you say, my daughter was billeted with you for some time and I expect some clerk filled in your name an address in the next-of-kin box by mistake.'

'I expect that's what happened, sir,' replied Tovell.

'Her mother and I will go and see her tomorrow. Fortunate that I'm on leave. She should never have done what she did, you know. As commanding officer of the station her place was to stay on the ground. If there was something wrong with the damn equipment it was for others to climb up the mast, or whatever. A girl that clever should never have been there anyway: she should have been at headquarters or better still, she should have been with other boffins at some laboratory.'

Tovell grinned and, looking his former boss in the eye, said, 'With respect, sir, I recall there were a lot of rumours going around that you had turned down various jobs at HQ. "A true officer of the line," they said. "He'd rather get his hands dirty in the trenches with us poor devils." Seems to me it's a case of, "like father like daughter", sir.'

Major-General Bradshaw smiled. 'Maybe you're right, Tovell. They won't let me get my hands dirty now, I'm afraid. They think I'm too old. Oh, they promoted me but the only areas they let me command were the dummy camps we set up to fool the Nazis prior to the invasion. Now I command a desk in Whitehall.' As Tovell climbed into the cab, the general commented, 'I see from the badge in your lapel that you're in the Home Guard. Stood down now, of course. Which battalion?'

'202 Battalion, sir,' Tovell replied.

'That doesn't surprise me. You're the perfect candidate. I bet they recruited you at the beginning – at the formation.'

'Yes, sir. They did.'

'Well, thanks again, Tovell. And regards to your wife.'


A few days later, when Tovell arrived home from making deliveries, there was another surprise waiting for him: Alec was asleep in his mother's armchair by the cooking range in the living room. Tovell looked across at his wife, quietly setting the table. 'Aren't we lucky?' she whispered. 'He's spent the last few months dodging the Nazis in Norway. He was so hungry that I think he must have been half-starved. He's been asleep all afternoon.'

'Have you told him about Claire?' Ginny shook her head.

Although they had spoken quietly, the noise was enough to wake Alec. When he saw his father, he immediately got up and embraced him. 'Your mother says you've been in occupied Norway. Did you get shipwrecked or something?'

Alec nodded. 'Our boat foundered when we were landing some agents on the coast. The pilot and I went with the agents. They were meant to set up a radio telegraphy station but they were too ill to do it at first; in fact one of them died a few days after we'd landed. When the other one eventually recovered we helped him set up his equipment and then got as far away from him as possible so we wouldn't endanger him. Various families sheltered us which was very brave of them. We were going to try to reach the border but the Resistance passed us down the line and one of our own Dog Boats from Lerwick embarked us a few days ago. I just hope the rest of the crew got to neutral Sweden alright. By the way, as I was waking up, did I hear you mention Claire? Is she here?'

Alec persuaded the nurse to let him see Claire by claiming that he was her fiancé. She announced him as such when she took him to the bedside.

'What are you doing here, Sailor?' Claire demanded as soon as the nurse had left the room. 'I asked your parents not to tell you. I don't want to see you.'

'Oh, I soon prised the information out of them,' Alec replied, grinning. 'You're almost shouting at me. That's a good sign. You're obviously feeling a lot better than when Mother and Father saw you ten days ago.'

'Why did she say you were my fiancé?'

'Because I told her I was. The fact that you haven't had the courtesy to reply to my proposal is immaterial. I never had any intention of taking "no" for an answer.'

'I don't know what you're going on about. You've never proposed to me. You never even fancied me.'

'That isn't quite true. I was a fool and I explained it all in my letter. It took me long enough to write – bloody days in fact.'

'What letter? I never received any letter.'

'I gave it to Bobby to post because I didn't have the address of your new station and I was being sent to the Shetlands. I only got back yesterday'

'You're making it up.'

'No, I'm not. Bobby will tell you. And Marshall: he saw me struggling over it and guessed it was a proposal.'

263

'Well, they would back you up, wouldn't they? I know what you're doing and it won't work.'

'Claire, believe me: I proposed to you last September. Everyone else had realized we were a couple ages ago; it just took me longer. I was an idiot; I admit that. You were right: we were meant for each other ever since we were children. I love you, Claire and I realize now that I always have.'

'Well that's typical of you anyway. You were always like this when we were young: never wanting any of the sweets until it was too late and I'd eaten them all. Well you're too late now.'

'It's not too late for us to be together. I can look after you – '

'No, you will not! That's typical of you too. You were always finding wildlife with a broken leg, seagulls covered in oil – anything you could take home in a box. This is one injured animal you're not taking home. You didn't want me when I was whole so you're certainly not getting me now. In fact, there's something sick about a person who only wants something that's damaged. Makes you feel big and powerful, does it?'

'It's not like that Claire. This has got nothing to do with you being injured or me feeling sorry for you – or wanting to take care of a wounded animal. I proposed to you last September and I feel exactly the same about you now as I did then and I want to marry you for exactly the same reasons as I did then.'

'I don't believe you. Go and find some other broken down wreck to make you feel a hero.'

'You're so bitter I can see I'm going to have to visit you a lot of times before I can convince you. But at least one good thing has come out of this disaster – you've made contact with your father again.'

'Hah! You should have seen the fuss they made of him when he arrived - when they saw his general's pips. Doctors, nurses, everybody - falling over him. It made you want to be sick.'

Alec laughed. 'That sounds more like my Claire.'

'I'm not your Claire. Now go away and stay away.'

'Alright but first I have to give you this. I promised Will that I would. He made it for you – with Mother's help. Apparently, its name is Tiger Two. And he said to tell you that the rhyme is the same. He said you'd know.'

Slowly, Claire lifted her gaze and looked at the small stuffed animal

Alec held out to her. Her eyes filled with tears and she said quietly, 'Put him where I can see him – please. Thank Will for me. Now go away, Sailor. I want to cry and I can't even blow my own nose.'

# II

In the weeks which followed, Claire regained the feeling – and the pain
– in her lower body and underwent further surgery on her injured legs.
Her wrists and hands – which had crashed against the metal struts of the
radar mast as she fell – healed too and she was able to use them again.
Eventually, she was moved from the RAF hospital at Uxbridge to various
rehabilitation units and military convalescent homes. The Tovells visited
her whenever they could, relying on public transport where possible
rather than using their precious petrol coupons. Alec went to see her too
whenever he had sufficient time off between watches to make the journey.
He even managed to find a jeweller's shop in Norwich which was still in
business; but she refused to accept the engagement ring he had bought for
her. Nothing he could say would convince her that he had proposed to
her long before her accident. All he could do was curse the fact that the
letter he had agonized over had been lost and hope that, once she was
moved nearer to their base, Bobby and Marshall would be able to
convince her of its existence.

The daily routine had to continue and Tovell followed the practice of most
people in a farming occupation of attending to his animals first thing and
then returning to the house for breakfast. By this time the newspaper had
usually arrived and he would devour the news along with his meal.
Information, much of it pointing to the fact that the war in Europe was
coming rapidly to a close, rolled off the presses in February and March: the
fall of Warsaw; the Russians pushing the Germans steadily back; an
armistice with Hungary; the Big Three, Churchill, Roosevelt and Stalin,
meeting in Yalta in the Crimea; Dresden, described as a big railway and
distribution centre, raided by the RAF by night and the USAAF by day;
Montgomery crossing the Rhine; the enemy retreating rapidly and the
Americans linking up with the Canadian and British ground forces. On the

Home Front, there was news of firewatchers being stood down, barrage balloons declared obsolete and gun batteries no longer operational.

But it was an article in an April edition which really caught Tovell's eye. He thought about it so intently after he had finished reading that he even forgot to eat for a while. Then he left the table without saying a word and, to Ginny's surprise, instead of passing the newspaper to her as he usually did, he folded it and carried it with him as he crossed the room and disappeared up the narrow staircase.

Somewhat mystified by this departure from her husband's normal routine – he never went upstairs once he was dressed ready for work – Ginny finished her breakfast, cleared the table and was washing the dishes in the stone sink in the scullery when she heard him come back downstairs. Realizing he was behind her and not bothering to turn round she said, 'I'll just finish these and I'll be outside to help you. Where are we working today?'

'We're not,' replied Tovell. 'We're having a few hours off.'

'What!' Ginny exclaimed. 'We can't do that. The country's worse off than ever for food. The government keeps telling us growers and farmers that we mustn't slack.'

'A few hours won't matter,' said Tovell, patting her bottom. 'And you can get out of these slacks – and the rest of your working clothes – and put on that nice blue dress. The one I've always liked.'

'My best frock! It was the last thing I bought in 1939. I don't wear that on weekdays and anyway it's a summer one,' Ginny protested. She wiped her hands on a tea towel and turned around to face her husband. 'Good gracious!' she exclaimed at the sight of him. 'You're wearing your uniform. Whatever for? The Home Guard's finished.'

Ignoring the reference to his attire, he replied, 'I told you we're having a few hours off. We'll drive into Cromer afterwards and find a restaurant; have a meal together. I can't remember the last time we did that. And before you start arguing that you have to be here when Lizzie gets back from work, let me remind you that you don't have to be anymore. Since Molly started at the same school last September, Lizzie's taken her with her on her bike and there's no reason why, for once, they can't get their own meal. Just leave them a note.'

'You said "afterwards". After what?'

'After we've been where we're going first.'

Ginny stood up on tip-toe so that she almost reached Tovell's chin and sniffed. 'You haven't been finishing off the rest of the ginger wine from Christmas, have you?' she asked teasingly.

'Cheeky. You know I haven't. Now hurry up and get changed.'

'Tell me where we're going then.'

'I'll tell you when we get there.'


Tovell drove for only a few miles, parked the wagon, got out, lifted Ginny down from the cab and taking her by the hand, led her through a gate into a field. 'This is what I wanted to show you,' he announced. 'This is where I've been sleeping all those nights when you suspected I might be in some other woman's bed.' Ginny was so flabbergasted that she just looked at Tovell open-mouthed. 'I'm not as insensitive as you think,' he continued, grinning at her. 'I know when I'm getting the cold shoulder.'

'When have you ever got the cold shoulder?' Ginny asked, slightly flushed with embarrassment.

'Whenever I've been absent for a few nights and you've been wondering if I really have been on *military* exercises.'

Ginny, who was not usually at a loss for words, could only mutter, 'You always seemed so tired; I just wanted you to catch up on your rest.' Then she remembered Tovell's original statement and demanded with her usual vigour, 'What do you mean, you slept here? It's an empty field.'

'No, it isn't. Take another look,' said her husband.

Ginny looked carefully around. 'It's empty – well, except for that dead tree over there.'

'Exactly! And that's where I've been sleeping.'

'Up a tree!'

'No, under it. Come on; I'll show you.'

'Not in these shoes, you won't. I'm not walking across a muddy field in these: they'll be ruined. It was your idea I should wear my best clothes. And why you should want me to do that just to visit a field ...'

'Stop arguing, woman! I'm going to carry you.' So saying, Tovell swept her up in his arms and began to march the few yards to the tree. 'Light as a feather! You see, you're still the sweet young thing I married.' He deposited her gently in front of the tree-trunk. 'Right, this is it.'

'This is it?' Ginny looked around bemused. 'If you curled up against this night after night, I wonder you didn't catch pneumonia.'

'I told you – I slept under it.' Whilst Ginny watched in astonishment, Tovell placed his fingers in a knothole in the gnarled trunk, releasing a catch, and a section of the bark swung inwards revealing that the dead tree had been hollowed out. The top of a ladder was just visible and indicating it, Tovell said, 'I'll go down first and put the light on and then I'll help you down.'

Moments later, when they were standing twelve feet below ground, Tovell said, 'It's a concrete bunker. The Royal Engineers built most of it although we helped with a lot of the work. There are Operational Bases like this all over the country. I think my battalion, 202, covered only northern and eastern England. There were other battalions for Scotland, Wales, western and southern England – so I believe.'

'But why didn't you tell me about this?' asked Ginny, still dazed.

'I couldn't,' replied her husband. 'The whole idea – I believe it started with Churchill himself – was to form a secret army. We were to be an underground resistance force which would hide in these bunkers once the Nazis invaded. If you remember, I told you at the beginning that you and the children must get away inland as soon as an invasion started and that you mustn't wait for me. That was because I would be here. We were to remain operating behind enemy lines causing as much chaos and destruction as possible. Come. I'll show you round.'

Tovell lead Ginny into a separate room full of metal racks. 'As you can see, this is the armoury. We stored our automatic weapons, ammunition and all our sabotage equipment here. There's enough explosive in this place to blow up and booby trap every significant position for miles around. Once the war is definitely over, I expect the Army will have to go round to all OBs like this one and collect or destroy this stuff. Otherwise I'll have to do something about it: I was the patrol leader here.'

'To think you were here and I never guessed …'

'I was recruited first – because of my years in the regular army and because I knew how to live off the land, I suppose.' Tovell lead Ginny back through the door to the larger of the two rooms. 'Then I recruited the others. As you can see from the six bunks, there were six of us. They had to be men with local knowledge who could live rough and would keep their mouths shut. We never knew the names of men from any other unit, or where they were located, even though we shared specialist training sessions – weekend and summer camps – with other units. I reckon the principle there was, you couldn't betray what you didn't know. The whole thing was set up like the resistance movements in the occupied countries on the Continent – you only know your own cell and not any other.'

'The whole idea frightens me,' said Ginny, wandering around the room.

Tovell followed, pointing out various areas. 'We had a stock of food to last a month and here – see – was the ventilation shaft. It comes up in a clump of dense bushes. We were allowed to cook a little, although mostly we ate cold food. We weren't allowed to fry anything, of course, because of the smell and the fumes. This little door leads to our escape route: a tunnel which comes up through a trapdoor into a cowshed. Here, come and sit down with me – this was my bunk.'

Ginny seated herself beside Tovell as he took a booklet and a wallet from his top pockets. 'This was our main training manual.'

'The 1938 Norfolk Calendar was your training manual!' Ginny exclaimed in surprise, reading out the title from the front cover of the booklet.

'That's right,' answered Tovell with a laugh. 'Look inside. It's a guerilla fighter's Bible. Everything a would-be saboteur needs to know. I had to keep that hidden away but more upsetting was that I had to keep these hidden away too.' Opening the wallet, he took out the photographs of Ginny and the children. 'I'd kept these with me for years but we were warned never to carry letters on us which would identify us with specific villages – for fear of reprisals if we were captured – and never to carry family photographs. Our commanders reasoned that if we were taken prisoner, and the Gestapo's usual torture methods failed, they would take the families hostage and use them to force confessions out of us. The thought of you being in their hands was almost too much to bear.'

'Oh, Tovell, I'm so sorry,' murmured Ginny, burying her head in his shoulder.

'There's nothing to be sorry for, little darling, because it didn't happen. But the invasion came very, very close. Heaven knows what made Hitler change his mind and invade Russia instead of us. And they were worried at the time that we invaded Normandy – D-Day – that if it failed he would invade us then. Our training was intensified for a while and we were given special orders. But it's all working out in our favour now. Clearly, no one in power expects us to lose or they wouldn't have released information to the press about the Resistance Units.'

'Is that what you were reading about in the paper this morning?'

'Yes. I couldn't believe it when I first saw the headline. Apparently, the War Office has announced that we've been in existence, as a secret army, since 1940. And that was what set me thinking.' Tovell's tone softened, he put his arm around Ginny's shoulder and kissed the top of her head. 'I got to thinking about what you'd suspected I was up to all those nights when I was on patrol or asleep in my little bunk. And then I thought, you were being accused of it, so why not do it? Underneath this coat you're wearing a skimpy little blue outfit, aren't you? Now what's a soldier to do when a lovely lady in an alluring dress sits down on his bunk beside him? The temptation would just be too much for him.'

'Aha, so now I know why we're both dressed up like this.'

'It just goes to show that you girls are not the only ones who can get creative …'

# III

Anticipation mounted and again people were taking bets with one another: this time about the date of VE Day – Victory in Europe Day. War correspondents sent home harrowing accounts of the ordeals of newly-released slave labourers and of many Nazi atrocities. Pictures in the papers showed the corpses of Nazi victims piled high in concentration camps – evidence, as everyone said, of why we had gone to war. On the thirteenth of April, Churchill hurried to the House of Commons to request that it adjourn immediately - out of respect for President Roosevelt, who had just died. By the fifteenth, churches were putting up notices that a service would be held there on the evening of the day hostilities ended. Lizzie was heartened on the nineteenth with the announcement that prisoner of war camps were being liberated by the Allies. On the twenty third came news that the *Lutzow,* Germany's last pocket battleship had been sunk by planes of Bomber Command and, on the twenty fifth, the announcement that Berlin was surrounded and in flames.

The news which particularly saddened Ginny concerned the plight of the Dutch. Alec told her that he and Arthur had been at sea when the convoys of planes had flown over to drop supplies to them. He said that the Germans, who were rapidly retreating from Holland anyway, had been warned not to fire on our food-carrying Fortresses and Lancasters but that they, in their rescue ships, had stood by at sea just in case. Ginny heard on the wireless that many of the rations which had been dropped were of special pre-digested food because that was all that starving people could manage to keep down. 'Just think, Tovell,' she cried. 'That so easily could have been us suffering like that.'

'I know, sweetheart,' he replied. 'And I fear as each country is liberated there's going to be a similar problem. Let's just pray there are good crop yields and a bumper harvest this year.'

Arthur and Margaret had been cuddled up together at the rear of the Coliseum cinema on the night of the twenty-fifth – although not on the back row itself, feeling they should leave that to the non-married couples – when another message flashed up on the screen. This time it was to announce that the Americans, driving the enemy forward from the west, had met up with the Russians driving the enemy before them from the east. Cheers went up from all parts of the auditorium and loud clapping was accompanied by cries of, 'Nearly over!'

By the twenty-seventh the news bulletins spoke of the help the Italian patriots were giving the Allies and that the Germans had almost been driven out of Italy – and that Mussolini had been captured. The British Government was sufficiently confident on the first day of May to order local councils to issue instructions for Victory-in-Europe Day, and for the two following days which would be public holidays. There were sobering pictures in the papers that day too: of the bodies of Mussolini and his mistress hanging upside down; and worse still, of prisoners at Dachau, machine–gunned to death as the Americans advanced on the camp to liberate them.

Rumours abounded the next day that Hitler was dead. On the seventh came the wonderful news that Germany was surrendering unconditionally. All U–boats had been ordered to cease hostilities and all ships of the *Kriegsmarine* ordered not to scuttle as every one of them would be needed to transport food to beleaguered Europe.

Tuesday eighth of May was declared VE Day. The Tovells listened on their wireless during the afternoon to Winston Churchill making the formal announcement of peace in Europe, and then they went to church. They were joined by family and friends, images of the concentration camps in everyone's minds and relief in their hearts that they had been spared such horrors of occupation. Later that evening, Lizzie and Molly joined them to listen together to the historic broadcasts from each of the Services involved in the war effort. They heard the King make a speech in reply, followed by Eisenhower, Montgomery and other leaders.

'I'm glad that was all rather subdued,' said Tovell as he switched off the wireless set. 'It wouldn't have been right for us to have been patting ourselves on the back. We were very lucky to have come through it and it's thanks to our Armed Services that we have. But there are hard times ahead before we fully recover. I dread to think how many years it's going to take us to pay back what we owe America from earlier on under the Lend Lease scheme. The papers have been talking about negotiations going on with the United States at the moment to secure yet another loan and that too will have to be paid back.'

'We'll certainly need a loan from somewhere,' Lizzie agreed. 'We must be nearly bankrupt. The only things our factories have been turning out for years are armaments and no one will want to buy those now. It'll cost a fortune to re-tool industry so that we can start making goods for export again. It could take decades to recover from this war.'

'I think it wouldn't be right to be too jubilant when so many of our boys are still struggling against the Japs in the Far East,' said Ginny with feeling. 'Mary was praying for her Albert when we were at church today.'

'I was praying that Peter would be home soon,' Lizzie said quietly. 'When I got the card from him saying his camp had been liberated I thought he'd be on the next plane.'

'I expect he's at some airfield queuing up right now,' said Tovell kindly. 'When I delivered in Yarmouth the other day I saw Arthur. He said all these Liberators and Fortresses we keep seeing flying over here are carrying our boys back home. I don't suppose we added up the numbers of our own servicemen taken prisoner over the years; but from what the papers have been saying, it must have been hundreds of thousands. You'll see, Lizzie – Peter will turn up on the doorstep anytime now.'


The day after VE Day there was an open air party in Haisbro for all the children from the village and the surrounding countryside. All the households contributed something in the way of food and there were games and races on the cliff top, well away from the barbed wire, in the field on the other side of the road from Lydia's cottage. The authorities had given permission for bonfires to be lit and the men's contribution was to build as big a bonfire as they could. Although it was not Guy Fawkes Day, they made a guy and gave him a little moustache, the significance of which was lost on the children but not on the adults. Ted at least was complimentary about their efforts. 'Cor blast bor, that looks just like the blighter. Pity someone dint stick him on a bonfire years ago: wouldn't have been a war then.'

Ted had brought the five evacuee children and their mother to the party in the farm cart drawn by Bessie. Ginny had noticed that as soon as they had arrived, one of the Italians who had been standing with a group of fellow prisoners, had left his comrades and walked briskly over to the wagon. Ted had acknowledged him, climbed down from the vehicle, hitched Bessie to a nearby fence and then walked away. The Italian had bowed to Joan as she sat on the driver's seat and had then presented her with a bunch of wild flowers. Ginny had nudged Tovell at that point and both had watched in amusement as the Italian had lifted Joan down from her seat and kissed her hand. He had then helped Peggy down from the rear of the cart. From his facial expressions and gesticulations - and her coy response - he had clearly been complimenting her on her appearance. Lastly, he had lifted the younger children down. He had then offered Joan his arm, which she had taken rather bashfully, and escorted the laughing family to the tables set out under the watchful eye of the lighthouse.

Ted, having inspected the bonfire and given his opinion, joined the Tovells. Ginny immediately referred to the cosy scene they had just witnessed. 'Ah, yes, that was Enrico,' Ted announced. 'I knew I could leave it to him to do the honours. He and his pals have been in these parts some time now. They were taken prisoner in North Africa as I recall. O' course, since the Italians made their peace with us in '43, them there prisoners have done pretty much as they like. The young master often asks the camp commandant to send him Enrico – every time old Billy our herdsman is sick, in fact. The master he say them there cows give a greater yield of milk when Enrico's looking after 'em. I reckon that's 'cause he talks to 'em all the time like they're ladies. I've heard him. That Italian charm of his must work on all females – the four-legged kind as well.'

'I expect the next thing we'll hear is the government saying all evacuees must return home,' said Ginny wistfully. 'If they've a home left standing to return to, that is. I'll miss the littl'uns and I expect you will too, Ted.'

'That's a fact,' Ted agreed. 'But the littl'uns don't want to go. Young Roger's really put his foot down. He say Enrico's learning him to be a herdsman and that's what he's going to be. He loves all the animals, does Roger. That'd be a real wrench for him to have to go back to London after all the years he's been here. Must be nearly five year, I reckon.'

'They'll have to send the prisoners back as well,' Tovell said. 'There must be plenty of Germans as well as Italians working on our farms. They'll be missed – given how short of food we are. And there have been plenty of German prisoners – the ones who weren't members of the Nazi party, I gather – working in gangs repairing the roads and clearing up the bomb damage. Mind you, the Russians are occupying plenty of German soil at the moment and if they're allowed to stay there, a lot of Germans may not want to go back.'

'Well, that's another thing – Enrico don't want to go back. He told me so,' Ted said.

'But he must have a home and family in Italy. It's his duty to go back,' Ginny protested.

'That's the problem. He had a home and family there but not any more,' Ted explained. 'He'd never worked on the land afore he was taken prisoner: he was a fisherman. He and his two brothers had their own boat. We bombarded the coast afore we landed in Italy and his boat, home and family were all bombed. Only his two brothers survived and they wrote and told him. So he say there int much point in him going home: 'cause there's nothing and nobody there.'

'The poor man,' Ginny murmured. 'All you seem to hear about are sad stories like that.' Then, seeing Mary and Janet approaching with little George, Ginny said, 'We'd better change the subject.'

Ginny was not depressed for long. Mary was proud to tell the group that her grandson had taken his first steps and, with encouragement from her and Janet, he happily demonstrated his newly acquired skill. His admirers were clapping and cheering his faltering efforts when Tovell shouted, 'Look who's here!' Peter was walking towards them with a smiling Lizzie on one arm and an excited Molly clasping his other hand.

Lizzie called out to them as they came closer. 'Father was absolutely right. Peter had just arrived on the doorstep as we got home from your house last night.' They all embraced Peter and friends and neighbours standing nearby – including Lydia and new husband, Richard – rushed forward and joined in the welcome.

Alec was in the North Sea on VE Day when the signal went out at noon to all ships of the Royal Navy to "splice the mainbrace". He was just a few miles off the Norfolk coast, east of Haisbro Sands. He raised his tot of rum in silent salute to the lighthouse and to friends and family living nearby – and to Claire. His Dog Boat was back on escort duty protecting convoys now that their cargoes were even more precious than ever. Whilst people ashore had been talking of a phoney war in 1939, the *Kriegsmarine* had challenged the Royal Navy from day one. So it was at the end of the war and the previous month, April, had seen continued attacks by German E-boats and S-boats; there was evidence that they were still operating in numbers when twelve E-boats were encountered laying mines in the Scheldt Estuary on the thirteenth of April. The E-boats and S-boats, however, had obeyed the command on the seventh of May to cease their attacks but there was news of some U-boat commanders refusing to surrender as ordered – hence the need to go on protecting the convoys.

For Alec and many other gunboat crews, Sunday the thirteenth of May was their real VE Day when they watched a pre-arranged ceremonial. The admiral commanding the E-boats based on the Dutch coast, together with the senior officer of one of those flotillas, crossed the North Sea in two E-boats flying white flags of surrender. The admiral had come to formally hand over the charts of minefields to the British admiral who was Commander-in-Chief Nore. The E-boats were met fifty miles off the East Anglian coast by ten motor torpedo boats which had been selected to represent all those craft which had battled with the E-boats over the years. They took up their positions on either side of the two E-boats and escorted the German admiral into the port of Felixstowe. Once docked, the admiral boarded the barge of the Commander-in-Chief Nore.

Alec and Marshall, their Dog Boat anchored at a discreet distance, watched from the bridge through their binoculars. 'I'll have to tell the missus about this, sir,' exclaimed Marshall. 'Do you see, the entire crew of the C-in-C's barge is made up of women? Every one is a Wren.'

'Yes, you're right. Even the coxswain piping the German admiral aboard is a Wren. I'll have to tell Claire: she'll like that too.'


People were still listening to snippets of war news as May came to a close: the Russians were confident that one of the four charred bodies they had discovered earlier really was Hitler's; Lord Haw–Haw had been captured; the Americans had bombed Tokyo; the Japanese had retaliated with a new weapon - Kamikaze pilots dressed in ceremonial robes crashing themselves onto Allied ships. The worst news, as far as Ted was concerned, was that Churchill had resigned, bringing the Coalition Government to a close, and had called for a General Election to be held in July.

June was given over to campaigning by Labour, Tory and Liberal politicians. The BBC allowed all three parties to take it in turns to broadcast. By Election Day on the fifth of July, everyone had had enough. 'They're all behaving like little boys,' said Ginny in exasperation. 'They've been the best of pals all these years, working together in the coalition, praising each other. Just look at them now: being downright rude and calling each other everything. They should be ashamed.'

The election results would take three weeks to come through because of the need to include the votes of the thousands of servicemen who were still abroad. It would be Churchill, therefore, as head of the Caretaker Government, who would go to the Potsdam Conference with the new American president, Truman, and with Stalin, to begin the task of mapping out the peace agreement. By the time the conference opened on the nineteenth of July, the reports from the Far East were good: the Americans were continuing to drive the Japanese from the Pacific islands; the British were forcing them out of Burma and had taken the capital, Rangoon. On the twenty-sixth, Britain and America issued surrender terms to the Japanese from the conference, with the ultimatum that attacks on Japanese towns and cities would increase. On the same day, the election results were released. Labour won by a huge majority; Mr Churchill left the Potsdam Conference and Mr Attlee replaced him. Japan rejected the surrender terms, declaring she would fight to the bitter end. On the seventh of August, America dropped the Atom Bomb on Hiroshima, the next day Russia declared war on Japan and advanced into Manchuria; a second atomic bomb was dropped, on Nagasaki, on the ninth.

Margaret and Arthur were nestled together, asleep in bed in her room at the Westgates, when they were awakened by a cacophony of sounds: fireworks exploding, horns blaring, hooters and ships sirens wailing, guns firing. They sat up in bed and as Margaret was about to speak, Arthur stopped her. 'Listen a minute! I can just make something out: the ships in the harbour are sending out a message in Morse code. Can you hear it?'

Margaret listened too. 'Yes! Three dots and a dash!'

'V for victory!' they both cried out together. Hastily grabbing dressing gowns, they sped downstairs to find Bill and Gladys Westgate already in the kitchen listening to the wireless.

Bill looked up as the young couple dashed into the room. 'It's all over!

The Japs have surrendered!' Margaret hugged her grandparents in turn, Bill offered Arthur a manly hand and Gladys kissed him. 'The announcer says today is a public holiday and so is tomorrow,' Bill told them. 'We can really celebrate now. Peace at last.'

'I'll put the kettle on,' said Gladys.

'I think we deserve something a bit stronger than tea in the circumstances,' said her husband.

'You can have what you like but I'm having tea,' Gladys declared. 'It's sustained me all through the war and if it was good enough then it's good enough now. But I could have a drop of whisky in it if you like.'

Everyone laughed then Margaret said, 'What's the date? Has it gone midnight?'

'Yes,' replied her grandfather, 'so it's officially the fifteenth of August.'

'That means it's only a matter of days short of six years since the war began,' said Arthur.

'Nineteen days to be exact,' said Margaret. 'Who would have guessed it would last so long – and kill so many.'

'We've got to look to the future now,' said Bill, cheerfully. 'Mustn't dwell on the past. We've got to make up for lost time. You two need to get yourselves out of the RAF for a start.'

'They're not closing the Air Sea Rescue Unit at Gorleston,' said Arthur. 'They've already announced that it will be maintained although I expect the operation will be scaled down. At times we've had as many as twenty launches there and we won't need that number in peacetime, surely.'

Bill frowned. 'Well, so long as you get demobbed by the start of next summer season, I suppose that will be alright. Sam and I can manage for what's left of this summer. We've only been able to open a few attractions and as you know, it's just the central beach which has been cleared of mines so far.'

'But it's lovely to see the children playing there again after so long,' said Gladys, 'and to see the posters advertising the show on the Wellington Pier. Let's hope all the theatres will be up and running by next season.'

'And that the military soon give up the hotels they requisitioned,' Bill added. 'I hope they get out soon. I dread to think the state some of our places are in. We'll have our work cut out to get them all in good order and redecorated before next year's visitors start arriving.'

'At least we'll have two more pairs of hands to help,' said Gladys, beaming at her granddaughter and her husband.

'Nan - and you, Granddad - seem to be assuming Arthur and I are going to come and work for you. We haven't decided what we're going to do yet. The war only ended minutes ago,' Margaret protested.

'We don't expect you to work for us, Margaret,' Bill explained. 'What we hope is that you and Arthur will join us – that you will come into partnership with me, your Nan and your father, in all our various enterprises.'

A couple of miles away at the Fishwharf, Alec "spliced the mainbrace" with his men then went in search of his half-brother, Bobby. Together they walked along the quayside until they came to HMS *Miranda*, the base for minesweepers. When they found the boat their mother's brothers were on, they cupped their hands around their mouths and yelled their uncles' names. Amazingly, their shouts were heard above the celebratory din, and the two men came to join their nephews on the quay. Both were hoping that they and their vessel would be released from service by the following month so that they could take part in the Home Fishing.

'Do you realize, bor, that there's been no herring fishing since the '39 season?' said one of them.

'Them old fish have had five year to breed undisturbed – except for the ruddy U-boats. The sea must be teeming with 'em. It should be a bumper harvest,' said his brother.

'Surely you won't be released straight away? You'll be needed for minesweeping duties more than ever now we've got the Germans' charts of their minefields,' Bobby reasoned.

'There are plenty of purpose-built minesweepers here now so maybe they will release the fishing boats, especially as the food situation is so dire,' Alec argued.

There the meeting ended as more shipmates from the minesweeping flotillas hailed the two men and they bade their nephews goodbye with the exhortation, 'Give our love to your mother.'

# IV

Ginny was as relieved as everyone else that the war was finally and completely over. She was also very pleased when, a couple of days later, she received a letter from Claire saying that she had been released from medical care and was staying with her parents on the North Norfolk coast. In a postscript she added that the latter would be away the following Sunday. Ginny needed no further hints and wrote straight back the same day saying that she and Tovell would be visiting, and bringing Will with them, on Sunday afternoon. The youngster had wanted to visit Claire before but Ginny had felt he would be too upset at seeing his friend whilst she was far from well.

Claire opened the front door for them and welcomed them loudly and enthusiastically. 'Hello, Matey. I've missed you. Haven't you grown!' she exclaimed as she hugged Will. 'I know you're a big boy now and probably too grown up to sit on my lap, but if you hop on, I'll take you for a ride in my chariot. Hang on tightly because we'll be going fast.' Claire spun her chair around and Will did as he was told. They dashed along the marble-tiled floor of the hall, Claire spinning the wheels with her hands as fast as she could. They arrived in a very large sitting room at the end of the corridor and Claire helped Will to get down from the wheelchair. The French windows, which led out onto the garden, were slightly open. 'Come in, everyone,' Claire called out to the Tovells as they hesitated in the doorway. 'We can sit outside if you like to have our tea and cakes. It's very warm today and the terrace is sheltered from the breeze.'

'That would be nice,' said Ginny. 'Will would probably prefer that, wouldn't you, Will?' Ginny had noticed how quiet the boy had become at finding himself in such a large room, the walls adorned with gilt-framed pictures and lined with glass cabinets displaying china ornaments. He would have found such unfamiliar surroundings daunting anyway but the alcoves either side of the chimney breast were even more intimidating, filled as they were with strange wood carvings, many of them hideous-looking masks.

'Yes, this room is a bit scary if you're not used to it,' said Claire. 'After the last war my father was posted all over the place and Mother insisted that she wouldn't be left behind again. It didn't bother her, once I was school age, leaving me behind,' Claire added ruefully. 'Of course, I was the last one – the afterthought – the postwar baby. My brothers and sisters were pre-war and no trouble to her. They've always been the goody-goodies whilst I've been the black sheep of the family. So all this awful stuff is what my mother collected on their travels. Come on, Matey. We'll all go outside.'

Tovell pushed open the French doors and Claire propelled her wheelchair through them.

As she passed him, Tovell said, 'You're wrong, you know. I spoke to your father when I came to tell him about your accident and it was quite clear to me that he had a high regard for you. He was proud to tell me how clever you are.'

'Well, he's never told me that,' Claire retorted.

'From what I remember of him, I should think he would find it difficult to tell a child face to face, how much he cared. But I'm sure he did and still does, Claire.'

'Oh, he belongs to the stiff upper lip brigade alright. "Never betray your emotions" has always been his motto.'

The bitterness in Claire's voice made Tovell decide to lighten the tone of the conversation. 'So your parents are away at the moment. Are they in London?' he asked casually.

'Yes,' Claire replied. 'They're in London at some regimental do.'

'I'm surprised they left you alone when you've only just come home,' Ginny remarked.

'Oh, they haven't left me alone, more's the pity,' Claire answered. 'The old retainers are still here keeping an eye on me. I bet they're secretly gloating at seeing me in this contraption,' she declared, slapping the sides of her wheelchair. 'I can just hear what they're saying behind my back: "she's got her just deserts at long last".'

'I'm sure they're not saying anything of the sort,' said Ginny, shocked.

'But you don't know what a horrible child I was. I made their lives hell – all but Nanny Barker's, of course.'

One of the old retainers – an elderly maid wearing a black dress with a white lace apron and cap – arrived at that moment pushing a trolley. 'Will you take tea now, Miss Claire?' she asked without any hint of animosity.

'Yes, please,' Claire replied, smiling warmly at the old lady. 'Will's hungry, aren't you, Matey?' Will grinned at Claire and nodded his head vigorously.

'Cook thought the young gentleman might like some jelly and blancmange and she's found a bit of icing sugar to decorate his ginger bread.'

'That's lovely, Maud,' Claire said. 'Please thank Cook for us. We'll help ourselves.' Will, though overawed by his surroundings and the strangely-dressed old lady, managed a mumbled "thank you" himself.

Once the maid had returned to the kitchen, Ginny said to Claire, 'I think you were telling us fibs: they obviously adore you.'

Claire grinned at Ginny. 'Let's just say that perhaps they've forgiven me my childhood pranks and tantrums.'

Whilst they ate the beautifully prepared tea, they chatted happily and the conversation eventually turned to a discussion about Bella. 'Father sent for her when I was still in the hospital at RAF Uxbridge. She was stabled near to my new station but she wasn't as happy there as she was when she was with you. The people didn't give her the loving care and attention which you gave her. She isn't that happy here either. She doesn't get the exercise she should. I'm afraid our groom-cum-gardener is rather elderly too. You and Will must go and see her before you leave. The stables are over to the right. You can't miss them.'

'Perhaps you should exercise her yourself,' said Tovell archly.

'I wish I could but it would take a block and tackle to get me mounted and dismounted. I don't fancy that indignity,' Claire replied.

'I thought the last place you were at had got you walking,' Tovell continued.

'Yes, that's right. I can stand and walk now provided I use both my crutches. But I can only manage a few steps. It hurts like hell too. Father thinks I should give up on my old legs and get tin ones. I'd be more mobile then, he says. He's probably right but, call it vanity if you like, I'd rather keep my own even though they're not much use.'

'If you can't get up into the saddle, why not hitch Bella to some sort of little cart,' Tovell suggested. 'Our old doctor – Doctor Lambert – did all his rounds in a pony and trap. He swore he'd have nothing to do with motor cars. His son's the opposite, of course.'

'I wouldn't be able to climb up to the driver's seat.'

'You're an engineer, aren't you? Surely you could devise something to help you.'

'I'm not that kind of engineer.'

'I'm sure you can think of something if you put your mind to it. Perhaps you could come up with an idea that would help other servicemen in the same boat as yourself.'

'I'll give it some thought.'

Ginny interrupted then, winking at Tovell as she spoke. 'You boys have finished your tea. Why don't you go and visit Bella?' Tovell took the hint and ushered Will away to the stables.

'Now you've got rid of them, what do you want to say to me?' asked Claire.

'Oh, dear. You don't miss much, do you?'

'It's only my legs which don't work properly any more,' replied Claire with a wry smile.

'Yes, you're quite right. I do want to talk to you,' Ginny confessed. 'Have you told Alec you're here?'

'No, I assumed you'd do that.'

'Claire, I know I said I'd never interfere again – '

'But you're going to.'

'Yes, because you're making a terrible mistake. From the things you've said here today about how you view your childhood, I'm beginning to understand why you can't accept that Alec loves you unconditionally – for real, if you like. But he does, Claire. Alec loves you and that's the only reason he wants to marry you. It's not because he feels sorry for you – believe me. If only that confounded letter hadn't gone astray you'd know he was telling the truth.'

Claire shut her eyes and gripped the arms of her chair tightly. She said nothing for a few moments and then she looked up at Ginny. 'I know he was telling the truth,' she said quietly.

'You know … How do you know?'

Claire put her hand into the top pocket of her blouse and drew out a folded envelope. 'This came yesterday. The letter's dated and the little things he mentions in it show he wrote it while they were standing by at sea during that disastrous Arnhem offensive. It must have been lying around somewhere for months after that because it didn't reach my station 'til the day I was stupid enough to try to make a repair on that damn mast.' Claire opened the envelope up and showed Ginny all the addresses scribbled on it and crossed out. 'It's been following me around ever since: Uxbridge first then all the rehab and convalescent units.'

'Claire, that's wonderful news,' Ginny cried. 'So everything is alright now. He'll be so pleased. I can't tell you how upset he's been because you keep refusing him.'

Claire slowly folded up the envelope again and put it back in her pocket. She shook her head and said sadly, 'It was a beautiful proposal; if I'd have got the letter before, I'd have been over the moon - but not now. I'm as well as I'm going to be and that's not saying much: I'm a cripple and there's no getting away from that fact. I might even get worse as I get older – the doctors have warned me of that. When you love someone you have to think of what's best for them and Alec can do a lot better than me.'

'You're wrong, Claire. He only wants you. He feels you were always meant for each other and he's full of regrets that he didn't see it years ago.'

'That's how I feel and I don't want you or anyone else to interfere. And I want you to promise me that you won't tell Alec that I've received the letter.'

Ginny looked at Claire and saw how earnest she was. 'Alright, I promise.'

'And promise me also that you won't tell Tovell – or anyone else.'

'I promise,' said Ginny reluctantly.

'Good. Now we can go and join the boys and Bella. She'll be pleased to see you too.'

Claire led the way, travelling quite fast in her wheelchair. Once they got to the stables, Claire asked Will if he would like to ride Bella. He was delighted at the suggestion, Tovell saddled the horse and they all spent a happy half hour in the paddock.

When it was time to leave, Ginny asked Claire if she was allowed to tell Alec of her whereabouts. 'Yes, if you must,' Claire replied. 'But I don't expect to be here for very long.'

'You haven't got to have another operation, have you?' asked Tovell, anxiously.

'No, thank goodness,' Claire answered. 'Some one came to see me on Friday from the RAF. It seems they don't intend to kick me out. This chap said the fact that the war had ended didn't mean they would stop developing radar and the like. He said that would continue for decades and that they needed people like me to train technicians and to teach each new development. I'm supposed to let him know when I feel ready and then they'll send me for a confirmatory medical. I'll be assigned to a training facility after that.'

'That's great news,' said Tovell. 'That must have cheered you up no end.'

'It certainly did. Now that I know I can still be useful, I don't feel I'm ready for the scrapheap – not just yet.'

## V

The following Sunday, Ginny was in the scullery looking out at the bright summer sunshine and toying with the idea of walking to St Mary's for morning service. When she heard young voices and the wheels of a cart trundling into the yard, she opened the back door and was surprised to see Ted tying Bessie to the hitching rail and the five evacuee children tumbling from the wagon. They all ran to greet her and after each one had been hugged the three older ones dashed off, dragging their younger siblings with them, to find the animals they had loved when they had lived at the smallholding. 'Uncle Tovell's working out there somewhere,' Ginny called after the children.

Ted had no intention of putting himself in a situation where he might be asked to help with something – he embraced a strict code which regarded any kind of work on the Sabbath as a sin – so he rushed through the scullery into the living room. Picking the Sunday paper off the table en route, he plonked himself down in Tovell's armchair, called out Ginny's name and said cheekily, 'A nice cup of tea would go down a treat, gal'.

Ted had not eaten any meals at the Tovells' - apart from Christmas ones - since Joan's arrival and although Ginny had complained in the past about having to feed him so frequently, she had missed him once he was not forever gracing their table. Nevertheless, the thought that she might be expected to produce Sunday dinner for him and five children without any warning, was not a happy one. She followed him into the living room and stood in front of him with her arms folded. He looked up from his paper and grinned impishly at her.

'I'll make you a cup of tea,' said Ginny, sternly, 'if you'll tell me why you've turned up unannounced on a Sunday morning with all them littl'uns in tow – '

'Put the kettle back over the hob, gal,' Ted ordered, gesturing towards the cooking range, 'then I'll tell you.' Once Ginny had complied with his wishes, he continued. 'Enrico's come a-courting. That's what I suppose he's up to – might be wrong. He turned up on the doorstep all spick and span and wearing a suit someone must have lent him – 'cause it was too small – and red roses in his hand. He usually brings wild flowers so I reckon he must have pinched them from someone's garden. Anyway, I thought I'd better bring the littl'uns out of the way and let him say his piece.'

'Well, I never!' Ginny exclaimed. 'But how does he think he's going to support a family?'

'He's got a job now,' Ted declared. 'He asked the young master yesterday. Old Billy kept going sick as you know and he finally snuffed it last Thursday. Poor old bugger must have been worse than we thought; he wasn't just putting it on after all. Anyway, Enrico's the new herdsman and he's got old Billy's cottage. That's bigger than mine so it'll suit 'em all a treat.'

'That's good news but taking on five children is quite a responsibility,' Ginny observed.

'Ah, between you and me, they're part of the attraction. It turns out, Enrico had six littl'uns of his own in Italy – all killed by the bombing.'

'Oh, dear! How terrible! But does Joan realize this: that he wants a ready made family as much – or even more – than her?'

'I reckon she knows: she's no fool. But she also knows she could do worse.'

'I've only seen him the once – at the Victory party. What's he like? Is he kind?'

'You wouldn't meet a kinder feller. He'll be devoted to Joan and those kiddies.'

'That's alright then – so long as he's kind.'

'You int heard the half of it yet, gal. The young master's getting hitched an' all. He's marrying one of them Land Army gals – one o' the best workers.'

'Do you mean Janet, Mary's friend?' asked Ginny in amazement.

'Funny you should say that,' Ted replied. 'I've got a sneaky feeling he asked her first and she turned him down. No, he's marrying Bertha - that strapping great mawther – strong as an ox. She's a jolly sort of gal – always cheerful, always laughing. I reckon he's done alright.'

'That will mean Joan will lose her job. That's a pity: the money came in very handy with all them littl'uns.'

'She won't lose her job – not if I know the young master. He won't want Bertha spending her time in the house, will he? She's an experienced man; he'll want her out there on the farm working alongside him – to "plough the fields and scatter", as the hymn says. She'll be cheap labour, won't she?'

'That's not very nice,' said Ginny. 'Not a very romantic reason for proposing to someone.'

'Don't you worry about young Bertha: she's perfectly capable of sticking up for herself. She'll see she gets her fair dues. But you've gotta laugh at the way things turn out. That old bitch of a mother of his would be turning in her grave if she knew. Yep, it's a rum old do. War's a wicked thing but some good can come out of it - that that can.'


Alec arrived home next day but his brief leave started off badly when he became embroiled in an argument with Ted. The Tovells had just finished breakfast when Ted arrived. Seeing Alec whom he hadn't met for some time, he immediately asked his opinion on the election results. 'I know you're upset about your hero being ousted as Prime Minister, Uncle Ted, but voting in a Labour government was the will of the people. Labour got a huge majority.'

'Maybe so but that still int right,' Ted declared. 'Churchill brought us through the war and how did we reward him? With a kick in the teeth!'

'Uncle Ted, Churchill is as admired and appreciated as ever but he was heading a coalition government and party politics didn't come into it during the war. People were not voting against Churchill but against the Tory Party. They didn't want things to go back to the way they were before the war.'

'Why not?' Ted demanded. 'I reckon things was alright before the war and they're alright now.'

'For you, yes,' Alec insisted. 'You've got a pretty good boss who treats you fairly but a lot of people were not as lucky as you. Those people wanted change and that's why they voted Labour.'

'I always vote according to what the master votes – always have done.'

'But it's a secret vote, Uncle Ted. You don't have to vote the way the master tells you. What the heck have we been fighting six years for if it isn't for freedom and democracy and the right to vote as we wish?'

'That's as may be; but I know which side my bread is buttered,' stated the old man and he promptly walked out of the back door.

Ginny, who had been washing the dishes, hurried after him with her hands dripping. 'Ted, what was it you came for?' she called out. 'What did you want?'

'Can't remember, gal!' he yelled back as he urged Bessie out of the yard.

'Oh, dear! I don't like him going off in a huff,' said Ginny as she returned to the scullery. 'He's too old and fragile to risk getting himself into a paddy. I don't know why that farmer of his still expects him to work – he must be in his late eighties by now.'

'Stop worrying, love,' said Tovell. 'I'd hardly describe Ted as fragile. He's old, yes, but he's fit and well. And as for working, his guv'nor leaves it to him what he does and I don't think that amounts to very much. He keeps him on out of kindness really: he knows Ted wouldn't last another day if he were banned from pottering on that farm.'

'Sometimes, talking to him is like talking to a brick wall,' said Alec with feeling. 'I know I shouldn't have got angry but that was a very frustrating encounter. When I've cooled down, I'll go and look for him.'

'He's an old man and very set in his ways,' said Tovell. 'You won't change his views no matter what you say.'

'I'll go after him nevertheless. Mother, did you tell Claire I was due home?'

'Yes,' replied Ginny. 'I wrote to her as soon as you dropped me a line to say when you would be home. I told her you were planning to visit her – as you'd mentioned as much in our letter.'

'I just hope I can convince her this time. And get the right answer out of her at long last, of course. I thought taking Bobby and Marshall to visit her, when she was moved to Suffolk, would make a difference but it didn't. She'd convinced herself I was going to instruct them what to say and she wouldn't believe a word they told her about that damn letter.' Ginny could not look at her son as he continued. 'But I have to come to a decision about what I'm going to do next and she needs to have her say.'

'If you take up the offer to stay in the Navy, you're going to be away from home and away from Claire a lot of the time,' said Tovell.

'I know, Father, but after six years I'm not sure teaching is the calling for me.'

'I still think it was good of that woman – another teacher's wife, you said – to take over the job you'd been offered and keep it open for you,' said Ginny, relieved that the conversation had moved away from the matter of the letter.

'She's been doing it all through the war so I don't expect she really wants to hand it over to me,' said Alec. 'That doesn't seem right either. And then there's that big house in Oxford which is back in my hands again. What am I going to do with that? I still don't want it.'

'Mr Collins is adamant that you're to have it,' said Ginny. 'And he doesn't care if you sell it – he told your father and me so, didn't he, Tovell?'

'Yes, you're mother's right. But you must decide. Talk it over with Claire – if she'll listen. When are you going to see her?'

'I thought I'd go this afternoon,' Alec answered. 'I'll find Ted first and try to placate him then see if I can have a word with Bobby. I know he's on a few days leave and you said he was stopping at Mary's. I might go and see Aunt Lydia too. Then I'll come back for an early bite to eat and be off to Claire's. Father, can I take Rajah Two?'

'Certainly!' Tovell replied. 'He'll enjoy the exercise. If you have time, take him up onto the cliff top. They've cleared away the barbed wire and all the mines from the beach. The whole area's been declared safe for the public so it should seem like old times.'

Alec, mounted on Rajah Two, found Ted Carter eventually. From his jovial manner, the old man had clearly forgotten their little spat of the morning and after a few exchanges of pleasantries, Alec rode off. Next, he stopped at Mary's house in the village, hoping that his half-brother was there.

'You've just missed them,' said Mary. 'I made them a few sandwiches so they could have a picnic on the cliffs or on the beach. I reckoned it would do Bobby good to spend some time alone with his son – just the two of them. You're sure to spot them along there somewhere.'

Alec felt obliged not to leave immediately so he asked if there was any news of Albert. 'Yes, I had a letter from him yesterday. He'd written it some weeks ago but he was alive and well then, thank the Lord. Dropping them atom bombs on Japan and killing so many seemed very harsh but I reckon the Americans were right: the Japs would never have given up otherwise. You only have to look at them suicide pilots crashing themselves onto ships to realize that. The war would have kept on for years more and who knows how many of our boys would have been killed.'

'I bet you're glad Albert was in the 2nd Battalion Norfolk Regiment and not the other three battalions – the ones which were taken prisoner when Singapore fell.'

'Yes, I wept when I read what the Japs had done to them – killing, starving and torturing them and working them to death on their damn railway. That's another reason I didn't feel that sorry about the atom bombs.'

'At least it's all over now, Auntie Mary, and those poor prisoners and your Albert might soon be home.'

'Yes, Alec, but you can't help wondering if we really won the war. We've still got to queue up at the shops where we're registered for food and, in fact, foodwise we're even worse off now than while the war was on. Our rations have been cut down again and the newspaper said today that bread will be rationed soon and that hasn't happened before. Admittedly, we haven't had the nice white bread we had afore the war – only that grey brownish muck full of old husk to make the flour go further – but at least it wasn't rationed.'

'We've a lot more mouths to feed now, Auntie Mary,' said Alec. 'Did you read what the papers said after the Channel Islands were liberated? There wasn't one cat or dog to be seen. They had to send a relief convoy there straight away. They're near to starvation in all the liberated countries and, of course, in Germany too.'

'I don't see why we should feed them – they started it all.'

'Don't blame the ordinary families – it was the Nazis. If you listen to my father, it's the men who made the peace treaty after the last war who were responsible for starting this one: for passing such harsh terms on Germany that they allowed someone like Hitler to come to power. Let's hope the men who are drafting the present treaty will have more sense or their mistakes could cause no end of trouble for us in the future.'

'I don't know about all that, Alec. I just know I don't feel very sympathetic towards the Germans.'

'It was the Nazi fanatics to blame, Auntie Mary. Fanatics anywhere, whatever they believe in, are the danger. If you're obsessed with a cause – any cause - and don't temper your obsession with reason and common sense, then you're as lethal and destructive a weapon as those atom bombs.'

'That's all a bit over my head, young Alec. Perhaps I'd better just settle for being a good Christian, and as a good Christian, for letting them bloomin' Germans have my bread.'

Alec visited his godmother and his former tutor next. They walked with him to the garden gate and waited whilst he unhitched Rajah Two from the tree and mounted him. They were standing there, arm in arm, when he turned round in the saddle to wave to them from the road. He was pleased to see them so happy but at the same time their happiness only added to his feelings of despondency. They had not been much help either with his dilemma about his future. They had been happy to talk through the various alternatives with him but felt that only he – together with Claire – should arrive at a decision.

As he was about to turn the horse towards the cliff top, he chanced to look into the field opposite. Two Land Army girls were working there and a third one was sitting down on the far side of the field with her back against the hedge. Alec recognized her at once because sitting beside her was Bobby and on her lap was young George. The two adults were laughing at the toddler's antics: he was trying to feed a sandwich to Janet. Alec smiled at the happy scene and then, with a sigh, he urged the horse forward.

They turned right onto the cliff top and as they passed in front of the lighthouse, Alec looked up at it, imposing yet benevolent, its bands of red and white gleaming in the sunshine. 'Why can't you work your magic for me, too?' he muttered. He allowed the horse to trot a little further along then he dismounted and wrapping Rajah Two's reins around a bush, he sat down on the grass at the edge of the cliff feeling quite downhearted. He wondered whether he was missing the company already – the camaraderie of service life. He would certainly miss Marshall: he had been great company. But Marshall probably would not miss him because he had his wife – he had Dorothy. And he was in no dilemma about his future. He had always been a regular Navy man who had signed on for years and years. He had been a chief petty officer for some time now so he had no soul-searching to do: he knew exactly where he was going. Alec envied him.

Alec also knew that he had been fortunate to be invited to stay on in the Navy. He had returned from Norway to find that he had been promoted to Lieutenant Commander in his absence and that he had been decorated for his spectacular success against the three E-boats the previous September. He had also spent this final year of the war as the Senior Officer of his flotilla. He knew that such a background would ensure him a good future career; but how would Claire feel about it? Father was right: they would be apart a great deal of the time if he stayed in the Navy. Would Claire enjoy life as a Navy wife? But then, she did not want to be his wife at all, did she? Marshall was so lucky to have his Dorothy.

Alec, more dejected than ever thought back to how he had felt the last time he had been on this cliff top before war was declared. He remembered that he had had a sense of foreboding. It was incredible to think that six years had passed since then. He had been almost twenty two years old; now he was almost twenty eight. Family friends like Ted and Mary still treated him and saw him as the boy they once knew but away from them - in the world he had lived in for the last six years - he had never been a boy. And now he felt much, much older than twenty eight years. So much had happened – that was why. Those first two years in destroyers he had seen life – and death – but it was the last four years that had aged him. The crews had always been so young; but gunboats were only for young men. He and Marshall had always been the oldest on board. It was like that in all the boats: the captain and coxswain were always the oldest members of the crew. That was what had aged him – and matured him. The enormous responsibility of all those young lives in his hands; the split second decisions that were his alone and which could mean the difference between life and death. How could he follow four years of that? How could he settle down to a mundane existence in this strange new peacetime world? How could he go from being somebody – to his crew, the amount of power he had wielded had made him a god – to being nobody.

But he was not the only one facing this dilemma. There must be thousands like him who had had a purpose, had a goal, had standing and respect, and now had lost it all. What was he saying - that he wished the war had gone on forever? No, of course not. All the pain, all the suffering and tragedy, all the cruelty and brutality which should never have happened in a civilized world, had to end and should have ended long before this. He had been so lucky to come through it unscathed – unlike

Claire. And he had not one, but two jobs waiting for him. Thousands who had not been so fortunate would be envying him now. They were the ones who had every right to feel despondent; not him. He should be happy; not wallowing in this sense of anti-climax. He must not be one of those people who spent their whole lives looking back; feeling that all that mattered was in the past. He must look ahead, strive for new goals; achieve something worthwhile in the future. But what? What was there that could possibly be worthwhile in his future? If only Claire were with him life would be worthwhile; the future would be meaningful …

But there had been times in those years when he had not felt old and mature; when he had felt young. Those times had been when he was off duty and away from the base. He had relished the joys of youth then; he had acted his age; he had embraced the make-merry-for-tomorrow-we-die philosophy like everyone else. Claire had wanted to do that; but he had not embraced it with her, had he? And now it was too late; now she did not want him.

He remained there on the cliff top sitting cross-legged for some time, gazing out to sea. Children's laughter made him look down towards the beach. Father had been right: with the barbed wire, the mines and the tank traps all gone, it was as it had been six years before. That was the last time he and Claire had galloped Rajah Two and Bella through the shallows. Now he felt even more depressed. If only he could put the clock back. All the carefree times they had spent together here as children – all gone forever. Would Claire ever be able to ride Bella through the shallows again? If only he had not been such a fool; if only he had recognized his feelings for what they were; if only he had been able to convince her; if only … He had so many regrets.

He slumped forward, resting his elbows on his knees and his head on his arms and closed his eyes. He could still hear the children down below him chattering and giggling as they ran back and forth playing in the waves. The warm sunshine and his depressed state of mind, which made him feel exhausted all the time, caused him to fall asleep. He dreamed that he and Claire were children again, down there on the beach exercising their horses. His tubby friend was teasing him and racing him. He could hear the sound of the horses' hooves and the trundle of wheels. Did they ever take a cart onto the beach? No, he wasn't dreaming now. Someone had driven a horse and cart onto the cliff top. He hoped it was not old

Ted – or anyone else he knew. He did not feel like talking: he was not in the mood for social chit chat. Perhaps if he bent his head lower and kept his eyes tightly shut they would think he was asleep and go on by. Rajah Two gave a little whinny and Alec could hear the rustle of the bush as the animal pulled on his reins. Damn it, he would have to look up in a minute and restrain the horse.

Then he heard a familiar voice say, 'Hello, Sailor. Want to come home with me? Very cheap rates.'

# EPILOGUE

HMS *Norfolk* took King Haakon and his family back home to Norway on 5th June 1945.

The memorial to the men and women of Allied Coastal Forces who served in HMS *Midge* is in the Town Hall, Great Yarmouth, Norfolk.

The memorial to the Marine Branch, Royal Air Force and to No24 Air Sea Rescue Unit, RAF, Gorleston, is at Brush Quay, Gorleston, Great Yarmouth, Norfolk.

The memorial to the Wrens who died in the 1943 air raids is in St Nicholas Church, Great Yarmouth, Norfolk.

The Royal Norfolk Regimental Museum is at The Shirehall, Market Avenue, Norwich, Norfolk.

The Memorial Library to the 2nd Air Division of the 8th United States Army Air Forces is at The Forum, Millennium Plain, Norwich, Norfolk.

Britain paid the final installment of the war loan debt to the United States of America on 29th December 2006.